dirty

MEGAN HART

dirty

Recycling programs
for this product may
not exist in your area.

ISBN-13: 978-0-7783-1435-6

DIRTY

For questions and comments about the quality of this book, please contact us at CustomerService@Harlequin.com.

www.Harlequin.com

Printed in U.S.A.

To Unagh and Ronan, who bring me more joy than
I ever imagined possible, and as ever and always, to DPF,
because the rest of the world gets to peek inside my head,
but you actually have to live with me. I love you all!

ACKNOWLEDGMENTS

This book would not have been written without the support and friendship of the following:

Natalie Damschroder and Lauren Dane, who read my book and held my hand through all of Elle's adventures (and who told me they loved Dan);

Scissors and Piston, my fellow Maverick Authors: long live the Power of the Three!;

CPRW, the most fantastic and supportive group of writers I'm honored to know;

Kelly, Sal and the rest of the Manor crew for the hours and hours of entertainment, and to Jena for the cowboy hat dancing and delicious emo angst! *MWAH*

The staff and owners of Mary Catherine's Bakery in Annville. Thanks for the space to sit, the coffee to drink and the encouraging words.

Special thanks to Mary Louise Schwartz of the Belfrey Literary Agency for believing in me, and to Susan Pezzack for giving me the chance to share this book with the world.

And to all of my family and friends who supported me, but most particularly my mother, Emily, for supporting my dreams since childhood, my father, Don, for helping to shape the person I've become and my sister, Whitney, for being not just my sister but my best friend.

Chapter 01

This is what happened.

I met him at the candy store. He turned around and smiled at me. I was surprised enough to smile back.

This was not a children's candy store. This was Sweet Heaven, an upscale, gourmet candy store. No cheap lollipops or chalky chocolate kisses, but the kind of place you went to buy expensive, imported truffles for your boss's wife because you felt guilty for fucking him when you were both at a conference in Milwaukee.

He was buying jellybeans, black only. He looked at the bag in my hand, candy-coated chocolate. Also in one color.

"You know what they say about the green ones." The rakish tilt of his lips tried to charm me, and I resisted.

"St. Patrick's Day?" Which was why I was buying them.

He shook his head. "No. The green ones make you horny."

I'd been hit on plenty of times, mostly by men with little

finesse who thought what was between their legs made up for what they lacked between their ears. Sometimes I went home with one of them anyway, just because it felt good to want and be wanted, even if it was mostly fake and they usually disappointed.

"That's an urban legend made up by adolescent boys with wish-fulfillment issues."

His lips tilted further. His smile was his best asset, brilliant and shining in a face made up of otherwise regular features. He had hair the color of wet sand and cloudy blue-green eyes; both attractive, but when paired with the smile…breathtaking.

"Very good answer," he said.

He held out his hand. When I took it, he pulled me closer, step by hesitant step, until he could lean close and whisper in my ear. His hot breath gusted along my skin, and I shivered. "Do you like licorice?"

I did, and I do, and he tugged me around the corner to reach inside a bin filled with small black rectangles. It had a label with a picture of a kangaroo on the front.

"Try this." He lifted a piece to my lips and I opened for him although the sign clearly said No Samples. "It's from Australia."

The licorice smoothed on my tongue. Soft, fragrant, sticky in a way that made me run my tongue along my teeth. I tasted his fingers from where they'd brushed my lips. He smiled.

"I know a little place," he said, and I let him take me there.

The Slaughtered Lamb. A gruesome name for a nice little faux-British pub tucked down an alley in the center of downtown Harrisburg. Compared to the trendy dance clubs and upscale restaurants that had revitalized the area, the Lamb seemed out of place and all the more delightful for it.

He sat us at the bar, away from the college students singing karaoke in the corner. The stools wobbled, and I had to hold tight to the bar. I ordered a margarita.

"No." The shake of his head had me raising a brow. "You want whiskey."

"I've never had whiskey."

"A virgin." On another man the comment would have come off smarmy, earned a roll of the eyes and an automatic addition to the "not with James Dean's prick" file.

On him, it worked.

"A virgin," I agreed, the word tasting unfamiliar on my tongue as though I hadn't used it in a very long time.

He ordered us both shots of Jameson Irish Whiskey, and he drank his back as one should do with shots, in one gulp. I am no stranger to drinking, even if I'd never had whiskey, and I matched him without a grimace. There's a reason it's also known as firewater, but after the initial burn the taste of it spread across my tongue and reminded me of the smell of burning leaves. Cozy. Warm. A little romantic, even.

His gaze brightened. "I like the way you put that down the back of your throat."

I was instantly, immediately, insanely aroused.

"Another?" said the 'tender.

"Another," my companion agreed. To me he said, "Very good."

The compliment pleased me, and I wasn't sure why impressing him had become so important.

We drank there for a while, and the whiskey hit me harder than I thought it would. Or perhaps the company made me giddy enough to giggle at his subtle but charming observations about the people around us.

The woman in the business suit in the corner was an off-duty call girl. The man in the leather jacket, a mortician. My companion wove stories about everyone around us including our good-natured bartender, whom he said had the look of a retired gumdrop farmer.

"Gumdrops don't come from farms." I leaned forward to touch his tie, which featured a pattern that upon first glance appeared to be the normal sort of dots and crosses many men wore. I, however, had noticed the dots and crosses were tiny skulls and crossbones.

"No?" He seemed disappointed I wouldn't play along.

"No." I tugged his tie and looked up into the blue-green eyes that had begun vying with his smile for best feature. "They're harvested in the wild."

He guffawed, tilting his head back with the force of it. I envied him the free and easy way he gave in to the impulse to laugh. I'd have been afraid people would stare.

"And you," he said at last. His gaze pinned me, held me in place. "What are you?"

"Gumdrop poacher," I whispered through whiskey-numb lips.

He reached to twirl a strand of hair that had fallen free from my long French braid. "You don't look that dangerous, to me."

We looked at each other, two strangers, and shared a

smile, and I thought how long it had been since I'd done that. "Want to walk me home?"

He did.

He didn't attempt to make love to me that night, which didn't surprise me. He didn't try to fuck me, either, which did. He didn't even kiss me, though I hesitated before putting my keys in the door and smiled and chatted with him before saying good-night.

He hadn't asked for my name. Not even my number. Just left me buzzing from whiskey on my doorstep. I watched him walk down the street, jingling the change in his pocket. He faded into the darkness between the streetlamps, and then I went inside.

I thought about him the next morning in the shower while I washed the scent of smoke from my hair. I thought about him while I shaved my legs, my pits, the curling dark hair between my legs. When I brushed my teeth I caught sight of my face in the mirror and tried to imagine seeing my eyes as he had.

Blue with flecks of white and gold visible upon closer observation. A feature many men praised, perhaps because telling a woman she has pretty eyes is a safe way of judging whether they can next move on to putting a hand on her thigh. He hadn't mentioned them. He hadn't, actually, complimented me on anything other than the way I'd drunk the whiskey.

I thought about him as I dressed for work. Plain white panties, comfortable in cut and fabric. Matching bra, a hint of lace, enough to make it pretty but designed to support my breasts rather than flaunt them. A black skirt cut just above the knee. A white blouse with buttons. Black and white, as always, to make the choices easier and because something about the pure simplicity of black and white soothes me.

I thought about him on the ride to work, my headphones tucked inside my ears to discourage random conversation from strangers. The shield of modern times. The ride was no longer than it ever had been, nor shorter, and I counted the stops the way I always did and gave the bus driver the same smile.

"Have a good day, Miss Kavanagh."

"Thanks, Bill."

I thought of him, too, as I climbed the cement steps to my office and pushed through the doors precisely five minutes before I was due in my office.

"You're late today," said Harvey Willard, the security guard. "An entire minute."

"Blame the bus," I told him with a grin I knew would make him blush, though the blame was not upon the bus but upon my distracted gait that had made me slow.

Up the elevator, down the hall, through my door, to my desk. Not one thing was different, but everything had changed. Not even the columns of numbers in front of me could wrest my mind from the puzzle he'd presented.

I didn't know his name. Hadn't given him mine. I'd thought it would be easy, two strangers looking to fill a mutual need. A standard seduction. One that didn't need names to complicate it.

I didn't like men knowing my name, anyway. It gave

them a sense of power over me they didn't deserve, as if by gasping out my name when they jerked and spasmed they could cement the moment in place and time. If I had to give a name, I gave them a false one, and when they shouted it out in come-hoarse voices it never failed to make me smile.

I wasn't smiling today. I was distracted, disgruntled, discombobulated...I'd have been disenchanted if I'd ever been enchanted to begin with.

I worked the problem in my mind like I'd figure a calculation. Separate the equations, decipher the individual components, add the pieces that made sense and divide them by the parts that didn't. By lunchtime I still hadn't been able to relegate him to a memory.

"Hot date last night?" Marcy Peters, she of the big hair and tiny skirts, asked. Marcy is the sort of woman who will always refer to herself as a girl, who wears white pumps with too-tight jeans, whose blouses always show a little too much cleavage.

She poured herself another cup of coffee. I had tea. We sat at the small lunchroom table and peeled open sandwiches delivered from the deli, hers tuna and mine, as usual, turkey on wheat.

"As always" came my reply, and we laughed, two women bound in friendship not from qualities in common or mutual interests but because our alliance forms the cage that protects us from the sharks with whom we work.

Marcy fends off the sharks with a blunt and unassuming, forthright presentation of her femininity. Of herself as woman all-powerful, all-intriguing, all-encompassing. She is blond and buxom and not above using her attributes to get what she wants.

I prefer a more discreet approach.

Marcy laughed at my response because the Elle Kavanagh she knows does not go on dates, hot or otherwise. The Elle Kavanagh of her acquaintance, junior vice president of corporate accounting, makes the cliché of the lady-librarian-with-spectacles-and-bun look like Lady Godiva.

Marcy doesn't know anything about me, or my life outside the walls of Triple Smith and Brown.

"You hear the news about the Flynn account?" This was Marcy's idea of lunchtime conversation. Gossip about other employees.

"No," I said to appease her and because she always did manage to dig up the best stories.

"Mr. Flynn's secretary sent the wrong files over to Bob, who's handling the account, right?"

"All right."

Glee danced in Marcy's eyes. "Apparently, she e-mailed Mr. Flynn's private expense account, not the corporate one."

"It has to get better."

"Apparently, Mr. Flynn likes to keep track of how many hundred-dollar hookers and bootleg cigars he buys!" She wriggled in her seat.

"Bad news for Mr. Flynn's secretary, I guess."

Marcy grinned. "She's been blowing Bob on the side. He didn't tell Mr. Flynn."

"Bob Hoover?" That was unexpected news.

"Yeah. Can you believe it?"

"I guess I can believe anything of anybody," I told her

honestly. "Most people are far less discriminating about who they take to bed than you'd think."

"Oh, really?" She gave me a ferrety look of interest. "And you'd know this because…?"

"Pure conjecture." I pushed away from the table and threw away my trash.

Marcy didn't look disappointed, only more intrigued. "Uh-huh."

I gave her a sweet and bland smile, and left her alone to meditate on my mysterious sex life.

The fact is, people *are* far less discriminating in who they fuck than anyone wants to admit. Appearance, intelligence, a sense of humor, wealth, power…not everyone has these qualities, and fewer have more than one. But here's the truth. Fat, ugly and stupid people get laid, too, the media just doesn't report on it like they do when the lovers are gorgeous film stars. Men don't need to be clobbered over the head with the sight of your tits to know you're looking for action. Even pent-up librarian types can get fucked with their panties around their ankles and a brick wall scraping bloody welts on their backs.

At least, this one can.

Or at least I'd been able to three years ago, which was the last time I'd gone out looking. I hadn't been looking for action at Sweet Heaven, merely jonesing for chocolate. So why, then, had I let him take me away? Why had I asked him to walk me home and been so disappointed when he left me on the doorstep with nothing but a wave?

That I hadn't been looking to find someone that day only

exacerbated my private torture. If I'd found him in a bar instead of Sweet Heaven, if my hair had been loose about my shoulders, if my blouse had been unbuttoned, would he have asked to come inside my door? Come inside my body? Would he have kissed me on the stoop, his hands slipping around my waist and pulling me against him tight?

I would never know.

I thought of him all that day and all the next, and the wanting of him grew and grew in my mind like pouring water into a vase filled with stones. Thinking of him consumed my waking moments and seeped into my dreams, leading to sweaty nights amongst tangled sheets.

I studied my face incessantly, wondering what he had seen that day to take me from the candy store and to the pub, but not to bed. Had I failed somehow? Had I said some wrong thing, revealed some flaw, laughed too loudly or not quickly enough at his humor?

I knew I was obsessing. That's what I did. Turned things over and over in my brain to pick them apart from every angle. Analyzed and calculated and pondered.

I could not forget the way his breath smelled when he leaned over to whisper in my ear, "Do you like licorice?"

I could not forget the warmth of his hand on mine when he congratulated me for downing that first shot of whiskey.

I could not forget the flash of his blue-green eyes or the small but perfect cleft in his chin or the faint freckles on the bridge of his nose and forehead or his voice and laugh, the slow deep honey of it that had made me want to lean against him and rub myself on him the way cats do, purring.

The last time I picked up a man in a bar and let him take

me home, he'd ejaculated all over my skirt and cried beer-scented tears all over my face. Then he'd called me names and demanded I pay him back for the drinks he'd bought me. It had been one last bad encounter in a string of them. Boys who didn't know what to do with their pricks, older men who thought two seconds of fingering counted as foreplay, sweet-faced lads who turned into abusive bastards the moment the doors locked behind them.

Celibacy had become the better option. A challenge I set myself that became habit. The day I'd met him in Sweet Heaven it had been three years, two months, a week and three days since I'd had sex.

Now, with thoughts of him on my mind, that nameless stranger, I couldn't stop thinking of sex. A man I passed on the street could catch my gaze and my cunt would clench like fingers closing on a flower. My nipples rubbed with constant friction against my bras. My panties tugged incessantly at my clit, urging me to stroke that small button over and over, no matter the place or the time or the circumstance.

I was horny.

My assignations had never been about any sort of amorous feelings. They'd been about filling an emptiness inside, of chasing away the dark cloud I could usually escape but sometimes…could not. I went to bars and parties and the park to pick up men who might take me away for a few hours, might make me forget everything in my head. Sex had been a choice I made to ease an ache inside. I knew it. I knew why I did it. I knew why I looked like a librarian and acted like a whore.

Until now it hadn't mattered. I'd met men who made me laugh, who made me sigh, even a few, very few, who'd made me come. Until now I had never met one I couldn't forget.

For two weeks I stuttered along this way, my concentration knitted together by strands of habit rather than any effort on my part. My work didn't suffer, only because the numbers came so easily to me, but everything else did. I forgot to mail bills, pick up the dry cleaning, set my alarm.

The spring days were still easing into night early enough that sometimes my ride home on the bus was done in darkness. I sat in my usual seat, the one at the back, my coat and briefcase folded neatly over my lap, my legs crossed high up at the thigh. I stared out the window and imagined his face and the smell of his breath, and then, with the rocking of the bus to aid me, I began to get myself off.

At first, just a gentle squeezing of my thigh muscles done in time to the thump of the bus wheels on the pavement. My pussy swelled. My clit became a tiny hard nodule pressing against the soft fabric of my panties. My hips, hidden by the coat and briefcase, rocked on the plastic seat. With both hands folded sedately on my lap, nobody looking at me would have any idea what I was doing.

Streetlights cast bars of silver on my lap and made swiftly moving lines of light that slid up my body and away, leaving behind darkness interrupted a minute later by another streak. I began to time my pace to the passing of the lights.

Sweet tension curled inside my stomach. My breath caught and held, then hissed out between my parted lips when it began to burn inside my lungs. I kept my eyes fixed on the window and the sights outside it, but I saw none of them. I saw the ghost of my face reflected now and again in the window glass. I imagined him looking at me.

My fingers curled on top of my leather briefcase, holding tight. My foot moved up and down, up and down, squeezing my thighs together, rubbing my clit in a small but perfect motion. I wanted so badly to touch myself, to stroke my fingers in circles around that hard button, to slide them inside and fuck myself while the bus sped on toward its destination—but I didn't. I rocked and squeezed, and each lamp we passed urged me that much closer to climax.

My body shook from holding so still when it wanted to writhe. I had never done this before, this furtive dance toward completion. Masturbation was done at home alone in the bath or in bed, straightforward and swift, a release of tension. This, here, was almost against my will. My thoughts of him, the movement of the bus, my celibacy, had all conspired to set my body burning with a fire only orgasm could quench.

Sweat slid down the line of my spine and into the crack of my buttocks. That touch, that light tickle, so much like the feeling of a tongue along my skin, sent me hurtling over the edge. My cunt tightened as my body tensed. My nails scratched thin lines in the leather of my briefcase. My clit jumped and spasmed, and bolts of pure bliss radiated through my entire body.

I shook in silence, drawing less attention than if I'd sneezed. I turned the gasping sigh into a cough that barely turned heads. In another moment looseness pervaded me, and boneless, I slumped a bit in my seat as the bus eased to a stop.

My stop.

I got off on trembling legs, certain the smell of sex had to be clinging to me like perfume, but nobody seemed to notice. I exited the bus into a spring mist, and I lifted my face to the night sky and let it kiss me all over, not caring that it flattened my hair and dampened my blouse.

I had made myself come on a public bus thinking of his face, and I still didn't know his name.

For better or worse, that solo touch on the public transportation eased some of my need. The numbers came back to me, filling my mind with their steady stream of plus and minus. I threw myself into my work, landing several big accounts that had been the responsibility of Bob Hoover, now too busy getting lunchtime blow jobs from Mr. Flynn's secretary to handle the load.

I didn't mind. More work meant greater opportunity to show the higher-ups I deserved my title, my corner office, my extra vacation time. It meant I didn't have to invent reasons to stay late at work so I'd need to choose between going home and facing an empty house or heading out to some meat-market bar and testing my strength of will.

"Sex," Marcy declared in the lunchroom, "is like this chocolate éclair."

She'd brought me a powdered sugar doughnut. "Full of cream and makes you feel like you want to puke after?"

She rolled her eyes. "What the hell sort of sex do you have, Elle?"

"None, recently."

"I'm shocked." Her tone made it clear she wasn't. "But no wonder, with an attitude like that."

She might have big hair and trashy taste in clothes, but Marcy could make me laugh. "Tell my why sex is like that éclair, then."

"Because it's tempting enough to make you forget everything else you're supposed to do." She licked some chocolate off the top. "And it's satisfying enough to make you glad you did."

I sat back in my chair a little, watching her. "I take it you had some sex last night?"

She made a mock-innocent face, and I realized something. I liked her. She fluttered her eyelashes. "Who, little ole me?"

"Yes, you." I put the doughnut back in the box and snagged the last éclair. "And you're dying to tell me about it, so stop wasting time and get to it before someone else comes in and we have to pretend to be talking about business."

Marcy laughed. "I wasn't sure you'd like to hear about it."

I studied her face. "You think that about me, don't you. That I don't like sex?"

She looked up from her gooey plate, her smile sincere, and something passed over her expression. Something a little like pity. It made me frown.

"I don't know, Elle. I don't know you well enough to say, really, but you act like you don't like much of anything sometimes, except work."

Hearing something you already know shouldn't ever be a shock, but it usually is. I wanted to answer her right away, but my throat had closed and my eyes burned with tears I blinked against to keep from falling. I put one hand on my stomach, which had lurched at her words in recognition of the truth of them.

Marcy, despite her appearance and occasional dumb-blonde performance, is anything but stupid. She reached at once for my hand and closed her fingers over mine before I could pull it away. She squeezed my hand and let go fast enough to keep me from startling.

"Hey," she said softly. "It's all right. We all have buttons."

Right then, at that moment, I had the chance to make Marcy my friend. A real one, not a business acquaintance. I have stood on the edge of so many things, so many times, and I most always back away. If there is a time when telling the truth will open a door, I lie. If a smile will forge a connection, I turn my face.

But this time, surprising myself and probably her, I didn't.

I smiled at her. "Tell me about your date last night."

She did. In detail enough to make me blush. It was the best lunch I'd ever had.

When it was time for us to go to our separate offices, she stopped me with another squeeze of my hand. "You should come out with me sometime."

I let her squeeze my hand because she was so earnest, and we'd had such a good time. "Sure."

"You will?" She squealed, the hand squeeze turning into an impromptu, full-length hug that made my entire body stiffen. Marcy patted my back and stepped away, and if she noticed that her embrace had turned me into a wooden effigy, she said nothing. "Great."

"Great." I smiled and nodded.

Her enthusiasm was infectious, and it had been a long time since I'd had a girlfriend. Any sort of friend. I caught myself humming later, at my desk.

Euphoria doesn't last under the best circumstances, and when I pushed open my front door to find the light on my answering machine blinking steadily, mine vanished.

I don't get many calls at home. Doctors' offices, sales calls, wrong numbers, my brother Chad…and my mother. The red number four mocked me as I dumped my mail on the table and hung my keys on the small hook by the door. Four messages in one day? They had to be from her.

Hating your mother is such a cliché comedians use it to make audiences laugh. Psychiatrists base their entire careers upon diagnosing it. Greeting card companies stick the knife in further by making consumers feel so guilty about the way they really feel about their mothers, they'll willingly pay five dollars for a piece of paper with some pretty words they didn't write, echoing a sentiment they don't feel.

I don't hate my mother.

I've tried to hate my mother, I really have. If I hated her, I might be able to put her out of my life at last, be done with her, put an end to the torture she provides. The sad fact remains, I haven't learned to hate my mother. The best I can do is ignore her.

"Ella, pick up the phone."

My mother's voice is a nasal foghorn, bleating her disdain as a warning to all the other ships to stay away from me, the reason for her disappointment. I can't hate her, but I can hate her voice, and the way she calls me Ella instead of Elle.

Ella is a waif's name, an orphan sitting in the cinders. Elle is classier, crisper. The name a woman called herself when she wanted people to take her seriously. She insists on calling me Ella because she knows it annoys me.

By the fourth message she was detailing how life didn't seem worth living with such an ungrateful excuse for a daughter. How the pills the doctor prescribed for her nerves weren't working. How she was embarrassed to have to ask Karen Cooper from next door to go to the pharmacy for her when she had a daughter who should be quite capable of taking care of her, but for the fact she refused.

She had a husband who could go for her, too, but she never seemed to remember that.

"And don't forget!" I jumped at the suddenness of her voice ringing out from the small speaker. "You said you'd visit soon."

There was a brief moment of hissing static at the end of her message as though she'd hung on the line, convinced I was really there and ignoring her, and if she waited long enough she'd catch me out.

The phone rang again as I looked at it. Resigned, I picked it up. I didn't bother to defend myself. She talked for ten minutes before I had the chance to say anything.

"I was at work, Mother," I managed to interject when she paused to light a cigarette.

She greeted my answer with an audible sniff of disdain. "So late."

"Yes, Mother. So late." The clock showed ten after eight. "I take the bus home, remember?"

"You have that fancy car. Why don't you drive it?"

I didn't bother to explain yet again my reasons for keeping a car in the city but using public transportation, which was faster and easier. She wouldn't have listened.

"You should find a husband," she said at last, and I bit back a sigh. The tirade was close to ending. "Though how you ever will, I don't know. Men don't like women who are smarter than they are. Or who earn more money. Or—" she paused significantly "—who don't take care of themselves."

"I take care of myself, Mother." I meant financially. She meant spa treatments and manicures.

"Ella." Her sigh sounded very loud over the phone. "You could be so pretty..."

I looked into the mirror as she talked, seeing the reflection of a woman my mother didn't know. "Mother. Enough. I'm hanging up."

I imagined the way her mouth pursed at such harsh treatment from her only daughter. "Fine."

"I'll call you soon."

She snorted. "Don't forget, you promised to come visit."

The thought made my stomach fall away. "Yes, I know, but—"

"You have to take me to the cemetery, Ella."

The woman in the mirror looked startled. I didn't feel startled. I didn't feel...anything. No matter what my reflection showed.

"I know, Mother."

"Don't think you can weasel out of it this year—"

"Goodbye, Mother."

I disconnected her, though she still squawked, and immediately dialed another number.

"Marcy. It's Elle."

Marcy, bless her, revealed nothing but pleased surprise at my desire to take her up on her invitation to go out after work. It was exactly the reaction I needed. Too much enthusiasm would have made me rethink; too little would have made me cancel.

"The Blue Swan," she said confidently, like she was reaching for my hand to lead me across a bridge swaying over an abyss. In a way she was. "It's small but the music is good and the crowd's eclectic. The drinks are pretty cheap, too. And it's not a meat market."

So kind of her, really, to keep assuming I was afraid of men. She didn't know I had once slept with four different men in as many days. She didn't know it wasn't sex that scared me.

Her kindness made me smile, though, and we made plans for after work on Friday. She didn't question my change of mind.

Still staring at the woman in the mirror, I hung up the phone. She looked as if she was going to cry. I felt bad for her, that woman with the dark hair, the one who only ever wore black and white. The one who might have been pretty if she'd only take care of herself, if only she weren't smarter, if only she didn't earn more money. I felt sorry for her but envied her, too, because she, at least, could cry and I could not.

A figure in black waited for me when I got home from work on Thursday night. Black sweatshirt, hood pulled up over black-dyed hair. Black jeans and sneakers. Black-polished nails.

"Hi, Gavin." I put my key into the lock as he stood.

"Hi, Miss Kavanagh. Can I give you a hand with that?" He took my bag before I had time to protest and followed me inside. He hung it neatly on the hook by the door. "I brought your book back."

Gavin belongs to the neighbors on my left side. I'd never met his mother, though I'd often seen her leaving for work. I'd heard raised voices a few times through our shared walls, and it made me conscious about keeping my own television turned low.

"Did you like it?"

He shrugged and set the book on the table. "Not as much as the first one."

I'd lent him my copy of C. S. Lewis's *The Horse and His Boy.* "Lots of people only read *The Lion, the Witch and the Wardrobe,* Gav. Do you want the next one?"

At fifteen Gavin was a typical Goth wannabe with his Jack Skellington wardrobe and liberal use of eyeliner. He was a nice kid, though, who liked to read and didn't seem to have many friends. He'd shown up at my door about two years earlier, wanting to know if he could mow my grass. Since I had a patch of grass about the size of a small compact car, I didn't need a lawn boy. I'd hired him, anyway, because he'd looked so sincere.

Now he spent more time borrowing from my library and helping me strip wallpaper and sand floors than he did on my sad excuse for a lawn, but I liked him. He was quiet and polite and far cheerier than any Goth kid should have been. He was good, too, with tasks I found too tedious to tackle, like scraping the wallpaper paste residue left behind when we peeled off two decades worth of home decor from my dining room walls.

"Yeah, sure. I'll get it back to you by Monday."

He followed me to the kitchen, where I put a box of chocolate cookies on the table. "Whenever you get it back to me is fine."

He helped himself to a cookie. "Do you need any help stripping tonight?"

We looked at each other as soon as the words had escaped his lips, and I blinked. He looked stricken. I had to turn around so as not to embarrass him with my laughter.

"I'm done," I managed to say. "I could use some help priming the drywall, though, if you'd like to help."

"Sure, sure." He sounded relieved.

I pulled out a frozen pizza and put it in the oven. "How've you been, Gav? I haven't seen you for a few days."

"Oh. My mom…she's getting married again."

I nodded, pulling out plates and glasses to set the table. We didn't always talk much, Gavin and I, which I think suited both of us fine. He helped me renovate my house, and I paid him with cookies and pizza, with books and with a place to go when his mother was out, which seemed to be quite often.

I made a noncommittal noise as I poured milk into the glasses. Gavin got up to get the napkins from my cupboard and set out two. He washed his hands before he sat back at the table. His black polish had chipped.

"She says this guy's the one."

I glanced at him as I set out grated cheese and garlic powder. "That's nice for her."

"Yeah." He shrugged.

"Will you be moving?"

He looked up, dark eyes wide in a pale face. "I hope not!"

"I hope not, too. I still have an entire dining room to paint." I smiled at him, and he smiled back after a moment.

I didn't have to be a mind reader to see something was bothering him, nor a genius to figure out what it was. I could have played the part of mentor. Asked him sympathetic questions. We didn't have that type of relationship, though, the sort that shared secrets or heartfelt revelations. He was the boy who lived next door and helped me around the house. I don't know what I represented to him, but I doubted it was a guidance counselor.

The buzzer went off on the oven, and I served us both sizzling slices of pizza. He added garlic powder. I used the grated cheese. We ate discussing the book I'd lent him and debating whether or not the next episode of the cop show we both liked was going to reveal the name of the killer. Gavin helped me load the dishes in the dishwasher and put away the leftover pizza. By the time I came downstairs after changing my clothes, he'd already spread out and taped down the tarp to protect the floor and opened the can of primer.

We listened to music and painted for a few hours until he had to go home. Before he went, he browsed the shelves in my living room and picked out another book.

"What's this one about?" He held up my battered copy of *The Little Prince.*

"A little prince from outer space." That was the easy answer. Anyone who's read Antoine de Saint-Exupéry's classic story knows there's far more to it than that.

"Cool. Can I take this one, too?"

I hesitated. The book had been a gift. It had also sat on my shelf gathering dust for years without so much as a glance from me. "Sure. Of course."

He gave me a real grin, then, the first of the evening. "Great. Thanks, Miss Kavanagh!"

He let himself out, and I stared for a moment at the empty space the book had left behind before I started cleaning up.

That night I dreamed of a roomful of roses and woke with a gasp, eyes wide open to the darkness. Turning on the light chased it into shadows cowering in the corners of my room but could do nothing for the darkness lingering in my thoughts. I lay in my bed for a few minutes before admitting defeat and reaching for the phone.

"House of Hotness."

I had to smile. "Hi, Luke."

I've never met my brother's lover. They live in California, a world away from my safe nest in Pennsylvania. Chad doesn't come home. I hate flying. So far, it's just never worked out.

We weren't strangers despite this, and his reply warmed me. "How's my girl?"

"I'm fine."

Luke clucked into the phone, but didn't comment further. A moment later Chad got on the line. He wasn't so taciturn.

"It's after midnight there, sweetie. What's wrong?"

Chad is my younger brother, but you wouldn't know it by the way he pampers me. I settled further into my blankets and counted the cracks in my ceiling. "Can't sleep."

"Bad dreams?"

"Yes." I closed my eyes.

He sighed. "What's going on, punkin? Is your mother getting on your case again?"

I didn't bother pointing out that she was his mother, too. "No more than usual. She wants me to go with her."

I didn't have to tell him where. Chad made a disgusted noise, and I had no trouble picturing his expression. It made me smile, which was why I'd called him.

"You tell Puff the Magic Dragon Queen to leave you the hell alone. She can drive her own damn self wherever the hell she needs to go. She should lay off you."

"You know she can't drive, Chaddie."

He launched into a tirade of cursing and colorful insults.

"Your creativity and vehemence leave me in awe," I told him. "You are truly the master."

"Do you feel better now?"

"I always do."

He snorted. "What else is going on?"

I thought of the man I'd met in Sweet Heaven. "Nothing."

Chad paused to give me time to add more, and when I didn't, he snorted again. "Ella. Baby. Honey, love muffin. You don't call me after midnight your time to talk to me about the Dragon Queen. You've got something else on your mind. Spill it."

I love my brother with all my heart, but I wasn't going to tell him about my sudden lustful fixation on a stranger who favored odd ties and liked black licorice. Some things are too private to share, even with someone who knows all your deepest, darkest secrets. I mumbled something about work and the house, which he seemed reluctant to accept but did, anyway.

The conversation drifted from my pathetic mental state to his work in an elder-care home, his plans to meet Luke's family, the dog they were considering buying. He had a cozy little life, my brother. A good job. A nice house. A partner who loved and supported him. I relaxed as he talked, my body melting into my bed and sleep beginning to tease me into thinking it might return.

Then he dropped the bomb on me.

"Luke wants to talk about having kids." His voice had dropped to a whisper.

I might suffer from occasional social awkwardness, but even I know the appropriate response to that announcement is not "What in the holy fuck are you thinking?" but rather "Oh, that sounds nice."

I didn't say either one. "What do *you* want, Chaddie?"

He sighed. "I don't know. He says I'll be a great dad. I'm not so sure."

I didn't doubt my brother would make a wonderful father. I also knew why he feared the thought. "You have a lot of love in your heart."

"Yeah, but kids…kids need a lot of…stuff."

"Yeah."

We sat in silence for a few moments, separated by distance but connected by emotion. At last he cleared his throat. He sounded more like his usual self when he spoke again.

"We're just thinking about it. I said we should get a dog first. See how we do with that."

It was more than I'd ever wanted to commit to, a pet. "You'll be great, Chad. Whatever you decide, you know I'm here for you."

"Aunt Ella." He laughed.

"Aunt Elle," I corrected.

"Elle," Chad agreed. "Love you, bunny muffin."

As far as pet names went, bunny muffin was among the more bizarre. I didn't quarrel with it. "Love you, too, Chad. Good night."

We disconnected and I settled back onto my pillows, my mind whirling with his news. A child? My brother…a father?

I fell back to sleep with visions of laughing babies in my head, which was marginally better than the dreams of red roses.

Friday came faster than I'd expected. I'd never been to The Blue Swan, but it was everything Marcy had said. More an intimate-coffee-shop setting with a dance floor than a dance club, it featured a steady pulse of electronic dance music, soothing blue lights and soft couches, an interesting array of drinks and stars scattered across the black-painted ceiling.

Marcy introduced me to her new beau, Wayne. He looked like the junior executive he was, complete with a hundred-dollar haircut and trendy designer tie, plain, without skulls and crossbones. He shook my hand and, to give him credit, did not overtly check out my breasts. He even bought my first margarita.

Marcy grinned. "Planning on getting wild, Elle?"

"Ah, one drink's not a big deal. Not everyone's a lush like you, babe." What might have been condescending sounded fond from Wayne, his arm outstretched along the bench behind her to toy with the long, curling strand of her hair. "Trust me, Elle, we'll be carrying Marcy out of here."

Marcy made a face and nudged him, but didn't look displeased. "Don't listen to him."

"Hey, so long as it gets me laid," Wayne said, "I don't care how drunk you get—"

She slapped him in earnest this time. "Hey!"

She sent me an apologetic glance, but I shrugged, not as embarrassed as I think she expected. The fact was, I liked drinking too much to be a hard drinker. I liked the oblivion, the way a few drinks softened the edges of my mind and chased away even the ever-present need I felt to count, catalog and calculate.

Alcohol is the noose with which my father keeps trying to hang himself. I understand why he does it. He is, after all, married to my mother. Now, retired and in his sixties, drinking is my father's career and hobby all in one. Maybe it's his shield. I don't know. We don't talk about it. We aren't the only family with a white elephant in the living room, but who ever cares about anyone else's family when their own is the one they have to live with?

"So, you work with Marcy?" Wayne earned points for what appeared to be sincere interest.

"Yes. She's in public accounting and I'm in corporate, but we both work for the same company."

Wayne grinned. "Me, I'm in murders and executions."

"Wayne!" Marcy rolled her eyes. "He means—"

"Mergers and acquisitions. I got it."

Wayne looked impressed. "You know *American Psycho.*"

"Sure." I sipped my drink.

"Wayne thinks he's Patrick Bateman," Marcy explained. "Aside from that pesky bad habit of slicing up prostitutes with a chainsaw."

"Well," I said carefully, watching him, "nobody's perfect."

His smile rewarded me, and then he laughed. "Hey, Marcy, I like your friend."

She looked at me. "Me, too."

Sometimes you share a moment with someone that has nothing to do with where you are, or what you're doing. Marcy and I giggled, girly in a way I wasn't used to but enjoyed nevertheless. Wayne looked at us, back and forth, until he shook his head with a shrug at our feminine absurdity.

"To murders and executions," he said with a lift of his beer. "And to all things materialistic and shallow."

We toasted his words. We drank. We talked, though much of what we said had to be shouted over the music. I relaxed, letting the alcohol and music loosen my tense shoulders.

"It's my turn," I protested when Wayne made to order one more round of drinks.

He held up his hands. "I'm not gonna argue. My mama told me a woman's always right. You go right on ahead, Miss Kavanagh, and buy the next round. I'm comfortable enough in my masculinity to accept a woman's generosity."

"Oh, ho ho," said Marcy. "You mean you're drunk enough you don't feel like getting up to go to the bar."

Wayne grinned and pulled her close for a kiss that made me feel like a voyeur. "That, too."

That was my cue to leave them for a few moments. I needed to stand, anyway, to gauge my own level of inebriation. Two drinks took me a lot farther than they had three years ago.

A space opened up at the bar as I approached, and the bartender gave me his immediate attention. I knew he was paid to flirt as much as he was to mix drinks, but his smile still flooded me with warmth. I'm no more immune to my sense of self being reflected in the light of another's esteem than any other woman. I smiled back and ordered two more beers and a bottle of water for myself.

"She doesn't want that. Get her a shot of Jameson."

I didn't turn to face the voice that had haunted me for the past three weeks. I nodded at the 'tender waiting my approval, and he slid the shot glass toward me without another word.

"Hi," said the man from Sweet Heaven, and I turned.

"Hi."

The crowd had grown as the night wore on, and now it jostled us closer. He looked down at me, his smile bemused. In the blue neon light his eyes looked darker than I remembered.

"Fancy meeting you here."

My fingers curled around the shot glass, but I didn't lift it. "Yes."

His gaze traced the lines of my face; I felt his look as if it was a touch. Someone pushed toward the bar behind him, nudging him forward another inch. He reached to grab my arm just above the elbow, so the sudden impact didn't make me stumble. He didn't let go.

"Aren't you going to drink that?" He nodded toward the shot without taking his eyes from mine.

"I've reached my limit."

More people pushed to the bar behind each of us, pressing us together. His hand slid down my arm to rest on the curve of my waist. A touch so casual anyone watching would assume we'd known each other for years. A touch so blatant it made my breath catch.

"So, you're a good girl."

Another man who'd called me a girl would have earned a stomp to his foot and maybe the drink in his face. For him, my mouth curved. Closer we drew, magnets attracting, one to one, without the pressure of the people around us.

"Depends on your definition of *good.*"

His fingers splayed against my side, his thumb drifting back and forth along the smooth fabric of my shirt. "Are you flirting with me?"

"Do you want me to?"

"Do you want to do what I want?" My pulse pounded at his question, murmured directly into my ear.

We'd already aligned thigh to thigh, belly to belly. If I turned my head, our mouths would be close enough to kiss. His breath caressed my ear and the slope of my neck exposed by my upswept hair.

I nodded. "Yes."

"I want you to drink that shot."

I did without a second protest. It burned in my gut and shot liquid fire through every vein. He hadn't moved anything but his hand, which now lingered at my lower back, keeping me tight against him though the crowd at the bar had eased a bit and there was no longer a need for us to remain so close together.

"Take down your hair."

A command, but voiced as a request, and I reached to undo the clip holding it on top of my head. Released, it tumbled over my shoulders and halfway down my back. It brushed his face, still so close to mine.

"Dance with me."

He pulled back to look into my eyes, his smile less bemused and his gaze brighter. Hungrier. He didn't move his hand.

"Is that…what you want?" My hesitation sounded coy, and I hadn't meant it to. I'd meant to sound sultry, to play the game.

He nodded, solemn. His eyes stared into mine, hard, and I could see nothing else. Could feel nothing else but the spots on my body where his body touched.

"That's what I want."

I gave him what he wanted. The dance floor, even more crowded than the bar, left little room for maneuvering, but most people weren't really dancing. Bouncing up and down in time to the rhythm, maybe, and wiggling, but not dancing.

He took me by the hand, fingers laced, and put us in the center of the dance floor. One step, and he drew me close to him. Another, and his hands fit my waist like they'd been made to match my curves. Three steps and his thigh slid between mine. These points of connection grounded me, kept me tethered.

There could be no talking here, for even a shout would've been difficult to hear above the pounding throb of the music. The bass thumped its pulse in the pit of my stomach, the hollow of my throat, my wrists, between my thighs. The crowd surged around us like the ocean against rocks, parting and retreating to return in the next instant, surrounding us. It pressed in on us as the song changed and brought more dancers onto the floor.

He wasn't smiling anymore, like this was serious

business. Like he could see nothing else around us, like his world had narrowed to only me. I shivered at the look.

When he put his other hand on my side, up high, just under my breast, I startled but had no place to go. No retreat. I looked up, into his eyes, those light-and-dark eyes, and lost myself in them.

We moved together, and my hand slid from his shoulder to cup the back of his neck. The edges of his sandy hair tickled my knuckles. The heat of his hand branded me through my blouse. Heat flared, too, in my belly where it rubbed against his groin.

It had been a long, long time since I'd danced with anyone, an eternity since I'd had a man's hands on me, since I'd seen my own desire reflected in another's gaze. It stole my breath and drew my tongue out to lick my lips. The motion caught his attention the way a cat will watch a mouse.

His hand slid up my back to tangle in my hair, tip my head back, bare my throat to his mouth as he bent to slide his lips along my skin. I felt myself gasp but couldn't hear it. He pulled me closer, and I gave in to his whim.

The crowd had become one body moving to the music's sensual beat. One entity with us in the center of it, pressed so close I could no longer be certain where I ended and he began. His hand slid up to embrace my breast through my blouse. I blinked and saw nothing but his face shadowed with blue and green, the colors pulsing in time to the rhythm.

Nobody watched us. Nobody saw. We had become part of something bigger and yet remained separate from it. The couple next to us kissed, their tongues tangling as their hands stroked and kneaded each other. The dance floor had become an orgy of lust. I smelled it, tasted it, saw it reflected in his eyes and knew he saw it in mine. The song changed again, blending into the previous one without break.

Bodies all around us pressed us together. Sweat slid down my spine and shone on his forehead. Everything had become heat and beat.

His cock pressed hard against my belly. The sensation parted my lips in silent reaction, and his gaze watched my mouth again, his expression tense, as though he was in pain.

It wasn't pain that thinned his mouth. I knew it by the way his jaw tightened when another surge of the crowd rocked me against his body. The hand on my ass splayed, then stroked upward to reach the small of my back, then down again to caress and press me against his erection.

I was lost. Lost in his eyes, in his touch, in the pounding pulse of music and lust. Lost in my own desire, which I'd denied for so long and now could no longer fight.

I saw the shift in his gaze and knew the exact moment when he recognized my reaction. If he'd smiled smugly or leered, I'd have fled. Instead, his eyes narrowed slightly, and his expression became a mixture of determination and helpless admiration. He looked at me as though he didn't care if the song ever stopped or if he never looked at another woman again.

His hand slid down my hip to my thigh. His fingers caught the hem of my skirt, inching it up as we danced, until he could slip his hand beneath it. He cupped me, the heel of his hand pressed against my clit on the outside of my panties.

The crowd moved us, so he no longer had to. The hand on my rear kept me secured close to him. Another shift of the crowd, and his fingers moved to dip inside the lacy edge of my panties and find my slick heat.

His eyes widened so slightly only someone staring into them as I was could have noticed. His lips parted in an unheard gasp or groan. My body jerked as his flesh came in direct contact with mine, and a groan tore from my throat.

His fingers teased my folds before gliding up to caress my clit. If not for the support of his hand and the crowd crushing us on all sides, I'd have stumbled. The touch speared straight to my core. My fingers gripped his shoulder in a sudden, tight hold, and his gaze flicked there as he winced. I'd hurt him but could do nothing about it. Every stroke he gave my clit made my fingers dig involuntarily into him.

Now he looked determined, admiring and quizzical, but the last passed in a moment as he circled my tight nub and watched the reaction I couldn't hide. Now he looked… honored, was the only way I could think to describe it, if I could do any thinking at all, which was becoming impossible.

Everything had become this man. His hand. His eyes. His cock, still pressing on my hip and now throbbing, hard, hot. He licked his lips, and my clit pulsed in immediate response beneath his fingers.

He tangled his fingers in my hair again, massaging the

base of my skull and keeping me from moving away. We danced, each movement rocking me against his hand until in moments I was on the edge.

I'd been feeling this way for weeks. Breathless, aching, body burning for release, unable to focus on anything but the pleasure building between my legs. My nipples tightened, and his gaze fell to my breasts.

It was impossible to see his face flush, not with the flashing blue and green neon coating everyone in science-fiction shadows, but I knew he was burning, as I was.

This was incredible, impossible, and at last I put my hand on his chest to push him away. I couldn't do this. Couldn't let some stranger get me off on the dance floor, not like this, I didn't do this…

But I was going to. Oh, yes, I was going to come, right there. Right then. I was going to come on his hand like we were the only two people in the world, and it didn't matter if anyone saw me, I was tipping over the edge so hard and so fast I thought I might faint from the pleasure.

His breath blew hot against my skin as he nuzzled my ear, whispering something I shouldn't have been able to hear but was unable to ignore.

"Let go."

I shattered, biting my lip to stifle the cry that tore from my throat. My pulse pounded in my ears and throat while my clit spasmed over and over, each beat of climax pulling another low moan from me.

His arm tightened around me, holding me close as I rode his hand, body shuddering and jerking. He kissed my jaw and the side of my neck. He stopped his fingers moving and cupped me again, perfectly, keeping the pressure there without working my oversensitized flesh into pain.

I tried to breathe and at first could not. I tried again, my body limp and languid and sated, and found not only breath but along with it the scent of him. I thought I would never again see blue and green neon without remembering the way he smelled.

It seemed to me everyone around us would know what had just happened, but if anyone did they showed no sign of it. The crowd moved and swayed in its own orgasmic rush, intent on finishing whatever piece of ecstasy its members were knitting for themselves.

The man I was with put a finger to my chin and lifted it until I looked up. He bent to kiss me. I turned my face at the last second so his mouth landed on my cheek and not my mouth. My pulse pounded in my throat.

"Okay," I thought he said, though the music made it impossible to hear him.

"Hey, watch where the fuck you're going!"

"The fuck *you're* going, asshole!"

Two dancers had collided, their faces red with exertion and slick with sweat. Fists upraised, they began the steps of another sort of dance, one that would lead to bloodshed and broken teeth.

My partner took me by the elbow and steered me away, out of the crowd on the dance floor and through the one in the rest of the bar. He led me to a small booth. I looked around for Marcy and Wayne and saw they'd moved to the bar, both of them laughing and kissing.

The booth had a half-circle bench. He let me slide into

it first, then took the place beside me. My heartbeat had begun to slow, my legs to firm, my breath to no longer catch in my throat. From the waitress who appeared beside us I ordered a sparkling water with lime. He ordered the same.

I could not look at him, though moments before I had been unable to look away. Heat that had nothing to do with the room temperature crept up my chest and throat, along my cheeks and the back of my neck.

I had done things in the past that would have made a hooker proud, but always in privacy. Never in public, and never with anyone whose name I didn't know. Strangers to me, yes, with nothing but a few hours acquaintance to recommend them, but even when I gave them a false name I always learned theirs.

He said nothing until after the waitress had brought our drinks and we had both sipped. I wanted to press the cool glass to my forehead, but refrained. I sat stiffly on the edge of the faux-leather bench, acutely aware of the closeness of his arm to mine and how he could have, but did not touch me.

"What is this?" he asked.

Back here the music muffled his voice but didn't drown it out. He didn't have to shout for me to hear him. He didn't have to lean forward to murmur in my ear.

I said nothing for a moment, uncertain how to answer. He reached for me. I thought he meant to touch my face, or put his arm around my shoulder, and I stiffened. His hand caressed my hair from crown to ends, brushing it off my shoulders to hang down my back and expose my profile to him.

"What's your name?"

Such a simple question, the sort asked at cocktail parties and in parks, an international query you might hear anywhere. Not out of place in a bar like this, where names, vital statistics and phone numbers were exchanged between singles the way women will exchange recipes for pound cake. Recipes for love.

"Elle."

He waited before answering, long enough that I broke and looked at him. He smiled at me. His fingers twisted a strand of my hair.

"I'm Dan."

He held out his hand. Socially groomed to take it, I did. He curled his fingers around mine, held it tight, drew me closer.

"Pleasure to meet you, Elle.

"Thanks for the drink. I should go."

But I didn't. I looked up at him. He looked at me.

"What is this?" he asked, voice pitched low but still audible.

"I don't know." I shook my head, and my hair fell forward again, over my shoulders.

"Do you want to know?" He moved closer.

Now we sat thigh to thigh, his hand still enclosing mine. The heat from his body seeped through my clothes, but I shivered.

I knew arousal. I knew desire. Lust. This was something else, all three and something different, too. This was tumbling headfirst down the rabbit hole, this was standing on the edge of the cliff and preparing to leap, this was nothing and everything all at once.

"Yes," I whispered, sure he couldn't hear me. "I want to know."

He took my hand and slipped it beneath the table, into his lap. I'm sure I gasped like a virgin, though I was anything but. He placed my palm flat on the bulge of his erection. He didn't do anything so crass as to move my hand, not even to rub it against him. He leaned forward to speak into my ear, my hand on his straining cock and his covering it lightly.

"I've known you forever, haven't I?"

I could only nod in reply and close my eyes. I curved my hand over him. His trousers were smooth under my fingers and beneath them I felt the outline of him. I moved my hand and he twitched. His other hand slid around under my hair, his thumb pressing the pulse on the side of my neck. His mouth brushed my earlobe, his voice tight, low, thick with need.

"Who are you?" He asked me. "Some kind of angel? Or a devil, maybe…?"

I turned my head to bring my mouth close to his ear. "I don't believe in angels or devils."

I stroked him slowly, infinitesimally, a gentle curve and straightening of my fingertips undetectable to anyone watching. He got harder. Hotter. I traced the line of his cock, then lower, my hand cradling the softer bulge below.

His hand tightened on my neck. "You look like a goddess when you come, did you know that?"

Sex makes bumble-tongued fools even out of the most eloquent, but the beauty of it is that it also tunes our ears to hear the meaning of words that, spoken under other circumstances, would make us laugh or cry or frown.

"I'm not a goddess."

"Not a goddess. Not an angel. Not a devil." His breath, whiskey-scented, washed over me. The wetness of his tongue caressed my earlobe, making me shiver again. "Are you a ghost? Because you can't be real."

In reply, I took his hand and put it on my chest, over the place my heart had begun its triple-thumping once more. "I'm real."

His thumb passed over my nipple, which tightened. His hand covered my breast, but he didn't fondle me. He held it against me, and I knew he could feel the beat of my heart.

Then he took his hand away and took mine from its place on his crotch. He moved back in his seat a little. His hair had fallen tousled over his forehead. His face was somber, eyes bright with reflected neon.

He reached into the pocket of his shirt and pulled out a business card. He put it on the table between us, then pushed it in front of me.

"The next time I watch you come," he said, "I want to be inside you."

Then he got up from the table and left me there, alone.

"Daniel Stewart." His name, embossed in fine black script upon heavy, cream-colored card stock. Expensive, elegant, without a hint of the whimsy he'd shown me in Sweet Heaven. So much and so little to be learned from a business card.

I waited a week before I called him.

"Next time," he'd said, as if there could be no doubt there would be a next time.

That easy confidence set me back, but more than that was the realization I wanted there to be a next time. I wanted to see him again, wanted to feel his hands on me, wanted to come with him inside me, as he'd said.

I wanted all those things, and the wanting frightened me. Knowing his name, where he worked, glimpsing that part of his life from something so intimately anonymous as his business card, all of it had me tossing and turning each night in my bed. Solace came from my hand, a finger gently circling my clit as I imagined his face and the scent of him. I came hard, alone, gasping and unfulfilled, and knew there would be a next time, just as he'd said, even though it took me seven days to give in.

His secretary took the call and passed it on. I imagined a tone of smugness, curiosity, jealousy. Was he fucking his secretary? Did she imagine me as a client, colleague, sister, lover? She asked only my name and if Mr. Stewart would know what this call was in regard to, and when I answered yes, she put me through without hesitation.

"Elle." His voice, warm, like honey dripping into tea. "I was just thinking about you."

"Were you?"

My own office door was closed. I sat back in my chair, the curling cord of my ancient phone tangled in my fingers. I closed my eyes.

"I was."

"What were you thinking?"

"I was thinking," he said, his voice sending a slow shiver of delight down my spine, "that you weren't going to call me."

That made me smile a little. Surely he'd had no doubts? "You knew I would."

"I didn't." I heard an answering smile in his tone and pictured the upcurve of his mouth. "I thought you'd forgotten about me."

"I haven't."

"So you'll be coming to meet me for lunch today."

The assumption was no more forward than what he'd said when he handed me his card, and there was no sense in playing coy. "Yes."

"Good."

He gave me directions to a restaurant, though I knew how to get there. I wrote anyway, my pen making smooth marks that belied the unsteadiness of my hand. I hung up the phone, uncertain of how the conversation had ended, and looked to see that I had written his name, over and over, in handwriting that looked like it belonged to a stranger.

"Daniel Stewart. Daniel Stewart. Daniel Stewart."

La Belle Fleur had a pretentious name but good food, nonetheless, and was central between both our offices. It took me fifteen minutes to get there in a cab. I'd told my secretary to reschedule my afternoon appointments.

"Miss Kavanagh?" The maître d' smiled as I pushed through the double glass doors and into the small foyer. "You're meeting Mr. Stewart?"

I must've looked surprised, because he cast his eyes around the small, wood-paneled area and lowered his voice as though he were revealing the chef's recipe for a secret sauce. "He described you perfectly. And told me to expect you."

"Ah." I nodded. "I see."

He beamed, a small, spare man with a head of perfectly groomed hair and a tiny mustache to match. "Right this way."

I'd eaten at La Belle Fleur dozens of times. Clients liked its nice atmosphere and good bar. Colleagues chose it because the food was decent and reasonably priced, despite the fancy decor. I saw several faces I recognized, and I smiled and nodded as I passed.

Every step I took was a triumph over my shaking legs.

Dan's name echoed in my head as I followed the maître d' through the maze of white-cloth-covered tables toward a smaller back room, the doorway half-hidden by an embroidered screen for privacy.

"Mr. Stewart has booked a table in our Jolie room."

And there he was, Daniel Stewart, at a small table in the corner. He stood when I came into the room. Today he wore a dark-blue suit, a pale-blue shirt and a tie with a hula girl imprinted on it. He didn't approach me, made no move to touch me, not an awkward social half hug nor a handshake, and I found myself both grateful and disappointed.

"Hello."

Foolish to feel shy after what he'd done to me at the Blue Swan, more foolish still when I knew I'd let him do it again in a heartbeat. We stared at each other across the elegantly set table, until the maître d' cleared his throat to draw my attention to the chair he'd pulled out for me, and I sat. Then we stared a few more moments until at last he spoke.

"I wasn't sure you'd show up."

I dropped my gaze and studied every bead of condensation on my water glass before I looked up at him. "I wasn't sure I would, either."

"I'll have a glass of merlot," Dan said as the waiter appeared. "The lady will have a glass of the cabernet. We'll both have steak salads with the house dressing and fries."

Then he sat back in his chair again and looked at me as though he were waiting for something. I had an idea of what it was. I sipped my water before I gave it to him.

"Should I be flattered or offended at your assumption you know what I wanted?"

"I know what you want, Elle." His smile, slow and easy, spread across his face. It reached his eyes. It made me smile back at him.

"Do you?" I knew this game, had played it before. I always won. They never knew what I wanted.

Dan nodded, his eyes moving over my face as though memorizing every line and curve. Then, without leaning closer or lowering his voice, he said as though discussing the weather, "You want me to put you up against a wall."

I looked at him, my fingers tightening on the wet sides of my glass. Slippery. Cold. It would have felt delicious to put them to my forehead, or the base of my throat, against the heat rising along my skin. I kept them on the glass. I swallowed, throat dry, but didn't drink.

There was no sense in denying it, but I would have, had he said the words with a leer or even if he'd moved closer to create a sense of intimacy.

"After lunch" was all he said, and I knew in that moment I had, at last, met my match.

We spoke over our food, sipping our wine. He asked me questions about myself. He had an easy way of drawing out information, a subtle use of interest and follow-up to make it easy to give him what he wanted. He didn't push, didn't pressure, didn't judge. He asked about my education, my job, my hobbies, and I answered. He didn't speak again of what I might or might not want him to do to me. It didn't matter.

By the end of the hour, I was so turned on, the simple act of crossing my legs made me shiver at the way my panties pulled across my clit. My nipples rose rock hard inside the satin and lace of my bra, which shielded them from poking through my shirt but stimulated them mercilessly. I was so wet my thighs slid across each other. My hands shook with wanting, and I fisted them on the tablecloth to keep him from seeing.

"Now," he said at last, when the waiter had taken away our dishes and left the check. "You're going to go to the ladies' room."

His eyes kept me locked in place; after a moment, I nodded. "Yes."

Dan smiled. "I'm going to pay the check."

"Yes."

"You'll wait for me, because that's what you want."

Again, I answered yes, the word nearly unintelligible from the hoarseness of my voice. I got up from the table, for a moment unsure if my legs would hold me. I steadied myself with a hand on the back of my chair. I laid my napkin on the table. I took my purse, and I went down the short hall toward the ladies' room.

It wasn't empty when I went in. I smiled at the woman who smiled at me, but my face must have shown some sort of strain because she gave me an odd glance and hurried through washing her hands. I washed mine, too, for something to do while I waited.

My heart hammered, the beat of it loud in my ears. I splashed water on my cheeks, my throat, the insides of my wrists. I placed my hands flat upon the sink and looked at my flushed face in the mirror.

This is the face of a woman about to get fucked, I

thought, deliberately harsh to make it all seem real. *He's going to come in here and fuck you, Elle.* My pulse leaped until I fancied I could see it in the hollow of my throat.

I looked into my own eyes, the pupils dilated so wide the black almost overtook the normal blue gray. What was I doing here? I watched my tongue snake across my lips, wetting them, and I imagined his tongue tasting me. I moaned involuntarily, low, embarrassed yet aroused even more that I was already so helpless with desire a mere thought could make me make a noise.

I saw him in the mirror first as he came in. He came up behind me, his eyes locked on mine in our reflections' transposed gaze. The mole on his left cheek now on his right, my slightly higher right eyebrow arching now upon the left. His hands slid into place on my hips, his thumbs finding the twin dimples at the small of my back even through my shirt.

He said nothing. If he'd spoken, I'd have bolted. He didn't speak. He was bold. Unfaltering. And even so, the glimpse of his face in the mirror showed that same odd mix of emotion in his eyes. Lust and admiration, with a sense of being honored.

He moved me with no hesitation to the last stall, the largest, and he locked the door behind us. Now I couldn't see him, but he didn't let me doubt what he wanted. He put my hands up, palms flat, against the cool ceramic tile. His hands slid beneath my skirt, over the tops of my elastic-topped stockings, then between my legs. He held me from behind, fingers curving upward to brush my clit.

I shuddered. I pressed my forehead against the wall. Closed my eyes. My thighs opened, and he spread them wider by sliding his foot between mine and pushing my right foot away from my left. His finger circled against me through the now-damp fabric of my panties.

I heard the small clatter of a metal buckle being undone, followed by the soft sigh of a button eased from its hole. The purr of a zip parting.

His fingers dipped down, then up, to slide inside my panties. He muttered a curse when his flesh met mine. He stroked a finger along my folds as though testing how slick I had become for him.

His chin pressed into my shoulder. His mouth nuzzled beneath my ear and I tilted my head to the side to allow him access to my neck.

The hand he'd used to loose himself now inched up my skirt. My fingers curled against slippery tile, finding nothing to grab. I bit back a moan when air hit my skin, the soft expanse of bare thigh and buttock exposed by my stockings and the edge of my panties. His palm caressed me, traced the curve of my ass.

I breathed in and in and in, forgetting to let the air from my lungs come out, too, until at last it hissed from between my lips in a long, shuddering sigh.

"You want this."

His words were not a question, yet they demanded an answer.

"Yes."

He put a finger inside me, then two, stretching me a little. He stroked me, in and out, a parody of what he would do with his cock. And I, shameless, trembled at that small touch and pushed myself against his hand to take him in as far as I could.

"My purse," I murmured, wondering if he'd balk and preparing for this all to end if he did.

He withdrew. I sighed a protest. He laughed, the sound broken by the harsh intake of his breath.

"Give me half a minute, Elle," he whispered into my ear.

I heard the jingle of my keys, then the crinkle of paper and sound of tearing, then a low groan as he eased on the condom. He paused, breath still hot against my neck, and a bolt of electric desire arced through me. It centered in my clit and radiated out through the rest of my body. Even my fingertips tingled. I imagined if the lights were off, I'd be glowing with it.

He pulled my panties over my hips and down past my knees, then pressed his cock against me. He nudged it along the cleft of my ass, then pushed between my thighs. His hand guided it toward my entrance, and he dipped down, then up, to push inside me.

"Fuck," he muttered, then bit down on my shoulder as though to stifle a further outburst.

I gave a strangled cry when he filled me. It had been so long I was almost too tight, but I was so wet with arousal there was no friction. Only a delicious fullness.

He put his hands over my wrists, his front along my back, and slid my hands down on the wall until I bent more at the waist. I hadn't thought he could move inside me any more, but that small shift in angle let him nudge my tender cervix, and I gave another low cry at the tiny spark of pain that did nothing to diminish the pleasure.

"Christ, you're hot," he murmured. "Like a fucking furnace..."

He began to move. Slow, smooth strokes at first, his hands anchoring my hips to keep me from moving. Then, after a few moments, faster. Harder. One hand slipped around front to press my clit in time to his thrusts.

The door to the restroom opened. Dan stopped for a moment, then kept on, pulling out and pushing inside me with excruciating slowness. His finger circled faster.

I heard voices, two chattering women who used the stalls at the far end of the room without a break in their conversation. One of them peed forever, a waterfall of piss, and a bubble of laughter leaked out of me.

My shoulders shook with the effort of keeping it inside. His breath puffed in silent glee on my neck. Stars, the result of lack of oxygen, danced in my vision and I drew in breath after shallow breath, trying not to make a sound.

I laughed, and laughing made me come, writhing against his hand and moving on his cock while he kept his movements almost stationary for silence.

They used the sink, still chattering. If they heard us, they paid no attention. Perhaps we managed to be quiet enough, or maybe the saga and drama of their lives was so enthralling nothing could tear their attention from it. I only know that the second the door closed behind them Dan began fucking me in earnest.

Hard and fast. The hand on my hip gripped tight enough to leave a bruise. The stroking hand stopped and held me. I came again, smaller but no less pleasurable, and throbbed on his palm.

His teeth grazed my neck. His mouth moved to my shoulder, and he muffled his outcry against my shirt. His cock jerked inside me, and he thrust once more, hard enough to smack my forehead on the tile wall.

It hurt, but it made me laugh again. Sex in real life is never like in the movies. The choreography's always off. Most people, though, don't like to laugh during sex. Something's wrong there. It's supposed to bring joy, isn't it?

Dan's hand squeezed my sides gently before he pulled out. My skirt fell back around my thighs, and I reached to pull up my panties from their place around my knees. He flushed the condom, tucked himself away, zipped up his pants, every movement businesslike and efficient like he'd done this dozens of times before. For all I knew, he had.

"I took care of the check," he said, his voice suddenly too loud for the small space, and then he walked out.

What had I expected? I chided myself. The same face looked at me from the mirror, but this time the fading flush on my throat and cheeks were a sign of a woman not about to be fucked, but one who has already been. I searched my eyes for some sign of change, something inside me to indicate how this should make me feel. Remorse? Guilt? Smug satisfaction? I saw no evidence of them in my gaze, couldn't feel it. All I could think of was the way I'd laughed and climaxed simultaneously.

Even so, I lingered at the sink to wash my hands and pat a dampened paper towel across my face. I fixed my hair, freshened my makeup, sprayed cologne to mask the scent of sex.

The parking lot had emptied, the lunchtime crowds gone. I came out into late-afternoon sunshine that had me pulling my sunglasses from my bag. A spring breeze plucked at the hem of my raincoat.

"Hey."

I turned to see him standing just outside the front doors. He flicked a just-finished cigarette onto the pavement and took two strides to catch up to me.

"You took a long time," he said. "I was beginning to think you weren't coming out."

I took a second to answer. "I didn't know you were waiting for me."

Something flickered in his eyes I couldn't decipher. "No?"

I shook my head slowly.

"Why would you think that?"

"Because you were finished. I figured you needed to get back to work."

I'd taken a cab to the restaurant, but the bus stop was only a block away. I started walking. He let me go four steps before he followed me.

"So…you think I just left you there?"

I nodded again, keeping my eyes straight ahead. It was true. I hadn't expected him to wait for me, had believed he'd gone. I hadn't been ashamed of what we'd done until I found him waiting for me. When it became clear he expected not just a quick lunchtime fuck, but conversation after.

"That's the sort of guy you think I am." He had a way of phrasing questions in such a way he answered them himself.

I glanced at him. "Well, Dan, I don't know what sort of guy you are, other than you're careful, which I appreciate."

Darkness passed over his features and he reached to grab my arm when I made to move forward again. "Elle—"

I extricated myself from his grip with firmness that could not be misconstrued. "Thanks very much for lunch, Dan."

He let me get six steps this time before he followed. "Is that all you think I wanted? Is that what you expected?"

How could I explain to him, who seemed so affronted, that it was not only what I had expected, but all I wanted. Twenty minutes of oblivion to make me stop thinking.

He took two more quick steps to end up in front of me, walking backward to keep us face-to-face. "Elle."

"That's my bus." I pointed at the one pulling up to the stop. I could be there in another minute, get on, go back to work.

"You're not getting on that bus."

"No? I think I am."

He stood in front of me so I had to step around him to keep moving. He matched my move with one of his own, graceful, as though we were dancing. He wasn't smiling, but then, neither was I.

"Elle," he said warningly. "Don't walk away from me."

I might have liked it when he was leading me unerringly toward sex, but I didn't like his assumptions now. "I'll walk wherever I want."

Again he stepped in front of me. The bus, its driver apparently taking Dan's side, pulled away. I glared. This time he let me move forward.

"Now you have to talk to me," he said.

"No," I retorted. "I don't."

"But you want to."

"Look," I said, whirling on him. "Just because I let you fuck me doesn't give you the right to tell me what to do!"

"I didn't say it did!" He frowned. "I think it at least gives me the right to have you not think I'm an asshole."

"I don't think you're an asshole."

He moved closer. "Then what do you think I am?"

"I think you're a man," I replied, not caring if that offended him.

Dan didn't look offended. He grinned. "Glad you noticed."

I wanted to be angry with him. I wanted to feel disdain. Yet as I'd waited for shame or remorse in the bathroom, anger and disdain eluded me, too.

"Look," I said finally. "We had a nice lunch—"

"We did."

"And what happened, after—"

"Also nice. We forgot dessert."

I paused. "But let's not kid ourselves it was anything more than what it was. All right?"

"Elle," Dan said seriously. "Why not?"

The bus stop was ten steps away, but I kept walking past it. He followed. I walked faster.

"Why not?" He asked again, softer this time, and reached to grab my elbow.

I didn't pull away this time. I let him turn me. He put both hands on my elbows, holding me in place.

"Why not?

A thousand explanations raced through my mind, but only one slipped from my tongue. "Because it's not what I do."

"Take off your sunglasses. I want to see your eyes when you talk to me."

I sighed, belabored, but complied. He met my gaze, searching my eyes like they held a clue, a key, a treasure map. His fingers curled on my arms.

"Why not?"

I could only stare at him for a long moment while traffic passed us by and birds chattered among the branches of a tree in springtime bloom. "I just don't."

"You don't what?" The tone was gentle, the words non-threatening, but I could give him no answer. "You don't date?"

"No."

He studied my face. "But you fuck in bathrooms."

I jerked from his grasp and set my feet to the sidewalk again. "I've never done that before."

This time I thought for sure he'd let me go. I made it to the corner before he reached my side again. I didn't look at him.

"I want to see you again."

I stopped, shoulders hunching in resignation that this conversation would not end until he was satisfied. "Why, Dan?"

"Because I didn't get to see your face this time."

Just like that, desire sliced me open like a samurai sword and left me gasping for breath. I hid it with a shake of my head and a scowl. He didn't grab me to stop me this time, just murmured my name in a low voice that halted my feet as though I'd stepped in glue.

"Because you have the sexiest laugh I've ever heard in my

life, and I don't think I could stand knowing I'd never hear it again."

Why is kindness so much harder to believe than cruelty?

I didn't want to believe him. I wanted to think he was full of empty words. I wanted to walk away from him. I wanted all those things, but in the end, had none of them.

"I don't date." The reply sounded lame, even to me.

Dan grinned. "So we won't date."

"What," I asked, refusing to smile though the corners of my mouth insisted on tilting upward, "will we do?"

"Whatever you want, Elle," Dan said. "Whatever you want."

Whatever I wanted. An easy thing to promise, but not so easy to request. I didn't know what I wanted. I only knew I couldn't stop thinking about him.

Marcy cornered me by the coffee machine. "Where'd you go on Friday? You ditched us!"

"I got a headache." The lie tripped easily off my tongue. "You two were looking pretty cozy by the bar, so I just snuck out."

She seemed satisfied with that answer, then prattled on about her night with Wayne. The cologne he wore. The brand of shampoo he preferred. The way he liked his eggs. She stopped midsentence to stare at me.

"What?"

I'd been transfixed by her commentary, but now I finished pouring my coffee. "Nothing."

I didn't want to tell her I envied her. I wasn't sure I did. I'd been in love before, with disastrous results.

“Did something happen at The Blue Swan?”

I shook my head. “No. Should it have?”

“Hell, yeah.” Marcy tossed her blond hair over one shoulder. “It should have. Definitely. But…nothing? We lost you after you went to get the drinks. Thought maybe someone swept you away.”

“Oh.” My laugh sounded forced and lame. “Nothing like that, I’m afraid.”

She didn’t look convinced, but I didn’t give her any more of the story.

Dan didn’t wait to call me the way I had.

“Hello, Miss Kavanagh. Daniel Stewart calling.”

“Yes, Mr. Stewart. How can I help you?”

“I read a good review about the film showing at the Allen Theater this weekend. I’d like to make an appointment with you to see it.”

“An appointment?” He’d caught me washing dishes left over from breakfast. I cradled the phone against my shoulder while I swirled a soapy sponge over my bowl and rinsed it.

“Yes. I believe you said you didn’t go on dates.”

“I said I didn’t date. Not that I didn’t go on dates.”

“Ah. Fine line, there.”

I imagined him running a hand through his hair, maybe wearing a T-shirt and jeans. He’d have a leather couch. Big-screen television set. Plants a housekeeper watered and plucked the dead leaves from.

I finished with my dishes and set the kettle on to boil water for tea. “I go on an occasional date.”

That wasn't quite true. I hadn't been on a date in a long time. Longer than I'd forgone sex, as a matter of fact.

"You're changing your story on me, Elle. That's not fair."

"Life's not fair." I wiped off my table and replaced the napkin holder in the center.

"Elle." His voice reached through the phone and stroked me from head to foot. I closed my eyes. "You want to go with me to the movies."

I leaned against my counter, an arm folded across my stomach to support the one holding the phone. I thought for a moment. "Yes. I do."

"Good," he said, as though that settled things. And it did.

He took me to an arty, independent film with subtitles, the plot of which I had difficulty untangling but enjoyed anyway for its lush visuals. We had dessert in the theater's attached coffee shop, where he challenged me to a game of Scrabble in which he spelled words like "cleft" and "slick" for a triple word score. We traded limericks, and he seemed impressed I knew so many. We laughed so loudly we turned heads, and I didn't even care. He didn't touch me, though I wanted him to.

He invited me back to his apartment for drinks. I agreed. I wanted to see the place where he lived. I wanted to see his bed.

He served me Guinness in a pint glass and didn't insist on using coasters, though his furniture looked new enough to require them. He settled down beside me on his leather couch as easily as though we'd spent months together instead of hours, and he asked me questions about the movie as if he cared about the answers.

I'm not completely socially incompetent. I do have to know how to interact with clients, give presentations, make appointments, shake hands and make small talk. I can do those things sufficiently, if not with ease. If anything, I would imagine people would describe me as aloof, taking my silence at times for standoffishness rather than awkwardness. I'm still the girl who sat in the front of the class, ready to answer all the teacher's questions. I just lost most of the answers somewhere along the way.

Dan didn't make me think too hard. He led me through the maze of conversation without hesitation, as easily as if he'd taken my hand to keep me from stumbling over a crack in the pavement. He talked a lot about himself, but not in an obnoxious way. It soothed me to hear his anecdotes of high school soccer games and college frat parties. I didn't have stories like that. Normal stories. Hearing the tales of others fascinated me. Maybe it should have made me bitter with envy, but it didn't, not any more than a fairy story made me envy the princess who could weave gold from straw.

Anyone who's ever spent time with someone who seems enthralled with every word you say knows how intoxicating that can be. His eyes watched my mouth move. He listened to me, engaged me in conversation, drew forth answers that surprised me with their honesty. I told him about my house and my job, my favorite television show and the fact I love anything chocolate but not hot fudge.

All because he listened. Was I so starved for admiration his good manners seemed like more to me? No. It was him, Dan, entirely, and the fact he listened to learn about me, not as a reason to have me learn about him.

I was in the middle of a sentence when he leaned in to kiss me. The contact startled me. I hadn't been expecting it, hadn't had time to turn my face. His mouth was soft and warm on my lips. I tasted salt from the popcorn. His hand came up to touch my face, strong fingers on my cheek.

I couldn't do it. I couldn't kiss him on the mouth, that gesture more intimate than taking him inside my body. I turned my face, broke the kiss, didn't finish my sentence.

"No?" He asked, breath hot on my ear.

"No."

He slid his hand down to caress my breast. "But this."

I turned my head to look into his eyes. "Yes."

Something flickered in his gaze. Got harder. His hand slid up to cup the back of my neck, his fingers threading through my hair. He pulled, tilting my head back and exposing my throat.

"And this," he said, pressing his lips to the spot where my pulse beat, beat, beat, skipping.

His teeth grazed my skin, and I gave a little gasp. "Yes."

His mouth trailed lower, to the jut of my collarbone. His fingers tightened in my hair, and I gasped again at the mingled pleasure/pain. He sucked my skin between his teeth, the tip of his tongue circling against it. His other hand found my breast and he thumbed my nipple erect. His hand slid lower, between my legs.

"And this."

"Yes…" The word sighed out of me.

"Stand up."

I did.

"Take off your clothes."

My hands went to the buttons on my shirt. I slid them from the holes, my fingers trembling. Fear and fierce desire can almost feel the same, sometimes. I slipped off the shirt, let it fall to the floor in a way I'd never done if alone.

I wanted to see his eyes fill with desire, hear him hiss in a breath at the sight of me. Dan watched me, his face unreadable. I flushed, heat creeping up my throat to paint my cheeks. I wanted to put my hands on them to cool them. Instead I undid the button and zip on my skirt and let that puddle to the floor, too.

I wore fine things beneath my clothes, panties and bra of black lace and satin and flattering cut. The bra pushed my breasts together, creating creamy-skinned cleavage. The panties rode low on my hips and cut high in the back to reveal the curve of my ass. The black looked darker against my skin, pale from being kept out of the sun, and I knew he could see the darker triangle of the hair between my thighs.

I stood in front of him, trying not to shake, though the desire that had made my fingers tremble now made my legs want to buckle. I'd been naked in front of men before. Had let them look at my body, judge it, praise or find flaws with the curve of belly, the jut of my hipbones, the weight and shape of my breasts. For them, I'd worn my body the way I wore my clothes, as something practical to be used for a purpose. A function.

In front of Dan, I'd become more than hip and thigh and cunt. He looked at my body knowing my real name, the way I drank my tea, the sound of my laughter. My nakedness came from what he knew about me, what I had let him know, those tiny, irrevocable intimacies I never share with anyone.

"The rest. Take those off, too." His voice had grown thick, proof of his desire, and it gave me courage.

This part I knew. How a glimpse of pink could render a man mindless. We all have the same parts, us women, yet every man I've ever been with has looked at me as though he's never seen a naked woman before. There is power in our bodies that men don't have, secret and hidden places they yearn to explore over and over. Women's bodies hold the mystery of blood and life, not just pleasure.

I reached behind me to unhook my bra, the movement thrusting my breasts forward. I watched him watch me as I let the straps fall down my shoulders. As I let the cups fall away to reveal my flesh.

He leaned back against the couch, his cock pushing at the front of his khaki pants. I wasn't the only one flushing. Red tinged his cheeks, too, and he licked his mouth as he watched me.

"The panties."

I hooked my thumbs in the sides of the lace and eased them over my hips. I did it slowly, enjoying the look on his face as he focused. I parted my thighs and cocked my hip, slid the fabric down my ass and over my thighs, then let them fall to my ankles. I stepped out of them and stood, at last, completely naked.

"Fuck," he muttered and ran a hand through his hair. "Turn around."

I did, one rotation.

"Touch yourself."

The request surprised me but I was already complying. I held my breasts, my nipples responding to my touch as quickly as if my hands were his. I slid my thumbs over the tight buds, then ran my hands down my sides, over my belly, down my thighs. I put one hand over the hair between my legs, cupping my center and pressing the heel of my hand against my clit.

"Fucking hell, you're hot."

My flush grew deeper, more blush than flush this time. His praise thrilled me and eased the fear that always accompanies being naked in front of another.

"Elle," Dan said, "tell me you want me to fuck you."

Simple words to describe an act with so much variation.

"Oh," I said, my voice hoarse. "Dan, I want you to fuck me."

I don't think I've ever wanted anything more. I will never forget the feeling of standing naked in front of him that first time. How he looked at my body as not pieces, but as a whole, woven together by those small things about me I'd allowed him to know.

He was on his feet without hesitation. His hands on my hips pulled me against him as his mouth found my throat. He kissed me there, then on my shoulder, then bent his knees to reach the tops of my breasts. His hands roamed my skin, cupped my buttocks, pressed the small of my back, traced the edges of my shoulder blades.

"Put your arms around me."

I did. He put his hands under my thighs and lifted me. It was sudden and took me unawares. I am not a small woman and he not a large man. It didn't matter. I wrapped my legs around him, the fabric of his oxford shirt rubbing my clit deliciously enough to make me whimper.

He took me to the bedroom and kicked the door shut behind him, I don't know how. I could only hang on and pray we didn't end up on the floor. He didn't drop me. He laid me down on the bed as skillfully as if it had risen to meet us. He covered me with his body, kissed me all over. Every place but my mouth, because I had told him no.

Together we worked the buttons on his shirt with far less grace than I'd used on mine. One flew off and spanged against the wall. Another refused to come free and tore the hole until it slipped out. His skin beneath was smooth and covered with crisp, curling hair over muscles that shifted under my fingers as he tore his arms from the sleeves. Then his hands were on me again, sliding up and down, and my hands were on his belt buckle, tugging. He reached to help me, his teeth biting into my shoulder when I reached inside to grasp him.

I gasped at the bite and tightened my grip involuntarily. He gasped too and gave another muttered curse. He sat up to push down his pants and the boxer briefs beneath, rolling onto his back to get them past his thighs and down his legs. He kicked them off, one foot at a time, and I watched his body become revealed to me.

I could say his body was perfect and every part of it beautiful, because it was. Not because he had no flaws, but because I wanted him so desperately I couldn't see any.

He rolled on top of me, skin to skin. He was hard where I was soft. Rough where I was smooth. Straight where I curved. Man and woman, puzzle pieces, meant to fit.

He took my nipple between his lips and I arched beneath him. He laved it with his tongue, then suckled gently. It tugged within my womb, and my cunt spasmed. His hand slid between my legs. His fingertip, unerring, found my clit and circled it. He dipped down to my folds and brought slickness from inside me to smooth his touch.

I put my hand on his head. His hair was soft and long enough for me to grasp and tug. Pleasure made me pull too hard, and he muttered *ouch* against my breast.

I loosed my grip but kept my hand in its place. He moved to the other nipple, offering it the same treatment. Every tug he gave sent another spasm through my insides. My clit swelled under his touch. I felt it grow, felt the blood rushing to that small bundle of nerves from all over my body. I floated in that pleasure, gave myself to it, welcomed the oblivion of ecstasy.

His mouth grazed my ribs. His tongue swept my skin, tasting me. He murmured against me, words I couldn't understand but didn't need to.

His cock stretched hot along my thigh. He rubbed it against me, his hips pumping slowly. I thought of how he'd feel thrusting inside me and moaned.

"Damn it, you've got a sexy voice."

I looked down at him, uncertain if I'd be able to form a coherent sentence. "Hush."

He grinned up at me, his hand moving, moving, making me shake. "You do."

Compliments embarrass me. I shook my head a little. My hair spread out around me on the bedspread.

He looked at me again with that same odd expression of

query and acceptance; a man being handed a gift he's not sure what he's done to deserve but taking it without hesitation.

"Elle," he said. "I'm going to watch your face this time, and I'm going to be inside you. Do you want that?"

I nodded. My fingers tangled in his hair. "Yes."

He left me for a moment to reach inside his nightstand drawer, and I was grateful I didn't need to insist, or get up to get my purse, too far away in the living room. I reached for the condom, but he shook his head.

"I need to do it."

He must have seen a question in my eyes, because he smiled. "I don't want to finish before we've started."

His honesty made me want to be honest with him. To give him something real. But I had given him enough already with inconsequential revelations he didn't realize he was so privileged to have.

I got up on one elbow to watch him, glad for the chance to see him. Like the rest of him, his cock was near perfect. Pretty, even, of average length and girth and color but somehow lovely. He slipped the condom on, stroking the latex down to the base. Thus shielded, he leaned in to look into my eyes.

He positioned himself on top of me, using his arms to keep from crushing me. His cock nudged me, and I parted for him and tilted my hips to allow him entrance. He rubbed the tip along my folds, pushing in a little before reaching between us to guide himself all the way inside.

I moaned when he did, and he did, too. He stopped when his cock hit my cervix. I had a hand on his biceps and felt him trembling. He put his forehead against mine, his eyes closed for a moment before he opened them. Then, without taking his gaze from mine, he began to move.

He'd said he wanted to fuck me, but that one word can mean so many different things. Dan moved inside me with slow deliberation, every stroke smooth. I put my arms around his neck to bring his mouth back to my neck. He obliged me by kissing me there. I tilted my head to offer him more, and he took it. He pressed his teeth to the spot he'd bitten but didn't bite this time. His tongue smoothed the spot.

He slid his hands beneath my rear to tilt me against him and change the angle. His pelvis bumped my clit with every thrust. The intermittent pressure pushed me higher. Made me wetter. Delicious friction, no need for lubrication, our bodies worked exactly the way they were meant to.

Skin on skin. Cock in cunt, a perfect fit. He moved. I moved. He gave, I took. I hooked my legs around his thighs, urging him against me.

He murmured my name. I answered with his. Connecting. We were connecting, and even in the oblivion of pleasure I could not forget who I was with. I didn't want to. It mattered to me what mouth kissed me, whose hands stroked me, whose penis filled me.

It mattered, suddenly, that it was this man, and the mattering made my body stutter. I froze. My heart, already pounding, skipped a beat.

A woman's orgasm is such a fragile thing, dependant as much upon her mind as on her clitoris, and though my climax had been swelling inside me, ready to spill over, I lost it. My body shifted, my thoughts atangle with self-discovery. I had let him in.

He couldn't know, of course, that because I had told him my true name and the way I drink my tea, sex would suddenly become so complicated. I had let him fuck me in a bathroom stall, after all. He couldn't know that sex was something I did and intimacy something I did not. Dan could not have known those things, but he looked into my eyes at that moment anyway as if he did.

"It's all right," he told me, as confident in that as when he'd ordered lunch for me. "Elle. It's all right."

He rolled me so carefully we didn't part and then was beneath me. He adjusted my legs and put my hands on his chest. My fingers curved around his ribs. He put one hand on my hip. The other slid between us, his thumb pressing my clit.

"Move," he whispered. "Move the way you want to."

And though I'd stuttered, though the moment I'd almost lost had less to do with sex and more to do with fear, I did as he said. I moved. I rocked against him, finding a pace that satisfied me and brought me back to where we'd been.

He helped me, shifting when I shifted and easing his thrusts when I changed the angle. He moved his hips at my guidance, and even when his breath became ragged he kept his thrusts smooth.

I let my head fall back to feel my hair tumble down and stroke the top of my ass. I wanted to lose myself again, to give up to the same sweet nothingness, but though my body filled with pleasure, I couldn't find it.

"Come for me," he whispered. His thumb stroked me as he helped me rock against him. "I want to watch you."

I shuddered. I opened my eyes. My body knew better than my brain. He looked at me, and I at him, and I gave him what he wanted.

Everything drew tighter, knotting, until I unraveled. I cried out. My fingers dug into his skin. His thumb ceased moving and stayed still, the pressure enough to keep me surging. He thrust harder, faster, both hands moving to pin my hips. He grunted when he came, so close behind me it was almost simultaneous.

We lay together in silence, after, not touching. Sweat cooled on my body, but it felt good. I felt good.

At least for a little while, before I began to calculate how long I'd have to wait before I could get up to leave. I listened to his breathing deepen. Maybe he'd fall asleep, and I could sneak out.

He let out one small, entirely adorable snore. I got up and padded to the bathroom connected to his bedroom, where I used the toilet and the sink. His washcloths were thick, plush and blue, to match the paint and shower curtain. I used his mouthwash, sniffed his cologne, admired the surprising cleanliness of his floor and counter. He had a rubber duck in his bathtub, and I marveled over it for a minute. The hint of whimsy.

Still naked, I came out of the bathroom to find his eyes open.

"You're the first woman I've ever been with who practically counted the seconds until she could leave."

"Really?" I asked from the doorway. "I've been with plenty of men who've done it."

I went to the living room to pick up my discarded clothes

and put them on. I'd slipped on my panties and was hooking my bra when he came after me.

"Why don't you date?" He asked from the doorway. He'd slipped on boxers printed with a pattern of marching jelly-beans, and I was vividly reminded of meeting him at Sweet Heaven.

"Dating complicates things." I slid my arms into my sleeves and did up the buttons. I put on my skirt, zipped and buttoned it, tucked in my shirt. I smoothed the wrinkles.

"How do you figure that?"

"Dating," I said, "implies a level of emotional connection for both parties to either create or work toward creating."

Dan crossed his arms over his chest. "And?"

I sighed. "I don't have time for that."

He made a low noise of disbelief. "You mean you don't want to have time for it."

"Semantics."

He watched me look around for my purse but made no move to help me find it. "You said you did go on dates, sometimes."

I shot him a smile. "Sometimes. Not for a long time. And a date is not dating. Dating implies more than once."

"Ah." He looked bemused. "Which leads to the emotional corruption."

"Connection—" I looked up. He was teasing me. "That, too."

"How long has it been since you went on a date?"

"Not counting our appointment?"

He held up a finger. "That was an appointment, not a date."

"Right." I didn't have to think hard. "Four years, eight months, three days."

I found my purse in the moment of silence my answer had created. I rifled through it, checking for car keys and cab fare. When I looked up, Dan was staring at me.

"How long since you'd had sex?"

"Three years. Give or take."

"Are you counting from tonight or the time in the bathroom?"

"I'm counting from the time on the dance floor." I zipped my bag closed and slung it over my shoulder. "Because… that was sex."

He watched me get ready to leave. His expression didn't tell me if he was shocked, angry or admiring. At last he ran a hand through his sandy hair, spiking it, then passed the same hand across his mouth.

"Good night, Dan."

His words caught me with my hand on the knob to his front door. "You want to see me again. I know you do."

I turned to look at him. "More than once, you mean?"

"You've already seen me more than once," he pointed out.

"So then I should say no."

I didn't want to say no. The sex had been fantastic. More than that, his company had been comfortable. Dangerously so.

"I don't date."

"I'll make another appointment."

"Why?" I asked, point-blank. "You've seen me come with you inside me. What's left?"

I think I really shocked him then. I meant to, anyway. I wanted to chase him away from me.

He stood up straight and glanced to the bedroom before striding over to me. He was tall enough so we didn't stand eye to eye, but not so tall I had to crane my neck to meet his gaze. His face had gone hard, and though I shouldn't admit it, the sudden sense of danger, of wondering if maybe I'd pushed him a little too far, sparked a thrill through me.

"You're smiling." He wasn't. "Do you like to play games, Elle? Is that it?"

Some men like to use their size or their fists to intimidate women. Dan looked angry, but he didn't touch me. I didn't move, didn't retreat. He put a hand on the door frame next to my head.

"I didn't get you off good enough?"

"That's not it. You were very good."

He didn't look pleased at the compliment. "Not good enough for another round?"

"You didn't ask me if I wanted to fuck you again," I said matter-of-factly. "You asked me if I wanted to see you again."

"You can't do the first without the second, Elle."

He was fast. Clever, without being arrogant about it. I liked that. Liked him.

"If you want to fuck—" I began.

"Is that what you want?" His voice dipped lower. "Just a quick fuck?"

"No," I said. "Sometimes I like them to be slow."

He put his other hand on my hip, pulling me step by reluctant step against him. "I can give you that."

He was hard again. I felt him on my belly. I put my arms around his neck and let him press me close along his body.

"Can you?"

He nodded, solemn, hands cupping my ass now to rub me against his erection. "I told you. Whatever you want."

"It won't work, you know. It never does. People get attached—"

He laughed. "I won't get attached."

I smiled. His bare skin was warm beneath my hands. "Nobody thinks they will. But they always do."

"And that's why you don't date."

"That's why."

He rocked me against him, slowly. "Because men get attached to you."

"Some have, yes."

"And you don't?"

I splayed my fingers on his shoulders, my thumbs stroking the ridge of his collarbone. "I did once."

He bent his head to run his mouth along my neck. "But other than that, you've broken the hearts of scores of fools who got attached to you."

"I don't like to think so, no. I've tried to avoid it."

"Why? It doesn't get you hot, thinking of all those broken hearts in your wake?"

"No."

"Because…you'd feel guilty."

"Yes…" The word became a hiss as his tongue stroked my skin.

"And that's why you don't date."

"Haven't we gone over this?" I looked at him, pushing him away a little to see his face.

"Don't worry, Elle," he whispered, pulling me closer again. "I won't get too attached."

How can I explain exactly how he made me feel? Even now, looking back, I can remember everything about that moment. The feeling of his hands on me. The scent of him, cologne and sex. The way his mouth curved at the corners and the way the first hint of stubble glinted on his cheeks. I hold a perfect picture of him in my mind: Dan in that moment. The moment he convinced me to stay.

I had time to regret my decision the next day when I got out of the cab in front of my house wearing the same clothes I'd worn the night before. I'd showered, brushed my teeth, washed my face. But there could be no mistaking the crumples for anything other than the sort of wrinkles your clothes get when they've been tossed without ceremony on the floor because you're about to get well and thoroughly fucked.

"Hi, Miss Kavanagh." Gavin waited on his own porch steps this time, but as they were scant inches from mine it made little difference. "I thought you might need some more help today with the dining room."

What I really wanted was to fall face-first into my pillows and go back to sleep. I gave Gavin a narrow smile as I put my key in the lock. He was already behind me.

"It's so early," I told him. "Don't you have anything else you'd like to be doing today? It's a gorgeous Saturday."

"Nah." He watched me fumble with my lock, which sometimes stuck on humid days. "Need some help with that?"

"I got it." I didn't. I was tired and he was crowding me, peering over my shoulder to look at the stubborn lock.

"Gavin!"

We both turned. Mrs. Ossley came out onto their front porch, her hands on her hips and a frown contorting what would have otherwise been a pretty face. She stopped when she saw me with her son. Her gaze swept me up and down. I owed her no explanation for my clothes or early-morning return, but that didn't stop me from feeling I wanted to give her one. Her frown gave way to an insincere smile.

"Gavin," she said, her voice sweet enough to rot teeth. "Leave Miss Kavanagh alone. You have to get ready to go."

Gavin backed away from me a step, but didn't go next door. "I don't want to go."

Her smile didn't waver. "I don't care what you want to do. Dennis has been talking about this all week."

Gavin didn't move toward her, though his entire body seemed to shrink in on itself. "I hate the Civil War, I don't want to go to the Civil War Museum. It's going to be boring." He looked at me. "Besides, I promised Miss Kavanagh I'd help her paint her dining room."

"Miss Kavanagh," his mother said through her teeth, "is perfectly capable of painting her own dining room."

"Yes, Gavin," I said quietly, meeting her gaze without looking away. "I am. You should do what your mother says. You can help me after I get home from work this week. I'll be taping off the moldings."

He muttered and grumbled but hopped down my two

concrete steps and took the ones to his house in one stride. He pushed past his mother without a word. She didn't look at him as he went inside.

We looked across the narrow gap between our porches. She didn't seem much older than I, despite having a fifteen-year-old son. She still smiled, and at last I relented and smiled at her with as much sincerity as she'd given me.

"Have a good time at the museum," I told her, finally fitting my key into the lock and opening my door.

"We will. My fiancé, Dennis, is taking us."

I couldn't have cared less about her fiancé, but I nodded at her anyway and started inside my house.

"Gavin spends a lot of time with you," she said, stopping me.

I turned to face her as I took my key from the lock and put it in my purse. "He likes to borrow my books. And he's been very helpful with my renovations."

She glanced inside before looking back at me. "I have to work long hours. I can't always be here for him."

I couldn't tell if she was explaining herself to me out of guilt or warning me off. "He's always welcome to come over here, Mrs. Ossley. I appreciate his help."

She looked me up and down again. "I'm sure you do."

I waited for her to say more and when she didn't, I repeated my hopes they'd enjoy the museum, and I went inside. I closed the door behind me and leaned against it for a moment. We'd never shared more than a wave in passing before, even though we'd been neighbors for five years. I supposed there were better conversations we could have had. Then again, there could have been worse.

I didn't care to ponder on it too much. My bed called me, and I went to it to seek a few hours rest before I got on with the rest of my day.

There was no hiding from Marcy on Monday. She took one look at me and squealed like she'd been stuck with a cattle prod.

"Ooooh, girl! You've done it!"

I kept my eyes on my reflection as I carefully applied sheer lip gloss and powdered my nose. "Done what?"

Marcy was touching up, too, though she'd brought a fully equipped tackle box into the bathroom. She had every color of eye shadow known to man and some I was convinced came from an alien planet, all with matching lip and eye pencils, blush, foundation and powder. She had so many lipsticks laid out the counter bristled like a coral reef full of tubeworms. She shook one at me.

"You've gone got yourself a man."

Her words took me aback, so I smeared instead of smudged. "I beg your pardon?"

She raised a plucked-to-perfection brow. "A man, honey. Don't deny it. You've got the FFG all over you."

I shook my head, laughing. "What's FFG?"

"Freshly fucked glow, honey," she said, lowering her voice in deference to the bathroom acoustics, but only for a moment. "Spill it."

"I don't have anything to spill." I swiped the sponge from my compact over my nose and cheeks, then tucked it and my gloss back in the small emergency kit I keep in my purse.

"C'mon. I told you about Wayne."

She was right. The bonds of feminine friendship did require reciprocation. And truthfully, I wanted to talk to someone about Dan. Marcy, sad to say, was my only friend.

"His name is Dan Stewart. He's a lawyer. I met him at The Blue Swan."

"I knew it!" She didn't seem to mind that I'd lied to her before.

Marcy owned more brushes than Picasso, all shapes and sizes and kept in a rolled-up leather case. She whipped out one now and used it to dab at the lipstick. I watched, fascinated as she drew in her lips like a paint-by-numbers picture.

"So he's got a good job. Big deal. Has he got a big dick?"

I coughed and blushed. I don't know why. I've heard worse. Said worse.

"It's adequate," I said.

"Oh," she said sympathetically, blotting her lips on a square of tissue. "Small?"

"No! Marcy, good Lord!"

"Adequate? C'mon, Elle." She turned to face me. "Cut? Uncut? Long? Short? Thick? Thin? What?"

"Jesus, Marcy. Who looks that closely?" I bent to scrub my hands.

"Who doesn't?" She began packing away her box of paints and powders.

"He has a very nice penis," I told her. "Aesthetically pleasing and fully functional."

She rolled her eyes. "Spare me, would you? You're acting like this is no big deal."

I pushed open the door to the bathroom and started for my office. She followed. She didn't stop at my doorway, either, but came right in and made herself at home.

"Have a seat," I offered wryly. "Can I get you a drink?"

"Give me one of your diet sodas," she said. "I know you hide 'em in that minifridge."

I handed her a can and settled behind my desk. "Don't you have work to do?"

"Yes." She cracked the top open and drank, not seeming to care she was ruining the lips she'd just worked so hard to paint.

"Shouldn't you go do it, then? Instead of interrogating me about my sex life?"

"Who's interrogating?" She cried. "I'm just asking."

I had to laugh at her. "Marcy, we had sex. It's no big deal."

She frowned. "Sugar, that's just sad. It should be a big deal, otherwise why bother?"

She had a point, one I'd made for myself when I'd sworn off the act altogether. "It was worth the bother, all right?"

"So he was good."

"He was good, Marcy!" I shook a pen at her. "You nosy bitch!"

She put a hand over her heart and looked wounded. "You say that like it's a bad thing."

I sighed, resigned. "He took me to the movies, and we went to his place, after."

I didn't mention the dance club or the bathroom at La Belle Fleur. Marcy oohed, anyway. She leaned forward on her seat.

"Did he put the moves on you right away, or did he pretend he wanted to show you his soda can collection?"

"I think we both knew why I was going back there. And he doesn't collect cans, at least that I can tell."

"Phew," she said. "Because that's total turn-off."

I laughed again and shook my head. "I'll keep that in mind."

Marcy drank some soda, then set the can on the edge of my desk. "Elle, if you don't mind my saying so—"

"Would you stop if I did?"

"Hell, no."

I waved my hand. "Then by all means, carry on."

"I think it's good you got out."

Her words touched me, and I smiled. "Thank you, Marcy."

She nodded, then winked. "So you'll be seeing him again."

My smile dimmed a bit before I answered. "Yes."

"Geez. You sound thrilled. What's the matter, he chews with his mouth open? What?"

I shrugged, studying the folders of work piled high on my desk. "No. He has very pleasant manners."

"Uh-oh," she said. "Very pleasant manners. An aesthetically pleasing penis. You're regressing, girl, let me hear you say he's a great fuck and fun to be with."

There would be no resisting her. I knew that by now. Yet I gave in to Marcy not because she could be an insistent, nosy bitch, but because I'd never have admitted my thoughts out loud had she not pushed.

"I like him."

"So what's the problem?" She looked concerned. "That's a good thing."

I shrugged again. I had my reasons for not wanting to like him. For avoiding relationships. They were shitty and pathetic reasons, but I had them.

"You don't have to marry him."

"Heaven forbid," I said, startled at the thought. "Good God, no."

She held up her hands. "Just saying. What's wrong with going out, having a good time, getting laid?"

"Nothing's wrong with it. I just…" I shrugged. "It's not really my thing."

"Maybe you should rethink what your 'thing' is," she advised, getting up. "'Cuz to be honest, honey, I don't think it works so good for you."

"Thanks for the advice," I replied.

"Sarcasm," Marcy said loftily, "is the defense of the guilty!"

With that, she swept from my office in a cloud of Obsession and left a sweating soda can to stain my desktop.

I had the bus ride home to think about what she'd said and what Dan had promised. No attachments. The idea was appealing, though ridiculous. People can't just fuck. They can't. One or the other gets caught up in emotion, someone gets hurt. We're not meant to separate sex from love; there's a reason why euphoria occurs in both situations. Sex and love nourish each other. You can argue it's humanity's way of establishing family groups and guaranteeing creation of the next generation, but the simple fact remains: the more often two people engage in sex, the more likely it is that one of them will fall in love.

How many times would it take, I wondered. I stared out my window at the streetlamps, counting them as I always did. The number never changed. I defined my life by numbers. What number of times would I take Dan inside my body before one of us felt that first pang of emotion?

And would I be able to stop if it were me?

It wasn't that I'd never had a boyfriend or never been in love. I had been, once. A long time ago. Head over heels, madly, passionately, devastatingly in love with the boy I thought might be my knight in shining armor. Funny thing about that shining armor, by the way. It tarnishes pretty fast.

By the time I got home, I had determined I was not going to see him again. There could be no point in it. It was useless, a satisfaction of the body that could lead to nothing but dissatisfaction of the mind. I knew it without a doubt. I wouldn't call him, I wouldn't see him, I wouldn't… wouldn't…would not.

By the time I got home, my mother had called three times and left messages so long they'd filled up the tape on my machine. And I, unable to hate her, found myself even unable to ignore her. I listened to her tirade, and then I picked up the phone.

"Who's this?" She sounded querulous. Old. I had to remind myself she was only in her early sixties and far from an invalid. "Ella?"

"It's Elle, Mother. Please."

"We've always called you Ella."

Then she was off on her rant, and I didn't bother correcting her again.

"Are you listening to me?"

As if I had a choice. "Yes, Mother."

She gave a low snort into the phone. "When are you coming home for a visit?"

"I'm very busy at work. You know that. I told you."

I listened with half an ear while I drew water into the teakettle and took out a microwave meal from the freezer. I grabbed one plate. One glass. One fork. Set one place at my table, which was big enough to seat four but never had. I didn't have dinner parties.

"I want you to take me to the cemetery, Ella. Daddy can't do it, he's not able to make the drive."

The fork clattered against the plate. "Mother, I told you before. No."

There was, incredibly, a long silence in which I heard nothing but the sound of her breathing. "Elspeth Kavanagh," she said at last. "The least you can do is put a rose on his grave once in a while. He was your brother. Aren't you ashamed of yourself, Ella? He was your brother, and he loved you."

The kettle screamed, saving me from the effort. With shaking hands I turned off the gas and poured the water into my mug. It slopped, stinging my hands. I hissed in pain.

"What's wrong?"

"I burned myself on some hot water."

And she was off again, with the best way to treat burns, and how I should have someone there to make sure I did it right, and someone there to take care of me. Because so obviously I couldn't care for myself. I ended the call as fast as I could. I looked at the tea, the food, the single plate.

"I know who he was," I said aloud to the empty room.

Dan answered the door with tousled hair and sleep in his eyes, which widened at the sight of me. It was the black vinyl raincoat and the stiletto shoes. The red lipstick and black eyeliner. I knew what I looked like. A parody of a teenage boy's wank fantasies.

I closed the door behind me. "Hi."

Dan smiled. "This is a surprise."

It is immensely satisfying to watch a man get hard at the sight of you. He wore flannel sleep pants, slung low on his hips. They tented admirably when I slid open the coat to reveal the little I wore beneath.

"How about this?"

He blinked, his gaze taking me in, toes to thighs to hips to breasts to throat to mouth and at last, to my eyes. He stared at me. My breath caught, my bold act more act than bold. For an instant I thought he'd fail me. That he'd ask me to sit down, offer me a drink. But only for a moment, because he gave me exactly what I wanted with his next words.

"Take it off."

I dropped the coat to the floor. I wore black thigh-high stockings and matching black lace bra and panties. Clothes from the back of my drawer I hadn't worn in ages. Power clothes, to make me feel sexy. They worked. Watching him watch me tightened my nipples.

"Get on your knees."

I did. He put a hand on my head, his fingers gentle and tangling in my hair. He nudged his hips forward, pushing flannel-covered cock toward me, and I reached for him. I touched him through the soft fabric, stroking, and his instant sigh of pleasure shot desire straight between my legs.

"Put me in your mouth."

He made it so easy for me to do what he wanted. I wanted that. I craved it. Having it made easy for me to not have to decide. I rewarded him with my acquiescence. He took away the responsibility, and I shivered with delicious, illicit joy. There is so much freedom in not having to choose.

I slid my fingers into the waistband of his pajama bottoms and slid them over his hips, then his thighs. Slowly, slowly I drew them down to his ankles. I let my fingers caress the sensitive backs of his knees. I studied his skin, the pattern of hair, darker than that on his head, the lovely thickness of his penis, standing at attention for me.

There are women who think getting on their knees for a man is demeaning. That putting a penis in their mouths is dirty, disgusting, a chore, a bother, something to suffer through, tolerate, an act to be borne instead of relished. In some cases I understand why they might find that to be true, but I pity them, nevertheless. They don't understand how much power they can wield from their place at his feet. How much they can gain by giving him pleasure. I looked up, meaning to speak, and the look on his face stopped me.

He put a hand on my hair. "You are so beautiful. Do you know that?"

I don't like the word *beautiful*. It's used for vases, horses, houses and flowers as much as it is for humans. *Beautiful* is a flattering lie.

I shook my head a little. “Shhh.”

His fingers smoothed along the top of my head, then down my cheek. “You want me to say something different?”

“I want,” I said, and pressed my cheek to his thigh, “you to tell me to suck your cock.”

His hand twitched on my head, and he groaned a little at my words. “Elle…”

I smiled. I kissed his thigh, nuzzling the hair, softer on the inside and higher up. I brushed the soft weight of his testicles with my lips, earning another soft gasp from him. “Say it.”

“I want you to suck my cock.”

I took him in my mouth, an inch at a time, steadying myself by holding on to his thighs. His grunt was reward. The way he pushed forward into my waiting heat another. The way he whispered my name as he stroked my hair yet a third. I took him all the way in until my lips brushed his belly and then drew out again, pausing at the head of his penis to offer a bit more suction. Then down again, slowly, breathing through my nose and concentrating on discovering every ridge and line along his length.

I wanted this. The taste of him. The sound of his breath getting faster. The feeling of the muscles in his thighs trembling beneath my fingers as he pushed his hips and put himself down the back of my throat the way I’d put the shot of whiskey he’d bought me the first day we met. I wanted this because in doing this I could think only of this. Of cock, of balls, of thighs, belly, moans, thrusts, of the salty, slippery taste of semen on the back of my tongue as his pleasure mounted.

"Elle." He murmured my name. "Elle, baby, stop. I'm going to come."

I didn't stop. I drew another moan from him as I used my tongue on the tender divot on the underside of his prick. I added my hand at the base, moving it along with my mouth so that he was never left without sensation. I used my other hand to cup his balls and stroke my thumb along them.

He pushed into me so hard it would have choked me had I not been gripping him so tight. I tasted him and his orgasm throbbed against my tongue. He gave a low cry. I took all he had and waited another moment or two until he'd finished, then pulled away from him with a last, gentle suck to end it.

I got to my feet. In my heels I could look directly into his eyes. He blinked, his hand finding my upper arm and holding it as though to keep himself from wobbling.

"Wow," he said at last. His eyes cleared.

I wiped my lips with my thumb. "Can I get a drink of water?"

"Yeah, sure." He pointed to the kitchen.

I walked across the living room and knew his gaze followed the sway of my hips. The water from his faucet was cold and quenched my thirst. It felt good on my cheeks, too, and on the back of my neck. When I turned from the sink, he was behind me.

"Thanks for the drink," I said.

"You're welcome." He'd pulled his pants up, though they

still slung low enough on his hips for me to see a hint of pubic hair.

"Well." Mission accomplished. I'd managed to erase the conversation with my mother long enough to make it easier to put from my mind. Not to forget. That was likely impossible. But far enough to at least ignore. "I'll be going."

He snagged my arm as I tried to pass. "You're leaving?"

I looked at his hand on my arm, then at his face. "I thought I would, yes."

"Why?"

I smiled. "Because I'm done."

Dan smiled, too, this time with a bit of a harder edge. The way he'd looked the last time I tried to leave. "What if I'm not?"

I gave a pointed glance to the front of his bottoms. "I think you are."

He smoothed his hand over my hip. "I don't think you are."

I tilted my head. "I didn't come here for that."

"You didn't come at all," he said, inching me closer.

"If I don't care, why should you?" I let him pull me next to him. His hands massaged my lace-covered ass.

"Elle, did you come over here just to suck me off and leave?"

"Yes."

He paused in stroking my butt to peer into my eyes. "Really?"

I nodded.

He looked surprised, and I took the opportunity to step away from him and head for my coat.

"Elle, wait."

I turned, one arm already in the sleeve.

He caught up to me. "I don't want you to leave. Stay here with me for a while."

"I'm not exactly dressed to play Parcheesi." I slipped the coat on the rest of the way and started on the zipper.

"You're really leaving."

"I'm really leaving, Dan."

"No."

I turned to look at him. "Most guys would love it if a scantily clad woman came over in the middle of the night, gave them a tremendous blow job and left without expecting anything."

"I'm not most guys."

"You…you didn't like it?" I covered up the hesitation in my voice with a quick cough and avoided his eyes. My cheeks burned. Without seduction to shield me, I felt foolish.

He came up behind me and put a hand on my shoulder, pulling me back against his chest. "I loved it," he whispered into my ear. "But I don't want you to leave just yet."

I shivered at his breath on my ear. When his lips touched my skin a second later, I bit my lower lip. His touch felt good, and I did want it. I wanted his hands on me.

I've never made excuses for liking to fuck. Never allowed what happened in the past to prevent me from accepting the pleasure my body brings me. Much had been stolen from me, but I haven't allowed that to be taken.

"You don't want to leave, do you?"

His hands came around my front. His fingers slid on the

slick vinyl, and he held my breasts. I couldn't feel more than the weight of his hands. The material prevented any more delicate stimulation. In another moment, though, he pulled down the zip, and cool air once again caressed my skin, already sweating though I'd only had the coat closed for a short time.

His fingers skidded along my damp skin, and this time when he cupped my breasts, the sheer lace tugged and pulled my nipples erect. I leaned back against him while he nuzzled my neck. His chest was broad, his skin warm against mine in the places we touched. His hands moved over me without haste. He slid his fingers along the lace of my panties, and my hips pushed forward into his touch.

"You smell so good."

I sighed and turned my head. He kissed the side of my neck as his fingers circled against me. His other hand slid inside my bra and rolled my nipple. I shivered at the dual sensation, and he must have felt it because his teeth came down on the curve of my shoulder and he bit me gently, making me moan.

"I love that sound," he whispered, kissing the mark he'd left. "You've got the sexiest voice. You make everything you say sound like it tastes good coming out of your mouth."

I blinked and turned my head to look at him. "What?"

He smiled. "Just seeing if you were listening."

I didn't have a reply. Most compliments take me aback. I know my strengths. I figure other people do, too. Anything else is flattery or insincerity.

He looked at me, his hand not ceasing in its slow seduction. "You don't like that, either?"

I put my hand over his to stop the motion, but though I

wanted to pull out of his arms I stayed still. "You don't have to do that."

"Do what?" He passed his thumb over my breast. "That?"

"No. Say things like that. You don't have to."

He looked thoughtful and turned me a little so we weren't craning our necks. "I want to."

I shook my head a little. "Why? I'm already here. You're already going to get what you want."

He frowned and let go of me. He crossed his arms over his bare chest. "Is that the only reason you think I'd say something like that?"

We stared at each other, both of us frowning. I straightened up and adjusted my bra strap, which had fallen over my shoulder. My cheeks heated as he looked me over, and this time it wasn't from lust. His gaze finally rested on mine.

"Elle," Dan said. "If you don't like me saying that sort of thing, then I guess I won't. But telling you to suck my cock's okay?"

I smiled a little. "Yes."

"Just like fucking you in the bathroom was okay but not asking you on a date."

"Yes."

He ran his hand through his hair, spiking it higher until I itched to smooth it. He took a deep breath and looked back at me. "And you can come over here anytime you please dressed like something out of my ninth grade wet dreams and get me off without letting me return the favor."

"Yes." I smiled a little wider and put my hands on my hips. "Though I haven't left yet."

He studied my face for a minute longer. "Come here."

I did, obedient, acquiescent, my heart skip-tripping again. He put his hand on the base of my skull, fingers tight in the back of my hair. He tugged my head back, then took a finger and traced the line of my throat, ending in the hollow of my collarbone.

"You like it when I tell you what to do."

I murmured in assent. The fingertip trailed lower, over the swells of my breasts and down. He touched my navel briefly, then slid his hand back between my legs. My arousal had faded with our conversation, but now it began to return.

"Why?"

"Because I think all the time," I whispered. "And sometimes it's nice to not think anymore. Sometimes it's nice to just...do."

"Or be told what to do."

"Yes."

His fingers slid back and forth over my panties, between my legs and up to stroke my clitoris. His other hand kept me still as he looked into my face with such intensity I wanted to look away.

"Has it really been three years since you fucked anyone?"

Stung, I pulled away from the hand in my hair and stepped back. "Yes. Why would I lie about that?"

"Why does anyone lie about anything?" He made no move to come toward me.

"Yes. It was three years."

"Come here."

I almost didn't. But then I did. It took two steps. He grabbed me a little harder this time, and I winced though he hadn't really hurt me. He pulled me close to his body and put his hand between my legs again.

"Are you going to tell me what you like, or am I going to have to guess?" He asked, stroking me. "Do you like to be tied up? Spanked? You want nipple clamps and hot wax?"

"Hot wax?" I tried to pull away again, but he held me fast. His gentle stroke, stroke, stroke between my legs never erred. Heat bloomed beneath his fingers and spread.

Dan smiled, eyes ablaze. "No hot wax?"

"I'm...I'm not..." In truth, I was having a bit of difficulty expressing exactly what I was or was not interested in. The longer he stroked me, the fewer words seemed to form on my tongue.

I put a hand on his shoulder to support myself as his hand moved a little faster. He hit all the right spots with the right amount of pressure, the right pace. I'd never been with a man who could get me off as easily as I could myself.

"You like me telling you what to do."

"Yes."

He bent to nuzzle and nip at my neck. The graze of his teeth on my skin pumped my hips forward against his hand. My fingers tightened on his shoulder.

"I like telling you," he whispered. "It looks like we both win."

He took me into his bedroom and pushed me onto his bed. Not like he wanted to hurt me, but a little rough. I was too aroused to mind.

"Touch yourself."

I hadn't been expecting that. "What?"

"You heard me." He stood beside the bed and stared

down at me, his expression implacable. "I want to watch you get yourself off."

"If I wanted to do that, I could go home." I got up on one elbow.

He shrugged and pointed at the door. "So go ahead."

I hesitated, trying to judge him. "You…want me to touch myself."

"Yes."

I'd never done that in front of anyone before. It wasn't even part of my fantasy repertoire. I did it anyway, because he told me to. I lifted my breasts in my hands and ran my thumbs over the nipples. It wasn't the same as if he'd been doing it. I pulled the lace down below my breasts, then licked my fingers and ran the wet tips across my nipples. That felt much better, and I drew in a quick breath.

His eyes followed my every movement. The front of his pants had begun bulging again, and that sight triggered more desire. I pushed my hand into the front of my panties and found the hard nodule of my clit. I pinched it as I pinched my nipple, working both small tight buds at the same time.

"You like that?" Dan asked. "Is that what gets you off?"

"Yes."

"Can you make yourself come that way?" His voice dipped a little deeper.

"Yes," I said, as my hand moved faster. I slid a finger down to bring some slickness up over my clitoris. I shuddered.

"Take off your panties. I want to see you."

I did as he said, my eyes on his face the whole time. When I pushed the scrap of lace to my thighs, his eyes centered on my pussy, and I felt his gaze there as if it had physical weight. I touched myself again with him watching me.

He got on the bed next to me and I thought he meant to take over, but he only watched me intently. The scrutiny made me falter a bit, but I continued on. I kept the pace steady, even, trying to lose myself in it.

"Is it difficult for you?" He looked up at me and put his hand on my belly.

It took some effort to speak. I had to lick my lips first. "Sometimes."

"Even when you're doing it to yourself?"

I hitched in a tiny laugh, my hand pausing. "It's hard to do it with you watching me like I'm going to test you on it later."

I hadn't realized how much I was hoping he'd smile until he did, and relief swept through me. He bent to press a kiss to my shoulder. Then another to my neck. His hand moved down to cover mine and he moved them both in the same measured rhythm I'd set for myself.

"Is it multiple choice or an oral exam?"

I gasped as he spoke, because he'd slid his finger inside me. He pushed in another, stretching me a little, moving back and forth. The small flame of desire leaped to life.

"You're so tight," he said against my shoulder. "And hot. And wet."

He moved his fingers as he spoke, and it was good, but not quite enough. I wanted more. I lifted my hips to his hand and rubbed my clit faster.

"Do you want me to fuck you?" He asked into my ear.

"Yes."

"Yes, what?"

"Yes, Dan, I want..." The words caught in my throat not from lack of desire but too much of it. "I want you to..."

"Say 'fuck me.'"

"Fuck me."

He reached to the nightstand and sheathed himself, first in latex, then in me. He hit my core immediately, and I cried out. He fucked me hard and fast, with very little effort into caring for my comfort...and it was fantastic. I came hard, like lightning striking, and then again like the rumble of far-off thunder. He came a moment later, holding himself up on his hands.

Breathing hard, he looked down at me. A drop of sweat dripped from his face onto my lips, and I licked it away. He withdrew, took care of the condom, then rolled on to his side and pulled my back against him. Spooning.

"Did you like that?" he asked. "When I told you to touch yourself?"

I thought about it, believing he deserved an honest answer. "I didn't not like it."

His hand made a roller coaster's journey along the slope of my hip and curve of my waist. "What's that mean?"

"It means I liked you telling me to do it. I wouldn't have done it if you hadn't."

He traced a pattern on my skin, his voice thoughtful. "And you'd do anything I told you to do?"

"Haven't I, so far?"

He didn't answer for a moment. "How far will you go?"

I didn't turn to look at him. Very carefully didn't. "As far as you'll take me."

He was silent for another moment.

"You really do it, don't you," he said in a low voice. "Keep it separate."

The sex had left me drowsy. I put my hand over his where it rested on my belly. "Yes."

He kissed my closest shoulder blade. "Always?"

"Yes, Dan. Always."

I waited for him to say more, but he said nothing. I listened to the sound of his breathing until I blinked and somehow the room had gone dark and he'd covered me with a blanket. He snored lightly beside me on the pillow, one hand still touching me as though to make certain I was there. I listened for a minute, the touch of his fingertips an anchor I didn't expect to enjoy so much.

Then I got up and helped myself to a pair of his sweat-pants and a button-down shirt. I might have been crazy enough to come across town in my underpants when it was barely night. I wasn't going to tempt fate by doing it now.

I was not totally without heart, even back then. I did my best to hide it, but it was there. I did turn back to look once more at him sleeping before I slipped out the door.

Chapter 06

When asked the question "What are you thinking about," many times the answer returned is "Nothing." It's a lie. Nobody ever really thinks of nothing. The human mind doesn't stop. Doesn't go blank. It's a tricky thing, the mind, always working on some problem or idea, even when it seems to be quiet.

I never think of nothing. The closest I come to a blank mind is when I am counting, fucking or drinking. The rest of the time, my thoughts are like a hamster on a wheel, running endlessly but getting nowhere.

Chad, the one person who knows me better than anyone else, understands this. It's why he sends me care packages full of cartoons and expensive chocolate, and cards with inspirational sayings on them. He knows quotations and goodies won't fix me, but he sends them anyway because it makes him feel good. I've never argued with it. I like expensive chocolate and cartoons that make me giggle. I gift him with designer fruit baskets and body lotion and restaurant gift cards. It's the way we take care of each other since we don't live close enough to do it in person.

"The guy left a package for you." Gavin must have been waiting for me to get home from work, because his door opened as soon as I put my foot to my steps. "I signed for it. I hope that's okay."

"Sure, Gav. Thanks. Want to bring it over?" I let us both inside and tossed my coat and my bag onto their hooks. The package from Chad was small and square. I set it on the kitchen table while I went to change my clothes.

Gavin had already begun cracking open the cans of paint I'd lined up along the wall. Plain white. Nothing fancy. The chair rail would be dark mahogany to match the furniture I'd bought at an auction. I watched him work as I opened up the package from my brother.

"How was the museum?"

He shrugged. "Sucked."

I didn't ask more. I slid out a box from its brown paper wrapping and shook it. Nothing rattled inside. I expected magazines. Chad liked to store up copies of celebrity gossip tabloids and ship them to me with hand-written comments in the margins.

A composition book slid into my hands. The hard black-and-white cover was scuffed and a little bent, but in good condition otherwise. My fingers rubbed cool cardboard. I laid it flat on my palms and watched it shudder with the shaking of my hands.

"The Adventures of Princess Pennywhistle."

Once upon a time, there lived a princess named Princess Pen-

nywhistle. Princess Pennywhistle had long, curly blond hair and eyes so blue they made the sky jealous. Princess Pennywhistle lived in a castle with her pet unicorn, Unique.

Princess Pennywhistle. I hadn't thought of her in years. Now here she lay in my hands, time making her story unfamiliar to me.

Gavin wandered into the kitchen to help himself to a glass of water and saw me sitting with the book in my hands. "What did you get?"

I lifted it to show him. "'Princess Pennywhistle.' It's a story my brothers and I wrote when we were kids."

"You wrote stories?"

I wasn't sure if I should be affronted at his expression of surprise. "This one. Yes."

"Wow." He looked impressed. "That's cool, Miss Kavanagh."

I traced the cover's black-and-white swirls with one fingertip. "Princess Pennywhistle had lots of adventures with her pet unicorn, Unique. She never had to wait for a prince to rescue her, either."

"She kicked ass, huh?"

I looked up to see one of Gavin's rare grins. "She sure did."

"How come you stopped writing about her?"

I set the book on the table. "Because I grew up."

He reached to pick it up and flip through the pages. "Can I look at it?"

"It's not *The Little Prince,*" I told him. "But...sure. If you want."

He grinned again. "Thanks. I write stuff, too, sometimes."

"Maybe you'll let me read something you wrote." I looked inside the package for a note or a card, but Chad hadn't included anything but the composition book.

Gavin had flipped some more pages. "Maybe. Hey! Pictures!"

He held up the book to show me a drawing of the brave princess, done in colored pencils. Unique, looking a bit more like a mule with a deformed growth on its head than a unicorn, pranced beside her. My throat tightened at the sight of the illustration, done so long ago by childish hands.

"'Princess Pennywhistle and the Garbage Monster,'" Gavin read, still turning pages. "'Princess Pennywhistle and the Glass Tower.'"

She'd gotten out of that one with a hammer.

"'Princess Pennywhistle and the Black Knight.'" Gavin had turned toward the back of the book.

Unfamiliar from the passage of time, but not forgotten entirely. I reached for the book. "I think...maybe we should get to painting, Gavin. You've got school in the morning, and I've got to go to work."

I put the book back into the envelope without looking at his face. I knew my abruptness had startled him, maybe even made him feel bad, but I ignored it. I put the envelope with the imprisoned Pennywhistle inside it away in my desk drawer, and I went into the dining room.

Later, when Gavin had left and I'd showered to get rid of the paint on my hands, I pulled out "Princess Pennywhistle" again. She'd been brave, that blond princess with eyes that made the sky jealous. Brave and strong. She'd broken free of the Glass Tower, defeated the Garbage Monster, visited the Kingdom of the Rainbow People and freed them from the Evil Black-and-White Witch. She'd been full of color and joy and confidence, until the end. When she'd met up with the Black Knight, who'd stolen her smile.

Why had she become that girl without color and joy and confidence? The one who was afraid? That was not the real question.

The real question was, why had I?

When the phone rang, I didn't leap to answer it. The movie on the television and the popcorn on my lap were more interesting. My mother could talk to the answering machine.

When the machine clicked on and a male voice began speaking, though, I dumped my popcorn on the floor and grabbed up the phone. I had a moment to realize I was acting like a girl who'd been waiting for that special boy to call. Probably because that's exactly what I was.

"Hello?" I made my voice sound casual, though I felt anything but.

It had been a week since I'd shown up at his door in my underwear. A week since I'd left him sleeping. He hadn't called. I hadn't, either, though I'd dialed a number of times and hung up, like a schoolgirl.

"What are you wearing?"

I looked down at my soft flannel pajamas. I'd washed them so many times the plaid pattern had faded mostly to grays and whites. "What do you want me to be wearing?"

Dan's voice shifted a little. I imagined a smile. "Nothing."

Such a small thing, that little bit of flirting, but all at once I felt as if air had rushed into my lungs, and I hadn't realized I'd been holding my breath. "Nothing but a smile."

"Do you often sit around your apartment wearing nothing?"

"Do you often call up women out of the blue without identifying yourself and ask them what they're wearing?"

"No." I heard shuffling, as though he were switching the phone to the opposite ear. "But you knew who I was. Didn't you?"

"You mean this isn't Brad Pitt? I'm so disappointed."

"Are you really wearing nothing, Elle?"

I laughed. "No. Why?"

"Why did you leave without saying goodbye?"

I looked at the mess of popcorn on my floor, my laugh fading away. "It seemed easier at the time."

He made a noise of disbelief. "For you."

"Yes, Dan." I sighed. "For me."

He was silent for a while, but he didn't hang up. Neither did I. It would have been rude. The irony of that didn't escape me; that I could leave without saying goodbye but not hang up the phone on him without doing the same.

"I want to take you someplace," he said finally. "I need a date."

I considered a moment before answering. "Is this an emergency?"

"Sort of. Yes."

I started to clean up the popcorn as I spoke to him. "And you think I'll…suit?"

"Elle," Dan said, "you'll be perfect."

"Flattery doesn't always get you everywhere, you know."

"It's a good start." He shuffled some more, enough to make me wonder what he was doing. I could easily imagine him running his hand through his hair, his habits already familiar though I barely knew him. "You want to do this for me."

I paused in gathering the kernels from my rug. "Do I?"

His voice shifted again, a little lower, a little huskier. "I think you do. Yes."

"What, exactly, do I want to do?"

"You want to put on something stunning and come with me tomorrow night."

"Where?" I had nothing stunning. I also had no plans for tomorrow night.

"A place I have to go. Dinner. Formal."

"And you want to take me? In something…stunning." I thought about it. "What do you consider stunning? I don't have anything formal."

"I'll have it delivered to your office. You'll wear what I choose. You'll come with me to this dinner."

He'd provide the dress and the dinner. I'd provide my company. There had to be a catch.

"And if I do this for you," I asked, not because I necessarily wanted anything else but because the question seemed logical to ask, "what's in it for me?"

"If you do this for me," he said, "I'll fuck you again."

Crude. Yet it made stomach drop to hit my toes, and a little gasp eeked out of me. "You're awfully sure of yourself."

"You said you'd go as far as I'd take you. Did you change your mind?"

As far as he'd take me. "No."

"I thought you might have. When you left like you did."

"No, I…" I wasn't sure what to say. "I didn't think—"

"Didn't think what, Elle? That I'd give you what you want? That I'd take you where you want to go? Did you think I'd let you go after that night, just because you keep making it so hard for me?"

"I don't know." I didn't know; that was the truth. I didn't know what I wanted from him, only what I didn't. What I couldn't want.

"How many times have you touched yourself this week, thinking about me?"

Again he made me gasp. The heat in my face made me glad for the anonymity of phone conversation rather than face to face. "Every night."

I heard the grin in his voice. "You thought about me, then."

"Yes!" I swept popcorn back into the bowl. "I did."

"Don't frown. You're prettier when you smile."

"You can't see my face, how do you now I'm frowning?"

"I can hear it in your voice," he said. "You're not as much of an enigma as you'd like to be, Elle."

That annoyed me, and I stood with the full-again bowl to dump the poor wasted treat into the trash. "Are you always this arrogant?"

"Always," Dan said. "I'll send the dress tomorrow."

"Maybe I don't want to go with you tomorrow night."

"You want to" was all he said, and then he hung up.

The package came the next day. I set it on my desk and stared at it the entire morning. I couldn't work for looking at it. I calculated the length, width and depth. Figured the volume. Touched the brown paper around the outside.

But I didn't open it.

"What's with the package?" Leave it to Marcy to bust in and demand to know my business.

"It's a dress, I think."

She settled on the edge of my desk. "You think? You don't know?"

"It's a dress." I tapped my pencil on my tablet. "Don't you have work to do?"

"Yes. But I came to see your dress."

"You didn't even know," I said, "that it was a dress."

"But I knew you got a package." She shifted my papers over to push the package in front of me. "Open it."

"Do you make it a point to know everyone's business, or just mine?" I picked at the edges of the paper wrapping the box. It had arrived by courier with my name on it. No return address. No indication of where it had come from.

"Silly question."

I looked up at her. "Right. Everyone's."

"Where'd you order it from?" Marcy reached across to pull the scissors from their place in my pencil caddy. She handed them to me with as much ceremony as if I were at a ribbon-cutting ceremony.

"I didn't order it. It's a…gift." I slit the paper carefully and pulled it off. The name on the box beneath made Marcy let out a low, impressed whistle. I just stared.

Kellerman's is a very exclusive, very expensive boutique. I'd looked in the windows many times, but never gone inside. It's the sort of store that sells "frocks." Day frocks, evening frocks, clothes with purposes so specific you needed a guidebook to decipher their use.

"Wow." For once Marcy seemed almost speechless. Not quite but almost. "Very nice."

I touched the embossed lettering but hesitated to open the box. How had he known my size? What I liked? What I didn't? What if the dress were red, the color I hated most of all and wouldn't wear? What if it had big, poofy sleeves like some 1980s prom gown and made my ass look fat?

"Open it," Marcy said, impatient. "I want to see."

I lifted the lid and set it aside. Tissue paper cradled the garment within. I lifted the first piece. More paper.

"They wrap those things like mummies," Marcy said. "C'mon, Elle. Let's see."

At last I lifted the dress from its shroud of paper and held it up. It was black. Long. Strapless.

Gorgeous.

Small, sparkly beads sprinkled the fitted bodice, boned for support, and down the skirt. A slit ran from the floor-length hem to so high on the thigh it might as well have been the waist. The skirt looked as if it would swirl around the wearer's ankles when she danced.

"Very nice," said Marcy. "Doesn't look like you, I have to say. What made you pick it?"

"I didn't." I touched the material with tentative fingers. How could I wear such a thing? So lovely. So revealing.

As if a black vinyl raincoat over lace panties wasn't revealing.

I never claimed not to be a dichotomy. I know very well the schism in me, and its source. I know why I hate being told what to do as much as I crave the freedom of having responsibility taken from me.

I looked at my work clothes—white shirt, black skirt, everything prim and proper and modest—and then back at the gown. It screamed, "Sex!" and that was only on the hanger.

"It will look absolutely fabulous on you, doll." Marcy smiled. "Try it on."

"Here? Now? No! I've got work to do. I couldn't..."

She put up a hand. "Say no more. You didn't buy this dress. Do I have to guess who did? Mr. Lover Boy from The Blue Swan?"

"Dan."

"Dan bought you this dress?" Marcy said. "Just for fun?"

"No. He wants me to wear it tonight. He's taking me out."

"Very nice," Marcy said, her subdued answer a sign she was more impressed than she'd admit.

I touched the material again, trying to imagine myself wearing such a creation in public. Worse. On a date.

"Look," she said. "He got you shoes, too. Oh, and a wrap! And a bag...damn, girl! The man has taste, and obviously money. And—" Marcy reached inside and pulled out a strap, a wisp of lace, a garter belt "—he knows what he likes."

"Put that back," I said sharply. "I don't even know if I'm going to wear any of this stuff."

Marcy looked at me with a raised brow. "Sure you are. You'll look beautiful."

I frowned, shaking the dress but not quite willing to put it back in the box. "It's very..."

"Sexy."

"Yes."

Marcy shrugged. "You don't think you can be sexy, Elle?"

That wasn't it. I knew very well I could be sexy. I could put on red lipstick, let down my hair, squeeze my breasts into a pushup bra and my ass into tight pants.

"I don't think I need this to be sexy. This…this is a parody."

"Maybe that's what he wants."

I thought she might be right, and could I blame him for wanting a parody when I had given him the cliché already? I stroked the dress's fine, soft fabric, then looked into the box at the shoes. Hooker heels.

"Where's he taking you, might I ask? Dressed like that?"

"I don't know."

Marcy laughed. "Hope it's not a funeral. You'd make a dead man rise in that getup, Elle."

She left me to ponder that possibility. I was sure he did not plan to take me to a funeral. So where, then, did he want to go?

Princess Pennywhistle wouldn't have been afraid. She'd have put on the dress and gone to meet the Handsome Prince. I looked again at the shoes, the wrap, the lingerie. He'd spent a lot of money. Bought black. My size. The Prince Who Paid Attention.

I smiled at the thought and put the dress and all its accessories away. Dan had been right. I wanted to go with him. It didn't really matter where.

I met him in the lobby of a swanky downtown hotel with real trees growing from its marble-tiled floor. A fountain made water-tinkle music in the hush. Chandeliers glittered overhead. I searched but didn't see him.

"Elle."

Dan's voice turned my head. He looked good. Damn good. His tux fit as though it had been tailored for him, like he owned it instead of renting. He took my hand and pulled me close to him, aligned my body with his. His hands went to my waist.

"Nice dress."

"This old thing?" I looked down at it before meeting his gaze again.

"It looks perfect on you." He kissed my cheek, a soft brush of his lips on my skin that became a nuzzling of my neck. "And you smell delicious."

I shivered at the movement of his lips on my skin, my nipples perking. The display of affection made me uncomfortable, but I didn't pull away. He kissed the curve of my shoulder and then took my hand.

"Shall we?"

"Where are we going?" I asked as he led me across the lobby toward one of the ballrooms at the end.

"My class reunion."

I stopped short so fast he kept going for a couple of steps. Our arms stretched out. "You're taking me to your class reunion?"

He nodded toward another couple dressed in formal wear heading for the same set of doors. "Yes."

I wasn't sure what I had expected of the evening, but not that. "Why?"

He gave another man a small wave and a smile of recognition, then pulled me aside into a small conversational grouping of chairs around a gas fireplace, lit even though it was the middle of May. He looked over my shoulder, smiling for the benefit of others, not me, as he explained.

"I wasn't going to come tonight, but then Jerry—my friend Jerry Melville, he's in arbitration—told me Ceci Gold was going to be here tonight."

I studied his face. "And Ceci Gold would be…?"

"Head cheerleader. Prom queen. Class president. Harlot who broke my heart."

"Ah." I glanced around. "You were high school sweethearts?"

"No. I jerked off to her picture in the yearbook like every other guy in the class, but she never looked at me twice. Three years ago we met up at The Hardware Bar on ladies' night. She was celebrating her divorce with Blue Maui shooters."

"I see." I did, much better.

Dan's eyes were fixed over my shoulder, watching the other couples heading through the doors. He smiled, nodded, waved, his pleasant expression belying the content of his conversation.

"She took me home that night and tried getting in my pants but was so drunk I felt too guilty to fuck her. I spent the night on her couch. She was so grateful for my behaving like 'such a gentleman,'—her words, not mine—that she asked me out for dinner. We dated for three months before she dumped me unceremoniously for a guy she met at the same bar on a night she wasn't too drunk to fuck."

"I'm…sorry?"

"Don't be." Dan focused on me, his grin losing some of its hard edge for a moment. "She was as conceited, high-maintenance and frigid a bitch as she was in high school. She gave me nothing but a headache and blue balls the entire three months I wasted on her."

"Ah." I tilted my head to look at him. "I thought she broke your heart."

He gave me a shark's grin. All teeth. "She fucked with me, is what she did."

"She made you angry."

"Yeah. She wasted my time. And she lied to me. She didn't have to do that. We weren't serious. Not in love. She didn't have to play me."

"Nobody likes being lied to." I found it interesting that three years later he still sounded so bitter.

"Jerry said she's going to be here tonight."

The dress made more sense now. "And you want to make her jealous?"

He put his hands on my hips and pulled me closer. "Yes."

"With me?" I had to consider that for a moment.

I hold no false ideas about my looks. The mirror shows me features many would call pleasing. I have long dark hair, greenish-blue eyes, skin that could be described as porcelain. I work at keeping in shape but have been blessed with a natural hourglass shape men seem to enjoy. I know, as my mother accuses, that if I 'took care of' myself I could garner much more male attention. I wear the clothes I do and keep to myself because I want attention on my terms, only. So yes, I know I'm pretty, but mostly I prefer being plain.

Dan kissed my cheek again, lingering over it. "Definitely."

"I'm not so sure I'm a match for a former prom queen," I told him with a small frown.

He ran a hand across my hair, which I'd pulled into a loose chignon. He tugged a strand to curl next to my face. "You will blow her out of the water."

We looked into each other's eyes for a moment.

"What makes you think she'll be jealous of you being with me?" I asked at last, ever pragmatic. "It doesn't sound like she cared that much."

"She'll care. Because she'll see you with me and even though she doesn't care about me, she's the sort who likes to imagine no man who's had her could ever move on. Besides, you'll drive her crazy."

The first part, at least, made sense. "How do you figure that?"

"You look gorgeous, Elle, and you don't act like a gorgeous woman does."

"I don't?" I sounded cynical. Because I was. "How do I act?"

"You act like an angel," he whispered in my ear and sent a shiver down my spine. "But you fuck like a demon. Don't you."

Angel. Demon. I was neither, or maybe both in his eyes.

"You want me to do this."

"I do, yes." He smiled. "C'mon, it'll be fun. Dinner. Drinks. Dancing."

"It's a date," I whispered, like we shared a secret.

Dan leaned in close, put his forehead to mine and whispered a reply. "Humor me."

Should I have been angry with him for what he asked me to do? For his assumption I would agree? Maybe. Yet there was something appealing in the way he presented the issue to me, as a done deal rather than something to negotiate. He acted as though I would do what he wished for the simple reason he asked it of me, but that's not why I agreed. I did it because he believed I could.

Chapter 07

I didn't need Dan to point out which one was Ceci. I knew her already, if not her, at least her type. She was tall, blond and built like…well, like a prom queen. She wore a red dress with lipstick to match, and my lip curled a little before I managed to smooth it.

It wasn't luck that put us at her table, but swift maneuvering of the place cards by Dan, who gave a chuckle so evil as he switched them that I had to step back and look him over.

"What?" He asked, catching my stare.

"I didn't think you could be so…mean."

"No?" He looked at me. "Does it surprise you?"

"No. Most people can be mean."

"But you thought I was a nice guy, and now you don't?" He took my arm to lead me toward our table.

"No," I told him. "I know you're not a nice guy."

"Hey." He frowned. "Yes, I am."

I raised an eyebrow and gave him a disbelieving look. We stared at each other for a moment, not caring that people were passing us by and that we were blocking traffic.

"You're teasing me." He sounded uncertain.

"Yes, Dan. I'm teasing you."

He shook his head with a little laugh. "You're devious."

"Sometimes."

"No," he told me, leaning in to kiss my cheek, close enough to my lips anyone watching would think he kissed my mouth. "I don't believe it."

He pulled away, admiration shining in his eyes. I warmed to it. We shared a smile, and I knew how rare this was for me, this rapport, even though he couldn't have.

"Dan?"

The feminine voice made me turn, and there she was. Prom queen. Ball buster. Blond bitch.

We faced each other. Two ice queens. I kept my smile, though I felt it morph from bemusement to calculating appraisal in that automatic way women have when we meet our rivals. It was okay, though. She was giving me the same look.

She cataloged me efficiently and without the subtlety to keep me from noticing. Her eyes took in my hair, my face, my body, my dress. Most of all, her gaze took in the way Dan's hand curled loosely around my waist. Possessing me.

"Hello, Ceci."

Her eyes flickered over me. The smile she gave him was no more genuine than the one she'd given me, but she put a lot more effort into it. She tried to make me invisible, a tactic that would have worked but for one small detail.

Dan wanted me to be sexy.

"This is Elle Kavanagh," Dan said, blandly polite. "Elle, this is Ceci Gold. She was our class president."

She shook my fingertips as limply as if I'd handed her a dead fish to shake instead of my hand. "Pleased to meet you."

I knew she expected me to say the same, but I didn't. I smirked, instead, and gave her the same sort of looking over she'd given me, because I knew she expected it.

Having sized each other up, we were free to stake our claims. She simpered at the man who came up beside her. Tall, dark-haired, wearing an expensive suit, he didn't look much like Dan. I smiled at him, too.

"Dan, this is Steve Collins." Ceci simpered. "My fiancé."

"Nice to meet you, Steve." Dan shook the other man's hand.

Steve, to give him credit, was either nice or self-confident enough not to posture. Or, as it seemed more likely, he didn't know his bride-to-be had picked up Dan in a bar and taken him home once upon at time. Either way, the men shook hands with more genuine sincerity than we women had.

"Looks like we're at the same table," Dan said, then to me, "should we sit down?"

We did. Boy, girl, boy, girl, just like in elementary school, which meant I ended up between the two men. The other two seats remained empty. We passed around rolls and chatted inconsequentially about what we might be served for dinner.

Ceci chattered about her job, party planner; her house, new; her upcoming wedding, ostentatious; and her plans for a Caribbean honeymoon, malicious. She kept her hand on Steve at all times. His shoulder, his hand, probably his thigh, too, as if when her hand disappeared under the table we wouldn't know what she was doing. Securing him to her. Proving he was hers, making it all right for her to flirt with Dan in front of Steve and me, because obviously she couldn't mean any of it. Not the fluttered lashes, or the pouting lips or the sly double entendres that sent her into bouts of giggles she'd have avoided had she known they wrinkled her forehead.

I said little, which I think she didn't expect. There are unspoken rules about bragging. The less I said, the more frantically she spoke.

"So, Elle, what do you do?" Steve asked finally, proving he really was a nice guy.

Ceci had opened her mouth to spout more inanities, but at her fiancé's question, she pinned me with her gaze. "Yes, Elle. What do you do?"

"I'm a junior vice president of corporate accounting and finance with Smith, Smith, Smith and Brown," I told him. "In other words, a glorified bean counter."

I couldn't have pleased her more. Accountants are nowhere near as exciting and sexy as party planners. Everyone knows that.

"Don't listen to her." Dan's fingers rubbed the back of my neck. "Elle's got a great position at Smith, Smith, Smith and Brown."

I glanced at him. "Do I?"

He smiled and leaned closer. "You do. I checked. You've got your own secretary."

I did, but that didn't necessarily mean anything. What exactly, had he checked? I didn't have time to ask, because Ceci took that moment to add her own comment to the conversation.

"Is he cute?" She was being transparently witty. "The secretary."

"Her name's Taffy," I told her. "And she's adorable."

"I guess bean counting must be a good business, then." She faltered, like she wanted to say more but couldn't think of what.

"It's good enough, I guess. It's steady work, and the money's nice. It's not as glamorous as astrophysics, but the pay's actually better."

That stopped them all.

"Astrophysics?" Dan's fingertips skated down my bare back, traced the line of the bodice, then rested flat against my skin.

"I have a Master's in astronomy," I explained nonchalantly. "With a concentration in celestial mechanics."

Blank looks.

"It's the science of the motion of celestial bodies under the influence of gravitational forces," I explained. I didn't expect them to understand what that meant, either.

I don't often tell people about my ostentatious beginnings, my attempt at glory, but I always love watching the looks on their faces when I do.

"Wow," Steve said. "That's impressive."

Dan half turned to face me, his hand moving on my skin, tracing the exposed bumps of my spine. I'd never told him about my degrees or the jobs I'd held before going to work at Triple Smith and Brown. Now as I talked about it both men looked as intrigued as if I'd been describing my kinky sex practices. Ceci didn't appear to like that much. Astronomy might not be sexier than party planning, but it's a hell of a lot smarter.

"Astronomy," she said with a small furrow of her otherwise perfect brow. "Horoscopes, right?"

Both men turned their heads to look at her, and she frowned. "What?"

"That's astrology," Steve said.

"Oh." She shrugged. "Same difference."

"They're both the study of stars," I said. "But astronomy has a lot more practical applications."

"What made you leave that for accounting?" Steve leaned in, probably unconsciously, but I noticed the body language. Ceci noticed it too and frowned.

"There might be billions of stars," I said. "But there aren't billions of jobs."

Steve laughed with a quick glance at Ceci, who didn't seem to share his good humor. "That must have been quite a change."

"Not as much as you'd think. It's all just numbers."

Ceci's laugh failed at being bell-like by a good measure. "Oh, you were the class brain, huh?"

"Class brain," I agreed, looking at her. "And I heard you were prom queen and class president."

"And voted most popular," she said without even bothering to hint at false modesty.

"Well then," I told her without even a hint of false insincerity, "it's a good thing high school was a long time ago."

Longer for them than for me, too. I hadn't realized Dan

was already in his thirties. I'd be twenty-nine on my next birthday. Time was running out, according to my mother, at least, but not as fast as it appeared to be for Ceci.

The first awkward silence passed around the table.

I glanced at Ceci, who was smiling so hard she looked manic. Her eyes went from the back of Steve's head to my face and back again, back and forth, fast. I felt sorry for her, so wrapped up in being adored she had no sense of herself without the admiration to tell her she was interesting. Of course, she was a bitch, too, that much was clear, and she had been flirting mercilessly with Dan for no good reason other than to build herself up and take me down. So my pity was short-lived.

"Ceci," Dan said. "I'm sure Steve won't mind if I steal you away for a dance. Would you, Steve?"

"Sure, go ahead."

Clever, clever Dan. I ducked my head to hide a smile, catching her gaze as I did. The expression on her face was priceless. Go with Dan and reaffirm he had, indeed, not been able to get over her, but leave Steve to discuss the mysteries of the universe with me? She nodded, her struggle clear to me, at least, then stood.

"Don't you worry, Elle," she said. "I'll take good care of him for you."

I smiled, catching Dan's eye. I had no worries. He wasn't my boyfriend. No attachments. She didn't threaten me.

"I won't worry," I replied, and turned back to Steve.

"So how long have you known Dan?" he asked.

"Not long." It had been three months. A lifetime and yet only a moment.

"You're a cute couple."

Maybe he was trying to be nice, or maybe he was doing what some people do when they're about to make an advance they want to be able to pretend is something else if it's refused. He smiled at me. Leaned a little closer.

"We're not really a couple."

"You're not?" Steve looked surprised, but I didn't miss the flicker in his eyes. Mr. Perfect was, after all, just a man. "Sorry."

"No reason to be."

We stared at each other across the table, and his glance flicked over my shoulder, to the dance floor. I didn't turn, but whatever he saw must not have pleased him, because he frowned. He spoke without looking at me.

"Would you like to dance?"

Then I did look, following the line of his gaze to where Ceci had draped herself over Dan, turning the upbeat ballad into some sort of sultry hoochie-coochie tango. Dan, for his part, looked as if he was having a good time, and somehow managed to give the impression that his hands were all over her when in reality they stayed perfectly still. It made me smile. He had talent.

"Sure. I'd like to dance." I let him take my hand, and by the time we got to the small square of wooden parquet the hotel had arranged for dancing, the music had changed.

"You all might remember this one." The dj cued up the next song. "From what I heard, it was y'all's prom theme."

"Oh, boy," I murmured as a late eighties love ballad came on. "Hold me back, I might cry."

Steve laughed and pulled me into a competent dance position a little too close to be casual but nowhere near what his fiancée was doing with Dan. We danced in silence for a few moments. The colored lights flashing on his face made shadows. His hand drifted a little lower, less on my lower back and more on my upper ass. I glanced at his arm, then back up at his face. He was smiling.

I looked at Dan. He smirked over Ceci's shoulder. Ceci, however, was not smiling. "If looks could kill" might be an old and clichéd turn of phrase, but it was true. It didn't seem to matter what she was doing with my date. Only what I was doing with hers. Or more appropriately, what he was doing with me, since I wasn't doing anything but not telling him to stop.

Another slow song came on. Steve drew me a little closer. I smelled his cologne, though I couldn't identify it.

"Smart women are so sexy," he murmured in my ear.

Steve had long legs, broad shoulders, white teeth and even features. He smelled good. He danced well. His hands were big enough to splat across my entire ass, something I was quickly discovering.

I didn't want to be dancing with Steve.

I looked over at Dan. He might have been holding a rag doll, for all the attention he paid the woman in his arms. Our eyes met. The song ended, and Dan left Ceci standing there while he came over to take my hand from Steve's.

"Pardon me," he said pleasantly. His eyes never left mine. "I think this dance is mine."

He took me in my arms without another word, without looking away, and held me close to him. My head fit perfectly on his shoulder, one of his hands at the small of my back and the other holding mine. He pressed his lips to my hair.

"Mine," he murmured, and we danced until the music changed again, became faster and no longer suited to slow dancing.

Then he took me by the hand and led me from the room, past a scowling Steve tossing back a shot of something at the bar, and an arm-crossed, pouting Ceci next to him. Dan took me down the hall, pushed open a door, led me inside the coatroom.

I didn't have time to ask him what he wanted, but then, I didn't have to ask. In May there were no coats to cushion me as he pushed me back. Only the jangle of metal on metal as he set the hangers swinging, and my gasp as he slid a hand beneath my dress and found me already wet for him.

"He wanted you." He fastened his mouth on my neck, just at the curve of my shoulder. "He wanted you so bad, Elle."

He stroked my clit with his thumb through my panties, then put his whole hand inside them. His palm pressed me, his fingers playing with my slickness. He put a finger inside me, and I muffled my cry with my hand, not caring if I smeared my lipstick.

"Would you have gone with him?" He asked in my ear, his hot breath blowing a loose strand of my hair.

I turned to look at him. "Tonight?"

"If he'd asked you."

"No."

His fingertip found my clitoris again and circled it, making my hips push forward. "You wouldn't?"

"No." My fingernails dug into the shoulders of his tux. "Absolutely not."

"Why not?" His other hand came up to caress my breast.

I pushed him away a little bit to look into his face. "Because I'm with you tonight."

He looked into my eyes, and his hand stilled for a moment before he started moving it again. "You're ready for me, aren't you. You're always ready for me."

An arrogant statement, but he made it seem like I'd given him a gift. He stroked me, made me shudder, then put my hand on the front of his fly.

"I'm ready for you, too." He smiled and moved my hand up down, stroking him through the fabric.

I looked automatically toward the door, which could have opened at any moment. "This turns you on. Sex in public."

He barely paused. "Sex anywhere."

I might have been indiscriminate when it came to choosing my partners before I'd met him, but until I'd met Dan, I'd never fucked in public. This would make three times. Thrice a charm. Or maybe our luck would run out this time, and we'd be caught.

I couldn't decide if the thought excited me or not. His touch did. His hands and mouth did. The way he looked at me did. And the way he said my name.

"Elle," he whispered. "I want you."

His touch skated me closer to the edge, and I wanted him, too. "My purse."

He nipped my neck, then looked up at me. "You really are always ready, aren't you?"

"I believe in being careful."

He shook his head a little, as though my answer amused him, but it took only a minute for him to put the condom on and slide my panties down to my thighs.

"Put your hands up. Grab the bar."

I grabbed the bar. It was cold. My fingers curled around it without effort, the tips of my nails meeting my palms.

He thrust inside me without resistance, his sole noise a grunt. His hands gripped my hips, lifted my leg to wrap around his waist. I grabbed the bar harder. My nails dug into my skin, but even that little pain wasn't a distraction to the pleasure of his cock filling me. He put his hands under my ass, holding me up as he moved.

It must've looked awkward, but I was spared the sight of it. No mirrors reflected the way he fucked me, nothing to show our faces twisted in lust. I looked at him as he looked up at me, and he slammed inside me so hard it moved my entire body.

I couldn't hold on to him. If I let go of the bars, we'd both fall. I couldn't move, either, balanced so precariously. It was all Dan, his job, his skill, and his brow furrowed in concentration as he moved.

I've said it before. I'm not small, and he's not large. Yet that didn't seem to matter now. He moved inside me without effort, his pubic bone hitting me in just the right place, over and over again, so he didn't have to slide a hand between us.

My orgasm surprised me more than it did him. I didn't think I'd come that way, skirt around my waist, hands numb from gripping a cold steel bar, heart pounding in anticipation of the door opening and our illicit behavior being discovered.

I came with a low, small cry, my eyes open and watching him, and he smiled. I closed my eyes immediately after, turned my head, but he didn't like that.

"Don't look away from me," he whispered, voice hoarse and breath short from exertion and arousal. "I love to watch your eyes."

There was no good reason for me to do as he said, not then, not ever. I want to make that very clear. No matter what Dan asked of me, I always had the ability to say no. I simply didn't take it.

I had the ability to refuse, and I did not.

I opened my eyes and looked into his, blazing with passion. That sounds funny, doesn't it? Do eyes really blaze with passion? Can they?

Yes. I don't know who said the eyes are windows to the soul, but I believe it. I saw passion there. And enjoyment. And as always, that hint of disbelief, like even though he was doing this he couldn't quite believe it.

I knew how he felt.

He fucked me harder. I adjusted my grip on the bars. The ring I wore on my right hand clattered on the metal. The hangers jangled. Our breathing sounded very loud.

His thrusts grew ragged, and beads of sweat formed on his brow. He bit his lip, shifting my weight and sinking into me one last time with a low grunt that brought a smile to my lips. It might be nice to be elegant and eloquent at the moment of orgasm, but most of us aren't. I watched his eyes flutter and the line of his throat as he swallowed hard. He put his face against my chest, bared by the gown's décolletage.

"I have to put you down," he murmured. "Ready?"

We disentangled with a minimum of awkward fumbling. I kept a hand on the bars above my head to keep me steady. My legs trembled.

My dress fell down around my ankles. He took care of the condom with a handful of tissues from a box on the shelf above us, zipped himself, tossed the evidence in the small brass wastecan by the door.

"Hey." He grinned.

"Why is everything so easy with you?" I asked him.

The words surprised me as much as my orgasm had. I think they surprised him, too, because his smile turned quizzical. He reached to smooth a curl that had fallen to my shoulder.

"What do you mean?"

Heat rose from my belly to my throat to cover my face. The dress revealed enough of it to be obvious. I couldn't meet his eyes anymore.

Shame and I are no strangers to each other. I'm well acquainted with the feeling. Oh, I force it away easily enough, pretend it's not there, deny it. Much of the time, I can even convince myself I have nothing to be ashamed of, and most of the time, it works.

Not then. It made me stagger, the shame that hit me in the gut like a punch. My ears rang with it. My vision blurred. I've fainted once or twice in my life, consequences of low blood pressure and anemia, or too much heat and too little hydration. I recognized the feeling. I ducked my head and kept my grip on the bar above my head, fearing if I let go, I'd fall.

"Elle? You okay?"

The solicitude in his voice was too much. I pushed past him, out of the closet, into the hall. I put my hands to my burning cheeks. I needed to get out of there, fast, and my feet found the swiftest route, toward the end of the hall and the door marked Exit.

I came out in a dark courtyard littered with cigarette butts and smelling of stale smoke. I gulped in blessedly cool night air as the metal door clanged shut behind me. The brick wall of the hotel still held the day's heat and was rough beneath my fingers. I let it support me for a minute while I breathed.

I wasn't crying, at least. But then, I didn't. Tears were a relief that had abandoned me a long time ago.

Sex is not wrong. Sex is not dirty. Not even sex in a public place with a man you barely know. It's not. Sex is a gift, a built-in human pleasure, something to enjoy and cherish and utilize. Sex rejuvenates. Sex replenishes. Orgasms are just one more miraculous function our body provides, no more shameful than a sneeze or the beating of our hearts. Sex is not dirty, not even in public places with someone you barely know. Liking sex, liking a man's hands on me, coming with him, letting him inside me…that doesn't make me dirty.

The night was cool, not cold, but I'd gone from heat to chill in minutes. Goose bumps humped my arms, and I rubbed them, furious with myself.

Sex is not dirty. I am not dirty. I'm not.

The door opened behind me. Dan came out. I straightened, the near-frantic motion of my hands on my arms ceasing abruptly.

"Hey," Dan said after a moment. "Elle, are you all right? Too much to drink?"

"No."

He stood next to me, but didn't touch me. I kept my gaze straight ahead, though I had nothing to see. Now I not only felt ashamed, but embarrassed.

He rustled in his coat pocket, pulled out a pack of cigarettes, offered me one. I took it, though I'm not much of smoker. He lit it for me, then one for himself, and we stood in silence while the red tips of our cigarettes glowed red in the darkness.

"Are you mad at me?" He asked after a while.

"No, Dan."

"Okay."

He tossed the butt to the ground, where it still glowed. He didn't crush it out. I watched the ember flare and go dark, then tossed my cigarette down to meet it.

"I'm sorry," I said.

He turned to look at me, his face in shadow. "I wish you weren't."

I swallowed, my throat tight, glad of the darkness that hid my face from him. "I think I should go."

"I wish you wouldn't."

"The night's almost over, anyway," I said.

"Elle."

One word, my name, but it fixed me as firmly as if he'd reached out and grabbed my arm.

"I don't want you to ever be sorry," Dan said. "Because I'm not."

I didn't mean to laugh, but that's what came out. One short, sharp laugh, full of cynicism.

"I don't imagine you would be."

He scuffed his shoe against the courtyard's stone floor. "You think I'm just the sort of guy who picks up women and fucks them all over the place."

"I don't know you!" My reply came out sharper than I'd meant it to.

"So get to know me," he offered. "I'm easy to know, Elle. I promise."

"I'm not."

I heard the smile in his voice. "No kidding."

"Do you…do you think I'm the sort of woman who just lets guys pick her up and fuck her all over town?"

"Are you?"

"Apparently." I sounded resigned.

He touched me, then. He put his hand on my waist and pulled me closer to him. He moved into the shaft of light from the security lamp. It made his eyes look very blue.

"So what if you do?"

I could only stare at him. He smiled. I didn't return it. His fingers moved on the slippery fabric of the gown he'd bought me.

"I don't think you're the sort of woman who picks up guys and fucks them all over town. No matter how many men you've been with."

"Seventy-eight." The answer slid from my mouth like an oil spill spreading between us.

He blinked and hesitated. "You've been with seventy-eight men?"

"Yes."

I waited to see disgust or censure cross his face, but he only reached up to smooth his finger around the curl of hair that had come loose from my chignon.

"That's a lot."

"Does it bother you?" I asked.

He looked thoughtful. "Does it bother you?"

"Yes, Dan," I told him after a second. "It does."

"Before you I dated lots of women. Does that bother you?"

"No." That was different. Dating women was different from picking up men and taking them home and fucking them to prove I could.

He inched me closer, adding his other hand to my waist. He smelled of cologne and sex. His shirt looked rumpled.

"I don't care what you did before. All that matters is what you do now."

I shook my head, silent.

"If you wanted pretty words, I'd find some for you. But something tells me you wouldn't believe them, anyway."

That tilted my mouth upward a bit. "That's probably true."

He pulled me in front of him to cradle me from behind, his hands linking through mine. His embrace chased away the goose bumps. He rested his chin on my shoulder and lifted our linked hands to point at the sky.

"What stars are we looking at?"

"That happens to be the Big Dipper."

He held me closer, keeping me warm. "How come you wanted to study astronomy?"

I leaned into him, looking up at the pinpricks of light

against the night's black sky. "I used to think I could count them all."

"The stars?"

I nodded. "I thought I could count them all, or at the very least, learn all I could about them. Figure out how they hung there in the sky like that without falling down. Find a way to reach them, maybe. Discover if there was life out there."

He laughed, low, his breath a brush of heat on my skin. "UFOs?"

"It's a legitimate field," I murmured. "But I never studied UFOs. No."

"Just the stars."

"Believe me, that was plenty."

We stood, quiet for a few moments. His thumbs traced repetitive lines on the fabric over my stomach. His lips pressed the skin of my shoulder.

"Do you ever miss it?"

"Every time I look at the stars," I told him.

"Did you ever figure out how many there are?"

I turned my head to look at him. "No. Nobody can count them. They're infinite."

"So…you gave up?"

I frowned, pulling out of his arms a little. "Abandoning a task that is futile and pointless is not giving up."

He didn't let me get far before tugging me back against him. "I know."

"So then why did you say that?"

I felt the lift and drop of his shoulders as he shrugged,

and the shift of his lips on my shoulder as he smiled. "I wanted to see what you'd say."

I said nothing.

"So how long did it take you to decide it was a futile and pointless task?"

I pulled away again to look at him. "Who says I have?"

We studied each other under the light of the stars. Then I looked away, back up to the sky. Dan looked up too, holding my hand, and we stared together at the night.

"I didn't give up," I said after a moment.

Dan squeezed my hand. "I'm glad."

"Me too," I said, and squeezed back.

"Ella." My mother's voice, as always, twisted my mouth. "Have you gained weight?"

The choice had come down to meeting her for lunch in a neutral location, having her come to my house or meeting her at hers. Dutiful daughter that I was, I'd chosen lunch. We both knew why, but neither of us spoke of it.

"Probably, Mother."

She sniffed. "No man's going to want a woman who doesn't take care of herself."

I'd been buttering a roll. Now I added extra butter and gave her a completely insincere smile. "I'm not worried about it, Mother."

She sniffed again, sipping water with lemon in it. I should explain that my mother is not old or infirm, or even in failing health, though she'd like to make the world pity her for being so. My mother is an attractive, well-preserved woman in her early sixties, who spends more money on her weekly beauty appointment than I do on groceries. A minor car accident more than fifteen years ago left her with an almost invisible scar on her left leg and the utter inability to drive herself anywhere, due to "nerves." And though we never discuss my father's drinking, she's not stupid enough to expect him to drive her anywhere. Frankly, I'd rather get over my nerves than be trapped at home with a man I hate and have to rely on the kindness of others to get me anywhere…but then again I have my own issues to work through and perhaps more of my mother's martyr complex than I'd like to admit.

The waiter arrived to take our order, and my mother ordered her usual, a house salad with dressing on the side. I ordered a cheeseburger and fries with a chocolate milk shake.

"Elspeth!" You'd have thought I'd ordered a roasted baby with a side of cute little puppy, from my mother's horrified expression. I'm not sure which offended her more, the food itself or the fact I was ordering something as plebeian as a cheeseburger in a restaurant as fancy as Giardino's.

"Mother," I replied, calm because that infuriated her more.

She shook out her napkin. "You do it to upset me, don't you."

"Oh, Mother. I'm just hungry, that's all."

She made no secret of her appraising look. "At least black is very slimming."

I glanced at my black sweater and black fitted skirt. I don't think there's a woman alive who doesn't wonder if her thighs could be thinner, her ass flatter. But overall, I've made peace with my body and the shape it takes.

"You'll get heavy again," she continued. "And after you got so slim, too."

I had been "heavy," as she put it, in self-defense, and slim from circumstance. It wasn't a diet I'd like to go on again.

"I'm happy with the way I look, Mother. Please drop it."

"Nobody's ever happy with the way they look," she said, echoing my thoughts of the moment before. "It's woman's curse, Ella. We're doomed to always want to be thinner, have bigger breasts and longer legs."

"I am more than tits and ass. I have a brain, too."

She wrinkled her nose at my use of language. "Well, nobody can see your brain, can they?"

As I'd told Dan, abandoning a task you know is futile and pointless is not giving up. It's being smart. I didn't bother arguing with her. She'd been giving me the same lecture for years. I sipped some water, instead, using the ice in my mouth to keep my tongue from snapping.

For once, she let it go. The detailed, gossipy story she began telling me next was a little better, in that it in no way involved me, my weight or my brain, but instead was the story of my mother's friend Debbie Miller's daughter, Stella, who'd just had a baby.

"…and she named it Atticus!" My mother shook her head, her opinion of such a name quite clear.

"Atticus is very nice name. At least she didn't name him Adolf."

"You've got a smart mouth," my mother replied, "to go along with that smart brain."

"I'm sorry." Funny how being an adult doesn't always change our relationship with our parents. I wasn't worried she'd reach across the table and smack me…but some part of me reacted as though she might.

The waiter brought our food, though I was no longer hungry for it. I sipped the thick shake anyway, just so she wouldn't have anything to remark upon.

"Ella," my mother said at last, her salad half-eaten and pushed away with a sigh. "I need to talk to you about your father."

"All right."

I put my own fork down and wiped my mouth with a napkin. I didn't speak to my father much. We talked if he answered the phone on the rare occasions I called the house, and my mother referenced him often in terms of her daily routine: "Daddy and I watched that show about psychic pets" and "Daddy and I are thinking about redecorating the kitchen," when really, the truth was my father spent the day in front of the television with an ever-full gin and tonic in one hand and the remote in the other.

"What do you want to talk about?"

I've seen my mother shed enough false tears to fill a swimming pool. She does it so expertly her makeup never runs. So when a tear glittered in her eye that smudged her carefully applied liner, alarm shot through me.

"Your father," my mother said, "isn't well."

"What's wrong with him?"

She made a little fluttering motion with her hands, and my alarm grew. She might be a martyr, but she was rarely without words. I watched her mouth work and nothing come out, and I had to link my hands in my lap to keep them from shaking.

"What's wrong with him, Mother?"

She looked around before she answered, like the other diners might care about what she said. "Cirrhosis," she whispered, then clapped a hand over her mouth as though she hadn't meant to say it.

It was no surprise, of course. My father had been a heavy drinker for most of his life. "Has he been to a doctor? What's wrong with him?"

"He's been too tired to get out of his chair, and he's lost weight. He won't eat."

"But he won't stop drinking."

She lifted her chin. "Your father deserves a little relaxer in the evenings. He's worked hard to support us all these years."

I didn't push her on it. "Will he have to go to the hospital?"

"I haven't told anyone," she whispered. She dabbed her eyes, and the brief moment of honesty we'd shared disintegrated.

"Of course not. We wouldn't want the neighbors to know."

She gave me a glass-edged glance. "Absolutely not. What happens at home stays at home."

What happens at home, stays at home.

How many times had I heard that, growing up?

We stared at each other across the table, two women any stranger would have guessed belonged together. I was the child who looked like her, with the same full mouth and the same crooked hairline. My eyes were more gray and hers more blue, but they were the same shape and size, wide set in a way that could make us both look innocent when we were not.

"Won't you ever forgive me?" I didn't want my voice to shake but it did. I gripped my napkin again. "Mother, damn it, won't you ever let that go?"

She sniffed again, like I wasn't even worth a response and I wasn't Elle anymore but Ella again, and I hated it.

She didn't deny my question though, or pretend she didn't know what I was talking about, and I set my gaze on my half-eaten burger in order to gain some perspective. The waiter saved me from blurting more by asking if I wanted a box.

"No, thank you."

That made her cluck her tongue again. "Waste!"

"I'm paying for lunch, so you don't need to worry about it."

"That's not the point," she told me. "Ella, you can't afford to go throwing your money away."

"Because I don't have a man to take care of me," I finished for her. "I know. Can we have the check, please?"

The waiter, caught between us like a dolphin in a tuna net, backed away. My mother glared at me. I had no more glare left inside me. I could only stare.

"The waiter doesn't even know you," I told her. "And what's more, he doesn't care."

"That's not the point." She shifted in her chair, frowning.

I couldn't fight her any longer. My lunch had settled in my stomach like a stone. I wiped my mouth again, then my hands, and set the napkin over my unfinished lunch so it could no longer accuse me.

"You really should come visit. Before it's too late."

Ah, simple. The real purpose of this lunch had raised its head at last. I shrugged.

"I'm very busy with work."

She reached forward, too fast for a woman who complained her fibromyalgia made her too clumsy to do her own cleaning. She flicked open the top button of my blouse, exposing my skin. Her face twisted.

"Work. Is that what you call it?"

I put my hand over my throat in automatic response, then rebuttoned my shirt over the small purple mark she'd exposed. "I have a job—"

"Are you a whore?" She sneered. "Is that your work? Or maybe it's not just work that keeps you from doing what any decent daughter would do. Maybe it's something else? Maybe you're too busy being…dirty."

Unless you're staring into a mirror it's impossible to know what your own expression looks like, but I felt mine go cold and blank. It must have looked something like that, because her mouth twitched in the familiar way that meant she'd triumphed, earned a reaction from me. Oh, the games we play, even when we know we can't win.

"Are you screwing your boss, Ella? Is he the one who gave you that suck mark?"

"I thought you were worried I'd never find a man," I replied in the same sickly sweet tone she'd just used.

We share more than eyes and hair. We share a keen sense of vengeance, too, my mother and I. She's the queen of holding grudges, but I might well be the duchess. I learned how words can wound more than a knife, and I learned it from the best.

She shook her head. "I'm so ashamed of you, Ella."

I said nothing. Not a word, and thus, won. She couldn't stand against silence. She needed fuel to continue her tirade, and I gave her none, though my tongue ached later from biting it.

She stood, clutching her fashionable bag. "Don't bother to walk me out. I'll catch my own cab. And, Ella, you really should visit, if not for me, at least for your father."

"And for the neighbors, maybe?"

And thus, I lost, because I couldn't manage to keep my silence.

My mother didn't believe having the last word was most important. An aggrieved sigh could be far more effective, and she gave me one before she swept off, carrying her righteous indignation around her like a cloud.

Me, I paid the check and then, my father's daughter despite my best efforts, I went to the bar down the street and found a spot in the back where I wouldn't have to speak to anyone.

The painting in my dining room progressed with painful slowness. Guilt plucked me every time I saw the paint cans and bucket of brushes soaking in my laundry room, but closing the door solved the problem neatly. I blamed Dan. Since the night of his class reunion a week ago, he'd called me almost every night. Our schedules hadn't allowed for more than phone conversations, which was fine with me. Most nights when I got home from work all I wanted to do was reheat something for dinner, shower and crawl into bed. Dan seemed to understand and hadn't asked for another appointment. I was a little disappointed.

None of that was helping my dining room. I love my house. It was the first thing that was really mine. I bought it before I even bought my first car. My house is my haven, my refuge.

But I hated the dining room. Not for its odd shape that wouldn't easily accommodate a table and chairs and sideboard. Not for its lack of windows, or the horrendous hanging fixture I hadn't yet replaced. I hated the dining room because it mocked me with its state of disrepair, and because every time I passed it I was reminded of how unmotivated I was to finish the task I'd begun.

I'd bought what had once been a decrepit row home in a part of town the mayor called "underprivileged." The neighborhood hadn't been great, but it was getting better. The city government, attempting to revitalize the downtown Harrisburg area, had put substantial financial support into projects assisting its efforts. It was nice to have neighbors who drove sports cars instead of stealing them.

I'd renovated, not remodeled, preferring to keep the house's original rooms intact, though it meant some inconvenience in such matters as closets and bathrooms. I'd worked room by room as money and time allowed, hiring professionals to repair damage done by time and neglect but doing all the cosmetic work myself.

Not that I had a flair for decorating. Like my wardrobe, I preferred to keep my decor simple. Neutral. White walls. Sturdy furniture, most of it acquired piecemeal from auctions and thrift stores, not because I couldn't afford new but because I liked old pieces. I had some framed black-and-white art, a few candlesticks and vases, mostly gifts. I had built-in bookshelves filled with books, and a working fireplace to read them by.

Tonight I also had Gavin. I had seen little of him for the past week or so, though I'd heard the muffled sound of shouting voices from next door more than once. He waited for me on the doorstep, a book clutched in his hands. Despite the temperate weather, he wore a giant black sweatshirt, hood up, looking so much like Anakin Skywalker on his way to becoming Darth Vader, I couldn't help commenting.

"The dark side of the Force is just too hard to resist, huh?"

My joke fell flat. Gavin looked up from the shadows of his hood, his pale face not smiling. He stood up.

"Huh?"

"The dark side…never mind." I wasn't going to ask him if he'd seen the Star Wars epics. I unlocked my door and he followed me inside. "Come to help me paint?"

"Yeah."

He'd never been a chatty kid, but this was uncommunicative, even for him. I gave him a glance as I settled my mail and my bag on the table. He headed for the dining room, stripping off his sweatshirt over his head and hanging it neatly on the back of a chair. Beneath he wore a plain gray T-shirt. He bent to pry open the paint can, and the fabric pulled out of his jeans, exposing the knobs of his spine. He looked thinner to me than he had before. I hadn't seen his mother's car lately, which meant nothing other than she'd been out when I was home. Maybe she hadn't been home to make him dinner.

"Want something to eat?"

On his knees, he looked over his shoulder at me. "Sure."

I put a couple frozen pizzas in the oven and went upstairs to change into paint clothes. By the time I came down, Gavin had spread out the brushes and rollers and poured the paint into the trays. The oven dinged and he stood, turning toward me.

I stopped short at the sight of his arms. The sleeve of one had pushed up on his bicep, exposing skin normally covered. He had lines there. Three or four, thin and angry red lines. Cuts.

"What happened to your arm?"

He pulled the shirt down lower to hide them. "My cat scratched me."

I used the excuse of pulling the pizza from the oven to not answer that. Maybe his cat had scratched him. Maybe he was telling the truth. I didn't mention it again.

He ate only two pieces of pizza instead of his usual four, but I didn't comment on that, either. I wrapped up the extra and set it on the counter.

"Take this with you when you go," I told him. "I won't eat it."

He smiled, a little. "Okay."

I stifled the urge to reach out and ruffle his hair. He was a kid, but he wasn't my kid, and he was fifteen. Fifteen-year-old boys aren't too fond of having their hair ruffled, I'm pretty sure.

We got to work, and he asked if he could put on some music. My CD collection seemed to surprise him.

"You've got some cool tunes, Miss Kavanagh." He held up the latest by a new alternative rock band.

I tried not to be offended by the unspoken addition "for an old lady." "Thanks. Why don't you put that on?"

He did, and we worked some more. Sometimes side by side, sometimes in different sections. He'd shot up over the past few months and now stood an inch or so taller than I, so I let him get up on the stepstool to do the parts closest to the ceiling.

"You know, Gavin," I said after a bit. "You don't have to call me Miss Kavanagh. You can call me Elle."

He looked down from his perch. "My mom told me I have to show respect for people."

"Your mom was right. But I don't consider you calling me by my first name to be disrespectful." I finished the last corner and stood back to put my roller in the tray. "I'm giving you permission."

He rolled some more paint onto the wall for a moment. "Okay. I guess I could do that."

The room looked good, though another coat of paint would finish it off. I started cleaning up. Gavin helped. The laundry room was small, and we bumped into each other, dancing with awkward smiles as he tried to put a roller in the sink while I tried to back out of the way. I knocked against the shelf where I kept my detergent and extra hangers. Some of them started to fall, and Gavin reached for them.

It was all innocent, aboveboard. He wasn't even touching me, just reaching around to keep the hangers from sliding off the shelf. We were laughing. I looked up to my back door, the window of which showed a face peering in.

I stopped laughing long enough to scream, embarrassed

a moment later by recognizing the face of Mrs. Ossley. Heart pounding, I pushed past Gavin to thumb open the lock. "You scared me."

"I knocked at the front, but nobody answered." She gave me a narrow-eyed smile. "Gavin. It's time to come home."

"I want to help Elle finish cleaning—"

"Now." Her tone brooked no argument.

"It's all right, Gavin," I said. "There's only a bit more to do. You go ahead."

"Lemme grab my sweatshirt," he said and went to retrieve it.

Mrs. Ossley and I stood in awkward silence in my tiny laundry room. She seemed disinclined to speak to me, and I had nothing to say to her. We were saved from true discomfort a moment later when Gavin returned, hooded once more, and followed his mother out the door.

I locked the door behind them, thinking I'd made an enemy of her somehow but not sure why.

It wasn't unusual for me not to hear from Chad for weeks on end. We kept in touch through e-mail and cards, with phone calls thrown in when one or the other of us realized it had been a long time since we'd spoken. Or one of us was undergoing a crisis. When I didn't hear back from my brother after I'd left a message thanking him for returning "Princess Pennywhistle" to me, I wasn't concerned. As the days passed, though, and even e-mails went unanswered, I knew something was going on.

His voice sank my stomach. He sounded like he had a mouthful of syrup, oozing, making him slur. "Hello?"

He perked up a little when he heard my voice, but the bubbly, effusive chatterbox who usually greeted me was gone. He mumbled on about being busy with work and the amateur theater group he'd joined, and about Luke's sister who'd just had a baby. Inconsequential things that filled the space between us but revealed nothing.

"What's wrong," I asked him after listening. "Tell me, Chaddie."

He didn't say anything for so long I thought we might have been disconnected but for the sound of his breathing. "I'm down, Elle. Just a little down."

"Oh, Chad." There wasn't much more I could say. Words couldn't replace a hug, no matter how heartfelt the empathy in them. "What are you doing about it?"

That roused him enough to chuckle a little. "Same thing I always do. Drown my sorrows in hot fudge sundaes."

It was better than in alcohol, which Chad never touched. "What's Luke say about it?"

Chad didn't say anything again after a moment. "He doesn't say anything about it. I don't tell him."

"He's got to know," I told him gently. "You live together. He can't not notice."

"We don't talk about it," Chad said. "Luke's happy all the time. I don't want to bring him down. I don't want to bring you down, Elle. I just need to get through this."

"You don't have to do it on your own."

"Forgive me if your advice doesn't really mean a whole lot," Chad said more snidely than I'd ever heard him speak. "Miss Island Unto Herself. Tell me something, big sis, when's the last time you cried on someone's shoulder?"

We went back to silence after that. I waited for him to apologize. He didn't, and after a minute I muttered an affronted goodbye and hung up. Sometimes, even when you know someone else is right, it's easier to be the angry one than it is to admit they're telling the truth.

I'd been invited to home parties before. Candles, cooking equipment, jewelry. I didn't ever go, though I was always polite and ordered something from their catalogs. Just because I didn't want to spend my time sitting around the living room of someone I didn't know giggling about products I didn't like didn't mean I wasn't smart about the way women work. Helping them out with their home parties engendered good feelings, and I usually ended up with a bunch of things to give my mother for Christmas and her birthday.

Marcy hadn't invited me to buy measuring spoons, earrings or dip mix. She hadn't let me get away with flipping through a glossy brochure and writing a check, either. She'd insisted I attend her home party, and I couldn't think of a good reason to turn her down.

Uncertain of the etiquette about these sorts of functions, I stood outside the door to her apartment for a full minute debating if I should knock or try the knob. Two women appeared in the hallway behind me and saved me from having to decide.

"Ooh, you're here for the toy party?" The taller one giggled.

The door opened. Marcy squealed. The other women squealed. I allowed myself to be dragged forward, hugged, my ear squealed into, my hand filled with a glass of wine, my rear end seated in a chair. Marcy passed around snacks. The women chattered. I sipped my wine without saying much. I didn't know anyone but Marcy and didn't have much to say.

I haven't been locked in a cupboard for my whole life. I know what sex toys are, even if I've never owned one. And even though my tastes in lingerie run to simple, lacy garter belts and pretty panties instead of leopard-skin thongs and stockings with holes, I have seen items of that sort in the stores.

I thought I was prepared for this party, my pen in hand, the order form in front of me. Three minutes into the hostess's spiel, I knew I was in over my head. By the time she passed out the penis pencil toppers, I was hoping I'd get out of there without thoroughly embarrassing myself.

I shouldn't have worried. Marcy, for all her bluster about sex, squealed and covered her face when the hostess pulled out the first item, and there were many other women there who blushed or peeked out through their fingers, too. Obviously the King Dong with detachable vibrating bullet wasn't something they saw every day, either. I relaxed. I wasn't as backward as I'd thought.

"Now, ladies," said the hostess, passing out pink papers to each of us. "It's time for Twenty Kinky Questions! And I'll be handing out some prizes, so be honest!"

We all laughed and bent over our pink surveys, which wanted to know how many partners we had, where the craziest place we'd ever made love was, if we'd ever slept with more than one man at a time. We were supposed to list our celebrity crush, if we'd ever cheat on our significant others, our favorite sexual position and more.

Dutifully, I filled out all the answers, being less than honest, though the hostess had admonished us to be truthful. There were simply some things I wasn't going to admit to a roomful of strangers. Not even for a free set of fur-lined handcuffs.

After demonstrating all the products and displaying all the lingerie, the hostess retired to Marcy's kitchen table to take orders while the rest of us replenished our wineglasses and giggled over pink plastic phalluses. I had a handful of cheese cubes in one hand and my wine in the other when Marcy cornered me.

"So. What are you going to buy?"

I showed her my order form, printed neatly with my penis-topped pen. She looked it over and took my pen to scribble something else on it, jerking the paper away when I tried to protest. With full hands I couldn't grab it back from her.

"Marcy, what are you doing?"

She giggled. "C'mon, Elle. All you got was the babydoll nightie! In white! Don't you want it in red, at least?"

"Absolutely not." I finished the cheese and grabbed at the order form. "No, Marcy."

"I'm getting the Deluxe Rodney Rabbit." She smirked. "I put you down for the Eager Beaver."

I looked at the paper. "Marcy—"

"C'mon," she teased. "Every woman should have a good vibrator. If you don't want to pay for it, I'll buy it. My treat. Consider it my contribution to your good health."

I didn't want to laugh, I really didn't. But she always made me, anyway. "I can take care of my own good health, thanks. And not with the Eager Beaver. I don't want to go to bed with wildlife."

"No?" She grabbed up the catalogue from behind me. "How about the Silver Bullet?"

"Do I need to worry about werewolves?" The wine had loosened my tongue.

Marc looked up with a grin. "The Mermaid? She's waterproof."

I looked at the picture. "Nothing with a face on it. Geesh."

She was cute, that Mermaid, with her smooth tail and flowing hair. Marcy flipped another page and let out a triumphant cry. She stabbed the page with her finger.

"That's the one for you."

I looked. "Blackjack?"

"You'll be screaming hit me baby, one more time, with the Blackjack. Made of smooth, contoured silicone and using our patented vibro-sleeve technology, the Blackjack is guaranteed to hit all the spots that count. Silent and discreet, the Blackjack enhances solo play or lovemaking." She giggled at the advertising copy.

"Clever," I said, looking at the picture again. Unlike the other cutesy vibrators, the Blackjack was about three inches long, shaped like a cigar, plain black. "Very utilitarian."

Marcy laughed and nudged me, her eyes shining. "Get that one."

I hesitated. "Marcy, I just don't…"

"Elle," she interrupted. "For fun. C'mon. Try it."

I looked around the room at all the other laughing ladies holding up slinky animal-print nighties and getting out their checkbooks. I looked again at the picture of the Blackjack. Then I looked at her.

"If one word of this gets out around the office—"

"It won't. Cross my heart."

I sighed. She'd won me over. I couldn't resist the allure. Marcy crowed and squeezed me, spilling wine down the front of my blouse.

"Here's to my good health," I told her as she bounced.

My cell phone rang, and she gave me another squeeze before leaving me to answer it. "Kavanagh."

"Kavanagh, Stewart here."

Dan. I crumpled the order form in my hand as if he could see it. I let out a strangled giggle.

"Elle, are you all right?"

"Fine." I smoothed the paper.

"I called your house but you weren't there. Thought I'd catch you on your cell. What are you doing?"

Two women had grabbed hold of the giant double dildo and were attempting to do the limbo with it. Raucous laughter drowned out my response for a moment, and I ducked down the short hall leading to Marcy's bedroom before I could answer. I leaned against the wall, phone pressed to my ear, the order form a guilty weight in my hand.

"Marcy invited me over to a home party."

"Yeah?" He sounded unaccountably pleased. "Pampered Chef?"

"Umm…no."

"Too bad. I need another cooking stone."

I couldn't blame the wine for the surreal, woozy feeling overtaking me. "You use cooking stones?"

He laughed, but sidestepped answering. "How long will you be there? Can you come over after?"

"I have to work tomorrow, Dan."

"Elle. It's only eight o'clock."

"Dan." I laughed. "You are becoming very demanding."

"I know." He sounded proud. "Come over after. You want to. You know you do."

My stomach jumped at the way he said it, and I closed my eyes for a moment. The wall felt cool against my cheek. I let the order form slide between my fingers, back and forth.

But in the end, I agreed, because he was right. I did want to. It would be good for my health.

Dan laughed when I told him where I'd been. His seawater eyes gleamed, encouraging me to describe the party. I never felt I was a good storyteller, but he was such a good listener I kept talking until I realized I'd blurted out twenty minutes worth of conversation about sex toys and crotchless panties, and I stopped myself short.

"Sounds like you had a good time," he said. "Twenty Kinky Questions."

Dan's wine was better than Marcy's, and I sipped it before answering. Wine made me expansive. I leaned back against his cushions. "I think society, as a whole, is so focused on sex and being sexy it's become a caucus race. Everyone runs and runs, trying to catch up to everyone else and in the end we all think we deserve prizes."

He laughed again, shaking his head. I frowned. "Are you making fun of me?"

He shook his head again, still smiling. "No. You're so sincere I can't make fun of you."

I put my wineglass down on the table. "You are."

"No." Dan scooted forward to put his hands on my upper arms. "It's cute. You're a little drunk."

I was, but indignant just the same. "It's cute that I'm a little drunk?"

He rubbed his hands up and down on my arms. "No. That you're so affronted by society turning us into sex maniacs. It's cute. And cute that you relate kink with something from *Alice in Wonderland.*"

I tried hard to be affronted some more, but with him so close to me it was difficult to maintain the temper. "You've read it, then."

"Yeah, I've read it." He moved closer again. "Does that surprise you?"

If I said yes, that might be insulting. I let my eyes wander around his living room and spotted his bookshelves. "Do you like to read?"

I got up before he answered and wandered to peruse his collection. Looking at the books someone has on his shelf can be as intimate as peeking in his medicine chest. Dan had several shelves of leather-bound volumes on law and other boring stuff, but below them were copies of paperback thrillers and hardback classics I recognized. Grinning, I glanced over my shoulder.

"You joined the Classics of the Month Club?"

He put on a hangdog look. "Yeah."

"Have you read these?"

The Heart Is a Lonely Hunter. Jane Eyre. Wuthering Heights.

Dracula. The Sun Also Rises. I ran my fingers over the spines and pulled one out. I sniffed it. There's something special about the way a good book smells.

"Yeah, I read them." He came over behind me, his arms around my waist as I fondled his books.

I put back the book in my hand and looked at the others. My fingers stopped again, and I turned to look at him. "You have *The Little Prince?*"

He chuckled. "Yeah."

I pulled it out. His edition was newer than mine, the cover unscuffed and the pages unbent. Someone with bad handwriting had inscribed the book "To Dan, with love." I showed it to him.

He shrugged. "Old girlfriend."

I looked back at the book. "Have you read it?"

He shook his head. "No. Should I?"

"Far be it from me to tell you what you should or shouldn't do" came my lofty answer as I put it back.

"You've read it."

I smiled. His hands gripped my hips lightly, and I did a sideways turn and step combination that took me from his grasp without making it seem like I was jumping out of his arms. I leaned against his shelves.

"I have. It's one of my favorite books."

"Yeah?" He looked over my shoulder, then back at my face. "Maybe I should read it, then."

"You don't have to on my account." I was a little embarrassed. *The Little Prince* is a children's book. Sort of. Revealing it to be my favorite had revealed something about myself.

"I know I don't have to." He moved closer. "Maybe I want to."

I ducked under his arm and headed for the couch again. "You might not like it."

"Or, I might." He followed me. "Want some more wine?"

I gave him what I meant to be a stern look. From the way his mouth tilted up, I think I failed. "I think you want me to get very drunk."

"Of course."

"So you can take advantage of me."

"You caught me out."

I kept my mouth from quirking into a smile, but only barely. "So you can do kinky things to me."

He laughed. "Sure. You got it."

I looked into his eyes as he sat beside me. "I got the lowest score on that test, by the way. I felt quite inadequate."

He made a sympathetic face. "Is that what prompted the rant?"

I nodded. Dan gave a soothing coo and patted my head. We laughed.

"Poor baby," he said. "What haven't you done that everyone else had?"

"Everything."

I'd had a lot of sex with a lot of men, but most of it had been dull and useless, ten minutes of haphazard foreplay followed by a minute and a half of frantic humping. People are not as imaginative as the movies make them out to be. Maybe I'd just been lucky in my conquests, never picking up the stray fetishist or serial killer. Maybe I'd just been careful to pick guys who didn't impress me with their imaginations…until Dan, and his hint of whimsy.

"Elle." He lifted a brow. "I know you've done some things."

"Not kinky things." I let him pull me closer, into the half circle of his arm around my shoulders.

"You don't think so?" He leaned over to nuzzle my ear with his lips. "I'd say letting me fuck you in the bathroom was pretty damn kinky."

"That wasn't one of the questions." At least not one I'd answered truthfully. I shivered at the deliciousness of his mouth on my skin. I leaned down and pulled the pink paper from my bag, resting at my feet. I handed it to him. "There you go. Twenty Kinky Questions. Learn the secrets of my sadly unkinky past."

Dan unfolded the paper and we leaned together to read it. His eyes scanned the page, and he looked at me to let them scan my face. He put his hand up to my cheek, his thumb rubbing over my skin, then over my lips.

"You were fifteen when you lost your virginity?"

That, at least, I'd answered honestly. "How old were you?"

"Older than that." He looked at the paper again. "You've only had one boyfriend?"

"Yes." I watched him think but was unable to guess his thoughts. "How many have you had?"

"None."

"Girlfriends, then." I knuckled his side.

"Four or five serious ones." He laughed and jerked away from my tickling. "Hey, cut it out."

We settled back against each other. He put the paper on the coffee table and turned to me. He looked serious, and I tensed.

"You've been with seventy-eight men but only had one boyfriend."

I nodded. "Yes."

I waited for him to ask me why. He didn't. Instead, he put his head against mine and said nothing. We sat in silence that could have been awkward but wasn't. The hand around my shoulder traced small circles on my upper arm. The other one took mine and settled it with his upon my thigh.

"Have you ever been with two men?"

"Have you ever been with two women?"

"Yes. Would that turn you on?" He asked me. We might have been discussing the weather. "Being with a girl?"

"I don't know. I've never tried it."

"But you'd like to be with two guys."

I nodded, wetting my lower lip with my tongue. "I think so."

He said nothing. Waiting for me to speak. I took a deep breath.

"I've had a lot of sex but…not a lot of…variety."

"Variety can be fun, Elle."

"I haven't had a lot of fun, then."

He tilted his head to look at me and gave a small nod. "I'd like to change that."

I chewed my lower lip. "I just…I don't know—"

"Hey." He interrupted me smoothly. "Would it make you feel better if you didn't have to know? If you could just do?"

I wasn't sure if it would or if it wouldn't. I've never cared for surprises. I live my life according to calculations, statistics, numbers, plans, rules. Lines. Grids. Everything I did revolved around order. Structure. Control.

Everything, until Dan.

"I'm a little uptight," I admitted. "I'm a lot uptight, actually. I'm very tense. A lot. And I have issues about control."

It seemed obvious to me, but Dan shook his head. "I don't see that about you at all."

"You don't?" I sat back from him. The wine was wearing off. "Tell me, Dan. What do you see?"

He smiled and looked me up and down. "I see a woman who's smart and sexy as hell."

He laughed at the look I gave him. "Elle, I mean it. Sure, you're a little…reserved. But you're not uptight. Especially not with a couple glasses of wine in you."

I waited a moment before answering. "Have you ever listened to a sound so long you've forgotten you were hearing it until it stopped?"

"Sure." His hand tightened on mine a bit. "Cicadas, the year they came out. They were so loud they sounded like a spaceship landing, but after a while it just became background noise until nighttime, when they stopped and I realized they weren't still buzzing."

I nodded. "White noise. That's the inside of my head. All the time. I'm never not thinking about something. I just… keep going and going, all the time."

I tried to gauge his reaction, but Dan didn't seem put off by this little revelation of weirdness. I amended my statement. "Almost all the time."

His thumb stroked my skin. "What makes it stop?"

"Drinking."

"That stops a lot of people from thinking."

I looked down at our hands, clasped with such intimacy. "And fucking."

"Sex makes you stop thinking so much?"

And counting, I thought but didn't say aloud. I nodded. "There had to be a reason why there were seventy-eight men, don't you think?"

He stayed silent while I studied our hands. I didn't want to look up at him, afraid the eyes that had encouraged me to speak would be filled with scorn.

"Come with me." He stood and pulled me up along with him.

My heart pounded, but I followed him to his bedroom.

"Sit down on the bed."

I did that, too.

He went to his dresser and pulled out a bandanna. He folded it, once, twice, and again, then placed it over my eyes and tied it behind my head. Instant darkness. A sliver of light below it. I let out a nervous laugh he didn't join.

Then, I waited.

Nothing happened. I heard him moving around the room, the soft shuffle of something that might have been him taking off his clothes, or maybe not. The drawer slid shut with a muffled clunk. He didn't speak.

I sat on the edge of the bed, my mouth slowly going dry with anticipation and anxiety. I didn't move. My entire life was about control, except here, in this one place. This time. With this man.

The little bit of humor loosened my muscles. His fingers whispered up my inner thighs. He teased the hollows high up on the insides, and I shivered. Beneath the blindfold, my eyes closed. My head fell back. I supported my weight on my hands.

When he touched between my legs, at last, I jumped a little. He stroked me through the lace, then pulled the panties off. His comforter felt silky and cool on my bare skin.

"Are you cold?"

I shook my head. His hands moved over my body again, up my thighs and over my hips, my belly, my breasts, up to my shoulders to encircle my throat with gentle pressure.

"You're shivering."

I licked my lips. "It's…the way you're touching me…"

His breath stroked my skin, and a moment later his mouth fastened on my throat, just over my pulse. I tipped my head back further. He nipped and nuzzled me. His hand went back between my legs. His fingers slid against me, then inside me, and I moaned.

"I love the noises you make when you get turned on." He murmured this directly in my ear as his moving hand urged another moan from my throat. "I love the way you get so wet for me, right away. I've never had a woman respond to me the way you do."

His fingers moved inside and against me and in moments I trembled on the edge of orgasm. Dan teased me, moving slow, his mouth tracing erotic patterns on my skin. He backed off, leaving me gasping. He touched me again, feathering strokes with a fingertip countered by firmer circles. My back arched.

He left me for a moment and came back. His fingers pushed the insides of my thighs and I felt his breath again. This time, not upon my neck, but against my belly.

Every muscle in my body went stiff, and I sat up. "No."

He rubbed soothing hands along my legs. "Relax. It's all right."

"No, Dan. I need to know that if I say no, you'll stop. I need to know that." I sat up, pushing away from him.

I put my hand to the bandanna to take it from my eyes. He put his hand over mine to stop me. We stayed like that a moment until, trembling, I put my hand down at my side. His shadow moved across my face, blocking out the sliver of light for a moment.

"Elle. I won't do anything you don't want me to. I promise."

I nodded. After a few moments he went back to what he'd been doing before, but it took me a while to relax into his touch again. He took his time. Moved slow. Easy. He murmured sweet words into my ear and nuzzled my skin while he stroked his hands over all parts of me. He eased me toward arousal with his fingertips and lips. His tongue painted calligraphy on my collarbone until at last he urged a sigh from me. Then a gasp.

Everything went away but him. It was glory, it was joy, it was pleasure, oblivion, infinity. It was sex, but there was intimacy too, a frightening thing I shied from but couldn't force myself to refuse.

When I came, I said his name. I sobbed a breath, and said it again. He pressed his hand against the pulse of my orgasm and held me as it flooded my body.

"What is it about you?" He whispered in my ear while my body still twitched. "I can't get enough of it."

My breath rattled in my throat like stones skipping on water. I had no words to give him. No explanation. I didn't understand it, myself. It scared me, but then so do roller coasters, and I ride them anyway, too.

New habits are as easy to gain as old ones are difficult to break. Dan became a habit slowly, a tiny step at a time, inch by figurative inch. If we didn't see each other, we talked on the phone. He sent me funny text messages and e-mails, and IM'd me late at night with inoffensively lewd innuendos that made me laugh and sigh in equal amounts.

The sex was fantastic. Varied. Eager. Exciting and slowly familiar, which was something I craved and feared at the same time. I had told him I would go as far as he would take me. It had been a bit of braggadocio, maybe, that statement. Dan took me to places I'd never been, had never allowed myself to go, and I let him take me there because, simply, he made me want to let him. I had given him my real name. I had given him my body. I could not, however, give myself. Not completely. I held back, and if he sensed there were still secrets I kept, truths I left untold, he didn't ask me about them.

I always went to his place. Never took him to mine. I didn't want to have to explain the stark furnishings, the lack of color, the absence of family photos. I didn't want to risk him overhearing my mother's messages. I didn't want to have to reveal myself to him.

He didn't push, and I didn't pull away. We coasted like

that, easing into comfort, and I tried to pretend there was less to it than there was. Three weeks or so passed that way, with him insinuating himself into my life so seamlessly I wished I couldn't remember what life had been like before I met him.

I did remember, and there were days when I thought it had been better and days when I admitted it had been worse, but every time I thought I would simply stop returning his calls he said or did something that made me see how purely silly such a thing would be.

As spring became summer, I no longer took the ride home into darkness. Therefore, it was no difficult feat to spot the garbage bags scattered all over the stoop next to mine. As I fit my key into my door, the Ossleys' flew open and Gavin stumbled out.

He wore the same oversize black jeans and gray T-shirt I was accustomed to seeing him in, though he'd left off the massive hooded sweatshirt. His hair fell in his eyes as he crouched protectively next to one of the bags.

I didn't mean to stare. I didn't want to. Whatever domestic drama was going on next door, I played no part in it. What happens at home stays at home. My key and the stubborn lock, however, seemed determined to block me.

"I told you! Clean your shit up or it's going in the trash!" Mrs. Ossley appeared in the doorway. "God damn it, Gavin, I work all day, I don't need to come home to a pigsty!"

"Then stay out of my room!"

On my other side of the tiny alley separating our houses, Mrs. Pease cracked open her door and peeked out. Mrs. Pease had lived in this neighborhood for forty years. She kept her house tidy and in decent repair, set out her garbage at the curb on trash days and had a cat I sometimes saw in the front window. Beyond that, she never bothered me. We shared a look through the crack in her door.

Mrs. Ossley looked up and saw me. She looked down at Gavin. I thought maybe she'd have been embarrassed to have been caught in such a display of belligerence. The glass she lifted to her lips a moment later showed me the reason she wasn't.

"Dennis is coming over tonight, and I don't need you junking up the place. Get your shit cleaned up," she continued as though I hadn't been there.

I wished I hadn't. Gavin stood up. He brushed hair from his eyes. His voice had gone high and shaking.

"Just stay out of my room! Stay out!"

"Your room is in my house!"

At last my key slid into the lock, and I vowed to treat it with oil to prevent this sort of thing from happening again. I closed the door behind me. My stomach churned, though it shouldn't have, really. Teens and their parents fought all the time about keeping their rooms clean. She hadn't hit him, so far as I could tell. There was no reason for me to be involved. There was no reason for the scene to make my hands shake.

Aside from the glass in her hand, the slur in her voice. The way he'd cowered at first when stumbling out the door and crouched, protecting a bulging plastic trash bag.

Not everyone who drinks is an alcoholic. Not everyone who gets drunk and screams and treats their children badly is an alcoholic, either. Some people would be utter assholes without the benefit of drink to lubricate their nasty tongues. I thought Mrs. Ossley might be that sort.

In the end, did it matter? It wasn't my business. She did have the right to expect her home to be kept neat. Teenage boys are notorious for creating mess. She had the right to demand obedience from him, her son.

But my mind kept going to the glass in her hand and the way he had cowered, though he stood taller than she by a good three inches.

It wasn't my business. It wasn't my concern. She wasn't hitting him, so far as I could see, and even if I knew that his story about the cat scratches rang false, I also knew it was unlikely his mother had made them. Mothers don't take razor blades to their children's arms and make perfect, aligned slashes. Kids do that to themselves. But it wasn't my business.

Not my concern.

Gavin was a good kid. Helpful. But he wasn't my kid.

I went up the stairs and shed my clothes, tossing them into an overflowing hamper that was a sudden surprising reminder of just how off track I'd let my schedule become. It had been days since I'd thought of doing laundry. Days, too, since I'd vacuumed or bothered to do more than toss my dishes in the dishwasher. If I needed a reminder that Dan was taking up a lot of my time, that was a good one.

Thinking of Dan, I took a shower, long and hot. Relishing the steam and the scent of the special lavender soap my mother would have sniffed at because it wasn't full of foreskins or whatever she used to keep herself from wrinkling, I washed my hair. The wet weight of it fell down to my lower back, the longest I'd ever worn it. Most of the time I kept it up or braided, so feeling it now, over my shoulders, down my back, heavy with water, surprised me, too.

It was like I was waking up after a long sleep, or maybe slipping into a dream, delicious in its surreality. The water on my skin, the heat, the scent of the soap, the feeling of my own hands moving over my body… I had felt them all before. Nothing new. Yet it felt new to me. I felt new to me.

I've never been much of a romantic. Facts and figures have always made more sense to me than flowers and fantasies. I love fairy tales not because I have ever believed they could be true, but because the ridiculousness of the themes they promote have always seemed to prove to me I am right in doubting them. A princess locked in a glass tower, waiting for a prince? Glass breaks. What sort of princess waits for a prince to save her, anyway? A stupid, unresourceful one. Princess Pennywhistle never waited for a man to rescue her. She did it herself.

A romantic nature had escaped me, but that didn't mean I was immune to the appeal of it. Just because I couldn't convince myself of its reality didn't mean I didn't want to believe in romance.

If there is a question about why him, why Dan, why did I want this man after so long without wanting any, I have no answer for it. Some people believe in fate or karma. Some believe in lust at first sight and others have faith there is one person in the universe for each of us, one true love we recognize immediately upon meeting.

I believe in numbers and logic, in calculations that can be proven, in results based on fact, not fate. I believe space abhors a vacuum and that we are all empty, just waiting to be filled.

I believe Dan and I were drawn together like stars whose gravity brings them closer and closer until they merge to create a sun. I believe I was empty and waiting to be filled, and Dan was there to do it. And I believe it could have been someone else, that we are not bound for one person in the universe, that another time or another man might have found the way to fill me. I believe that, but I am glad it was Dan who did. Dan had opened my eyes, but only because they were ready to open.

I stayed in the shower until the water ran cold and perked my skin into gooseflesh. The softness of my robe and the towel I wrapped around my hair added to my sense of being in a dream. So did the steam over the mirror, which I wiped away to stare at my reflection, staring for an outward sign of my inward change.

I couldn't see any, of course. My eyes didn't suddenly gleam with new light, the lines around them didn't disappear. My mouth had not all at once begun to curve upward of its own accord.

Naked, I sat on my bed to comb through my hair, easing the tangles until the comb ran straight through from crown to ends without snagging. The motion soothed me, almost hypnotic in its repetition. Sensual. The smoothness of my bedspread against my skin, the warmth of the night air coming in my open windows, the soft hiss of the comb through my hair all created a cocoon around me. Made me aware.

I smoothed scented cream over my skin and slid into soft

pajamas. I let my hair hang free around my shoulders. Every limb felt languorous, relaxed. I lay back on my bed for a few minutes, staring at the cracks in my ceiling and for once, not counting them. I made pictures from the lines. A bird. A woman's profile. A clock.

Something had shifted inside me, something I had no words to describe. For the first time in years, I didn't feel as though I stood behind a closed door, terrified for the moment it would open. The time had come for things to change.

My body and mind might have been content to drift along with thoughts of this new path, but my stomach grumbled its discontent, and I roused myself from my lethargy to move downstairs and feed it. Hours had passed since my return home. Night had fallen.

As I popped a frozen meal into the microwave, I heard muffled shouts through our shared kitchen wall. I had been in the Ossley house before I bought mine. It had been empty at the time, the layout a mirror image of mine. I'd chosen mine because the interior features had been in better condition, but I remembered the way it had felt to walk through both, one right after the other, creating a sense of déjà vu slightly offset by feeling like I'd walked through a mirror.

The microwave beeped. The voices next door grew louder. Something thumped against the wall so hard it rattled the picture hung over my kitchen table. A moment later, a motion in the window overlooking my postage stamp of lawn caught my eye, and I went without thinking toward the window.

The Ossleys' back door had been flung open, and a

golden rectangle of light illuminated their yard. As I watched, something flew out of the door and landed in their grass. A moment later, Gavin followed it.

"I warned you!" Mrs. Ossley shouted from the back porch. "Clean up your fucking shit or it's getting tossed, god dammit! Dennis is gonna be here in fifteen fucking minutes, and I don't want your shit all over the fucking house, Gavin!"

I cringed at the language and became aware, suddenly, that I was being just the sort of nosy neighbor I despised, peeking out the blinds. I stepped back from the window but could still see through it. Could still hear Mrs. Ossley's shouts through the open screen. More thumps and thuds as more things flew out the back door to land in the grass, and then I saw what they were.

Books.

The bitch was throwing books. One of them struck Gavin on the shoulder and fell in a flutter of pages to the grass. He bent to pick it up, his arms full of them. His face had twisted.

She threw another one, and I realized she wasn't just tossing them out the door. She was aiming for him. This one, a thick hardback, struck him in the hip hard enough to knock him back a step.

They say that people in tense situations can do things like lift cars or run into burning buildings. This wasn't as dramatic as that, but I did move fast, without thinking, and was out my back door and into my yard before I even had time, really, to ponder it.

A waist-high chain link fence separates our patches of

grass. Mindful of my privacy, I'd had it installed when I moved in. It had served to keep my neighbors from encroaching on my property, but now it kept me out of theirs as effectively.

"Gavin," I said. "Are you all right?"

He startled, though he had to have seen me flying out of my kitchen. He opened his mouth to say something, but his mother answered for him.

"Get inside the house, Gavin."

I looked over at her. Silhouetted in the light from her house, she was no more than a shadow. I had no trouble seeing the glass she still held. Apparently not even throwing books was enough reason to set it down.

Gavin bent to pick up the books she'd thrown.

"Leave that," she ordered. "Get inside."

"Mrs. Ossley. Is there a problem?" My voice sounded colder than I'd meant it to, and it must have antagonized her.

"No, Miss Kavanagh" came her retort, the words spitting out of her like they tasted of vomit. "Why don't you go back inside and mind your own business?"

"Gavin?" I asked quietly. "Are you all right?"

He nodded and moved toward the house, then paused to pick up one more book. This once had landed, open, in a puddle left from a late afternoon shower. The spine had bent and cracked, and a few of the pages fluttered to the ground when he lifted it. Mud splashed the rest of them.

It was my copy of *The Little Prince.* The one my childhood neighbor Mrs. Cooper had given me. He handed it to me over the fence, refusing to meet my eyes.

"I'm sorry," he muttered.

I had nothing to say as I took it from him. I could only watch him head inside. The shadow in his doorway moved aside to let him in, and the door slammed behind him, leaving me standing in my pajamas with a ruined book in my hands.

"This is the place you took me to, the day we met." I looked up at the sign, which showed a rather grisly drawing of a wolf's head, mouth tearing into the body of a sheep. "The Slaughtered Lamb."

"Very observant." He held the door open for me to go inside. "Let's find a table."

"I could hardly forget a place with a name like that. Do they serve food?"

"Very good food."

"Good," I said. "I'm starving."

We found a table toward the back and sat. He smiled as he handed me the menu, which featured traditional pub food like fish and chips and shepherd's pie. He grabbed the beer list.

"Me, too." He studied the list. "I'm glad you eat."

I laughed. "Of course I eat."

"No. I mean you *eat*," Dan said. "I take some women out and they just nibble."

"Oh." I kept my eyes on the menu and fought back a blush. "Well. No, I don't suppose I miss many meals."

"Hey," Dan said so I'd look up. "I like that."

"Do you?" As he had the habit of answering his own questions, I had a habit of posing ones that didn't need any.

He grinned. "Yeah. I do."

Compliments, unless they're about my mental prowess, fluster me. Not because I automatically assume the person giving them isn't sincere, but because I am never quite sure if they expect me to give them one in return.

"Good" was all I said, and looked up as the waiter approached. "I'll have the fish and chips, please, with malt vinegar and tartar sauce, and fries. And…a Guinness?"

I looked at Dan, who nodded. "Make that two. Of everything."

The waiter, who couldn't have been any older than the minimum drinking age himself, smiled. "Hey, a chick who drinks real beer. Cool. Most girls drink light beers."

Dan looked at me, then the young man. "She's something else, this one."

The waiter nodded, two men sharing an appraisal. "I can see that."

It struck me, their differences. Dan, clean-cut but not preppy, favored expensive business suits or khaki pants, oxford shirts, whimsical ties. Today he wore dark denim jeans, straight-legged, low slung and a white T-shirt beneath a scoop-necked black sweater of fine knit, light enough to wear in the summer heat, the sleeves pushed up on his forearms. Casual but not sloppy.

The waiter, in contrast, wore his jeans cinched with a

black leather belt studded with small spikes. His dark hair looked like silk, shorter in back and long in the front to fall over one eye. Tattoos covered his arms and multiple piercings ornamented his ears, his eyebrow. His nipples, too, I noticed through his tight white T-shirt. He had eyes of startling blue and a voice that spoke of too many cigarettes, pitched lower than you'd expect from someone so slender. He flashed me a smile of brilliant, white teeth, and I understood why the group of girls sitting in the corner had been giggling when we came in.

"What's your name, man?" Dan reached into his pocket and pulled out a pack of cigarettes.

He offered me the pack and I took one, a man's brand, not a dainty menthol or clove cigarette. I let him light it for me and sucked the smoke in deep, holding it long enough to impress both of them before letting it out in a series of rings.

"Nice," admired the waiter. "I'm Jack."

"Dan." They shook hands. Dan indicated me with a slight lift of his chin. "This is—"

"Jennifer." I gave the false name without pause.

"Nice to meet you, Jennifer," said Jack and he lifted my hand to his lips and kissed the knuckles.

I glanced at Dan, who smiled through smoke. I looked back at Jack, who could have been flirting with me, or just being silly. I didn't seem to be his type. Too old, too conservatively dressed.

"Be right back," he said. "Holler if you need me."

Okay. The look he gave me proved it. Definitely flirting. I watched him head toward the bar, stopping to elicit

I felt his hands on the hem of my skirt, pushing it up over my thighs. The bed dipped with his weight as he settled next to me. I straightened my back, and he put a hand on my shoulder, holding me still. His hand moved over my thigh, between my legs. His fingertips brushed my panties. Then he didn't move again.

Without sight, my other senses had heightened. I could smell his cologne and the wine he'd drunk. Hear the puff and blow of his breath. Feel it on my neck. I sat stiff and straight, muscles tense with waiting.

"Dan?"

"Shh."

I swallowed. The hand between my legs traveled up to unbutton my blouse and ease it off my shoulders. Cooler air caressed me. My nipples spiked. He took off my bra, too. His hands held my breasts. His thumbs circled my rock-hard nipples, and a moment later I cried out when I felt heat and wetness surround one.

His mouth. He suckled my nipple, still holding the other with his hand. I drew in breath after shallow breath. He moved gentle lips along the slope of my breast to capture the other nipple and suck that, too.

His hands roamed my skin. He unbuttoned my skirt and pulled the zipper at the side. He lifted me a little to take it off. Then I felt him between my legs, his hands on my thighs again while his mouth found my nipple. He pushed my legs wide apart. I tensed.

"Are you still thinking?"

"Yes." My voice sounded breathy and a little hoarse.

"Let's see if I can help you with that."

another round of giggles from the college girls. He looked over his shoulder at me and shot me that striking grin again.

"He thinks you're hot." Dan stubbed out his cigarette.

I'd barely smoked mine, but I put it in the ashtray to smolder. "Does he?"

"Definitely."

I gave him a thoughtful look. "Does that bother you?"

There was no reason it should. I was simply curious. Dan grinned.

"Nope. Why'd you give him a fake name?"

"I don't like just anyone knowing my name."

"So you usually give a fake one?"

I tidied the menus and put them back in their holder. "Yes."

"You told me the truth."

I looked into his eyes, and we shared another of those looks I couldn't quite describe. "Yes."

"Lying to someone about your name could cause trouble later, if you want to know them better and they find out you started off the relationship with a lie."

"I told you the truth," I said evenly. "Why should you care what I tell anyone else?"

"I guess I don't." He looked to the bar, where Jack was filling glasses with our Guinness. "Do you think he's good-looking?"

I studied the waiter. "He's young."

"That doesn't answer my question."

"He's cute," I said. "He's got that punk-band Goth look going on."

Dan lit another cigarette. "If you weren't with me, would you go home with him?"

I didn't answer right away, because Jack came back with our drinks. He set them in front of us, flashed me another grin and told us our food would be out shortly. He seemed disappointed when we told him we didn't need anything else right then.

"I might," I said when Jack had moved away to take care of his other customers. "I doubt it, but I might."

"Do you want me to leave, so you can?"

I think he was trying to shock me, or at least to gauge my ability to be shocked, but all I did was pick up my cigarette and make some more rings. Dan leaned back in his chair and drank his beer. His gaze speared me.

I speared him back. "Do you want to leave so I can?"

He glanced at Jack, then leaned in close to me. "I want to watch you with him."

The cigarette stopped on its journey to my lips. Dan's face was very close to my cheek. I gave my head the slightest tilt. "Do you?"

He nodded and nuzzled the spot just below my ear for a second. "Yeah."

I ground out the cigarette and pulled away from him to drink some beer. My stomach fell away and heat swirled within me. I drew my cardigan together at my throat then laid my fingers on the beads embroidered along the collar. I rubbed them with my fingertips before putting my hand flat on the table.

"You just want to watch?" I blinked and drank more beer as I waited for Dan to answer.

He looked at Jack again. "Did you have something else in mind?"

I, too, looked at Jack, who caught us both staring and gave me a small nod. I looked back at Dan, but when it came right down to it, the words wouldn't come out. What do you say to the man you're fucking when he asks you if you'd like to fuck another man?

"You want to fuck us both."

He always knew the right way to say it.

I nodded, unable to put voice to my assent, though the thought of it alone was enough to make me wet.

Dan looked thoughtful. "That would make you happy?"

"Happy?" I laughed. "I don't know if it would make me happy, but…I think I'd like it. Are you sure you wouldn't rather do that?"

I nodded at the group of girls in the corner. One of them was giving the other a lap dance, earning applause and appreciative glances from a covey of young men at the table next to theirs.

"Girl-girl action," I murmured. "Bisexuality is the new black."

Dan leaned forward again and loosed my hair from its twist. He finger combed it around my shoulders and slid his hands through it at the back of my neck as he whispered into my ear.

"If I asked you to fuck another woman, would you?"

I had to swallow against my dry throat before I could answer. "If you wanted me to."

"Fuck," he muttered. "Christ, Elle, you're so fucking…I can't…"

He pulled me into an embrace I wasn't expecting. He pressed his face into the side of my neck, breathing me in, his hands warm on my back. I sat, stiff, uncertain if I'd done something wrong or too right.

He sat up and looked into my eyes. "You're beautiful, you know that?"

I shook my head. "Don't say that. I don't like it."

He put his hands on my face, then traced my mouth with his thumb. "You've got the hottest fucking mouth. Do you like that?"

That made me smile. "I have a big mouth."

"Who told you that?" He stroked his fingers through my hair again, almost like he was petting me, a gesture that took me aback but pleased me at the same time.

"My mother. My brother."

"Ah," he said. "What do they know?"

I didn't answer. He traced one of my eyebrows. I felt silly, but let him do it.

"If I asked you to be with another woman, that would be for me. Not you."

I shrugged a little, bewildered at what he was getting at. "I guess so."

He took his hands away from my face and looked over his shoulder at Jack by the bar. "But that would be for you."

I had no words for a moment. "Dan," I said at last, and this time I was the one who leaned forward to touch him. I put my hands on his shoulders, our knees touching, our eyes meeting. "What is this all about? What is this? Why are we doing this?"

He slid his hands along my arms, circled my wrists, then

took my hands into his. "Fuck if I know. But I don't want to stop, whatever it is."

What sort of picture we made, holding hands so close like that, gazing earnestly into each other's eyes, I don't know. I didn't care. That simple touch excited me and yet grounded me, too. I was excited but not anxious.

Sitting there in the Slaughtered Lamb with Dan holding my hands and asking me if I wanted to take him and Jack to bed at the same time, the numbers went away. Like he'd turned off a switch in my brain the same time he'd turned one on between my legs. Desire made me forget counting, but it was Dan who made me feel comfortable enough to let it go.

I looked at Jack once more. "Do you think he would?"

"I think he'd give his left nut to get in your pants."

"Very nice," I told him. "So elegantly put."

Dan laughed and leaned forward to nuzzle my neck again. "Yes, Elle, I think Jack would love to fuck you."

He slid his hand under my skirt as he said the words, between my thighs, straight to my lace-covered cunt. He touched me, and my body jerked. He nibbled my earlobe, then pulled away while I tried to catch my breath.

I'd finished half my beer when the food arrived, but felt as drunk as if I'd had three. Jack set our plates in front of us and gave us silverware and napkins. I kept my gaze on the table as Dan made small talk with him, and he went away.

We ate. Grease slicked our fingers, and the malt vinegar puckered my mouth. The food was delicious, eating it a sensual pleasure heightened by Dan feeding me bits of his fish with his fingers. Messy, silly, but very, very sexy.

He sighed and pushed his empty plate away, wiped his fingers clean and patted his stomach. "Good stuff."

I hadn't managed to finish it all, but neither had I left much on the plate. Jack, who'd left us alone while we ate, appeared.

"Can I get you a box for that?"

I shook my head. "No, thanks."

That grin again. It transformed his face. I wondered how many skirts that grin had lifted. Probably a lot.

"Anything else tonight? Something else to drink?"

I shook my head again. Dan leaned back in his chair. His arm stretched out to grip the back of my chair. Possessive.

"Actually, Jack, we were wondering what time you got off work."

Jack didn't skip a beat. "In about half an hour."

I couldn't look away from him. The stud in his tongue flashed when he spoke, and I imagined what it would feel like on my skin. It would be warm from his mouth, I thought, and my nipples hardened.

"Then I guess maybe we'll have another round of Guinness," said Dan. "And wait for you?"

Jack gathered up our plates and trash while he answered Dan, but looked at me. "Sure."

It was as easy as that. I watched Jack walk away. This time he didn't look back over his shoulder at me. He brought us beers a few minutes later. Dan paid our check. We drank, and Dan talked, a steady stream of observations requiring little answer on my part, and I was grateful he didn't expect me to speak. I wouldn't have been able to. All I could think about was what was going to happen.

Dan chose the motel, and Jack followed us on his motorcycle. I stayed in the car and watched him smoke a cigarette while Dan got us a room. My palms hurt and I looked down to see my nails had made crescents in the skin. I rubbed the palms together to soothe the marks away.

Dan closed the door behind us all and locked it while Jack set his helmet and leather jacket on the chair by the window. I didn't know quite what to do, just that my every muscle felt stretched taut in anticipation, every sense heightened.

They made it easy for me. Jack moved forward and took me in his arms. He was taller than Dan by an inch, and at first it felt awkward, the adjustment, the way I had to tilt my face up higher to look at his. He held me against him for a moment and kissed my cheek, my neck, my jaw, like he knew I would refuse him my mouth.

Dan came up behind me and swept my hair to the side to kiss the back of my neck. His body pressed mine, his hands on my hips, pulling them back against his groin. Jack moved closer in the front, pushing his bulging crotch against my belly.

This was what I'd thought about sometimes, when I touched myself. Being surrounded. A man in front, a man behind, strong arms holding me and two mouths leaving wet marks on my skin. Sandwiched between them, I didn't even have to worry about standing upright, because they kept me from falling.

Two mouths. Four hands. Two erections, as yet shielded by clothes but impossible to ignore as they pressed their bodies to mine. Dan ran his hands along my thighs, inching up my skirt and sliding his hands beneath to find my bare skin. Jack tugged my shirt from my waistband and worked the buttons without fumbling. They both kissed me. My neck, throat, shoulders, back, over my clothes and under, leaving no spot unattended while they undressed me as swiftly as if they'd rehearsed it.

I stood in my bra and panties, still wearing my shoes. Jack glanced over my shoulder at something Dan did and nodded like they had an entire language I didn't understand. Dan nibbled the back of my shoulder, and Jack got on his knees in front of me.

I startled at how suddenly he dropped. His head was at my waist. I backed up a step in reaction, but Dan was there to keep me from fleeing. His sweater was soft on my bare skin.

"I—"

"Shh." Dan whispered in my ear. One hand curved on my rib cage, just below my breast. The other anchored my hip.

Jack put both his hands on my hips, one a little higher than Dan's. He leaned forward and kissed my belly. My muscles leaped, but their hands kept me still. His lips skated the edge of my panties, just below my belly button, and I tensed further.

Arousal had beaten anxiety, but anxiety was making a comeback. Jack was too close to putting his mouth between my legs. I didn't want that, didn't like it, couldn't have it, but I couldn't move.

"Shh, Elle, shh." Dan soothed me.

Jack kissed my hip bone. Then my thigh. Then…my knee. A giggle shot out of me as his hands closed around my calf and he stroked downward, lifting my foot to slide off my shoe. Then the other one. He looked up at me with that grin, a pretty boy on his knees in front of me.

"We'll take care of you," Dan said. "See?"

Jack nodded. "Are you scared?"

"No." I wasn't, then.

Jack grinned again. "Good."

He kissed my other knee and got to his feet. He took my hand. Dan left me for a moment to strip the comforter off the bed and then he took my other hand, and together they led me to lie down, my head on the pillows.

"Look at her," Dan said. "Fucking gorgeous, right?"

"Helluva hottie," said Jack.

Dan pulled his sweater and shirt off over his head. Jack did the same. They kept their eyes on me as they undid their belts, slid jeans over hips, kicked off their briefs and peeled off their socks. I envied their comfort with their bodies. If either of them worried about the other's pecs or abs or length, width and girth, they didn't show it. They simply stood naked it in front of me like they were offering themselves for my approval.

It was easy to give. Dan, a little shorter but with a broader build and more hair on his chest, was already familiar. Jack, taller, decorated with ink on his pale, smooth skin and the nipple rings I'd guessed at, had almost no hair at all.

But he had something else.

"Oh, my God."

Jack laughed, looking down at his cock. His pierced cock. The ring, large enough to look scary, lay against the side of the head.

Dan looked down. "Jesus, man. Why would you do that to yourself?"

Jack laughed again and stroked himself, up and down, hand passing over the ring. "I'll let her figure that out."

I blinked, fascinated. "Come here."

He obliged, crawling up the bed to kneel next to me. I got up on my knees to look closer. I touched him, and he made a little noise. I stroked him, up and down, the way he'd done. The ring rubbed my palm, the metal warm and smooth.

He sighed and put his hand over mine, pumping it up and down. "That's good."

Dan joined us on my other side. He unhooked my bra and took it off, then covered my breasts with his hands and kneaded them gently. He teased my nipples erect, his mouth hot and wet on my shoulder blade.

Dan put his hand down the front of my panties, rubbing me in circles while I stroked Jack. I moaned when Dan touched me, my clit already swollen with desire. With subtle movements of his other hand, Dan shifted me so I was no longer on my knees but sitting between his legs, my back against him, his hands making magic with my breasts and cunt and his mouth sucking gently on the side of my neck.

Jack's breathing had quickened and I looked up at him. His grin was no less bright, though his eyes were a little glazed, and sweat had beaded along his hairline. His hips pumped forward, into my fist. He put his hand on my hair, tangling and tugging it a little, which made me cry out and arch further into Dan's touch.

Dan's penis throbbed against my back. He let his finger slide lower, then up again to rub my moisture on my clit. Jack put his hand over mine, squeezing the fingers closed over the head of his cock, stopping me.

"Slow up," he whispered, that smoky voice making my body contract with pleasure.

"Gonna lay you down," Dan murmured.

He did, moving from behind me and pushing the pillows beneath my head to make certain of my comfort. The two men shared a look, and both reached to hook their fingers in my panties and ease them down. I lifted my rear to help them. Jack tugged the lacy material over my knees and tossed them on the floor, then knelt in front of me and bent my leg at the knee to rest my foot on his thigh. Dan caressed my other leg, then my hip and belly, his eyes on me, his smile reassuring.

Jack kissed my knee again, and I giggled again, the sound breathy and hoarse. He moved a little to kiss my calf, then the bone of my ankle. He took my foot between his hand and massaged it, then pressed a kiss to my instep. My whole body jerked, but his hands had closed around my ankle and kept me from kicking him by accident.

It had tickled, that kiss, but also sent a bolt of sensation so strong it felt like he'd slid his cock inside me. My thighs parted and my hips lifted in reaction. I bumped Dan's nose with my hand, and he winced, proving once again that really good sex needs choreography.

"Warn me next time you make her do that," Dan said.

Jack laughed, his eyes locked on mine. "I think she liked it."

I should have cared, maybe, that they spoke of me like I

couldn't respond, but I didn't. There was something sexy about it, the two of them talking about me the way I imagined men might talk about women when they think we can't hear. If they'd softened their words, tried for romance, attempted to woo me, the situation would have seemed ridiculous.

"She's got pretty feet." Jack kissed my sole again, letting his mouth linger, and again I moaned. "See how it makes her squirm?"

Dan nodded as he passed the flat of his hand down over my breasts to my belly. "She's wet. Touch her."

Jack put my foot down carefully and leaned forward to touch me. He licked his lips and again I saw the tongue stud flash. "I bet she tastes sweet."

Dan looked at my face when Jack said that. I must have looked panicked again, because he reached up to brush the hair from my face and cup his hand on my cheek.

"No," Dan said. "That's not for you."

Over Dan's shoulder, I saw Jack nod, as though he'd expected an answer like that. Dan looked into my eyes and then kissed the corner of my mouth. Respecting without complaint the distance I felt ridiculous for enforcing. I put my hand on the back of his neck and held him for a moment to stare into my eyes.

Whatever he saw there must have satisfied him, because he smiled and kissed the tip of my nose, then took my hand from the back of his neck and kissed the palm. He sat up.

"Suck her nipples," Dan offered. "She likes that."

Jack nodded and slid up my body to take my nipple between his lips before I even had time to take a breath. I'd been right about the tongue stud. Like the ring in his penis the metal was warm and smooth, and I gasped as he worked it against my flesh.

Dan took my other nipple in his mouth, and I looked down. One dark head, one fair, so close together but focused both on me. I wondered if they would kiss each other, or touch, and the thought of that made me gasp again, so Dan looked up at me.

I licked my mouth, and he smiled, glancing at Jack, who looked up from what he'd been doing. They shared a look, then both started laughing. It made me laugh.

"She's got a sexy laugh, doesn't she?" Dan asked.

"She's got sexy everything." Jack suckled my nipple again as his hand slid between my legs.

Jack stroked my clit, his touch different than Dan's. Less sure. I found the skipping hesitation of his fingers unbearably arousing. Everything in my body had begun to draw together, tighten, contract and tense. I had to force myself to remember to breathe.

Dan put his hand between my legs too, for one moment holding me while Jack kept up his uneven pace. Then I felt a finger slide inside me, followed quickly by another, and I made a noise.

"Fuck," Jack muttered. "Let's see if we can get her to do that again."

They had taken away from me the need to speak. They didn't expect me to answer, or to reciprocate. They took care of me, Dan sometimes murmuring direction to Jack, who took it without seeming to bristle. Two men working together to bring me pleasure.

I opened my eyes. They were both looking at me, but not

my face. Their expressions of concentration would have made me giggle if I'd had the breath for it. They both stared at my cunt like it held the secrets of the universe. Dan fucked me with his fingers while Jack kept his attention on my clit, but both seemed fascinated by my body and its responses.

It should have made me self-conscious but I was too close to coming to worry about whether or not they liked the way I'd shaved my pubic hair. My hips lifted, pressing harder against both of them. Dan looked up at me and withdrew, making me sigh in protest.

"Sit up, baby," he said tenderly, and helped me.

Together they moved me to the edge of the bed so my feet met the floor. Dan slid around behind me, straddling my back and pulling me to rest against his chest. Jack, who'd been busy putting on a condom while Dan arranged me, settled between my legs and put his hands on my hips.

"Doesn't it rip?" I had to ask.

He grinned and shook his head, that silky hair falling over his eye. "Nah."

My heart pounded in trepidation but I let Dan pull me back against him. My head fit on his shoulder, his lips at my temple, his hands clasping my ribs just below my breasts.

"Are you ready?"

It was sweet of Jack to ask, and I wanted to give him an answer but my throat had closed and I could only nod. He shifted his feet and gripped his cock at the base, guiding it to my opening. He didn't push inside me right away.

"Shhh." Dan whispered into my ear, brushing the hair off my neck so he could kiss me there. "Relax."

Jack pushed inside me, bit by bit. I tensed, expecting pain from the metal piercing his penis, but felt only a different sort of pressure. He was longer than Dan, and when he pushed inside me to the hilt I squeaked at the sensation. Jack looked up, brow furrowed in concentration.

"Christ, she's tight."

Dan's cock, pressed to my back, leaped at the words. "I know."

Jack swiped hair from his eyes and put a hand on my shoulder. He looked at me. "You all right?"

The solicitude from both of them touched me. Aroused me. They could have made this such a bad experience, but they weren't.

Again, I nodded, not trusting my voice. Jack smiled. Dan kissed my neck.

"Fuck her now," Dan told him.

Jack nodded and looked at me for confirmation. I licked my mouth. "Yes, Jack. Fuck me."

At the sound of my voice, hoarse with longing, Dan shuddered. Jack throbbed inside me. Then, with deliberate concentration, he began to move.

With Dan behind me, I didn't need to worry about falling. He supported me. His mouth on my skin transported me even as Jack's cock inside me did the same. Jack fucked me slowly for a few strokes, then hooked his hands beneath my knees, bending them, pushing me back harder against Dan and deepening the angle.

I cried out. Jack didn't stop, but he did murmur, "Okay?"

"Yes," I managed to say. "Oh…yes."

Dan's penis, hot and hard, rubbed my spine with Jack's

every thrust. Dan's breath got hoarse in my ear. He slipped a hand around to caress my clit while Jack pumped in and out of me, and the dual pleasure clawed my fingers into the bedclothes, scrunching the fabric in my fists.

I had imagined different ways two men would fuck me. One in my mouth, one in my cunt. One in each hand. One entering me from behind while I sucked the other one off. I had never imagined this, being held snugly from behind, my every need anticipated and granted.

I looked to the side, at the mirror over the dresser. As neatly as a painting, it framed us within it. Three people, a woman caught between two men who held her like she was something precious. I had to blink to make sure it was me.

Sweat from Jack's brow dripped onto my belly. His face contorted, but he kept his pace steady, not losing himself in climax just yet. The three of us rocked together. Dan took his hand from my clit for a moment to hold it in front of my mouth.

"Spit."

I filled his palm with saliva. He slid his hand between us and I felt his fingers close around his cock, lubricating it with wetness from my lips, and the thought of what he was doing excited me even more. In another moment he'd pulled me back against him again and returned to stroking my clit, but now his penis slid more smoothly against my skin. It fit into the groove of my spine as neatly as Jack's cock fit into the cleft of my cunt, and I thought of my body accepting and surrounding both of them and bringing them pleasure, and my cunt bore down in its first pleasure spasm.

Jack let out a grunt. His fingers dug into the backs of my knees. His thrusts got harder, jamming me against Dan. I was close. Jack was close. Dan seemed to be getting the short end.

"Dan?"

"Shh, baby," he whispered, fingers never ceasing their perfect circling. "I'm almost there."

I know we could have gone on for only a few more minutes, but I lost track of time. Everything became focused on the pleasure between my legs. Sights. Sounds. Smells. Sex.

We moved harder, faster. Skin slapped and sucked. Someone moaned. I cried out. Someone said my name, my real name, but I didn't care, too caught up in what was going on.

"I'm gonna come." Jack panted the words. He thrust harder. His eyes closed and his head tilted back. The smooth line of his throat mesmerized me.

"Come with us," Dan said. "C'mon, Elle. Go over."

I would have, even had he not urged me toward it, but hearing him speak helped me along. For one instant the universe had become a giant fist, closing. Then it opened, tossing out the stars and moons and planets and comets, and I went with it, surrounded by the cosmos. Pleasure so fierce it left me breathless arched my back and I heard myself cry out, wordless.

Slick heat spurted against my back and Dan's hand on my hip bore down hard enough to leave red marks. He groaned and thrust against me.

Jack thrust inside me once more with a shout, then stopped, shuddering. He moved a second later, once, twice, then stopped again, head bowed. More sweat dripped onto my skin. He shook a couple times, then loosened his grip on my knees and let them gently down.

We stayed like that for a moment, a tableau of satisfaction. Muscles in my back and legs ached, but not unpleasantly. Dan kissed my temple again and smoothed his hands up and down my sides, then cupped my breasts. Jack withdrew a moment after that and left me cradled in Dan's arms.

I wasn't quite sure what to say even after I'd regained the capability. I watched Jack take care of the condom with practiced ease. He turned, gave me that grin again.

"Mind if I take a shower?"

I shook my head.

"Toss me a towel, would you?" Dan asked.

"Sure thing, man."

Jack disappeared into the bathroom, tossed a towel toward Dan, who caught it, then went back in. The shower started running. I sat up, and Dan wiped my back with the towel using slow, gentle strokes.

I turned to look at him. He'd settled the towel across his lap. He smiled.

"Hey."

"Hey," I answered.

He reached out to smooth my hair from my face. "You all right?"

I was all right, but I paused for a second, waiting for guilt or anxiety to arrive. They didn't. All I felt was content and a sense of wonder as in "Did that really just happen?"

"I'm fine," I said.

"Good." His hand on the back of my neck, he pulled until

I leaned toward him so he could brush his lips across my cheek. "I'm glad. Was it what you expected?"

I laughed. "No."

"No?" He frowned. "Not good?"

"Better," I told him and let my hand touch his face for a second.

He grinned. "Well…that's good."

I chewed my lower lip for a moment. "Next time, we can get a girl. If you want."

He laughed and pulled me toward him again, into a hug I allowed but didn't really return. His hands caressed my back, and he breathed in against my hair. He held me like that for a few moments, then let me go.

"We'll see" was all he said.

Jack came out of the bathroom, towel wrapped around his waist, hair slicked back. He headed for his clothes, lifting them and shaking them to begin putting them on. He took off the towel and rubbed the rest of his skin dry, then rubbed his hair, tossed the towel to the floor and pulled on his boxers.

"You heading out?" Dan kept his hand on the back of my neck.

I, naked, suddenly wished for something to cover myself with. I stood, meaning to head for the shower myself. Jack gave me another of those brilliant grins, which made me feel less naked and more like giving him another try. He had a real talent, that pretty Goth boy.

"Yeah," he said to Dan. He laughed a little, shaking his head. "You were right, man, she is smoking hot. You two call me anytime, okay?"

I caught Dan's gaze. He didn't bother looking ashamed. Stunned, I watched Jack dress and leave the room, closing the door behind him. I backed into the bathroom, still steamy from his shower, and I turned on the water again.

"Are you mad?" Dan said from behind me as I pulled back the shower curtain and stepped inside.

I said nothing, just let the water cascade over me. Dan came to the shower, silhouetted through the plastic. He pulled it open, mindless of the water spraying onto the floor.

"Elle, talk to me."

I turned the tiny bar of soap over and over in my hands, creating palmfuls of lather. Jack had used this soap before me. Jack had fucked me. Jack had fucked me because Dan had asked him to.

"Should I be mad?" I asked finally, not looking at him. I rubbed my hands over my body, replacing the aroma of sex with the scent of harsh hotel soap.

"You told me you'd never done a lot of experimenting. I thought you'd like this. You did like it." He spoke without accusation or defense of his actions.

I looked up. "How did you know I would?"

He smiled. "You'd have told me no. We'd have gone home and left him there. No big deal."

I turned my face into the spray, deciding if I should, indeed, be angry. "Did you have a girl picked out, too? Just in case?"

The words came out more bitter than I'd thought they would. I opened my mouth to let it fill with water, to rinse away their taste. The water pounded in my ears, but I had no trouble hearing his reply.

"No."

I said nothing, then, unable to forget the way it had felt to have Dan behind me and Jack in front. How they'd held me between them and given me pleasure without expecting me to do anything but accept it, and how that had given them pleasure, too. How Dan had done this because he thought it would please me and for no other reason.

He got in the shower with me, and I made no protest, though I kept my back to him and didn't make any attempt to share the water. He reached around and slid a hand between my legs. He was gentle there, using his fingers and the water to clean me, not soap as though he understood it might irritate the sensitive flesh. He parted my folds and the water pounded my clit. His finger rubbed me, and my clitoris responded to his touch by getting hard.

The shower was small enough that even when he pushed me up against the back wall the water still poured over us both. My skin was red from it. His face had flushed. Steam wreathed us and the steady pounding noise masked the sound of our breathing.

He aroused me again with his hand between my legs and his mouth on my throat. Slippery with soap and water we slid against each other. I reached for his cock and stroked it, making him hard again, and that pleased me, that I should be able to rouse him again so soon.

"Did you like watching him fuck me?" I asked, looking into his eyes.

He nodded, hips pushing forward to pump his penis into

my fist. "Yes. But I like it better when I'm the one inside you."

We had no condoms in the shower, and for the first time with him I wanted him more than I wanted to be safe. That scared me, and he must have seen the fear in my eyes, because he pulled me close and held me under the water for a moment before moving back to look into my eyes. My hand hadn't stopped moving. Neither had his.

He smiled and made me smile, too, in the way he had of making everything so easy. "You're still so wet. Tell me I do that to you."

"You do this to me," I replied obediently.

"Say, 'Dan, you make me wet.'"

I smirked a little, eyes rolling to look up at the water falling around us. "Dan, you make me wet."

He circled more insistently and pumped himself harder into my fist. "Say, 'Dan, I love it when you fuck me.'"

"Dan…" His name became a moan as his touch sent me closer to the edge. "I…"

"I love it when you fuck me," he repeated, his own voice hoarse.

"I love it when you fuck me." I shuddered.

"Tell me you're going to come."

"I am," I said with a gasp. "Oh, fuck, yes…I'm going to come."

I did, a smaller burst of pleasure than when the three of us had been together but no less excellent for being less intense. My fingers gripped his penis harder, and I twisted my wrist, pumping him.

He muttered a curse and put a hand on the shower wall

to support himself as he leaned into my touch. He put his head down. Water parted his hair and ran down the back of his neck, made a river in the seam of his spine and the crack of his buttocks. I stroked him harder. Faster. With a hoarse shout he pushed against me, and I smelled the sea-musk scent of semen for but a moment before the shower washed it away.

He shuddered against me. "I think I need to sit down."

Alarmed, I twisted the faucet to cool the water. "Are you okay?"

He laughed. "Jeez, Elle, you're amazing."

I didn't feel amazing. I felt…exhausted. I needed to sit, too, but the shower was no place for it. I turned off the water and hooked the last two towels from the rack, handed him one and wrapped the other around my body before stepping out.

"Be careful," I cautioned. "According to the National Safety Council, eighty percent of all household accidents occur in the bathroom."

Dan got out and put the lid down on the toilet to sit on it. He rubbed his hair dry. "Can you get me a glass of cold water?"

"Sure." I took the paper lid off one of the glasses and filled it with water, handing it to him before filling another for myself. It slid down the back of my throat, refreshing.

"Thanks." He drank it down and set the glass on the sink, then stood and rubbed his body dry. He tossed the towel on the floor, lifted the toilet lid and began to urinate.

This intimacy sent me fleeing from the bathroom with burning cheeks and thudding heart. Why I should be embarrassed to watch him take a piss when I'd just jerked him off, I don't know, except that his comfort with the act triggered something in me. I recognized it as foolishness but didn't bother to fight it. Some people have a few buttons. I have many.

Dan came out of the bathroom a moment later and came up behind me to wrap his arms around me. I let him do it as I'd done all the other times, though I stiffened a little. He kissed my shoulder blade.

"What is it, exactly, about being hugged that you don't like?"

I shook my head with a little laugh, using that as an excuse to move from his embrace and start retrieving my scattered clothes. "Who says I don't like it?"

"You do."

"I've never said that." Skirt. Panties. Bra. Shirt. I found them all.

"Your body says it."

Dan seemed in no hurry to dress, or to leave. He sat on the bed, leaning back on his elbows, apparently completely comfortable in his nudity. I, on the other hand, had already stepped into my panties and was hooking my bra.

"Some people are more…tactile…than others."

He watched me pull on my skirt. "You don't think you're tactile?"

I shrugged, feigning disinterest in the subject as I put my arms through my sleeves and buttoned up my shirt. Dan got up and came around behind me again, his hands on my shoulders. I looked up, into the mirror that had earlier reflected our triumvirate and now showed only two. His eyes met mine once more in the reflection. He ran his hands up and down my arms to the elbow, then up again to my shoulders.

"You tense up when I touch you like this."

"Do I?" An old trick. Asking a question to avoid giving an answer.

He nodded, fixing his gaze upon my mirror eyes and holding me there. "Yes."

I shrugged again, a little. He moved closer, aligning himself along my back, and put his arms around my ribs, his hands gripping his own forearms. His chin nestled into the curve of my neck and shoulder.

"You didn't tense when we were on the bed and I held you this way."

I said nothing. He stared at me a moment longer, then let me go with a sigh. I finished buttoning my shirt and tucked it into the waistband of my skirt, doing up the zip and button. I smoothed the wrinkles and reached for my purse to find a comb, which I dragged through the wet weight of my tangled hair.

Dan dressed quickly and in silence. I didn't like the awkwardness where there had been none before. I knew it was my fault. I knew he wanted something from me, but I didn't know how to give it. It irritated me, that he couldn't just take what had happened at face value. That he wanted more.

I yanked my comb through my hair, forcing away the snags hard enough to bring tears to my eyes. The comb caught on one particularly nasty tangle, and I let out a curse when I couldn't seem to get through it.

Dan said nothing as he took my comb and lifted my hair.

I stood still, suddenly incapable of moving, as he worked the teeth through the knot, inch by inch. Strand by strand. Patient, gentle, never forcing the tangle but instead encouraging it to part. When he was done and the comb slid through my hair from crown to ends without catching, he handed me back the comb.

"I'll be in the car," he said, and left me to stand alone and stare at a mirror that had once reflected three and now only showed one.

I hadn't seen or heard from Gavin since the night his mother had thrown books at him in the backyard. I looked at his house every night when I returned home from work and listened carefully at my walls for sounds of violence, but all had remained quiet. I saw his mother leaving in the morning, sometimes, but she never spoke to me. Her glare said enough. A new car, belonging to the infamous Dennis, was parked on our street. He appeared to have moved in permanently, but if his presence eased or exacerbated the situation with Gavin and his mother, I heard no sign of either. I thought a few times of going over or calling to see if he wanted to help me finish off the dining room, but I didn't.

I'm not brave that way, with confrontations. It was easier to let it go, ignore the unease that had filled me that night and at the memory of the cuts on his arm. Easier to put it all from my mind.

The same way it had been easier to avoid talking to Chad after our argument. Thankfully, my little brother isn't as much of an emotional wimp as I am, and he's unafraid of reaching out.

He'd been smart, too, delivering the gift to my office to make sure I got it all right. A glass vase, filled with marbles and "Lucky" bamboo, tied with red ribbon. Far better than flowers.

I hadn't been in my door five minutes when the phone rang, Chad calling to be certain I'd received the delivery.

"Hello, punkin," he greeted before I could even say hello. "Peace?"

"Peace." I set the bamboo on the center of my kitchen table. "You're the best brother, you know that?"

"I try."

We chatted about our jobs. About Luke. About the books we were reading and the television shows we were watching. We didn't discuss my mother or father.

"Anything else going on with you, sweetie?"

I could tell Chad expected me to say no. "Actually…yes."

"Hmm?" It was easy to imagine him sitting up straight. "Spill."

"I'm seeing someone."

"What? I mean, great!"

I laughed, embarrassed at his reaction, even though I'd expected it. "You don't have to act like it's a miracle, Chad."

"Well, since I haven't heard about the Red Sea parting again or anyone walking on water, I'd say it's as close as I'm ever going to get."

His teasing didn't make me feel better. "Stop it."

"Oh, sweetie, I'm happy for you. You know that."

"I know. But it's..." I couldn't finish my sentence. I didn't know what to say.

"I know, Ella. I know."

I didn't correct him on the name. "His name's Dan. He's very nice."

"Uh-huh."

"He's a lawyer."

"Okay."

I appreciated the control Chad must have been exercising in not overwhelming me with questions. "He wears fun ties."

"How long have you been seeing him?"

"About four months."

Chad didn't say anything for a moment or two. "Wow."

"Stop. Just...please. Don't."

"Don't what?" He sounded defensive. "Don't jinx you? What?"

"Don't point out to me that this is the first man I've seen more than once in years. Since Matthew."

"Sweetie, Matthew's name shouldn't even cross your lips."

"Maybe I'm not as good at holding grudges as you are, Chaddie." I touched the curling stem of one of the bamboo shoots. "It's not like I'm still holding a torch for Matthew. He's not the reason why I haven't seen anyone."

Chad's snort told me he didn't quite believe me, but he didn't argue. "This Dan man, he's good to you?"

I chewed my lip before answering. "He is. Yes. So far, at least."

"And you like him."

"Yes. I like him."

"Good for you, sweetie." Chad sounded so sincere I didn't have the heart to tell him I had my doubts about Dan's place in my life. "Good for you."

"It's not that serious," I cautioned. "We're just seeing each other. It's not even exclusive."

"Are you seeing anyone else?" He always knew just how to poke me, one of the advantages and disadvantages to having siblings.

"No," I had to admit.

"Is he?"

"I don't know."

"And you're using condoms, I assume?"

"Chad, you don't need to lecture me on safe sex. But yes." I shook my head at his taking over the role of lecturer.

"Why don't you know if he's seeing someone else or not?"

"Because I haven't asked." The questions annoyed me, not only because they were nosy and prying, but because I had thought about asking them and simply never had. "I don't really care to know."

"How can you not care to know?" He sounded indignant on my behalf, and I loved him for it even as it annoyed me further. "He could be out banging half the city!"

"He could be! What difference does it make! He's not my boyfriend! I'm not his girlfriend, Chad. We're just seeing each other on occasion, and we sleep together when the mood strikes us. It's a very convenient arrangement. That's it."

"That's not just it, Elle," my brother said. "Not four months worth of convenience. I know you better than that."

"You don't know everything," I told him, the childish answer flying from my lips before I could stop it. "It just works out, that's all."

He greeted that answer with a small sigh. "Okay. But remember, Elle, even Princess Pennywhistle eventually found her prince."

I held the phone from my ear to glare into it, a gesture useless but satisfying. "Princess Pennywhistle is a made-up character. She's not real. She's fiction. And bad fiction, at that."

"Hey! Princess Pennywhistle is great! I can't believe you'd say that about her!"

I couldn't tell if he was joking or not. "Princess Pennywhistle was a know-it-all."

"At least she knew how to admit when it was time to stop fighting dragons and start saving princes," Chad said, and I hung up on him.

What Chad had said was enough to set the wheels turning. I'd been denying my feelings for Dan, convincing myself it was sex and nothing more. Something casual. No attachments. But I no longer could pretend that it wasn't becoming more than that.

Dan's office building was nice. Big. Lots of windows overlooking the street, and plants that looked healthy. A secretary who kept her hair silver and her glasses on a chain around her neck. His office, like mine, had a door and, like mine, a nicely engraved nameplate on it.

"Mr. Stewart said for you to go right in." The secretary smiled at me, no evidence in her eyes that she knew I wasn't there for a meeting. She gestured toward the door, closed, and I put my hand to the cool metal knob.

I counted. Fast, so fast nobody would know what I was doing, should they be watching me. I can do that now, not like in childhood when I had to count out loud, and slowly, and always gave myself away. I counted, multiplying the number of letters in his name with the number in mine and dividing it by two. No significance in the results, but the act of doing the calculation calmed me enough so when I turned the knob and opened the door, I could enter the room with a smile that didn't feel as though it screamed "faker."

He was on the phone when I entered. He held up one finger to indicate he'd be done in a minute, and I amused myself by looking around his office. He had framed diplomas on his wall. Good schools. He had some framed photos, a smiling Dan with people I didn't recognize. Family, some of them, I could tell by the resemblances. Others looked more like standard meet-and-greet publicity shots, two men shaking hands, their grins broad and somewhat fake, while in the background people mingled on a golf course or in a hotel ballroom.

He had a nice, broad desk. Flat. His computer squatted on a smaller desk behind him, so he could twist his chair to work on it while leaving his other desk free for paper-work. He had a little bit of work on his desk, nothing like the usual stacks of papers and folders and files found on mine. This peek into his personality amused me. The way he arranged the cup holding his pens, the cube of notepaper, the small container of paper clips, the stapler. The desk calendar, unblemished with doodles, but the blocks for every day filled with neat printing.

I set my purse down on his desk and came around behind him to look over his shoulder at some of the things he'd written. To my surprise, I saw my own name there. More than once. No notation as to what it meant, just the letters written in dark ink.

That he'd noted the days he'd seen me made me look at him, but his concentration still focused on his call. What did this mean, my name marked with importance apparently equal to such events as "meeting with John" and "Second Quarter reports due?" I checked today's date and found my name at the bottom of the block. He'd written it in a different color ink, perhaps only after I'd called.

He'd been keeping track. I had not. I wondered if I should feel guilty, that what we were doing meant more to him and less to me. Maybe he marked down the names of every woman he saw—and that reminded me that I didn't know if he was seeing other women. I checked quickly, but though he had, indeed, marked down some feminine names, all were incorporated with other things. None of them stood alone, like mine did, a name without explanation or with meaning discernable only to him.

"Sorry about that." He hung up the phone and reached for my wrist, tugging me down onto his lap before I had the chance to pull away. His chair swiveled. I had to grab his shoulder to steady myself. "You're a little early."

I was not early, I was exactly on time, but I didn't argue. "Your secretary sent me in."

"She's under strict orders to send all gorgeous women in to see me right away. No waiting." His tone was teasing as he tilted his head back to look up at me. His hand fell naturally to my hip, fingers warm through the thin linen of my skirt.

"Oh, really." I frowned, also teasing. "And you get a lot of gorgeous women coming to see you?"

"Not today," he said. "Today I have only one."

"Well." I pretended to try and get up from his lap. "I'd better get out of the way so you can see her, then."

He laughed, squeezing me gently. "Are you hungry? I thought we might hit the Sandwich Man. Grab something and take it to the River Walk? It's a nice day. How much time do you have?"

"As much as I want. One of the perks of being VP," I told him. "I get to take long lunch breaks."

He made an impressed face. "Ah, well, what do you know, I happen to have nothing scheduled for this afternoon, which means I can take as long as I want, too."

We smiled at each other, and I saw the desire in his eyes at the same moment I felt it flare in mine. His gaze shot to the door. "It's not locked."

"Are you expecting anyone to come in?"

"No."

His hand slid between my knees, then up higher. When he found the bare skin of my thighs above my stockings, he gave a little groan.

"You're killing me, Elle. You know that? Killing me."

"That's not good," I said. "I don't want to do that."

He shifted my weight on his lap, and his erection pressed my thigh. "See what you do to me?"

I leaned against him. "Very impressive."

His hand moved higher and around my hip to tug at my panties. "Why do you bother to wear these when you come to see me? You know I'm only going to take them off."

"Next time I'll remember."

He laughed. With coordinated efforts we undid his pants, removed my panties, sheathed him. The arms of his chair were open so I could slide my legs through and straddle him.

He fucked me hard and fast, but I'd been thinking about him all morning and didn't need much but a few strokes from my hand to get to the edge. He looked down between us, at my hand touching myself, my skirt pushed up around my hips, and he licked his lips before looking up to meet my eyes again.

"I love it when you do that," he murmured.

"This?" I rubbed my clit in slow circles as I rocked against him, my breath catching.

"That," he agreed. "That you don't need to wait for me to guess what you want, you just…ah, fuck, Elle."

We came together and he pulled me close as I put both my arms around him. We stayed like that for a moment, breathing hard, and then I extricated myself from him and pulled a small package of baby wipes from my bag to use.

He watched, amused. "You think of everything. Did you know we were going to do that when you said you'd meet me here?"

"I didn't know for sure, no."

"You're just always ready."

I grinned at him. "Dan. C'mon. Is there any other reason

we get together? Should I not assume this is going to happen?"

The moment the words left my mouth I knew they were wrong. Something perhaps meant to be thought, not spoken. His grin faded, brilliant blue-green eyes shuttered, and he looked away.

"Yeah. I guess you're right."

I'd hurt him, but wasn't sure how to fix it without acknowledging that something was wrong. Ignoring it was easier, and that's what I did.

He was quieter than usual on the way to the river. We stopped at the Sandwich Man and picked up sandwiches and drinks before walking the last block to cross Front Street. A lot of people had the same idea, a nice lunch in the fresh air. We had to walk a distance before we found a bench. We walked the way in silence I pretended was normal.

By that time I didn't have much appetite, but I unwrapped my food anyway and shook a little packet of mustard before tearing it open and spreading it along the turkey. Dan had ordered a sloppy steak sub with grilled onions and peppers I could smell from my seat.

"Whoa," I said, trying to lighten the mood. "Someone's going to need some gum."

He looked up at me without smiling. "Why? You planning on kissing me?"

I should have expected him, at some point, to get sick of me, but when it actually happened it felt like he'd taken an inch of flesh from some tender spot and twisted it. I looked quickly down to my sandwich. I put aside the empty mustard packet and put the roll back together, but I didn't eat.

Dan looked out toward the water. The Market Street Bridge bustled with cars, and the trees on City Island had turned green. On a nice summer day like today, the carousel and the kiddie train would be in full gear. Maybe tonight there'd be a baseball game at the stadium. Maybe I should ask him to go there with me, try the batting cages. Eat ice cream. Ride the carousel.

I didn't ask him to do any of those things. Those date type things. I could have. I even wanted to. I just…didn't.

Dan chewed. Sipped his soda. Swallowed. Wiped his mouth and fingers with his napkin. He ate without getting sauce or grease on his clothes, and I surreptitiously admired him. I had to struggle not to drip mustard on my skirt. I'd already splashed iced tea on my shirt.

We'd often sat in silence before but it had always been companionable. Comfortable, I realized with growing dismay. I'd grown comfortable with Dan, and today, we had become worse than strangers. We'd become people who had almost, but not quite, become friends.

I drank my tea but couldn't force the sandwich down my throat. I crumpled the napkin in my hands, shredding it. Small shreds of paper littered my skirt, and I brushed them away.

"I didn't mean it," I said finally. "What I said before."

"You meant it. Besides," he said with a shrug. "It's true. Isn't it?"

It should have been true, but I knew it wasn't. "I'm sorry, Dan."

He shrugged again, not looking at me. His eyes scanned the Susquehanna River, wide but not deep, its gray-green surface ruffled today by the breeze. He wrapped up the remains of his lunch and tucked it back into the bag, sucked the last of his soda until the straw crackled along the bottom, and put that in, too. He tossed it in the trash basket next to the bench.

"Ready to head back?"

I hadn't even eaten more than a few bites, but I nodded and packed it all up to toss. The trash basket was made of metal mesh, interlocking octagons formed by the intersections of the metal. I counted 123 of them before I turned back to him.

"Ready."

Dan had put his hands into his pockets and undone his suit jacket. The breeze pushed his sandy hair back from his forehead. The tree overhead cast dappled shadows on his face, looking in profile so different than full-on. I saw small lines at the corner of his eyes I'd never noticed before.

I didn't know his birthday, or if he had siblings, or where he'd grown up. I didn't know his favorite color, or if he'd played sports. I knew how he tasted and smelled, and I knew the length and girth of his penis, the curve of his ass, the pattern of freckles on his shoulder, the number of hairs surrounding his nipples. I knew he liked to laugh and that he could be kind or demanding, or kindly demanding or demandingly kind.

"My favorite flavor of ice cream is teaberry." As I said it, the flavor carried on memory burst on my tongue. "You can't find it many places, but that stand over there on City Island has it. And waffle cones."

One eyebrow raised, he glanced over his shoulder at me. "Yeah?"

"Yes." I nodded.

I didn't deserve for him to give me an inch, and he didn't. It made me respect him more, that he didn't trot after me like a puppy expecting a treat. He looked back over to City Island. The breeze flapped his tie. Today it featured Sponge-Bob Squarepants.

"Maybe we could go there sometime," I offered. "Get some?"

He looked at me again, and I saw in his face he wasn't going to buckle. But I liked that about him, that he didn't let me walk all over him. That he wasn't willing to let me use him. That he was willing to push me.

"Maybe we could," he said.

I gave him a tentative smile. One step forward. He couldn't know how much courage it took, but then...I didn't want him to know.

We stood apart like that for a bit longer before he took his hands out of his pockets. The smile he gave me wasn't as bright as usual, but it seemed real enough. "I've got to head back."

I nodded, disappointed but relieved, too, that he didn't want to walk and talk. A little at a time was all I could handle. I needed time to think about this, all of it. Where it was going. Where I wanted it to go, or not.

"Want me to get you a cab?"

I nodded again. My office wasn't within walking distance, especially not in business clothes.

"Thanks for lunch," I said before I got in the cab. I hesitated, watching another pair of lunchtime trysters saying goodbye with quite a bit more passion than we were displaying.

I watched him from the window as the cab drove away. He waved, a not-so-tall man in an expensive business suit and a tie that flapped in the breeze. I waved back.

I had the best intentions when I got into my car and started to drive. My childhood home wasn't far out of the city. A forty-minute drive, in Saturday traffic. Too close and too far, too.

The town of my childhood hadn't changed too much. Wide, tree-lined streets. Houses more than fifty years old, some of them turned into specialty shops or boutiques. There were a few more gas stations and chain restaurants, but other than that, I could have been riding my bike, my hair in pigtails. Maybe going to the library or the swimming pool.

Instead I drove my car and turned down the street toward my parents' neighborhood. The same houses, painted the same colors, greeted me. The trees had grown. Porches had been added or driveways paved. A vacant lot had sprouted an out-of-place apartment building.

I meant to visit my father. I truly did. My mother might be a martyr and a drama queen, but for her to admit his illness meant he was really sick. Dying, perhaps. I should talk to him before he did that. I knew all too well the empty feeling left behind when someone I loved died before I had a chance to make my peace with him.

Yet, when it came right down to it, I didn't pull into the

driveway. I stopped across the street to look at the house in which I'd grown up. My stomach twisted, acidic as if I'd drunk too much coffee.

The last time I'd been in this house had been the day I left to attend a college my mother didn't approve of. She'd told me never to come back, and I'd been too happy to oblige. Her tune had changed but mine hadn't. I hated that house and the things that had happened in it, and I couldn't go back. Not even to see my almost certainly dying father. I drove on by, made the turn at the end of the street and headed back toward the city I'd adopted as my home.

Marcy seemed surprised to see me when she opened her door, and no wonder. Night had fallen by the time I got there, and I hadn't called first. She opened the door to let me in, and I saw Wayne at the table as I stepped inside.

"Oh, I'm sorry. I'm interrupting." I turned to go, but she stepped in front of me.

"Don't be silly. We were just having something to eat. C'mon in." Marcy looked at me. "Elle. Come on. Want a drink?"

I'd been drinking already, a few shots of vodka at a bar down the street, but I nodded. "Sure. Whatever you're having."

They exchanged a look I could have interpreted if I hadn't already been blurred with booze. Wayne got up and went to the cupboard to pull out a bottle of lemon-flavored vodka and a couple of shot glasses. Marcy pulled some lemons from the fridge and the sugar bowl from the counter.

"Lemon shooters?" she asked.

I nodded again. “I’m sorry to barge in like this on a Saturday night. You must have plans.”

“Actually, we’re just waiting on some friends.” Marcy sounded embarrassed. “We’re going to play some games.”

“Board games?” I blinked at her answer. It seemed so incongruous with the picture of the Marcy I knew.

Wayne laughed. “Yeah. Board games. Some Saturday night, huh?”

His arm went around Marcy’s shoulders and he kissed her temple while she swatted him. They smiled at each other, sharing a secret. I watched them, feeling an outsider.

“I should go.”

“No, Elle, stay. It’ll be fun. I promise.” Marcy reached to pull me toward her. “Stay.”

I stayed. We drank. Marcy’s friends arrived, and we pulled out board games. Balderdash, Guesstures, Pictionary, Trivial Pursuit. We divided into teams, boys against girls, and we drank lemon shooters while we scarfed nachos and pretzels. The girls won two out of three, but the boys didn’t seem to care. I was the only singleton there, but nobody seemed to care about that, either. At least nobody mentioned it, and if there were any pitying looks shot my way I didn’t notice.

It had been a long time since I’d been part of a group like this. Laughing, playing games. In fact, I had to think about if I’d ever been part of a group like this. In high school I’d been quiet, a brainiac. My best friend Susan Dietz had moved away when we were in tenth grade and after that…well, after that, things changed. In college I’d had friends. Matthew had pulled me into his group and made me a part of it. Late-night laughing, drinking, playing games. Kissing and more under blankets while watching scary movies. I'd had a year, at least, of friends and parties and love, before that too had changed.

Those memories didn't make me melancholy. They were part of my past. The truth. Not all the memories were bad.

The party dispersed around 1:00 a.m. with much hugging and tipsy taunts about mental prowess. I was soundly squeezed and petted by most of the people there, as Marcy's friends seemed to be as hands-on as she was. I didn't really mind, although I'm not much of a hugger.

"I'm glad you came over tonight." Marcy wrapped her arms around me. I gave her back an awkward pat. She kissed my cheek, and I squirmed away with a laugh.

"Thanks for letting me stay."

"Are you gonna be all right getting home? Wayne can take you."

Wayne looked up from his flopped-out place on the chair. "Sure, Elle."

I shook my head. "Thanks, but I can take a cab. Don't worry."

I might've been drunk, but not so drunk I'd get in a car with Wayne, who'd been drinking steadily all night. He gave a languid wave and a goofy grin, then turned his attention back to the television. Marcy walked me to the door, stopping me just outside it and closing it partway behind us.

"I'm glad you came tonight. Are you all right?"

I nodded. "I just thought I'd stop by. See what you were up to. I didn't mean to crash your party."

"You didn't." Marcy glanced over her shoulder, then back at me. "You had a good time?"

"I did." I didn't have to fake a smile. "I haven't played a board game in…well, forever."

"You should come again." Pause. "Bring Dan."

I made a face before I could stop it, smoothing it with effort. "Sure. Okay."

"You won't? Did you stop seeing him?" She leaned in her doorway, arms crossed, and I realized Marcy had barely been drinking at all.

An awkward position to be in, deflecting questions from someone way less intoxicated than myself. "No. I'm still seeing him."

"Good." Marcy grinned.

I said nothing. She squeezed me again. This time I hugged her, too, if only so she'd release me sooner.

"Elle? Are you all right?"

Her question stopped me at the elevator, and I turned. "Sure."

"Are you sure? You look a little down."

I almost told her about my dad then, but it's not something that should be blurted out in a hallway at one in the morning. Especially not after the consumption of much alcohol. So I did what I do best. I lied.

"No, just a little tired." I smiled and waved at her as I got on the elevator, and the closing door cut off the sight of her concerned face.

Again, I had the best intentions. Plenty of cabs cruised past the block of bars and clubs still swinging in full gear. I'd heard this section of Second Street referred to as Hookup

Alley because of the crowds of young singles cruising it on club nights. The police probably called it something else. Their cars lined the street as officers patrolled in groups of two and three, keeping the rowdy and the horny in line. I headed for the bus stop, but I didn't make it.

Three years ago I'd been one of the regulars on Hookup Alley. I'd had no problem letting boys buy me drinks in exchange for a dance or a feel. Sometimes, lots of times, a hand job or even a fuck. Because I didn't dress like a tramp, or dance on the bar, my hookups were less like conquests and more like secrets. My little secrets.

Tonight I wasn't dressed for clubbing, but I went inside, anyway. The bouncer scanned my driver's license and took my ten dollars without cracking a smile. I had a better reception when I went inside. The club at this hour had a sense of desperation about it. Last call was in less than an hour. Time was running out to make the hookup. As I pushed through the crowd gathered around the door and entered the bar area, heads turned. Fresh meat had arrived.

Girls looked me up and down, checking out my clothes and turning to comment behind their hands to their girlfriends. Boys stared, their beers in their hands. And I? I, for my part, slipped into an old role with as much ease as slipping into a favorite pair of worn jeans that hug your ass just right.

I didn't stop to think about why I was doing it. Why, when I had Dan, I had come to a bar to see how far a stranger would take me. I moved through the crowd without making eye contact until after I'd ordered my drink. Then, sipping, I turned and surveyed them.

Striped shirts seemed to be in season, and two out of three men there wore them. The rest wore T-shirts emblazoned with clever slogans like Kiss Me, I'm a Pirate. I wasn't looking for a pirate.

The group of girls in front of me had clustered around three young men who appeared to be enjoying the attention. They bumped and ground individually with the ladies, all of them laughing and looking quite drunk. They made quite a spectacle.

The man next to me, tall, dark-haired, slightly older, pointed with his beer bottle. "Five girls. Three guys. Someone's gonna get left out."

He had to lean in close so I could hear him, and I didn't bother looking any further. I turned to him and smiled. I raised my beer in his direction, like a toast.

"They look like they're having fun," I said.

He nodded. The music here was inconsistent, one minute a hip-hop ode to the female posterior and the next a hard-edged rock ballad full of angst and woe. At the moment, the song had softened into a retro-pop tune that seemed to make everyone want to bounce.

He was cute. I leaned closer. He smelled good, even after a night sweating in smoke. I leaned back. Our eyes met. I let him take me out to the parking lot, where I got in the backseat of his car and he put his hand up my skirt.

I didn't ask his name, and he didn't offer it. I told him my name was Jennifer, and I was twenty-two. He seemed to believe me. He got into my panties with fumbling fingers as he unzipped his pants and put his erection into my hand.

He understood the etiquette of Hookup Alley and didn't

press for intercourse. He also attempted, at least, to get me off, and it wasn't quite his fault that he didn't. I made the appropriate noises and writhed beneath him, though I was as far away from coming as a woman can be without being dead.

He came after about five minutes of jacking, which was before my wrist started to ache but about four minutes after I'd lost interest. He ejaculated into my fist with a loud cry I hoped no passing cops would seek to investigate and collapsed on top of me like he'd passed out. We stayed that way for a minute or so, until I pushed him to get up.

We blinked at each other without saying anything for a moment. I wiped my hand on the tails of his shirt. He looked down with a grimace but didn't complain. I sat back from him and rearranged my clothes.

"Can I give you a ride home?" He scored points for chivalry, at least.

"No, thanks." I smiled. It wasn't his fault he'd been meant to be a distraction.

"Are you sure? Because—"

I got out of the car before he could finish. I didn't feel drunk anymore. This time, when I hailed a cab, I actually got in.

Chapter 12

My role as dutiful daughter might not have extended to visiting my parents' house, but when my mother called and invited me to meet them for dinner, I could think of no good excuse to refuse, especially when she told me my father was coming, too. My father, in a restaurant? The idea would have been laughable, if it didn't give me acid reflux.

It meant canceling an appointment with Dan. He said nothing when I told him I'd have to change our dinner plans. He didn't have to say anything. I could hear his frown through the phone.

"I've never met your parents," he said at last.

Silence fell between us again. I wished for an old-fashioned phone so I could twirl the cord in my fingers. I had to satisfy myself with tangling my hair.

"You don't want to," I said when I could no longer stand the quiet.

"Why don't you just give me a call when you're free, then."

I waited for what seemed an eternity before replying. "I don't want you to meet my parents."

"Why not?"

I didn't blame him for sounding affronted. "Because I barely want to go to this dinner, Dan. I can't subject you to it. Not only that, but it would be very stressful for me to have you there."

It was a very honest thing for me to tell him, but he didn't sound appeased.

"All families are stressful, Elle. But if you don't want them to meet me—"

"I don't want you to meet them," I interrupted. "There's a difference."

"Do you think I won't like you anymore if I meet them?" He sounded teasing. I didn't laugh. "Elle?"

"It's my mother," I told him. "You wouldn't understand."

"Never having met her, no. I guess I wouldn't."

I got the sense he was waiting for me to invite him along to dinner. The thought of that was enough to make me shudder. "You don't want to. Believe me."

"Actually," he said. "I do."

"Dan, you don't. Trust me."

"You don't want me to meet your family. It's fine. Have a good time."

I didn't want to fight with him about it, but I also couldn't imagine introducing him to my mother and father.

"It's complicated, Dan."

"Elle," Dan said. "It seems that most things with you are."

Then he gave me the dial tone and I stared at the phone before I hung it up. This time I didn't call him back.

* * *

My mother waited alone for me at the table. "Daddy couldn't make it."

"Why not?"

"He was busy, Ella. What difference does it make?" She stirred sweetener into her tea.

"The difference is, you told me he was going to be here, that's all."

She sniffed. "Why? I'm not good enough?"

"It's not that."

She pursed her lips at me. "If you're that concerned, you could come over to the house."

We stared at each other without speaking until the waiter came over and asked us what we wanted to order. She ordered for us both, food I didn't want but was grateful not to have to think about, and he went away. She talked on and on about my cousin's wedding, which I hadn't attended. I couldn't have cared less about the details, but it filled the space between us with words so we didn't have to actually speak.

She paid for dinner, and I allowed her to. We left the restaurant and I walked her to the parking lot, when it occurred to me I hadn't asked how she'd gotten there.

"I drove," she told me as she dug in her purse for her cigarettes and lighter. She lit up with the ease of a long-term addict. "I'm going to have to get used to it again."

For when my father was gone. She didn't say it, but I heard it. That simple admission revealed more to me about the extent of my father's illness than anything else she could have said, yet I found myself unable to respond with anything beyond a low murmur.

"Will you ever visit us again, Ella?"

I looked at her car, the same one they'd had for fifteen years, before meeting her gaze. "No, Mother. I don't think so."

She made a low, disgruntled noise. "Such a selfish, selfish girl you are. I don't understand it. Your father is sick—"

"That's not my fault."

"You know what?" She asked sharply. "I think it's time you just got over it. How about that, Ella? Just get over it. It's been ten years already. I can't keep bending over backward to apologize to you for things that happened in the past!"

I could only blink, listening to her tirade. "Mom, it's not about you, okay?"

"Then what's it about? Tell me, please, because I'm so interested to know." Her tone made that statement a lie. "Because I'd really like to hear how it's not because of me. I understand how you hate me, but you should at least come to visit your father," she added, like that made everything sensible. "He's not well."

"That's not my fault," I repeated, my voice steadier than I'd thought it could be. "And you're right. I think maybe I should just 'get over it.' But I can't."

She didn't seem to have much to say to that, but her cigarette got a vicious workout. "You keep holding on to the past like that, and you'll never have a future. I'm warning you."

"Good advice," I said mildly, "considering the source."

She glared. "Why do I bother? Why? When all you do is give me grief? Maybe I should just give up on you, Ella. Let you go your merry way. Forget about trying to have any sort of relationship with you at all. It's impossible to communicate with you. All you do is hear your own self."

What she said was probably true, though I didn't want to admit it. "Maybe you should just give up on me, then. Like you did with Chad."

Deep lines gouged her face as she frowned. "Don't talk to me about him."

"Maybe we need to talk about Chad." I said his name on purpose, to force her to hear it. "I think we need to talk about Andrew, too. About what happened. We never talk about it—"

"There's nothing to talk about." Her face smoothed, as if by magic. She blew a dainty stream of smoke from her nostrils.

I had spent a lot of years trying to forget. Not talking. The urge to stop hiding from the past flooded me there in the parking lot, and I could no longer pretend the past didn't affect my future.

"Mom," I whispered. "Please. I need to talk to you about it. About what happened. I can't not talk about it anymore. It's making me sick inside."

"You're sick inside, all right," she countered, poking at me with her cigarette. "You need to get over it! He's dead! He's gone!"

"That's not my fault, either!" I cried.

"It is your fault!" She cried back, then sucked more smoke into her lungs like it was more precious to her than oxygen.

I stood, stunned, watching her crush out the cigarette and light another in the next moment. Smoking is a dirty habit, bad for the teeth and skin, not to mention the lungs, and though I'd indulged on occasion I had never taken it up as habit. It had always surprised me that she had, considering the ravages cigarettes created on clothes and faces.

"It's not my fault he died." I meant the words to sound strong. I meant to believe them. "Andrew killed himself, Mother, I had nothing to do with it."

"You drove him to it," she snapped. "He was fine before you started working on him."

"You don't believe that." Yet I didn't find it hard to believe she did.

"I should never have stopped you when you tried it," she said. Smoke hovered in the air between us. It stung my eyes and throat, and I wished for tears to wash it away. "Then he'd be alive and you'd—"

"Don't," I said. "Don't you dare say it."

She looked at me, her face twisted with anger and grief. "You and Chad have been nothing but disappointments to me and your father. I don't understand what happened. Andrew was such a perfect son."

"You don't believe that, either. Do you? How can you say that?" I wanted to take her by the shoulders and shake her until she came back to reality. "Mother, he wasn't perfect! Nobody is. But him…definitely not."

"Bite your tongue, Ella."

"Were we both just afterthoughts?" I asked her. "Me and Chad? Parents aren't supposed to have favorites."

"Well, here's a clue for you," my mother said, and ground out her second cigarette beneath the toe of her expensive suede pump. "We do."

And then she got in her car and drove herself away.

* * *

"You should come home," I told Chad the next time he called me. "I miss you."

"I miss you, too. Come to visit me. It's nice here in California."

"Mother says Dad's not doing well at all."

"And have you been to see him, sweetie?"

Bless my brother for always knowing just where to stick me to press the guilt button. He's more like our mother than he'd like to admit. I had to smile, though, because he was right.

"No. Come home. We'll go together."

"You know something I don't?" I heard him scuffling with something. "Pop's got us both signed up as beneficiaries on some big-time life insurance policy? Because you know if I walk in his door he'll kick the bucket right away."

"He's dying, Chad. Do you want to let him die without seeing him again?"

"Don't." My baby brother's normal ebullience was not in evidence today. "Don't you start with me, Ella. They kicked me out, they told me to never darken their doorsteps again, they called me names."

"He didn't." I cracked the top on a soda and sipped it.

"He didn't stop her from doing it, and that's the same as if he'd done it himself. Just because he was too piss drunk to get off the fucking chair doesn't give him any excuses. And frankly," Chad accused, "I'm fucking surprised to hear this from you. You of all people, Ella."

"I wish you wouldn't call me that."

"Elle," he amended. "Sweetie, baby doll. I love you."

"I love you too, Chaddie."

"Don't ask me to come home. You know I can't."

"I know." I sighed and rubbed my forehead against the headache. "I know. But she keeps calling me."

I didn't mention the conversation in the parking lot.

"Tell her to fuck off," he said succinctly. "Bitch never did a damn thing for us. Not when we needed her to. Not when she should have. Let her reap what she's sown."

"Do you ever…Chad, do you ever think about…forgiving her?"

"Do you ever think about forgiving *him?*"

A harsh question, but one I'd been seriously pondering lately. "He's dead. What good would forgiving Andrew do now?"

"You tell me, baby doll." Chad made a comforting noise. It didn't make up for him not being able to hug me, but it was better than nothing.

"Why are we such awful, fucked-up messes?" I asked with a low chuckle. "Why, Chad. Why can't we just…get over it?"

"I don't know, honey. I wish I did."

"We should. We shouldn't let the past keep us from having lives!" I was angry and glad I'd shut my office door so my raised voice didn't carry.

He laughed. "Who are you talking to, here?"

"It's been years, Chad. Years of holding on to hurt. I'm tired of it. It doesn't serve me any longer. But I don't know how to let it go."

"Oh, sweetie."

We sniffled together, my brother and I, separated by distance but brought together in mutual misery.

"I'm seeing someone," Chad said before I could say anything new. "He's helping a lot."

"What happened to Luke?"

He laughed. "No, baby doll. Luke is still around. I mean seeing a shrink."

"Oh." I wasn't quite sure what to say to that. "Well. Good."

"You might think about it, you know. Talk to someone."

I shook my head, though he couldn't see me. "I talk to you."

"Do you talk to Dan?"

"No."

"Maybe you should."

"Listen," I said, annoyed. "Since when do you give me advice on my love life?"

"Since you finally got one," Chad replied.

I sighed. "He's a nice guy."

"So?"

"So, I just…I just don't want to get hurt again."

"Nobody does, sweetie. You gonna live the rest of your life worrying about it?" He paused. "Are you going to let Andrew do that to you?"

"I don't want to."

My brother sighed. "Then don't, Elle."

"Is it helping you? The shrink. Does he help?"

I took a piece of graph paper from my drawer and touched the point of my pencil to each box the blue lines made on the white paper.

"Yes," Chad said. "Talking about it helps. Puts things in perspective. Proves I'm not crazy. Our parents are the fucked-up mess, sweetie, not us."

"I don't need a shrink to tell me that." I laughed a little. "They put the fun in dysfunctional."

Chad laughed at my bad joke, too. "You know I'm always here to listen to you, sweetie. But really. I think you should think about talking to someone else. It could help you a lot."

"Will you think about coming home?" Silence wound its way through miles of wires to stab my ear. "Please?"

"I'll think about it."

I looked at the clock. "Oh, shit, I've got to go. I'll call you later, okay? And Chad, thanks."

"Anytime, sweetie. How many?"

"How many what?"

"How many whatever you're counting," he said, and I laughed.

"I'm looking at graph paper. A lot."

"Keep counting, sweetie."

"I will, Chad. Love you, bye."

I hung up the phone and stared at the graph paper, then pushed it aside. Chad had a boyfriend and a shrink, and I had neither. I had to decide if I wanted one or both. I knew I needed something.

Knowing what you need doesn't always mean you know how to get it, though. I'd spent a long time hiding in my cave. No matter how much I might want to come out into the light, I knew it would hurt my eyes. I was a fool.

A fool, but nevertheless too smart not to know I was the architect of my own demise, that it was time to put my past behind me. It was time to stop allowing the white elephants to stand unspoken of in my living room.

* * *

When I got back from the home improvement store, Dennis's car had stolen my spot. The inconvenience of parking across the street did nothing to dampen my enthusiasm for my new project. I carried buckets of paint, new rollers and trays inside and spread the tarp over my floor.

I began painting. Not white this time. Not for this room, the one in the house that had given me such trouble. This room I painted a deep, night-sky blue.

At the first stripe of it on the white I had to step back and set down the roller. I had to leave the room for a moment and draw a glass of cold water from the kitchen sink. I drank it down. I took a few deep breaths. I chided myself for being ridiculous, and with thumping heart, I went back into the dining room.

The second stripe of color was easier. The one after that easier still. And after ten minutes, the room had already changed. I painted for an hour without break, then stopped to stand back again and assess what I had done.

I know I'm a contradiction of clichés. I have always known it and understood my preference for black and white makes for a stark life without gray to cloud it. Looking at my blue wall, I didn't suddenly decide to throw away everything I'd held around me, or give up the things that gave me comfort. My blue wall was a choice I'd made, an urge toward change. And looking at it, even unfinished, made me smile.

I answered the knock on the door with paint still on my hands and cheek from where I'd brushed away my hair. "Gavin, hi."

"Hi." He looked still thinner than when last I'd seen him, but perhaps it was the black attire. The dark hue could have been the reason he looked paler, too. He held out a plastic bag from a local bookstore chain. "I brought you something."

I took the bag and looked inside, then pulled out a new copy of *The Little Prince*. "Oh, Gavin. You didn't have to."

He shrugged. "Yeah, I did. The other one got ruined, and it was my fault."

I waited until he met my eyes before I answered. "It wasn't your fault."

He shrugged again, shuffling his feet. "Yeah, it was. I made her mad. I shoulda cleaned my room, like she said."

I didn't say anything. Mrs. Ossley had a right to expect him to clean his room. Not a right to throw books at his head.

Gavin looked up. "I thought, maybe..."

"Actually," I said, so he didn't have to fumble, "I'm repainting the dining room. I could really use a hand."

He followed me inside, and I stood in front of the blue wall. Gavin looked it up and down, tilting his head like a curious puppy. After a moment he smiled, too.

"I like it." He nodded in approval.

I looked at it. "Yes. Me, too. I want to do the others this color, and the moldings in gold. And I bought this."

I showed him the rubber stamp in the shape of a star. "I'm going to stamp stars all over it, in a pattern."

"Wow, Miss Kavanagh, you're really going all out. Elle, I mean. You're really going crazy."

"A little crazy," I agreed. "Or maybe a little less crazy. I guess we'll see."

He looked so sad for a moment, my own smile turned down. He ducked his head and pulled off his sweatshirt, then went for the paint can to pour some out into a tray for his use. I watched him move. He scuttled, hunched, and I thought how having books thrown at one's head might make anyone prone to ducking.

We put on some music, and we painted. We got a little silly. When I used the end of a paintbrush to serenade Gavin with a cheesy boy-band drama song, he actually laughed out loud. I joined him. Every stroke of my roller laid down paint and seemed to lift me up a little farther.

I made grilled cheese sandwiches and tomato soup for lunch, comfort food I hadn't eaten in ages. He devoured his and demurred when I asked if he'd like more, but I got up to fix him another sandwich, anyway. His wrists looked as if I could break them with a glance.

"Hasn't your mom been feeding you?" I kept my tone light, but the question was serious. I didn't turn from my place at the stove. Confessions are easier given in anonymity.

"Mom's been too busy with Dennis to cook much. And work. She's been busy with work, too," he added, like admitting his mother's new lover took up all her time was something to be ashamed of.

It was, I thought, but not for Gavin. I slid a second sandwich onto his plate and dipped the last of the soup into his bowl. I sipped from my can of soda while he ate.

"Dennis moved in, huh?"

He nodded, head down over his food.

"How do you feel about that?"

Gavin didn't look up. "He's okay."

I sipped more cola. This wasn't my business, what went on next door. A fifteen-year-old boy was capable of making himself a sandwich if he had to. He didn't need his mother to cook him three meals a day, and I knew the house wasn't bereft of groceries because I saw their garbage cans overflowing with trash every week.

"And how are you?" I asked the question gently, watching the way his shoulders tensed at the question. "I haven't seen you much lately."

"Been busy," he mumbled. "Hadda go to summer school."

He tore apart the remnants of his sandwich but wasn't eating it. I didn't want to press him. Gavin was my neighbor, a nice kid, nothing more, and still my mouth opened and questions came out.

"Have you been reading a lot?"

"Yeah."

That, at least, urged another smile from him. "What have you been reading?"

He rattled off an impressive list of science-fiction and fantasy novels, some of which I knew and others I'd never heard of. He started eating again. When we'd finished, he helped me clean up the dishes and put them in the dishwasher. We turned the music back on and got back to painting.

My house is old, and I haven't yet fitted it with central air. The dining room doesn't have windows, and painting's hard, sweaty work. I saw the marks on Gavin's belly when he lifted his shirt to wipe his face.

Four, five, six of them. Straight red lines, the skin around them puffy and irritated. Not cat scratches, unless from a cat with extra toes and a wicked sense of aim.

And I could no longer ignore it. Because once upon a time, I had needed someone to push me for answers I was afraid to give, and nobody had. Princess Pennywhistle might have been able to defeat the Black Knight on her own, but I'd needed help and none had been given.

"Gavin. Come here."

He turned, the roller in his hand full of paint. Something in my face must have made him nervous, because he blanched. He put the roller down.

"What?"

I gestured. "Come here."

He did, with reluctance. His face had gone sullen. Guarded. He crossed his arms over his chest. We stared at each other for a moment before I reached over and turned off the music. The silence between us was very loud.

"Lift up your shirt," I told him.

He shook his head. I put my hand on his arm and my heart cracked at the way he winced. He didn't jump away from me, but I felt his muscles straining.

"I just want to see, Gav."

He shook his head. We were at a stand-off. He wouldn't acquiesce, and I couldn't force him to. I didn't ask again, but I also didn't let go of his arm. My fingers curled loosely enough on his biceps that he could have pulled away without effort, but he didn't. After another minute, he lifted the hem of his shirt to show me the wounds.

I kept my face neutral, looking at them. "These look sore."

"They're not too bad." His voice shook a little. Beneath my hand his arm had gone as hard as rock.

"Have you put anything on them? You don't want them to get infected."

"I…I don't…" He trailed off.

I put my palm flat against them for a second. "The skin's hot. That's not a good sign. What did you use?"

"A piece of glass."

I gave his arm a soft squeeze and stood up. "Come upstairs with me and we'll put something on them."

I went to the stairs, leaving him to come after me. I was almost convinced he wouldn't. That he'd flee. He followed me to the bathroom and sat obediently on my toilet while I opened my medicine cabinet and pulled out some antibiotic ointment, hydrogen peroxide and some bandages.

"Take your shirt off, it might be easier."

He pulled the T-shirt over his head and I put it on the sink. Faint white lines criss-crossed his chest, upper arms and stomach, though the only fresh cuts were on his belly. I cleaned them carefully, and though he hissed when the peroxide bubbled on his skin, he didn't pull away. I smeared them with ointment and covered them with bandages, but I couldn't make them disappear.

I sat on the edge of my tub, facing him. "Want to tell me about it?"

He shook his head, but again made no move to get away or even put his shirt back on. I capped the bottle and tube and threw away the bandage wrappers. I washed my hands. He still didn't get up. His shoulders shook, and I thought he must be fighting not to cry.

I didn't know how to do this. Be a confidante. I didn't know, exactly, how to make someone else's pain seem bearable. Faced with his tears, I was the one who wanted to flee. I put my hand on his shoulder instead.

"Gavin" was all I managed to say, and he burst into the terrified tears of a child.

Somehow I put my arms around him as he wept. His face was hot on my neck. He was so thin the bones in his shoulder blades hurt my hands, but I didn't let go.

"She never touches me," he whispered in a voice thick with shame and self-loathing. "She never hugs me or tells me she loves me. But she's always all over *him*."

I rubbed the knobs of his spine, trying to get him to stop crying. "Why do you cut yourself?"

He sat up, wiping his tears and leaving grimy streaks on his pale skin. "At least then I feel something, man. I get to feel something."

"Do you tell your mom about it?"

He hesitated, then shook his head. "I tried to, but she didn't want to listen."

I handed him his shirt and he shrugged into it. I handed him a tissue and he blew his nose, then wiped his eyes. He tossed the tissue in the trash without looking at me.

"Why do you think your mom doesn't hug you?"

"Because she hates me," he said. "I don't know."

I had no good answer for him. I wasn't the best person to be giving advice about mending relationships with mothers. I ran a washcloth under cold water and handed it to him.

"Wash your face."

He gave me an embarrassed smile, but did, then folded

it and hung it on the edge of the sink. "Are you gonna tell my mom?"

"Do you want me to?"

He didn't answer at first. "No."

"Gavin, I'm worried about you. I don't want you to hurt yourself anymore, okay? There are better ways to deal with stress and anxiety." I ducked my head to try and meet his gaze. I felt so old, all at once. Old and ineffective, telling him how to fix his life when I couldn't fix my own.

He shrugged. "Booze. Pot. No, thanks. My old man was a super pot head. I don't want to be a stoner. I'm trying to feel something, not go numb."

An astute observation from a fifteen-year-old boy.

"Cutting yourself isn't good, either."

He shrugged, looking down. "Are you gonna tell my mom or not?"

"What do you think she'll do if I tell her?" The edge of the tub was hurting my butt, but I didn't get up.

He shrugged again. "Dunno. Nothing. Yell."

"She might not yell," I told him. "She might try to get you some help."

He looked up at me, eyes bleak. "You think I'm crazy, don't you?"

"No, Gavin." I shook my head and reached for his hand. "I really don't. I know sometimes it can be easier to do things you know aren't good because it distracts you from the things that hurt."

He looked down at his hand, covered by mine. "She's getting married to him, and then she won't bother with me at all except to yell at me."

"Your mom loves you, Gavin. I'm sure she does, even if she doesn't act like it."

He snorted and pulled his hand away from mine. "Not all moms love their kids, Miss Kavanagh. It's a fact of life. Everyone wants to think they do, but they don't."

I knew that, too, but saying it aloud was too depressing. I was the adult here. I needed to find the magic words that would make him feel better. I couldn't find them.

"I should go," he said at last. "She'll have a cow if I don't clean up the living room before she gets home."

I nodded and sat back, watching him. "Gavin, you know if you ever need anyone to talk to, you can talk to me. Okay? About anything."

He shrugged, still looking down. "Okay."

I put my hand on his shoulder. "Anything."

He nodded. "Yeah. Thanks."

He got up and pushed past me, leaving me behind, hoping I'd done enough and knowing I hadn't.

Chapter 13

I worked hard on the dining room and finished it in a couple of days. Gold trim shone against the dark-blue walls, decorated with gold stars. Along the top, just under the crown molding, I painted a quote from *The Little Prince.* "All men have the stars, but they are not the same things for different people."

I liked the way it looked. Bold. It complemented the furniture in a way the stark white I'd originally planned never could have. The room I'd once hated more than any other in the house became my favorite.

That blue room gave me the courage to call Dan and invite him to go to the annual Susquehanna Art Show with Marcy, Wayne and me. It was an apology for not taking him to meet my mother. Neither of us mentioned the days that had passed without speaking. I wasn't sure he'd want to come, but he seemed to like the idea of meeting my friends.

We arranged to meet by the life-scale statue of the man

reading a newspaper on a park bench, but a delay with the bus had made me late. Consequently, I saw them before they saw me. Marcy and Wayne held hands, chatting, comfortable in a way I envied.

"Elle!" Dan waved and trotted over to me. "We were wondering where you were."

I wasn't sure if he'd hug me, but he did. "The bus got stuck in traffic. I see you've met."

He put his arm around my waist. "Yeah. I took a chance that the gorgeous blonde was Marcy."

Marcy tittered and leaned against Wayne. "He tried convincing me you told him that, Elle, but I didn't believe him."

I hadn't, of course, described Marcy as gorgeous. Blond, yes. Bubbly, certainly. Likely to be wearing stiletto heels and a tank top, definitely. In contrast to her casual attire I felt overdressed and a little grungy. Worried about being late, I hadn't bothered to change.

"Hi, Elle." Wayne reached forward to kiss my cheek. "Good to see you."

"Hi." I nodded.

Dan took my hand and squeezed it before linking our fingers. The action made me look at him, but for once he didn't seem to be reading my mind. I didn't pull away, though the possessive action made me a little nervous.

"Should we eat first?"

It took me a moment to register Dan was asking me. Marcy and Wayne looked expectant. Like it was up to me what we should do first? Like I was in charge?

"I guess so."

"Great, I'm starved." Dan squeezed my hand again.

This man had licked whipped cream from my nipples. I didn't need a shrink to tell me holding hands in public shouldn't have been an issue. Marcy and Wayne held hands. So did dozens of other couples walking past us.

But they were couples, pairs, lovers. And that was not us, Dan and me. He was a habit, a ritual, a way to pass the time. We were not a couple, oh, no. Not like Marcy and Wayne, not like the boy with the dreadlocks with the girl wearing a Ramones T-shirt. No. We were not a couple. Were we?

"Elle?" Dan's brow creased. "You okay?"

"Fine," I said, though I wasn't.

There were enough people to count, and I did that, dividing the total number by two. Couples. Two by two. Like something out of Noah's fucking ark…

"Elle? You look pale. Do you want to sit down?"

I shook my head. "No, I'm fine. Just need a drink. Let's get a drink, okay?"

I let Dan lead me through the crowd, Marcy and Wayne close behind us and Marcy chattering away even more than she does at work. I was grateful for the steady stream-of-consciousness gabble she spouted, as it left very little room for my own comments. Grateful, too, for the strawberry lemonade Dan bought and handed me.

I sipped it and he brushed my hair off my shoulders, his eyes still crinkled a bit in concern. He had, at least, needed to let go of my hand to buy the drink, and I made sure to hold it with both hands so he couldn't take it again.

Foolish. Stupid. I knew it. I did. I knew my reaction was unreasonable, but the heart has its reasons of which reason knows nothing. Blaise Pascal said that, and I've always found it to be true.

I'd invited him here. What's more, I wanted to be there, with him. Holding hands. A couple. My panic was unfounded, and I let it fill me anyway because I wasn't sure how to stop it.

"Oh, look." Marcy pointed. "Let's check out the wind chimes over there."

She and Wayne moved off ahead toward the stand where unique wind chimes made from kitchen utensils danced and clattered in the breeze from the river. Dan stayed with me, close but not touching me unless the crowd pressed us together. He put a hand to my elbow to help me cross a large tree root protruding from the grass, but then took his hand away again.

Marcy bought a wind chime. Wayne teased her. She solicited my opinion on it, and I told her I liked it, which I did. Dan sided with Wayne, who said it was ugly. They all laughed, and after a moment, I followed suit.

My eyes caught Dan's, and I saw a question there, but it wasn't the time for him to ask and so I pretended not to see.

We ate. We visited the stands. We tossed pennies into glass cups for chances to win cheap trinkets. We bid on silent-auction items.

If I was quiet, that was normal for me, and Marcy made up for it with her squeals and chatter. Dan and Wayne seemed to hit it off, standing together and talking about sports and other male-bonding topics while Marcy dragged me over to look at a display of truly hideous glass clowns.

"This one looks as if Bozo and Ronald McDonald had a love child and raised it in a toxic waste dump." Marcy pointed to one sad creature with the astounding price tag of twenty-seven dollars. "Jesus, Elle, what would you do with something like that?"

"I'd buy it for my mother," I told her.

"She likes glass clowns?"

"No." It was my first genuine smile of the night. "She'd probably hate it."

Marcy shook her head. "Shit, girl, remind me not to get on your bad side."

"Oh, Marcy," I told her. "Don't you know? They're both bad."

I'd meant to sound joking, but I'd looked toward Dan as I answered and the words sounded flat.

She gave me a funny look, her eyes shifting toward our men before meeting mine. "What's up, girlfriend?"

"Nothing." I shook my head.

"He seems nice," she offered.

"He is."

She looked at the men again. Wayne was gesturing, about what I couldn't begin to guess, but Dan was laughing. "So then…what?"

"Nothing," I insisted.

My smile must have convinced her, because she linked her arm through mine and giggled.

"Such boys. Look at them."

Dan laughed again, and he turned to see me. His smile widened. He gave me a little wave. I returned it. His tongue slid along his lips, and my heart thudded.

"You like him, don't you." Marcy's question caught my attention. "I can tell."

"I do like him."

Marcy has no sense of personal boundaries. She put her arm around me and rested her chin on my shoulder. It was a little sharp, and I winced.

"So?" she asked, "What's the problem?"

"No problem."

She didn't ask again. Wayne distracted her by pointing toward the pit beef booth, and Dan waved me over, and we all went to get something to eat. Marcy talked enough for all of us, and I got away with eating my sandwich and not saying much at all.

I like the art show. I like the booths and the artists and the carnival atmosphere, absent of the actual carnies. I even like the food.

This year, they had a band playing on a floating stage down by the river. We took our sandwiches and drinks to sit on the concrete steps leading down to the water. The band was good, playing a mix of oldies that pleased most of the crowd and didn't offend anyone. Marcy and Wayne sat close together, feeding each other French fries and sharing a milk shake. Dan and I sat a bit farther apart, not sharing anything.

This time, when he dropped me at my door, I didn't chatter the key in the lock or make small talk. I opened the door and went inside, holding it open for him to pass by me and into the house. I shut it behind us, and he followed me down the long, narrow hall to my kitchen.

He stopped in front of the dining room. "Wow."

I paused, feeling shy. "I just finished it."

He walked inside the odd-shaped room. "*The Little Prince.*"

I smiled, watching him read the words. "You know it."

He looked over his shoulder at me. "I read it, since you told me I should."

Nerves caught me again, and I ducked out of the room to head for the kitchen. I filled the kettle and started heating water for tea. A moment later, he joined me.

"This is nice, too." He looked around at my black-and-white existence.

"Thanks."

"I like that print."

He pointed to the black-and-white photograph I'd hung on the wall next to the back door. It showed a girl with long, dark hair obscuring her face. She sat on a low brick wall surrounding a koi pond, her arms gripping her knees. Ripples made rings on the water's surface. That picture reminded me of all the reasons I'd never invited him here, and why I'd kept pushing him away.

I waited for him to look at the picture again. Look harder. I waited for him to really see it, not just look at it.

He glanced over his shoulder at me. "Where'd you get it?"

"My brother took it."

The kettle whistled and I ignored him by scooping tea into the pot and pouring in the boiling water. Earl Grey, my favorite. I let the fragrant steam bathe my face before I put the teapot lid on to steep the tea.

"That's you."

"Yes."

"How old were you?" He stepped closer, hands in his pockets, to study the framed photo.

"Fifteen."

I set out cups, sugar, cream. I rustled in the cupboard and brought out some chocolate-dipped cookies, though my stomach churned from the horseradish I'd had on the beef. I had to move the container of bamboo to the counter to fit everything on the table.

He studied the picture a moment longer. "What were you thinking when he took it?"

The question startled me so much I dropped the bamboo. Made of heavy, clear plastic instead of glass, the container didn't break when it hit my tiled floor, but the bamboo, water and marbles flew everywhere, and I let out a heart-felt "FUCK!"

Dan was already moving forward to help me, and that annoyed me. It was irrational. Petty, even, but I waved impatient hands at him to move away as I grabbed a dish towel and bent to mop up the water.

"It will survive, Elle. Bamboo's hearty."

"Someone gave this to me." I soaked up the water as he gathered the twisting stems and set them on the table. "It was a gift. Now the roots are all broken!"

He scooped up marbles and put them back in the container. "It'll be okay."

I made a rude noise and got to my feet to wring out the towel. I had to turn my back on him to keep from saying something mean, something he didn't deserve but something I wanted to say, anyway. Does knowing you're about to be a bitch make it any easier? More justifiable? I didn't think so then and I don't now, but like a lot of things in my life, I couldn't seem to stop myself.

The clink, clink, clink of the marbles settling into the container made my shoulders hunch with tension, and I turned. "Don't crack it! It will leak!"

He looked up at me, his eyes narrowing. "I'm not going to crack it."

I scanned the marbles in the jar, those in his hand and the few left on the floor as he finished cleaning them up. "You missed three."

He looked around. "Where?"

"I don't know where," I snapped, irritable beyond justification. "I just know there were 287 marbles in that container and now there are only 284!"

He stared at me. Heat crept up my throat and my cheeks. I turned back to the sink. Behind me I heard him scuffling around, then the clink of the last three marbles being dropped next their companions.

"Elle." Dan came up close behind me, but didn't touch me.

"I was counting," I told him. "In the picture. I was counting the fish in the pond."

Whisper-soft, his hands rested on my shoulders. I didn't pull away, but neither did I yield to him. He sighed and took his hands away.

"How many were there?"

"Fifty-six."

"Elle. Turn around."

I did, reluctantly. I wanted to fight with him. I wanted, actually, to make him angry enough with me that he would go away on his own, and I'd be saved the trouble of making him.

"Did I do something wrong?"

The only thing he'd done wrong was make me like him. And how could I tell him that? "No."

"Then what?" He ran a hand through his hair. "You're acting like I pissed you off."

I crossed my arms over my chest. "You didn't."

"Then what?" He gestured from himself to me. "What's going on?"

"Nothing is going on!" I scowled. He scowled back. The phone rang and he looked at it while I made no move to answer. On the fourth ring, I jerked the handset from the cradle and thumbed the talk button. "Hello?"

"Hello, darlin'."

"Hi." I turned away from Dan.

"Is this a bad time?" Chad asked.

"Yeah. Can I call you later?"

"Sure, baby doll. You okay?"

"I'll call you later." There was no use lying to him. Chad could tell when I was upset.

"Sure, sure. Later, 'gator."

I disconnected and hung up. Dan had put his hands on his hips. I met his gaze with a steady one of my own.

He looked at the phone. Then at me. I couldn't help it. I smiled, snarky bitch. "Yes?"

He shook his head. "Do you want me to go?"

It wasn't what I wanted, but I nodded. "I think that would be best. Yes."

He stared at me a moment longer before letting out a hiss. He tossed up his hands. "Fuck it. Right. Okay. I'll go."

He couldn't have gone very far. Down to the newsstand

on the corner and back, less than ten minutes. I hadn't even had time to finish cleaning up the mess from the bamboo before my front door rattled beneath his knock. I almost didn't answer it, but the thought of him making a scene in front of my neighbors changed my mind. I yanked it open.

He had a bouquet of crimson roses. "I'm sorry."

If my expression showed half of the horror I felt, he could have had no doubt about my reaction. I stepped back with a grimace. There were roses when my brother died. Roses all around him. Roses at the funeral. Roses on his grave.

I hate roses.

"Elle?"

I put a hand over my mouth to keep from smelling them. "Take them away."

He hesitated, then leaned out the front door and tossed them into the garbage pail next to my small concrete porch. He came in and shut the door behind him. I put my hand up to keep him from coming closer.

"What kind of woman doesn't like roses?" He looked so perplexed I might have laughed if I wasn't still so distraught.

"I'm allergic to roses," I lied. "I told you to leave!"

"No." He shook his head. "Not until you tell me what the hell's the matter."

I pushed past him into the living room, but he snagged my elbow and turned me. "Let me go."

He didn't. "Is there someone else?"

"Why is that the first question men always ask?" I jerked my arm out of his grasp.

"Is there?"

"Fuck you, Dan." My throat hurt. My head hurt. I didn't want to be having this conversation, but it had begun and I didn't know how to stop it.

His hand went to the throat of his shirt, working the buttons. "If that's what you want."

I backed away from him. "Very clever. Get out."

He advanced on me, his shirt hanging open. I had never seen him look this way, like storms brewed in his eyes. They'd gone dark, no longer brilliant blue-green but the color of a lake before a storm. His mouth had thinned into a grim, determined line, and I suddenly found it difficult to believe I'd ever seen him smile.

"Don't tell me you don't want it."

I opened my mouth to tell him that very thing, but no words would come. I stammered something I meant to sound negative but only made him quirk his mouth into something too scary to be a grin.

He pulled off his shirt and started with his belt. I took another step back. My heart hammered. I couldn't look away from his face. His anger. His determination.

"Tell me, Elle." He frowned.

I took a few deep breaths. "I told you in the beginning, Dan."

"Yeah, you don't date." He sneered, looking me up and down. "You'll let me fuck you seven ways to Sunday, but you won't let me take you on a date. Elle, what difference does it make what we call it?"

"It makes a difference to me!" Tears would have eased the tightness in my throat, but even then I couldn't find them. "It's something, Dan, I can't—I don't—I just don't want…I don't…"

I shook my head, took another few deep breaths while he stared at me. "I don't want a boyfriend."

"Why not?" He buckled his belt again, with angry hands, then started on his shirt. "I'm good enough to get you off but not be your boyfriend? Is that it? You're ashamed? You're married? What?"

"I'm not married."

"Then what," he said, softer, buttoning his last button and moving toward me again. "Because I thought we were past this bullshit."

I let him touch me for a moment before I pulled away. I sat on my couch, a pillow hugged in my arms to create distance between us. I didn't indicate he should sit, too, but he did.

"I thought you liked fucking me." The explanation was lame, but the best I could manage at the moment.

"I do. I do, Elle. But I like being with you, too. Don't you like being with me? Just hanging out?"

He sounded vulnerable, and it made me hate myself. It made me hate him. I pulled on the tassels of my pillow and tried to find kind words, not cruel, to explain myself.

"I don't want a boyfriend," I repeated. "I don't want that commitment. A boyfriend is flowers and holding hands and having to buy cute little cards for holidays. A boyfriend is an investment, an emotional investment, and I don't want to give it and I…I don't want to expect it."

He made a noise low in his throat, and I wanted to smack him for understanding me even when I wasn't being clear. "You don't want to expect me to want to be with you, do things with you, that aren't just sex?"

"It's not that I never had one," I replied. "A boyfriend. I did."

"And he hurt you."

"It wasn't that simple."

"It never is." He rumpled his hair with a sigh. "But all other men should pay for his sins?"

"Something like that, yes." Yet again, that wasn't really what I meant.

"Elle…" Dan seemed at a rare loss for words. "We've been together for four months, and I still don't feel like I know anything about you."

The tassel unraveled beneath my nervous, twining fingers, and I balled the threads in my palm. "You know lots of things about me."

"Yeah. I know how to make you come."

"That's something, Dan."

He frowned. "It's not enough."

I looked up at him. "It has to be."

"Why, Elle?" He demanded. "Why does it have to be all?"

"Because," I cried, honest. "It's all I have!"

"I don't believe that."

"Believe it. I barely have enough of myself for me. I don't have enough for anyone else."

He rubbed his face. "Because of your ex?"

"No, Dan," I said more kindly that I'd thought I could. "Not because of him."

He stared at me, seeming lost. "Did he hurt you? Physically, I mean."

That surprised me. "No. Why would you think that?"

He lifted his hand, fast, and watched me flinch. "Because of that."

I shook my head. "No. He never hit me, if that's what you mean."

"But someone did."

"My mother has," I told him. "Not for a long time."

I could see he thought he was getting an insight from my admission, though he couldn't know my mother smacking me around was the smallest piece of my life's fucked-up puzzle. His expression softened, like he understood.

"Don't pity me," I said sharply.

"I'm not."

"She stopped when I got big enough to hit her back." I watched him again, taking a perverse pleasure in revealing this small truth.

Cocktail party secrets. The sort of things people reveal over drinks to strangers because it makes them seem open. I've always thought if someone reveals that their mother smacked them or their daddy drank too much to a stranger, what sorts of darker, more awful secrets are they hiding? I waited for him to tell me about his own horrid childhood, because it's what people do. Share the bad things that have happened to them to make you feel better. I'll show you mine if you show me yours.

"I'm sorry that happened to you. Not sorry for you."

"Bad things happen," I said. "Every day, all the time. To lots of people. She never chased me around with a butcher knife or anything."

"And yet you still flinch."

I shrugged. "You're angry and you're bigger than I am. Some things are habit."

He sighed. "What'd your boyfriend do? Cheat on you?"

"No."

"But he broke up with you."

The longer we talked the less urgent I felt to make him leave. He was defusing me in the way he had. Whether it was conscious or not I couldn't tell, but I wasn't unaware of it. I knew what he was doing…and as with so many other things we'd done, I let him.

I didn't want to. I didn't want to explain myself, to relive the past, to tell him the truth and why I was the way I was. Because the truth was, I might have told him I wanted him to go, but I didn't really want him to leave.

"We were young. I was nineteen. He was twenty. We met in college. His name was Matthew."

His name was Matthew, and the first time he kissed me, I thought I'd never be able to breathe again.

"You loved him?" His question sounded tentative.

"I thought I did. I thought he loved me. But what's love, anyway? A word."

"It's a feeling, too."

"Have you ever been in love?" I shot back.

He didn't answer for a full minute. "So what happened?"

"He thought I was cheating on him, but I wasn't. I wouldn't have." I narrowed my eyes at Dan, who didn't seem inclined to disbelieve me. "But he insisted. He'd found some letters he thought were from a lover. He called me a liar, and some other things. Slut, mostly, though being called a liar hurt worse. I should have lied and told him what he wanted to hear, but instead I told him the truth."

"He didn't believe you?"

"He did," I said, thinking about it.

"But if you weren't cheating—"

"It was a long time ago," I told him. "And like I said, we were young."

"And you're not going to tell me any more." He frowned.

"No, Dan."

"And you want me to go."

I looked into his eyes. "No. I don't."

He moved closer, encouraged, and put his hand on my shoulder. "Then what do you want, Elle?"

"I want you not to have to settle," I told him.

"Is that what you think I'm doing?"

"I know that's what you'll be doing. Because if you want more from me, you're not going to get it."

He said nothing for a long time. "When I read *The Little Prince,* I thought you must be the rose. You with your four thorns, convincing me you're able to defend yourself. But now I know you hate roses. So you must be the fox instead. So maybe what you really want is for me to tame you."

From a lot of men, that speech would have made me laugh, or roll my eyes. Then again, a lot of men wouldn't have read Antoine de Saint-Exupéry's classic story of *The Little Prince,* or bothered to try and understand it.

I reached for his hand and held it between both of mine. "The fox tells the Little Prince he is a fox like a hundred thousand other foxes. Just like the flower was like a hundred thousand other flowers."

Dan tucked a strand of hair behind my ear with the hand I wasn't holding. "But the fox asked the prince to tame him. To make it so they'd need each other and be unique to each other. And he did it."

“And then the prince went away, Dan, and left the fox bereft.” I looked down at my hands, holding his.

“Would you be sad if I left you?” He asked me, and at first I wasn’t sure how I would reply.

At last the answer came on breath as tremulous as a breeze wafting curtains from an open window.

“Yes. I would.”

He squeezed my hand. “Then I won’t.”

He pulled me close to him, my head on his shoulder, and for a long time that was all I needed or wanted to do.

I'd stopped into the break room to fill up my mug with coffee before the afternoon meeting when sex again waylaid me.

To be fair, it wasn't sex, exactly, but Marcy with waggling eyebrows and a whispered, "I've got it!"

She waved me over to the table toward the back, where she'd either been doing loads of cocaine or eating powdered doughnuts again. I looked at the napkin with its telltale evidence and looked for a bakery box, but she was good. All that remained were a few incriminating crumbs.

"What do you have, aside from a sugar high you didn't share?"

"No," she said with a meaningful pause to shoot a glance at the floor. "*It.*"

I looked at the bag at her feet. Nondescript brown paper, no logo on the side. The sort of thing porn magazines were delivered in.

Then I knew what it was. The Blackjack. You might think that after so many embarrassing escapades in my life, my blush function would be broken, but sadly, it continues to advertise my least discomfort. Heat spread from my chest, up my throat and all the way to my hairline. Marcy laughed.

"It's gorgeous," she told me. "I made sure to bring fresh batteries for you."

"Thanks. I'm sure it could've waited until I got home."

"Maybe. But I wanted to make sure you could use it right away." Her blue eyes glinted. "It's so cute, the way you blush."

"It's not cute." I set down my handful of files on the table and took the package from her. It was heavier than I expected, the cardboard tube unmarked, the same as the bag in which she'd brought it. A thought struck me. "You didn't... try it out. Did you?"

Her disgusted expression forced a giggle from me. "No, ew, Elle! Ewww!"

"Just checking."

"Aren't you going to open it?"

I shook my head. "Not here."

"Oh, c'mon."

Marcy should be classified a force of nature. There is no resisting her when she has her mind set on something. All she had to do was give me a look, and my fingers obediently began working the tape covering the box's lid.

"What do you use, the Jedi mind trick?" I grumbled, slitting the tape and prying open the cardboard flap.

Marcy hooted. "Mmm...Obi-Wan Can-bone-me."

"God, you're such a dirty pervert. You'll make Alec Guinness roll over in his grave." I pulled open the flap.

Marcy pursed her lips. "I'll roll Ewan McGregor over, thanks. C'mon, pull it out!"

I looked around the room, but it was still empty. I didn't hear anyone outside in the hall, either. I looked back at the box and then opened it up all the way.

The Blackjack lay cuddled in its bed of protective bubble wrap. It didn't look that sexy. In fact, if I hadn't already known what it was, I might have thought it was a large black candle or something, instead of a phallic-shaped sex toy.

"Take it out!" Marcy bounced with glee, peering over my shoulder "Let's see!"

"I thought you already saw it," I said, but obliged her by unfolding the bubble wrap.

"Oooh." Marcy cooed with pleasure. "It's so classy, Elle. Just like you."

"Oh, good Lord, Marcy." I wanted to clap a hand to my forehead. "Vibrators are not classy!"

"That one is."

It did have a certain aesthetic charm with its sleek design and deep ebony color. The small, ridged handle, made of molded black plastic to seamlessly match the rest of the device, fit comfortably in my palm. It had weight to it. Solid. For a moment my brain imagined it would make as good a weapon as it would a tool for lovemaking.

"Turn it on!"

"Marcy, no!" I pulled the Blackjack protectively against my chest to keep it out of reach of her grasping hands. "Jeez!"

Laughing, she poked my arm. "Oh, c'mon, Elle! Make sure it works! Here. I put the batteries in the bag."

She opened the package of batteries with one long fingernail and handed them to me, one by one. They slid into the Blackjack like bullets into a gun, and after a moment the toy rewarded us with a low hum. It buzzed against my palm, tickling.

Marcy giggled. I did too. We hunched like conspirators over it, Marcy making whispered lewd comments and me shaking my head.

"Ladies?"

I clutched the still-working vibrator against my chest, my wrist hastily twisting to turn it off. The voice belonged to Lance Smith, one of the Smiths in Smith, Smith, Smith and Brown. He was the youngest Smith, the third, and a nice guy with a family of three gap-toothed children and a plump wife who sometimes brought him lunch. She liked expensive chocolate truffles from Sweet Heaven. He was also my boss. I definitely did not want him to see my deviant little dildo.

"Lance," Marcy said. "Time for the meeting?"

"Yep. Elle, you've got the files on the charity information, right?"

"Sure, Lance," I told him cheerfully without turning around.

"Great. Oh, we're meeting in the big room today. Dad's coming. See you there in five."

Dad was the senior Smith. Walter. He'd retired two years before but liked to keep active with the firm's charitable contributions. He, too, was a nice man. I didn't want him to see my sex toy, either.

"We'd better get over there." Marcy's eyes danced with amusement. "We don't want to keep Walt waiting."

That wouldn't have been a good idea. And since my office was on the other side of the building, away from the meeting room, that meant I'd have to find a place to stash the Blackjack until afterward. I looked around, but putting it in the cupboard was too risky. My luck, someone would go looking for more creamer and find my Blackjack instead.

"Put it back in the box and just carry it with you," Marcy suggested as I looked around the room. "Nobody will know what it is."

It was the best suggestion, and I enfolded it back into the bubble wrap only to discover it no longer fit back into the box correctly. Voices in the hall alerted me to our co-workers heading down to the meeting room. Time didn't allow for vibrator wrestling.

"Just leave off the wrapping. Here." Marcy took the wrap and tossed it in the garbage while I slid the plastic, already warm from my hand, back into its cardboard sheathe. "All set."

I tucked in the flap and picked up my folders. "All set."

Marcy and I didn't often have much work-related interaction, since she dealt with personal accounts and I handled corporations. One project we were able to work together on was the company's annual participation in Harrisburg's Children Are Our Future event. Featuring displays, free food, demonstrations and giveaways by area businesses, the event raised money for children's charities in the Dauphin County area. I'd been on the planning committee for four years. This year they were asking participating companies not only to pay for booth space, but to make matching donations from their employees.

I settled my things at the table and greeted my coworkers with small talk while we waited for everyone to arrive. Lance caught my eye from across the table and quickly looked away. A few minutes later the rest of the committee had arrived and we began our discussions.

There wasn't much to plan. We'd reserved the booth space in one of the higher traffic areas of the event, which was going to be set up inside the Strawberry Square shopping center. The indoor mall with its food court and specialty shops had a convoluted layout, and the year before we'd been stuck in a back corner. We'd had to bring home almost our entire supply of goodies.

I listened to reports from the man in charge of setting up and tearing down the booth and from the woman overseeing the handing out of notepads, pens and magnets with the company logo and information to parents. For the children we had balloons and small gift bags stuffed with candy and plastic treats, as well as popcorn. Marcy would be manning the popcorn maker. I was handling the employee contributions and disbursements to the charity Triple Smith was sponsoring.

"Elle?" Walter Smith beamed at me from his chair at the head of the table. "What have you got for us?"

I shifted the box with my Blackjack inside it and flipped open my folder. I cleared my throat. I knew all of these people—some rather better than others—and yet I still felt awkward about speaking in front of them all. It was the way they stared, like my words mattered.

"The past four years we've built a good relationship with the Capital Area Sexual Abuse Awareness Foundation," I said. "Because CASAAF isn't a government-funded program, they continue to need our support. Last year they used the money we donated to purchase anatomically correct dolls that allow children to role-play their situations if they're unable to articulate them."

I paused, clearing my throat again, and wishing I'd thought to grab a bottle of water instead of a mug of now-cold coffee. "They also used the money to implement training in their volunteers to utilize the dolls. This year Barry Leis, the director, told me they intend to put the funds toward a series of summer camp programs about personal body safety."

"Very good," murmured Walter.

"Are there any objections to continuing naming CASAAF our beneficiary for this event?" I looked around the table, expecting as I did every year to get opposition and again having none. It reminded me I should have more faith in my coworkers. That people really do care.

We briefly discussed the possibility of having a bake sale to raise employee donations that Triple Smith would then match. I didn't bake. Marcy made a face, too. We decided on a candy sale instead.

Walter gave me another warm smile as I closed my folder. "Thank you, Elle. We really appreciate the work you've done toward this matter."

His praise warmed me, and I returned his smile. Then it was Lance's turn. The buzzing began when he stood up to go over the logistics of the event, who'd use what company vehicle to transport which items, who'd be in charge of petty cash, who'd be in the office on that day and who'd be at Strawberry Square. At first nobody else noticed, though the instant the low hum began I'd sat up straight in my seat. I deliberately did not look at the box containing my Blackjack.

I couldn't look at Marcy, either, who sat across from me. The buzzing stopped after a few seconds. I relaxed. Lance droned on, using his pointer to go over his lists up on the whiteboard.

The buzzing started again. Louder, this time. Marcy gave a strangled giggle she turned into a sort of snorting cough. My entire body went rigid and the only reason I managed not to let out a squeak was because I bit my tongue so hard I thought I tasted blood. Lance looked over at the two of us, his smooth forehead wrinkling a bit, but he kept talking.

Marcy was trying to get my attention, but I was trying to surreptitiously shift the Blackjack box so it would stop on its own. All I did was make it worse.

Marcy started giggling. People were staring, curious. I bit down on my lower lip and closed my fingers around the box. The vibration got louder. It sounded like a hive of bees.

There was no mistaking the interest the noise had garnered. Not so long ago the situation would have sent me into a panic. This time, all I could do was stifle my increasingly desperate giggles with my hand while I tried to shake the box and make it stop.

Lance paused in his speech and turned around again. Everyone stared. I grabbed the box and shook it, hard, which set the Blackjack into an even greater indignancy of rattling.

"It's a gift," I explained lamely over the sound. "For a friend. One of those automated cat toys…."

Marcy burst out into guffaws and slapped the table. This

wasn't an unexpected response from her, so nobody seemed to mind. On the other hand, I'm not sure anyone there had ever seen me react so extremely to anything.

Something about laughter is so contagious it infects anyone who hears it. Marcy's guffaws blended with Brian Smith's raised-brow chuckles and Walter Smith's bemused snicker, as well as the laughter of everyone else at the table. Including mine. I shook the box again, irritating it further, then banged it on the table.

It fell silent while we all still laughed. I laughed harder because none of the others in the room had any idea about what, exactly, had set us off. The room shared five more minutes of collective good feeling before we tapered off into small chuckles and got back to business. Lance finished up the meeting and we dispersed. I made sure to handle the box carefully.

"Elle. Can I see you a minute?" Lance asked as the rest of the room filed out.

I hesitated. By unspoken agreement, Lance and I kept our interaction as limited as possible. He didn't need to oversee my work but was available on the rare occasions I needed input, and he did my annual review in which I always got the highest rating and an above-average raise. For him to hold me back after a meeting meant he had something to discuss about my work, or so I thought.

"Sure." I smiled at him carefully.

He waited until the room had cleared of everyone else before he spoke. "I've never seen you laugh like that."

"Oh. I'm sorry." I sobered. "It was inappropriate. I apologize."

Lance shook his head. "No. You don't have to. I just wanted to tell you I've noticed you've been a little…different…the past few months."

I kept a frown from creasing my face. "Oh? If it's an issue with my performance—"

"No, Elle," Lance interrupted gently. "Your work's been fine. Great, actually. The clients love you. We're nothing but pleased with your work."

"I see." I nodded as though I did, when in fact, I wasn't quite sure where he was going with this and it made me nervous.

Lance smiled at me, and it was easy to see how much he resembled his father. "I just meant that you seem to be…happier. Lately. That's all. We like happy employees."

I shifted my folders to give my hands something to do. "I've always been happy working here, Lance. You should know that. Triple Smith is a great company to work for."

He beamed. "We try to make it so. But it's not just that, Elle."

He didn't say more, and I didn't need him to. We shared a look, one he broke first, and I understood what he meant. The understanding softened my voice when I answered.

"Thanks, Lance," I said. "Yes. I'm happy."

He nodded vigorously. "Good. Good. I'm glad to hear it."

It was nice he'd noticed. That was all we said, but really, all we needed to. I watched him leave the room ahead of me. People really do care.

I'd carried my garbage out to the curb when I noticed that for the second week in a row, Mrs. Pease's cans remained in the small alley between our houses. It wasn't like her to forget garbage day, and I didn't think she'd been gone because I saw different lights on in her windows every night. I peeked into her pail and saw nothing but a few scraps of paper at the bottom. They prompted me to knock on her door, something I'd only done once or twice before when we needed to exchange packages delivered incorrectly.

She answered the door after a few moments. She pulled her bathrobe tight around her neck as though the air chilled her, even though it was still summer and the night was warm enough to almost be uncomfortable. Her hair, normally styled in a perky set of tight curls, looked squashed.

"Oh, hello, Miss Kavanagh." She blinked at me, looking tired and pale but smiling at me, anyway. "What can I do for you?"

"I noticed you hadn't put your garbage out," I told her. "I thought maybe I'd check in on you and see how you were doing."

"Oh, aren't you a dear." She sounded sincere, too. "I've been a little under the weather lately, that's all. Haven't managed to have the strength to get around to taking out the trash, that's all. I thought my son might be by to do it. But…" She gave a shrug.

"If you need help, I'd be happy to do it for you."

She smiled again. "Oh, my dear, you really don't have to. I'm sure Mark will be by sometime soon. This week. I'm sure he'll be able to do it."

"If you're sure," I said. "It's really no trouble, Mrs. Pease.

It won't take more than a few minutes, and garbage collection is tomorrow. I'd hate for you to have to wait another whole week."

She hesitated, looking torn, then nodded slowly as if admitting something to herself. She stood aside. "If you really don't mind. I hope Mark comes by, but I really can't be sure he will, after all."

I'd never been inside Mrs. Pease's house before, but like all the homes along this block, the layout was almost identical to mine. She had a closet where I didn't, and her stairs had a landing instead of going straight up, but the rest was similar. I looked around her small, tidy living room, the television tuned to an old game show. Doilies decorated the arms of the overstuffed chair, and a knitted throw along the back of the couch reminded me of one my grandma had kept in her house. A lot of things about Mrs. Pease's place reminded me of my grandma's house. Cozy and warm.

"Come in, come in," she said. "The kitchen garbage is back here. Though living alone, as I do, I don't seem to make much trash."

She led the way through the narrow hall toward the kitchen at the back of the house. Unlike mine, which had been refitted with new appliances, flooring and countertops, Mrs. Pease's looked like it hadn't changed since the fifties. She waved a hand toward the pail in the corner between the back door and the refrigerator.

"Of course, when the kids lived here at home we had to take out the garbage every few days or it was unbearable!" She chuckled. "That was quite some time ago, though."

"How many children do you have?" I headed for the pail,

which wasn't overflowing but needed emptying just the same. I pulled the bag from the can and tied it shut as Mrs. Pease came forward with a fresh trash bag.

"Just two now," she said. "We lost our daughter Jenny in a car accident back in '86. But I see her children from time to time. They're in college now. Their dad remarried a long time ago."

I replaced the trash bag and asked to wash my hands at her sink, using soap that smelled of green apples. "And you have a son Mark."

"Oh, yes. My Mark. And Kevin."

"Do they live close by?" I wiped my hands dry on a soft dish towel and turned to see Mrs. Pease looking so sad it made me sad, too.

"Kevin's moved away," she said. "And Mark lives here in the city, but…I don't see much of him. He's very busy, my Mark. He's very busy."

Too busy to visit his mother and make sure her garbage was taken care of, I thought meanly. Guilt pricked me in the next minute. At least he visited her sometimes. I was an awful daughter.

"Thank you, dear," Mrs. Pease told me. "You're so helpful."

"You know, Mrs. Pease. I'm right next door, if you ever need anything at all. I'm happy to come and give you a hand."

She shook her head, her soft white hair looking like white cotton around her apple-doll face. "I don't want to trouble you, Miss Kavanagh."

"It's really not any trouble at all. Really." Nothing quite

like a guilty conscience to prompt unsolicited and slightly desperate offers to elderly next-door neighbors.

She bustled around her kitchen for a few seconds and pulled out a small tin of cookies. "Have a cookie?"

"Thank you." Sugar. They were good, still soft. "I've never learned to bake."

She gave a small, trilling laugh. "Oh, my dear! Every girl should learn to bake!"

I nibbled the cookie. "My mother wasn't particularly interested in domesticity."

Mrs. Pease might be feeling under the weather, but it hadn't dulled her perceptions. "You don't see her often, do you?"

I shook my head. I thought she might judge or lecture me, but Mrs. Pease gave a soft sigh instead. "Have another cookie, dear. And it's never to late to learn to bake."

I helped myself to another cookie, and she put away the tin. She wiped up some crumbs with a dishcloth and folded it on the sink. The second cookie was as delicious as the first had been, and when I finished I lifted her garbage.

"I'll take this out to the curb. Do you anything else to take? Anything from upstairs?"

"No," she said. "Though I might, next week, if you're able to stop by. I'll be baking cookies, Miss Kavanagh. You could watch, if you like."

We shared a smile. "I think I'd like that, Mrs. Pease."

I took her garbage out to the can and dragged it to the curb next to mine. I turned to wave goodbye to her before heading into my house, when a police car stopped next to me. I jumped a little, wondering instantly if I'd broken some ordinance or something, but the officer who got out of the vehicle didn't do more than nod at me before opening the back door.

Gavin got out. Not in handcuffs, as least, though he didn't look any happier for being unshackled than if they'd had him bound. He looked up and met my gaze, then dropped it immediately as the cop pulled him by the elbow toward his house.

This wasn't my business any more than anything else had been, but I stood frozen next to the garbage as the Ossleys' door opened and Gavin was yanked inside by his mother. I overheard raised voices from inside, though the officer who brought him home kept his voice pitched low and professional. He didn't go into the house. He and Mrs. Ossley spoke for a minute or so, words I couldn't make out, and then he left.

He gave me another nod as he got back in his car. "Evening."

"Evening," I said, pulled away from staring at the Ossley house by his greeting.

I couldn't ask him what had happened with Gavin. I looked back toward the house. Then I put the lids on the garbage cans and intended to go home, but my feet instead found the four concrete steps leading up to the house next door.

Mrs. Ossley opened the door, her frown becoming a grimace of fury when she saw it was me. "What the hell do you want?"

I refused to allow her hostility to take me aback. "I came to see if Gavin was all right."

She looked me up and down, her expression getting tighter and harder. She looked as though she'd bitten into an apple and discovered only half a worm. Even though she wore a pair of high heels, I stood over her by about two inches, and this seemed to irritate her further as she crossed her arms and looked up at my face.

"He's fine. You can go back home, now."

"Mrs. Ossley, I'm not really sure what I've done to offend you, but I can assure you, I'm only concerned about Gavin's welfare." I retreated a step under the force of her glare.

She laughed, the sound like barking, and then pulled a cigarette from the pack I hadn't noticed in her hands. She lit it and blew a runner of smoke directly into my face. I waved it away.

"I bet you are," she said. "I just bet you are."

Her obvious dislike and antagonism toward me tied my stomach into knots, but the memory of precise and self-administered wounds kept me from fleeing. "Can I come in?"

"You cannot!" She seemed aghast at the suggestion. "Go mind your own business!"

I looked over her shoulder to the sight of a man silhouetted in the hall. Dennis. A flutter of movement on the stairs caught my gaze, and she turned to see what I was looking at.

"Gavin! Get up to your room! Right now!" She turned back to me. "We'll deal with him, Miss Kavanagh. Go play with someone else's son."

She made to close the door in my face, but I put out a hand to stop her. Her words had made a nasty noise in my head. "I beg your pardon?"

"Oh," she said with another gust of smoke. "He told me all about you."

"He did?"

Again, she looked me up and down. I wondered what she saw. I wore work clothes, a mid-calf black skirt and a simple white blouse with buttons. Shoes with sensible heels. Compared to her outfit of a teal, low-cut lingerie-style top spangled with sequins, flowered short skirt and matching stiletto sandals, I wouldn't win any prizes in a fashion show. The outfit was staid and comfortable, but didn't deserve her look of disgust.

"Oh, yes, he did. He sure did. Told me how he helped paint your dining room." Her fingers hooked quotation marks in the air around the work *paint*.

"He did help me paint my dining room. He's been a big help, as a matter of fact. He's done a lot of work for me."

She snorted. This close, I could see the faint acne scars on her cheeks. She'd covered them with makeup, but they still shadowed her face here and there. I had no idea how old she was. Old enough to have a fifteen-year-old son, but maybe not that much older than me, after all.

"Yes, he's spent a lot of time over there. With you." More smoke. She had red-painted nails and red lipstick to match. It left crimson stains on the end of her cigarette. "I can't get him to clean up his goddamn bedroom, but he's got time to hang around over there painting your walls."

"I'm sorry, Mrs. Ossley. I told Gavin he needed to make sure he did his chores at home."

The hostility still flowing off her in waves made me want to step back again, but I stopped myself with a hand on her railing. Unlike mine, which I sanded and painted every spring, hers scratched my hand with its bumps and lumps of pitted rust. When I took away my hand, a red stain dotted the palm.

"Well, Miss Kavanagh," she said my name with a sneer that wouldn't have been out of place had she been calling me a worse sort of name. "I'm awfully glad to hear you're so concerned about my son that you have him doing your dirty work for you, but you telling him he should be a good boy and clean up his mess doesn't seem to matter much, does it?"

I still didn't quite know what had gotten her so upset, unless it had been my witnessing her bad behavior with the books. It was one thing to holler at your child. Another to pelt him with books. I'd have been embarrassed, too, if it were me.

"I have always appreciated Gavin's help," I told her. "And I've offered to pay him for his time, but he's never wanted to take any money for it. However, I understand if his helping me has caused problems in your house—"

"Oh, you *understand!*" she cried. "I'm sure you did want to pay him. Sure you did. Yeah, he told me all about that, too."

"He did?" I blinked, uncertain where this was going, but knowing at once it was going to end badly. "Mrs. Ossley, please believe me, I'm just concerned about Gavin. I think there are some things you should know—"

She cut me off again. "Don't you tell me what I should know about my own son!"

From over her shoulder, I saw again the flutter of motion

on the stairs. A figure in a dark, hooded sweatshirt hovered halfway up, halfway down. Mrs. Ossley advanced on me a step, and I countered with another back. Now with me on the lower steps she stood taller than I, and it seemed to give her fuel for her outburst.

"Mrs. Ossley," I said sharply. "Your son's been—"

The sight of Gavin's face, a pale blur in the shadows of the stairs, stopped me. This wasn't my business. But was it my responsibility?

"Gavin's been cutting himself," I told her with a lift of my chin to show her I wasn't going to let her nastiness stop me from trying to help. "I thought you should know."

She snorted. "Yeah, he told me all about that, too. About how you asked him to take his shirt off. What were you doing, asking a fifteen-year-old boy to take off his shirt? Can you answer that for me?"

Her accusation, not quite spelled out, but obvious just the same sent me back down the rest of her steps.

"Yeah, I'm asking you," she said. "All those nights he spent over there, doing work for you. How'd you pay him back? Huh? You get off on contaminating kids?"

"No." I had to take the time and forcible effort to swallow just to squeeze out that one word from my suddenly constricted throat. "Absolutely not. It wasn't like that."

"No? What was it like, then? You're a little old to be playing doctor, aren't you? What do you think a kid his age is gonna do when it's put out right there for him?"

I shook my head. "Mrs. Ossley, you are mistaken—"

Mrs. Ossley never seemed to have learned interrupting

was rude. "*'Mrs. Ossley, you are mistaken,'*" she mimicked in a high-pitched voice. "Are you calling my son a liar?"

"Did Gavin tell you I'd been…inappropriate?"

Inappropriate. The word didn't even begin to describe what it would have been for me to behave toward Gavin the way she was intimating I had. I tried to see his face again, but he'd retreated so far up the stairs I could no longer see him.

The other woman laughed cruelly. "He told me you wanted his help with a special project. That you offered him something to drink—"

It was my turn to interrupt, damn the rudeness. "He said I offered him alcohol?"

"Does it make you feel good to corrupt minors? Get them drunk, show off your body? Boys'll do anything for a glimpse of titty, won't they? I bet you thought you had a nice little thing going on!"

Her statement so boggled me I couldn't reply. It didn't stop her from continuing. Her voice got louder, cutting through the hot summer air.

"Bet you thought you could get him to do just about anything you wanted, huh? Get him to take off his shirt. Get him drunk. My son was a good kid until you got ahold of him!" Her voice rose on the last words and echoed down our street.

"What happens at home stays at home," I murmured without thinking. I wanted to beg her not to say anything more. Plead with her to keep quiet, to stop, to stop embarrassing me. I imagined curtains twitching aside and neighbors peering out to witness the lies.

"What? What did you say? You're lucky I don't press charges! But honestly, who'd do anything about it? He's a teenage boy, of course he's going to fuck a woman who—"

"I did *not* behave inappropriately with your son, Mrs. Ossley." My voice froze the air between us. It backed her up a step, but only for a moment. She was too full of her own self-righteous accusations to pay attention to my defense. "I did ask him to take off his shirt, but that was because I was worried about the cuts on his stomach. And yes, we've spent a lot of time together, but I have never…I've never…"

I couldn't go on. She took the chance to shake her finger at me. Gavin looked like her, I saw, even though her face had twisted and become ugly in her anger.

"I could have you brought up on charges of giving alcohol to minors! And for the other stuff, too." She crossed her arms over her ample chest. "Just because he went along with it doesn't mean you have the right to molest him!"

"Nobody deserves that," I told her.

She seemed to be waiting for more from me, but I said nothing. I couldn't. The things she'd said had sickened me. I backed up further and went to my own porch. She swiveled her body to follow me with her eyes as she lit another cigarette.

"You stay away from my son!" She shouted. "Or I will call the cops on you!"

I paused, my hand on my own smoothly painted railing. The curtains I'd imagined twitching all along the street seemed to be remaining closed. All except for one. The one on their second floor shifted, and I caught a glimpse of a white face shadowed by a black hood. It ducked out of sight as soon as it saw me looking.

"Don't worry, Mrs. Ossley," I told her. "I will."

Chapter 15

I didn't emerge from the cocoon of my past to become an uninhibited, emotionally healthy butterfly. Nothing is ever that easy. Sometimes grief is a comfort we grant ourselves because it's less terrifying than trying for joy. Nobody wants to admit it. We'd all declare we want to be happy, if we could. So why, then, is pain the one thing we most often hold on to? Why are slights and griefs the memories on which we choose to dwell? Is it because joy doesn't last but grief does?

The confrontation with Gavin's mother had left me shaken and determined to mind my own business from now on. Instead of tackling a new painting project, I enjoyed learning to bake cookies with Mrs. Pease, whose son did visit, eventually, if not as often as she'd have liked. And, I made an effort, a real effort, with Dan.

Since the extent of my cooking extended no further than sugar cookies at this point, Dan invited me to dinner at his place. I knocked on his door with a bottle of good wine in my hand, and the smile he gave me when he opened the door made me smile back. We did an awkward little dance for a moment before he took the lead and pulled me into his arms for a hug brief enough to remain casual but full of meaning just the same.

I felt a different kind of nervous around him. More anticipatory than anxious. I didn't mind it. I followed him to the kitchen and we opened the wine as we chatted.

"Pasta à la Dan," he said from the stove, where steam had wreathed his face. He turned, grinning. "My own special recipe."

I cast a pointed glance to the empty jar of expensive spaghetti sauce he'd left in clear view on the counter. "Uh-huh."

He raised an eyebrow. "You doubt me?"

I held up my hands and sat at the table. "Hey, anything I don't have to cook is fine with me."

He laughed and poured the pasta into a strainer, ladled it onto plates, layered the sauce over it and added a sprig of parsley. He slid the plate in front of me and sat down with his.

"Cheese?"

"That's a nifty gadget." I watched him shred Parmesan cheese in a minigrater like the kind they have in restaurants.

"Pampered Chef."

I blinked. "You really do like Pampered Chef?"

"Hell, yeah." Dan set the grater down and reached for the bottle of wine to refill our glasses. "Their stuff is excellent."

"I don't cook, so I guess I wouldn't know." That was true. "My domestic gene is broken."

He looked up. “Seriously?”

I smiled. “Seriously.”

He pushed the basket of garlic bread toward me. “Damn. Here I thought I’d finally found me a woman who’d cook and clean for me.”

I rolled my eyes and took some bread. “Whatever.”

He twirled some pasta on his fork and blew on it, then tucked it into his mouth and sighed in contentment. I watched him eat. It was nice to see someone take such enjoyment out of something so simple. That impressed me about him. He was just as happy eating home-made pasta as he’d been at La Belle Fleur. It was refreshing and a little paradoxical, that the man who put me up against a wall could be the same as the one now cooing over spaghetti.

“Not hungry?”

He’d caught me staring, and I looked down at my plate. “Oh, yes…this looks great.”

“Tell me something, Elle.”

“Like what?” I looked up from the bread I’d been tearing into small pieces.

Dan smiled. “Anything.”

I sipped some red wine and studied his face. “The sum of the squares of the shorter sides of a right-angled triangle will equal the square of the hypotenuse.”

“The sum of the what will equal the what of the what-what?” He shook his head. “What’s that?”

“Pythagorean Theorem,” I told him. “You said anything.”

“How about something about yourself?” He poured us both more wine. I’d barely realized my glass was empty.

“I wear a size seven glove.”

"Really?" He made a show of looking at my hand. "I'd have said an eight, easily."

"You make a habit of guessing women's glove sizes?"

He looked up with a grin. "I'm better at guessing bra sizes."

Another man saying the same words would have made me frown, but Dan…Dan got me to giggle. I put my hand over my mouth to cover it, but the sound slipped free. He looked pleased.

"I made you laugh. That's good, right?"

I ran my finger across my lip and bit my finger gently before taking my hand away. "That's good. Yes."

The food was good. The wine better. The conversation easy and flowing, and as relaxing as anything could be, for me. It helped that his plates had a multicolored pattern of dots on a dark background. Counting the dots between bites kept me occupied.

He kept my glass filled, the sneaky bastard, but I didn't mind. The wine was good, a rich, dark red with a fine flavor that was a pleasure to drink. I didn't realize how much I'd had until I stood and had to grab the back of my chair.

"Whoa," I said with a small laugh. "Wine."

"I'll take that." He stole the plate and silverware from my hands and put it in his dishwasher. He lifted my wineglass and reached for my hand. "Living room."

"You're always doing that," I told him, though I followed him willingly enough.

"What's that?" He looked up as he settled my glass on the coffee table and moved the pillows on the couch so I could sit.

"Telling me what to do."

As I sat, he grinned and leaned in very close, his mouth not quite touching mine. "You like it."

"And that," I breathed. "Telling me what I like."

"Am I wrong?"

I turned my head a little, smiling. "So far…I don't think so."

He nuzzled my earlobe. "But you'd tell me if I was. I'm sure."

I turned my head more, this time not to keep him from kissing me but to encourage it. "Of course."

He'd put both hands on the back of the couch, one on each side of me. His lips brushed the side of my neck, then down, stopping at the small bump of my collarbone. He licked it. I shivered.

"Because you don't really need me to tell you what you like. Do you?

"No."

"Because you already know."

I smiled at that. "Yes."

He pulled away and put a finger to my chin to turn my face toward him. "Or is it that you know what you don't like?"

I looked into his eyes. "That, too."

"Nothing wrong with that, Elle. Not a thing."

He kissed the side of my neck again, then sat next to me. I licked my lips, and his eyes followed the motion of my tongue before he looked back into mine. He stretched his arm out along the back of the couch, his fingertips an inch from my shoulder. I wanted to move closer. I didn't. Then I did.

"Thanks for dinner," I said after a moment of us staring without speaking. "It was delicious."

He buffed his fingernails on his shirt. "Aw, it was nothing. Really."

I reached for my wine and sipped it slowly. My head was buzzing, but unlike other times, when I'd sought oblivion, I wanted to savor the taste. Not get drunker.

We stared again in silence for what seemed like a long time. It became a game, like seeing who'd blink first. He put a hand on my shoulder, toying with the ends of my hair in a way that sent shivers creeping along the back of my neck.

"Elle."

"Dan." I liked the way his name tasted, like wine and garlic.

"I want to kiss you."

Chewing my lower lip is a bad habit but one I can't break myself of. Again, his eyes focused on my mouth. Self-conscious, I slid my tongue over the place I'd gnawed and forced myself to stop biting.

He moved closer, his hand moving closer to the slope of my neck. His thumb pressed against my pulse. He leaned in, moving with slow precision and concentration.

At the last second I turned my face. His kiss landed at the corner of my mouth, his breath hot on my skin and his lips soft. He didn't pull away.

"No?"

I wanted to give a glib answer. More than that, I wanted to turn and let him kiss me on the mouth, to feel his tongue on mine, to open for him. I wanted so badly to open for him, but I simply…could not. I gave a minute shake of my head instead.

Dan kissed my jaw, then down toward my neck, and his lips found the place his thumb had caressed. My heart thumped harder when he kissed me there, and I imagined he must be able to feel the rush of my blood beneath his mouth.

The hand on my throat moved down to cup my breast. A sigh eased out of me, followed by a quick intake of breath when he passed a thumb over my nipple, already straining against the lace. He tweaked it through my clothes, then put his hand flat over it again. A hand over my heart and his mouth on the pulse in my throat, so in two places he could feel my blood rush through my veins.

His other hand slid up to curl around the back of my head, fingers threading through the hair at the base of my neck and tangling a little. Tugging a little. He sucked on my skin as his thumb traced another path over my nipple, and every muscle in my body thrummed under his touch. He pulled me closer as the hand on my breast moved down to inch up my skirt over my thighs, and he curled his fingers over my knee, caressing the skin with soft feather touches that made me jump.

"Ticklish?" He moved to breathe the question in my ear.

"A little."

He slid his fingers higher, tracing little circles on my skin. "Now?"

I let out a small gasping giggle. "Yes."

"Want me to stop?" A little higher, stroking.

"No." A whisper.

Higher still, until his fingertips teased the lace of my panties. "Now?"

"No."

When he finally touched me I moaned. He bit down on my neck as he put his finger inside me. His other hand pressed my back as I arched against him.

"Tell me what you want me to do to you, Elle. I want to hear you say it."

Heat crept up my throat to burn my cheeks, and surely he must have felt it, but I gave him what he asked for. "I want you to touch me."

"Where?"

"There. Where you are—"

He moved his hand against me. "There?"

I nodded and had to swallow hard to answer him. "Yes."

"That feels good?"

He pulled back a little to look at my face. I blinked and faced him, acutely aware of our position, him with his finger inside me and all our clothes still on. He took his hand away, but slowly, so it didn't feel like he was abandoning me but rather taking the time to take care of me.

"Do you always wear skirts?" He smoothed the hem up and down over my thigh.

I leaned back against the pillows, my hand still on his shoulder, his collar between my fingers and the side of his neck. "Not always. But usually."

"I like that." He smoothed the skirt higher, exposing my thigh. He rubbed my skin. "You don't shave up here."

I blinked. "I…no."

Dan scooted down so fast I didn't have time to react until he kissed my bare thigh, just above the knee. "How come?"

"The hair is blond, and it's very fine. Shaving is more of

a pain than it's worth." My answer was honest but difficult to give, as his mouth on my leg distracted me.

"I love it" came his answer as he ran his fingers up and down my leg.

I laughed, moving back a little away from him. His position made me nervous. "Do you?"

He nodded, looking boyish with tousled hair and that grin. He held my leg in his hands and ran his thumb over my knee. "What happened here?"

"I fell."

He kissed the scar, and I frowned.

"Don't, Dan."

He looked up at me again. "Why not?"

"Because it's ugly."

"You think this scar is ugly?" He rubbed it lightly with the tip of his finger. "It's not. It's part of you."

I shook my head. "It ruined my knee."

"How'd you fall?"

"I was running, and I tripped. I landed in some gravel. It tore up my knee. Then, when it was healing, I ran into a coffee table and opened it up again."

He wouldn't let go of my leg. "How old were you?"

"Twelve." I didn't want to think about my scar.

He bent his head and again kissed the ragged, raised line. "It must have hurt."

"It did."

He kissed higher, on my kneecap, then just above, and then a little higher, nuzzling against the fine, downy hairs I didn't shave. My breath caught, and I wanted to pull away. I watched him, his eyes closed as he kissed higher, working his way up to my inner thigh, pushing my skirt along ahead of him until my panties flashed white against the black of my skirt.

"Stop!" I put my hand on top of his head, and he paused, his mouth hovering over the mole nobody ever saw.

He looked up at me, then deliberately kissed it.

"Dan, I said stop." I jerked away from him, though the pillows at the back of the couch made it difficult for me to get very far. I yanked my skirt down and pushed his hands away. Pushed him away.

He sat up, silent. He looked at me. I looked at him. My heart skipped, and I crossed my arms over my chest to keep my hands from trembling.

"What's wrong?"

"I don't…I don't like that."

"You don't like me kissing your mole?" He tilted his head and reached out to tuck a strand of hair behind my ear.

"No." I shook my head. "I'd rather you didn't."

"Because it's ugly?"

That was not my reason, but I lied and agreed. "Yes."

His eyes studied my face. His hand cupped my cheek before moving down to my shoulder. I waited for him to laugh at me or roll his eyes or scowl. To insist I do what he wanted. To press the issue. Men don't like being told no.

He sat back and unbuttoned his shirt, took it off, tossed it to the chair next to the couch. I knew his body already. Knew its smell and taste and the smoothness of his skin. His chest was paler than his arms, but not by much, his shoulders freckled like his nose, but with darker spots. He didn't have six-pack abs, though his stomach didn't bulge.

Curling hair a little darker than that on his head made a small vee in the center, surrounded the brown circles of his nipples, and made a trail down to his belly, where it furred more thickly as it disappeared into his pants.

He bent his arm, showing me his elbow. "Soccer, ninth grade." Set among the wrinkles of his elbow, the scar was almost invisible until he pointed it out. "Hit a rock when I took a dive to make a shot."

He lifted his arm, turning slightly to show me his side, where a small dimple with some distinct lines stood out from the rest of his skin. "I had a mole removed. The intern who did it botched the cut. I had to get four stitches instead of two."

He turned to show me his other side, pointing down close to the waistband. A darker freckle, larger than the others, shadowed his skin. "They told me to keep watch on this one, but so far, it's been fine."

"Why are you showing me this?" The display fascinated me, this step-by-step tour of his body's flaws.

He tapped the base of his throat, where another scar seemed to suddenly appear, though it had been there all along, I had just not noticed. "Campfire accident. My brother and I were dueling with our marshmallow forks. He speared me."

"Oh, God." I winced at the thought and put an involuntary hand to my throat.

"Hurt like a son of a bitch. Little prick missed my jugular, thank God, or else I'd have bled to death." He said it without rancor.

I sat up and touched the scar. "You were lucky."

He closed his hand around my wrist and pressed my hand flat against his chest. "The way I see it, Elle, scars are proof we can survive."

Beneath my palm, his heart thumped. Steady. Constant. Strong.

I looked into his eyes, then took my hand away. I unbuttoned my shirt and took it off the way he had. I reached behind me in the awkward, chicken-wing position into which women must contort themselves to unhook my bra, then coiled it on top of my shirt. Bared that way, I faced him.

Dan put his hands on my shoulders. His thumbs caressed the jut of my collarbone. His fingers curved to touch my back. His gaze traveled over me, inch by inch, and he lifted one hand to touch a mark just above my left breast.

"Curling iron," I said. "I wasn't paying attention."

He brushed a fingertip along the slightly darker skin, then bent his head and kissed it. I took in a deep breath, but this time I didn't pull away. He traced a finger down between my breasts to my belly, and pressed his palm flat on another scar.

"Appendix?" He asked.

I nodded. He smiled. Then he kissed that, too, his lips featherlight but not tickling.

Dan eased the elastic waist of my skirt over my hips, then off. He folded it as carefully as I would have and set it on top of my shirt and bra. He sat back and unbuckled his pants, and I helped him take them off, too. He pushed his boxer briefs down, and I slid out of my panties, my breath hiccupping a little, though we'd been naked together many times.

He pointed to a thin, white curving scar high up on his thigh, near the groin. "Thornbush."

"Ouch."

He grinned. "I was skinny-dipping in the neighbor's pond, and he came out with a shotgun. I didn't notice I'd left some of my skin behind until the next day."

I touched it, and his cock, half-erect, stirred. "You weren't skinny-dipping alone."

"Nope. I was with the neighbor's daughter."

That made me laugh a little. "No wonder he came out with the shotgun."

"Yeah. I got poison ivy, too. Not fun."

I looked up at him. "On your—"

He nodded. "Yep."

I grimaced. "Double ouch."

"Tell me about it. Though I did come to appreciate the lubricating effects of calamine lotion." He made a half-closed fist and pumped it back and forth a couple times.

I laughed again and shook my head. "I'll bet."

He pointed to another line on his shin. "Broke my leg riding my bike."

"You've had it rough," I murmured, with fondness. "Active little lad, were you?"

"Drove my mother crazy." He put a hand on my thigh again, close to the mole on the pale inner flesh. "It's shaped like a heart. Did you know?"

"I know."

He rubbed my thigh lightly but didn't bend to kiss it again. "Why don't you like it? It's pretty."

I shook my head. "I just…I don't like it. That's all."

He seemed to accept my answer. His eyes traveled over me again, cataloging the lumps and marks and lines that made my body unique. This time I didn't pull away. I let him see it all, and I tried hard not to blush or shake when he found them, one by one. The proof I had survived.

He turned my right wrist upward. I have two creases there, one at the base of my hand. One a little lower. A bit beyond that, I have another line. A scar. A bracelet, I've heard some call it, like it's an ornament. Something to show off. He touched it, then looked into my eyes.

"And this?"

"A mistake." I didn't pull my arm away, though I very badly wanted to. I wanted to cradle it against me, hide it. Actually, I wanted to forget it, but I never could.

"How old were you?"

"Eighteen."

He nodded, as though my age made sense. He turned over the other wrist, which bears the same two creases but is unadorned by a scar. He used a fingertip to rub the unmarked skin.

"Only one?"

"I'm left-handed. And I changed my mind."

He nodded again, then brought both my wrists together and lifted them to his mouth. He kissed them and once again I imagined how the rush of my blood must feel against his lips.

"I'm glad you did," he whispered against my skin, then looked into my eyes.

So many times I have run when standing would have better served me. I can't help it. Call it cowardice, or self-preservation. Call it learned behavior. I call it habit. And like any habit, it can be broken.

"Are you?"

He nodded and drew me closer, until we were eye to eye. "Yes."

I shivered, nipples peaking and gooseflesh raising on my arms. "It bled a lot. And it hurt. I didn't think it would hurt so much."

He didn't ask me why, though I might have told him. Dan settled my arms around his neck and pulled me onto his lap, straddling him, our foreheads touching. His cock rose between us, captured between my pubic bone and his belly. My knees pressed the back of his leather couch, but it was soft and didn't hurt.

"Everyone has scars, Elle."

His mouth was very close to mine. I smelled wine on his breath and felt it against my lips. He did not move. He did not push. He did nothing but breathe and look into my eyes, our faces so close all I could see was the blue-green brilliance of his gaze.

And I kissed his mouth.

Birds did not sing, fireworks did not explode. No bells rang. I kissed him like I'd never kissed a man before, and in a way that was true because it had been so long. I kissed him because at that moment I could not imagine not kissing him. I kissed him as proof I could survive.

His mouth parted beneath mine and our tongues met. I put my hands to his face and slanted my head to open further for him, greedy for his mouth now, wanting to taste him and touch him with this intimacy, even though I shook as I did it.

He kissed me back, taking what I gave and giving what I needed. No questions. No demands. He let me lead the kiss, and when I pulled back, breathless, he didn't ruin it with some smart comment. He only ran a hand over my hair and twirled his fingers in the ends.

Dan smiled at me with lips still moist from mine. I have seen clouds part for the sun. I have seen rainbows. I have seen flowers in the morning, covered in dew, and I have seen sunsets so brilliant with fire they made me want to weep.

And I have seen Dan smile at me, his lips still wet from my kiss, and if I had to choose which sight moved me the most I would say it was that one.

There seemed to be some words I should say. Something to mark the occasion. He saved me from it by leaning forward to kiss me again with firm confidence that gave me no time to shy away. His tongue stroked mine as his hand threaded through the back of my hair and brought him close.

We kissed a long time. Soft and hard, tiny feathering touches and deep soul kisses that sent shock waves of arousal through me. We kissed like we had nothing else to do, ever again. He breathed in, I breathed out, we shared air and spit and…trust. We shared trust.

His hands roamed my back, then down to grip my hips and press me against him. His penis throbbed between us. My clit rubbed against the base of it, and he rocked me, rubbing, and my arousal made both of us slippery.

His fingers dug into me, but I didn't mind. We were moving together, our bellies a cocoon for his cock. My breasts scraped his chest. He put a hand flat on my back, holding him close, his hips thrusting upward and every movement urging another burst of pleasure from my clit.

The pleasure ebbed and flowed, the contact indirect enough to keep me pushing closer and closer against him and at the same time hard enough to reward me. He ground me onto his cock, my pussy slick and hot and wet with desire and my clit its own tiny erection. His fingers curled under my ass to add a small up and down motion that made me gasp into his mouth. We rocked together without friction, smooth, skin gliding on skin.

His tongue thrust inside my mouth the way I wanted his cock to fill me, and I moaned. He moaned, his hands hot on my skin, moving me, using my body as a tool for his own satisfaction, and it drove me wild to think that I could get him so hot without even putting him inside me.

He rocked me harder, and I shuddered. *Just a little more. Just a little more.* Just a little more, a little harder, a little faster, a little deeper.

He thrust against my stomach, fucking against me, each movement bringing me closer and closer to the edge. Sweat molded us together. My clit burned. My lips burned. My hips burned from where he clutched them.

He murmured my name into my mouth, then tilted his head back against the pillows. His eyes closed, his face contorted, his penis leaped and throbbed and his body shook.

So did mine. I came, watching him take his pleasure from my body. Bright sparks of pleasure rocketed through me. My thighs jerked. Heat flooded between us as he emptied himself against my skin. I could smell him, musk and sex mingled with my own fluids, and the scent made me groan as my body shook in climax.

He pulled me closer, his arms around me. He held me while our bodies quieted. Our breathing slowed. I tasted the skin of his neck and found it salty. My head fit perfectly on his shoulder.

I didn't want to move. I didn't want to look at him. I didn't want to unglue us. It was too raw and new, this feeling of comfort. Too easily dissolved. I didn't want to lose it. I didn't want to chase it away.

We had to pull apart, of course, unstick ourselves from the aftermath of our passion. It was too physically uncomfortable to do otherwise. My thighs had cramped, something I hadn't noticed when surging toward orgasm but was quite unable to ignore now.

Dan rubbed my back and helped me to extricate myself from his lap. I thought I'd be embarrassed, but he gave me no time to be. His belly and chest glistened with the evidence of our actions. So did mine.

"Want to shower?" His calm reaction to the aftermath allowed me to be calm, too.

Genuinely calm instead of merely blank; I noticed the difference but made no comment. I nodded and held out my hand for him. I helped him up, laughing at the way he hobbled upright, apparently as stiff as I felt.

He looked down at himself, then up at me. He linked my fingers through his. He tugged me closer, oblivious to the stickiness that had made me so squeamish.

The kiss he gave me was tender and almost hesitant, like he feared I'd pull away again. I didn't. There could be no turning back now, I had crossed a line with him. Even I wasn't so fucked up to pretend it hadn't happened.

"Thank you," he said.

A simple phrase, but one that made me flinch. I hid it well, or so I thought, because I knew he didn't mean it the way it sounded. He couldn't know what the words meant to me, how they made me feel, what they made me remember.

I thought I hid it well, but I didn't realize how much he saw. He put a finger beneath my chin to make me meet his eyes.

"Elle, what?"

I shook my head. I didn't want to talk, didn't want words to ruin what we had done. I liked feeling close to him. I liked feeling that I could let him close to me. It made me feel normal. I didn't want to ruin it.

"Shower," I said, pushing past him and going through his bedroom to his bathroom.

I pushed aside the shower curtain and turned on the water. Hot. Steam began to fill the room, which was fine because it shielded the mirror so I couldn't see my reflection, and I got in the shower before he could say anything.

Thank you. He didn't know what that meant to me or why. It didn't matter what he'd been thanking me for—the sex, the kiss, for helping him up from the couch. He'd meant to be polite. Considerate. I knew that. And yet I still turned my face into the too-hot spray and closed my eyes, the words echoing in my head but spoken in another's voice. Someone who thought saying thank you after doing something wrong could make it all better.

He got in the shower behind me and reached around to

adjust the water so it cooled enough not to sting. The shower was big enough to hold both of us but small enough to make it close quarters. When he moved, our bodies brushed. Elbow against belly, thigh against thigh, shoulder to breast.

"Turn around."

I did, because he told me to, and because like so many other times, he knew what I wanted. Dan held up a blue washcloth and squirted shower gel into it, worked it to a creamy lather and turned me so I was out of the main part of the spray.

Then he washed me.

I know my mother did that for me in infancy and childhood, but I have no recollection of her doing it. I have suffered the touch of some and embraced it from others, but I've never had anyone bathe me. He started at my throat, eased the lathered cloth over my breasts, over my belly, my thighs, between my legs. He used soft, gentle motions, nothing rough, nothing hurried. He washed each arm, even each individual finger. He even knelt to wash my legs, lifting each foot to swipe it with the soap and rinsing them before he set them down so I wouldn't slip.

Water splashed my face and stung my eyes when he knelt at my feet. It turned his sandy hair dark and parted it in odd places. It pounded against his freckled back, turning his skin pink with heat and spray.

"We all have scars, Elle," Dan repeated as the water came down all around us, and then he stood aside to let it spray my body. Rinsing away the last of the soap.

Making me clean.

"I have something for you."

Dan pushed an envelope across the table toward me.

"What's this?" A gift?

"Open it." His gaze burned into me, set me back in my chair, fingers hesitating on the envelope's flap.

I pulled out two sheets of paper, stapled. Numbers. Data. Test results. I stared, reading the listings. Cholesterol. Red blood count. HDL. And then, on the second page, other results.

I gaped, and a tiny gasp of surprise eeked out of me. "Oh."

Gonorrhea, chlamydia, HIV. All negative. I folded the paper and put it back in the envelope. I cleared my throat and sipped some ice water. Dan looked expectant.

"Well," I said finally, when it became clear he was waiting for me to speak. "You're in very good health."

Now I knew how old he was, too, along with his blood type.

"I thought it might make you feel better."

I blinked. "About what?"

"Us."

I blinked again. "I'm not sure what you mean."

But I did.

Dan smiled. "Elle. I never asked you if you were on the Pill or—"

"You want to stop using condoms."

He shrugged, cheeks staining a bit pink. It was interesting to watch him blush, for a change. "Well…yeah."

"As a matter of fact," I told him, "I am on the Pill."

He grinned. "Good."

I sat back in my seat, arms crossed. We'd had takeout Chinese at his place, with the promise of a movie after on his big-screen TV, but now I wondered if his real reason for inviting me over was to bring up this subject.

I didn't say anything, let him sweat it for a few moments before I decided upon honesty. "I have never had sex on purpose without using a condom, Dan."

He chuckled. "On purpose? How do you have sex by accident?"

"It wasn't by accident," I said. "Just not on purpose."

I still held the envelope, and my thumbs rubbed the smooth paper in small, steady strokes of five at a time. Five. Pause. Five more. Another pause.

His smile faded. He looked stricken. "Elle?"

I shrugged and put the envelope down. "I get tested for everything you could possibly be tested for every year. I could show you my results, too. I don't have anything, either."

"Elle..." He reached across the table for my hand, and I let him take it. He turned his palm up beneath mine and linked our fingers together. "If it's important to you, I don't mind using them."

I looked at our linked hands. "This would mean we'd have to trust each other."

He squeezed my hand gently. "If you're asking me if I'm sleeping with anyone else, the answer is no."

I nodded a little, then looked into his eyes. "Well. I'm not, either."

I'm not sure if he expected me to give a different answer, but there was no mistaking the look of relief on his face.

"Good."

"You should ask me if I *plan* on sleeping with anyone else, Dan." I said this matter-of-factly, my sense of safety so ingrained it would have been impossible for me not to say it.

"Do you, Elle?"

I shook my head.

"I don't, either." Dan smiled. "Unless you want another night with Jack."

A bubble of laughter escaped me. "Jack can wear a condom, then. But...no, I'm not planning on that, anyway."

"Good." Dan grinned again. "But I don't think I'd want to watch you with anyone else again."

The implications of that gave me pause. "No?"

"No," Dan replied, and squeezed my hand again. "Definitely not."

He got up and came around the table to pull me to my feet. His arms fit around my waist so naturally I couldn't believe I hadn't been born to fit his hands.

He took me to his bed for our first time this new way, and in a way it was like the first time for us. He pulled down his comforter and laid me back on soft sheets, my head cradled by his down pillows. He undressed me and then himself, easing open buttons and unnotching zips, sliding fabric over the curves and valleys of our bodies until we both lay naked with nothing between us.

He kissed my face all over. Forehead. Each eye. The tip of my nose, my cheeks, a series of tiny kisses along my jaw and chin. He kissed my mouth almost chastely, a light, faint brush of lip on lip that withdrew so fast it was almost like it hadn't happened.

He drew his lips down the curve of my throat, pausing at the hollow of my collarbone to lick me. He mouthed up to my shoulder and followed a path down my arm. He kissed the inside of my elbow and my wrist over the scar, then pressed his mouth to my palm and closed my hand over it like he meant for me to save it.

I floated on these embraces, letting myself be worshipped and adored. His mouth skated down my ribs to the small curve of my belly. He blew a breath across my navel, making me shiver with longing. He nibbled my hip. My thigh. Across to the other, adding his tongue, and my body responded to his touch by opening, tensing, heating.

He brushed my pubic curls with his hand, and at that contact my eyes opened wide. I'd been floating with sweet erotic tension created by his mouth, but now my entire body tensed in a much less pleasant fashion. My legs, which had parted as he'd been kissing me, closed.

"Elle." Dan moved up my body to cover me with his.

I was grateful for the warmth, because I had begun to shiver. He propped himself on his elbows and looked into my eyes. His penis, hard but not insistently so, nudged my belly.

"Would you let me kiss you?" He murmured. "Just kiss you. That's all. I promise."

I gave a minute shake of my head. He reached up to smooth his hand along my cheek and trace his fingers along my eyebrows. This tender gesture made me draw a shuddering breath and my lips parted. I meant to speak. I couldn't.

"Do you trust me, Elle?"

I trusted him enough to agree to sex without a condom. I trusted him enough to believe him when he said I was the only one. I trusted him more than I'd trusted anyone in a long, long time.

"Yes, Dan. I trust you."

He smiled. "Let me kiss you, then."

I do not like that I allowed my past to close me off. I do not like that I let circumstances rob me of the ability to have a normal relationship with a man, to have friends, to be happy. I do not like it, but I had felt myself powerless against it.

I didn't want to feel powerless anymore.

"All right."

I tensed again as he kissed his way down my body. He hovered over me. His breath, warm, caressed me. I tensed more, so much that my muscles would ache the next day. I waited for him to betray my trust, to break his promise, to do more than he had said he would do.

Dan kissed me. Soft. Warm. His mouth pressed against

me, and I drew in a sharp breath that made my chest hurt. He kissed me again, but that's all he did.

"Do you want me to stop?"

"No." I shook my head. I had put a hand over my eyes. I tried to relax.

Somehow, covering my face made it better. This was different. This was Dan. It was all right if it felt good. It was supposed to feel good. It was all right if he kissed me there, if he used his mouth to bring me pleasure, because this was Dan. And it was all right.

I felt his mouth on me again. Another kiss. I kept my curls trimmed short, so his lips had no trouble finding my flesh. He kissed my clitoris. My fingers gripped my temple.

I cried out when he used his tongue for the first time. My hips jerked. I put my other hand over my face.

I wanted him to stop. I wanted him to keep going. He inched open my thighs with his hand and licked me again. I swallowed my cry that time.

His fingers traced my body's contours as he kissed and licked my clitoris. It felt good. More than good. It felt like lightning strikes of pleasure striking me. He was gentle but skilled, his mouth echoing more closely the movements I used with my own hand than anything he'd ever done with his. He used his tongue like water, trickling, flowing over my skin. Nothing harsh or jagged, nothing out of sync to jar me from the desire building.

I heard him moan and almost lost myself then.

If you have ever done something that terrified you because you knew it was going to be better, in the long run, you will understand how I felt then.

"Do you...want me to stop?" He sounded like he was having as much trouble speaking as I had answering.

"No," I breathed. I took a hand from my face and reached for his head. His hair tickled my knuckles as I twined my fingers in it. "No, Dan, please don't stop."

He took me to the edge of orgasm and held me there. It felt different, this summit, getting there this way. Less like I was going to fall and more like I was going to fly.

I didn't come so much as I released. Unraveled. I had always thought of orgasm as being like a coiled spring, wound tighter and tighter and exploding, but this time, with Dan's kisses to lead me, I eased into climax like leaves whispering in a tree or ripples on a pond. I felt every spasm, separate and distinct when my clit fluttered. My heart pounded in my ears. I didn't explode, I melted. Liquefied. Became a puddle of pleasure.

And after a moment, when I realized I was breathing again, Dan slid up my body and held me tight against him, looking down into my face. Admiration gleamed in his eyes.

"I want to make love to you," he whispered.

"Yes, Dan," I replied. "Please."

We both groaned when he slid inside me, bare for the first time. I hadn't thought it would feel much different, had believed it would be more conducive to his pleasure than affecting mine, but the brain is an underestimated sexual organ. Knowing he was moving inside me without a condom made as much of an affect as simply feeling him.

He paused, his face buried in my neck. "Oh, God."

I smoothed my hands down his back, feeling the groove

of his spine, the twin dimples at the base of his back. He pushed deeper into me, then pulled out, almost experimentally. Then in again.

He pushed himself up on his hands and looked down at me as he thrust faster, and I moved with him. Eager. My body welcomed him with slick heat. He thrust harder and I lifted my hips to let him get deeper inside me.

He cried out, hoarse, motion becoming ragged. The muscles in his arms and chest stood out. His face tensed, eyes closed, cords in his neck standing out.

"Dan," I urged, as he'd done for me more than once. "I want you to come."

His eyes opened. He gave a low cry. His body jerked, and he throbbed inside me. I imagined his heat filling me. He collapsed on top of me, heavy, but I welcomed the weight. His face on my neck was hot. He kissed my shoulder.

We stayed silent for a moment as our breathing slowed and the air dried our sweat and left us cool in the wake of our passion's heat. He rolled off me, bent to pull up the sheet and tucked it around us, then pulled me against him, my back to his front. I felt his penis, soft and wet and sticky against my buttocks, but was at the moment too tired to get up.

He kissed me between my shoulder blades. I tucked a hand beneath my cheek. His hand drifted up and down my hip, moving the sheet in a motion like waves rolling on the sea.

"He was older than me," I said. "Told me he loved me. Said I was the most beautiful girl he'd ever known, that he'd never love anyone else, ever again. That he'd die if he couldn't have me."

Dan's hand paused in its journey up and down my body for the barest blink of a moment before continuing. "Did you love him?"

"Not like he wanted me to." I closed my eyes, thinking he might expect tears with a story like this but knowing I'd shed none. I had disassociated myself from the memory in many ways, just as in many others it never left me alone. "But…I let him do what he wanted, anyway. He always said thank you, after, like that would make it okay. And sometimes he didn't just want me to do things to him. Sometimes, he wanted to do things to me. Like you did. I've never let anyone else."

He kissed my shoulder again, lips lingering before he spoke. "How old were you?"

"I was fifteen when it started. Eighteen when it ended."

His arms tightened on me for a moment, then a bit more when I didn't tense or pull away. "What made him stop?"

I pushed the sheet off. Sat up. Looked over my shoulder at where he still lay, now on his back.

"He meant what he said, I guess, when he said he'd die if he couldn't have me."

I waited for a platitude, a stifled gasp of horror, a grimace of shock. Dan only sat up and put his arms around me again, turning me into the circle of his embrace.

I waited for him to ask me who it had been, this boy who'd loved me so much he'd rather die than be without me, but Dan didn't ask and so I didn't tell.

Summer nights started later, and I was tired by the time darkness fell. We'd spent the day at a local farmers' market under the hot August sunshine, and I was too lazy now to bother getting up to go home. That had been happening more frequently—me being too lazy to leave. I'd even started leaving a toothbrush there and bringing a change of clothes.

"It's called two truths and a lie," Dan said from beside me.

"Like truth or dare?"

His overhead fan whirled, sending cooler air to caress us. I watched the circling blades and yawned, content at that moment to be semidressed, semiawake, semicogent.

"Sort of. You tell me two truths and one lie, and I'll try to guess which is the lie."

I turned my head the barest inch to look at him. He looked too damned fresh for having spent the day in the sun, which didn't seem to wilt him like it did me. It brought out the pattern of freckles on his nose and bronzed his cheeks, highlighting the crinkles at the corners of his eyes. He slid his hand beneath his cheek as he waited for my answer.

"Why?"

"Because it's fun," he said. "It's a drinking game."

"We're not drinking," I said, still too lazy and contented with the bed and the air to consider getting up.

"I'm afraid of heights. I once ate a worm. And my middle name is Ernest."

"Should I hope the third is a lie?" I rolled onto my side and put my hand beneath my cheek in conscious mimicry of his position.

He smiled. "You can hope, but it's true."

"I believe you ate a worm. So that means you're afraid of heights."

"Very good," he praised. "See how it works? Your turn."

If not for my utter lack of interest in moving, I'd have refused. Being churlish didn't seem worth the effort. "I once sang 'This Is the Song That Never Ends' 157 times in a row. I love the color red. And I've never been to Mexico."

"Easy," he said. "You hate red."

I watched him, curious. "What made that one so easy to pick out?"

"I've never seen you wear it. You won't pick something that's red when you have a choice."

"You've never seen me wear a lot of colors," I told him.

Dan smiled. "True. But definitely not red. Besides, it's easy to believe you've never been to Mexico, lots of people haven't. And you're the sort who'd know exactly how many times you've done something, so that one was a snap. I never heard that song, though."

"I could sing it for you," I said. "But it never ends."

I rolled onto my back again, to stare at the ceiling. I watched the fan blades whir in their lazy roundabout way for a minute. Dan didn't move. He stayed on his side, looking at me. I could feel it.

"You know about the counting?" I kept the question light, neutral, as though I didn't care.

He reached out and twirled a strand of my hair around his finger. "Yes."

"It's…it's that obvious?" I kept my eyes fixed on his ceiling. It had thirty-four cracks in it.

"No. But I noticed you always know how many there are of anything, it doesn't matter what. How many times we've gone round the block looking for a parking spot." I heard the grin in his voice. "How many marbles are in the vase."

"The day I dropped it."

"Yes."

I took an even breath, trying not to care he'd discovered such a thing about me. Such a strange, embarrassing thing. He had seen me in nearly every sexual position, yet this made me feel more naked in front of him than I'd ever felt without my clothes.

"You don't like me knowing."

I turned on my side, away from him. "No, Dan. I don't."

He touched my shoulder, then moved up behind me. His body fit along mine, hip to hip and thigh to thigh. Puzzle pieces. Like we'd been cut from wax and meant to mold together. He sighed, and his breath moved against my bare skin.

"Why, Elle? Why does it matter?"

I couldn't answer. Couldn't explain what counting meant to me. How I'd used it for so long to keep from thinking of things that would otherwise have hurt so bad…I couldn't answer, even to myself.

"It's embarrassing."

He said nothing for a few moments. His hand began a gentle pass along my body, from my shoulder, down my arm, over the slope of my hip and to my thigh, then back up again. His cock and belly pressed against my butt, and it occurred to me our nakedness had not aroused him. That we had reached the point where naked meant comfortable. His hands on me could soothe as well as arouse.

That I no longer felt vulnerable in front of him.

I closed my eyes against the sting of tears and pressed my fingers to my eyes to further hold them back. Dan smoothed his hand over me again and again in silence. I wanted to move away from him and I did not. I wanted to get out of bed, dress, go home to my clean, cool sheets and white, bare walls. To solitude.

"Elle," he said after a while. "I've never broken a bone. I've never ice-skated. And I'm not in love."

I'd seen the scar from the bike accident that had sent him to the hospital with a broken leg. I had seen photos of him on his grandparents' wintertime pond. "Dan. Don't."

He nestled closer to me and pressed his lips to the place he loved to kiss between my shoulder blades. "You are so beautiful, Elle, why won't you let me—"

The word gave me reason to move, and I sat, swung my legs over the bed. "No. Stop it. Don't Dan, you'll ruin it. You'll ruin this."

The bed moved as he sat, too. "How am I going to ruin this? What is this, can you tell me?"

I stood and started looking for my clothes. I did not want to hear what he had to say. Did not. Would not. I would not hear it, I would not listen.

"Elle, look at me."

"This is…sex," I said. "It's…acquaintanceship, it's the two of us finding someone we're compatible with in bed. It's friendship."

"That's not all it is," he said.

I found my shirt and pulled it on without bothering with a bra. Panties. The long gypsy skirt I'd worn to the market. I found one shoe, but not the other.

He watched me from his place on the bed. "What are you doing?"

"I'm getting dressed."

I caught his glance. The face which had, despite my best attempts, become so familiar to me, scowled. He hooked his fingers around his knees.

"I'm going home," I added.

"Why? Because I made you a little uncomfortable? What?"

"Yes!" Shoe in hand, I turned to look at him. "Isn't that reason enough?"

"No, it's not!"

His shout forced me back a step. I held up the shoe in my hand as though it were a shield, and the ridiculousness of my response sent heat to flood my cheeks. He looked offended, then angry.

"You act like you think I'm going to hit you."

I didn't look at him. "I don't think that."

"But you think I'm going to hurt you, right?"

He sounded so hurt and angry I had to turn away. I found my other shoe and held on to the dresser for balance as I slipped them on. *One plus one is two. One plus two is three.* I was counting and didn't care. Couldn't. I needed them, the numbers, the task, needed the distraction so I wouldn't have to look at him.

"You're doing it!" He accused, getting off the bed and stalking toward me. "Blocking me out!"

"I have to go."

I got to the doorway before he snagged my sleeve and yanked me back. I didn't fight him. He put his hands on my arms and turned me to face him.

"Elle, why do you think I'm going to hurt you?"

"I don't think you're going to hurt me," I said at last, each word pulling out of me like tearing thorns from skin and leaving the same bloody wounds behind. "I'm going to hurt you."

"No, you don't have to." He touched my face with soft fingers. "Elle. You don't."

"But I will." I looked into his eyes. "I will, Dan, I will, I know it!"

"No." He forced me to look at him, though his touch remained gentle. "You don't want to."

I jerked my arms away from him. "I didn't say I wanted to! I said I *would!* I don't want to but I'm going to, that's the way it is, that's what happens!"

"It doesn't have to."

If he'd pleaded I could have looked at him with contempt and gone my way. As it was, he talked to me the way he always had, right from the beginning. Like he knew me better than I knew myself. But he didn't.

"I need to go, Dan. Please. Don't make this harder than it already is." I buttoned my shirt with trembling fingers.

"It doesn't have to be hard."

I stopped and looked up at him. "You said you wouldn't."

In reply he gave a small shake of his head and held out his hands, fingers spread. Mea culpa. Forgive me. "I know. But—"

"No!" I cried. This time, my shout drove him back. "No excuses! You said no attachments, Dan! You said so in the beginning! I was very clear with you about what I wanted, and you said…you said you wouldn't."

I couldn't scream through a throat gone so tight I almost

could not breathe. I had misbuttoned, and anger and frustration shook my hands so much I couldn't loose the buttons from their holes to fix the mistake. I clenched my jaw tight, to prevent more words from flying free. I didn't want to do this. Yet it would be done, no matter what I wanted, and the powerlessness of it made me grip the misaligned tails of my shirt hard enough to leave wrinkles in the fabric.

"You agreed." A deep breath had let me speak without my voice shaking. "You said you wouldn't get attached."

He said nothing. He stood before me, unconcerned with his nakedness. I couldn't look at him that way, at his body I had touched with every part of mine. I reached for a pair of scrubs from the top of his dresser and tossed them. They hit him in the chest, and he grabbed them, pulled them on, saved me from the shame of having to fight with him unclothed.

"Elle, we've done everything a man and woman can do together, almost. We've done things I never dreamed of doing. That I never wanted to do with another woman. When I wake up and you're not here beside me, I miss you."

"You'd miss a dog or a cat, too, if you got used to it on your pillow and suddenly it decided to sleep on the chair."

He put his hands on his hips. "I miss you when you're not with me. When I see something funny, I always look right away to make sure you're with me to see it, too. And if you're not, I want to tell you about it, just to see you laugh. You're beautiful when you laugh Elle."

"Stop it! Stop saying that, you know I don't like it!"

Again I headed for the door, and again he blocked my way. "Why can't you let me inside?"

"You've been inside me at least a hundred times."

I knew the words were cruel. The tone crueler. I waited for his gaze to shutter or blaze in anger.

"You let me fuck you," he said quietly. "But you never let me inside you. Not really."

I stopped. "I'm sorry."

"Then don't go. Stay here with me. I'll make popcorn."

"I'll have to count it," I warned him, letting him pull me closer into his embrace.

"I'll help you," Dan said. "Every bite."

I let him cuddle me against him. "I'm sorry, Dan."

"Shh," he said. "You don't have to be."

I'd bought the book on a whim from the independent bookstore downtown, and given it to Dan wrapped in aluminum foil. *Three Hundred and Sixty-Five Sexual Positions*. With creative names like Cradle of Love and The Gay Blade, it promised to have something for every gender combination.

Dan had laughed when he opened it, but he'd also immediately started flipping through the pages. "This one?"

I looked at the line drawing that showed a man holding a woman upside down while, apparently, they gave each other oral. I laughed. "Oh. I'm so sure."

He looked at the book again. "Doesn't that look like fun?"

"No." I took the book and flipped the pages until I found one that seemed more realistic. "This one."

He looked at it. "Says we need a rocking chair."

I looked pointedly at the corner of his bedroom, where the cane-backed chair was almost invisible beneath the clutter of clothes, magazines and junk mail he habitually piled on it. It took him a second to clear it, another to turn with a grin. A moment more and his belt was undone, the zip pulled, his pants around his knees.

I watched all of this from my spot on the bed, the book still in my hands. "You are such a horndog."

He grinned, unapologetic. "Ah, but that's why you love me."

I ignored that statement and tossed the book aside as I stood and pulled my shirt over my head. My nipples were already erect, my cunt already getting slick.

We'd been lovers for five months. I did not want to love him. But I couldn't stop wanting to fuck him.

Dan stripped off the rest of his clothes and sat on the chair. His penis rose against his belly and he stroked it lightly as I wiggled out of my clothes. It wasn't much of a strip tease, but the heat in his gaze showed me it didn't matter that I wasn't swinging around on a pole or wearing six-inch platform shoes.

"Wait."

I paused, my thumbs hooked in the sides of my panties.

Dan made a twirling motion with his finger. "Turn around."

I did, my heart skipping at his low whistle of approval. I'd bought the thong on a whim and hadn't told him I'd be wearing it. The soft lacy fabric had been far more comfortable than I'd expected.

"Jesus," he muttered. "Let me see the front."

I obeyed, pleased at his reaction. The front was sheer peach lace that blended with my skin to make it look almost like I wore nothing.

"Leave them on." He stroked himself harder and leaned back in the chair.

I took my thumbs out of the sides and moved toward him. He reached for me, helped me slide my legs through the arms of his chair and settle onto his lap. We faced each other, this position familiar but for the wobbling of the chair under us.

"All those positions and this is the one you wanted to try first?" He tilted my head toward him to kiss me.

"It will be fun," I scolded. "Don't be so pessimistic."

"Elle, anything with you is fun."

That pleased me, too, and I couldn't hide the smile. I put a hand between us to tug aside the thin lace panel between my legs and Dan helped guide me down onto his cock with a sigh.

"Very nice," he said as I settled onto him. His hand came up to stroke my breasts and tug down the cups of my bra. He bent to kiss each nipple.

"It's not much use if you take them out. I might as well take it off," I said.

"Shh," Dan ordered, voice muffled against my flesh. "Fuck me."

Inelegant wording but it made me twitch in reaction. My inner muscles clamped him. I smiled again when he moaned a little. I did it again, working him as I pushed the floor to start us rocking.

Effortless sex. The movement of the chair took the place of any thrusting he'd have done. All I had to do was keep pushing. We rocked, moving him inside me. The lace of my panties rubbed my clit in a way that made me shiver and moan, and I let my head fall back as his mouth suckled my nipples.

I was almost ready to come when my phone rang. Dan looked up from my breasts, his face flushed. We didn't stop rocking. The phone kept ringing.

"Voice mail," I muttered, too close to even think of stopping to take a call.

He nodded and took my nipple between his lips again. The chair rocked harder, pushing him deeper inside me. The gentle rub-rubbing of my clit on his belly wasn't enough, and before I could slip a hand between us he anticipated it and pressed his thumb there. The touch jolted me closer. I made a mindless noise of pleasure.

My phone rang again. "Fuck," I muttered.

"I am," Dan said, and we both laughed.

It was the laughter that sent me over, that ease and comfortable manner he had. I came with a gasp, clutching his shoulder hard enough to leave a mark. My phone rang again, and this time I started to be more than annoyed.

Dan came a moment later with a muffled grunt and a thrust that made the chair skid along the polished wooden floor. We settled against each other, our breath falling into the same rhythm before the phone rang again and mine hitched in my throat.

"I'd better get it."

"Can you reach it?" Dan gripped my hips. "I'll hold you."

Of course it would have been easier to get up, but he'd tempted me into the hint of whimsy. I bent backward, hooking my bag with a finger and yanking it toward me as he pulled me upright again.

"You're very flexible," Dan said. "I think I saw a few positions in that book you'd be good at."

I laughed, though this phone call was making my stomach churn. One call would have been nothing unusual. Four meant my mother. I punched in the buttons to access my voice mail, listened to the message, deleted it. Calmly. Without outward reaction. But when I saw him looking at me quizzically, I knew that I'd merely thought I wasn't reacting, when in reality, I was.

"You just went the color of chalk." Dan rubbed my arms. "What's wrong?"

"It's my dad," I said in a faint voice not very much like my own. "He's dying."

Chapter 17

If I'd had my choice, I wouldn't have had Dan come with me. He didn't ask me, however, what I wanted, and so I found myself bathed, dressed and in the passenger seat of his car before I really had time to think. It was good he drove me. I'm sure I'd have had an accident. I couldn't even get the seat belt to click, as my fingers fumbled it too much. He had to reach across and buckle it for me.

We made it to the hospital in time for me to say goodbye, though I didn't have much to say. My mother had set up a vigil by my father's bedside, and she wasn't about to allow her position as the Martyred Widow to be preempted by the Prodigal Daughter.

I did what I could. I sat at his other side, holding a hand that felt as dry and brittle as sticks. This was the man who had taught me to read. Who had taken me fishing, taught me how to bait a hook. Taught me how to whistle like the boys did, with two fingers. This was the man who had walked me to the bus on my first day of kindergarten and had been the one to cry when my mother had not.

This man was my father.

He died without a few words of pithy wisdom. Without even opening his eyes. I waited, my two hands holding his, for some revelation. Something. Some sign he knew I was there. That he cared. That he was sorry, maybe, or maybe that he wasn't. I waited for acknowledgment, but in the end he just slipped away without bothering to give me anything, and I was outraged and disappointed and struck sick with grief, but I was not surprised.

My mother didn't seem to know he'd passed until I put his hand down and got to my feet. She looked at me with narrowed eyes and a small, hard smirk. "Coward" that look said. "Running away again."

"He's dead, Mother." I sounded cold and hadn't meant to.

She looked at him. Then she began to wail. She keened and howled like the mythical banshee. One that's come too late to warn the living of death but in time to shriek it's already happened.

Nurses streamed into the room. I was pushed aside, backed out, ignored amongst the bustle of their preparations, and I didn't care. There was nothing for me to do in that room. My heels clattered on the industrial tile in the hall. I heard them telling my mother to calm down. I heard them suggesting she be given "something." I heard silence a few moments later, but by then I was already at the end of the hall and pushing through the doors into the waiting room where Dan sat on a couch the color of frat boys' vomit and sipped coffee from a foam cup.

"Elle." He got to his feet. "How is he?"

"Dead," I said flatly. "And my mother is acting like the holy fucking ghost herself."

He grimaced and reached for me, but I stepped back. "I need a drink."

He held out the coffee to me, but I shook my head. Our eyes met. I don't know what he saw in mine, because I have a hard time recalling what, at that moment, I was feeling. If I was feeling at all. It seems likely I was angry, but the memory is cloudy, like viewing something underwater.

"There's a bar across the street," he said.

"There always is, isn't there?" came my oh-so-clever reply, and as I had done when we first met, I let him take me there.

It seemed fitting to toast my father's passing with a gin and tonic, since that was his drink of choice. I've never been so spectacularly drunk. Shit-faced. Pissed. Trashed, wasted, sloshed. Or, as my father had been fond of saying, before the alcohol had robbed him even of his desire for conversation, extremely well lubricated.

I remember walking into that bar, a nice enough little pub called The Clover Leaf. I don't remember walking out. I think I recall a long walk down dark streets, and singing, but that might have been a dream. At any rate, the next thing I do remember with any clarity is the inside of my toilet bowel and the sound of blood rushing in my ears as I heaved.

It shouldn't be difficult to imagine how a person such as me, a woman who barely feels comfortable around people when she is well, feels to have an audience when she is ill.

That it was self-inflicted was no comfort, and in fact made my shame worse. I squirmed with it like the worms on the hooks my father had shown me how to bait. I cursed with it. I'm sure I frankly wallowed in it.

Dan, who could have left without a word of judgment from me, stayed the whole time. He brought me ginger ale to sip and saltine crackers, which I promptly vomited again. He held my hair back, then found a ponytail holder in my drawer to do it for me. He rinsed and wrung cool cloth after cool cloth to put on the back of my neck. Most of all, he sat, rubbing my back, while I wept or puked, or sometimes both at the same time.

There's a reason why there are clichés. Because much of the time, they're true. That it's always darkest before dawn proved itself to me that night as I crouched on my knees and lost my guts over and over. While I lost my self-control.

He made a pillow for me from a towel and covered me with a sheet. I slept in the clothes I'd worn to the hospital. I woke with muscles aching, head pounding, stomach churning but staying in place. Dan slept next to me, propped between the tub and cabinet under the sink. His head had fallen forward. He snored.

He opened his eyes when I shifted. "Hey."

I said nothing, afraid to open my mouth. Afraid to move too much. It felt as though my head were going to fall off, which might have been a blessing, considering how much it hurt.

Dan reached forward. "How are you feeling?"

I swallowed with a grimace at the taste of sickness. “I feel like shit.”

He looked sympathetic. “You drank a lot.”

“Yeah.”

I rubbed my eyes and brought my knees to my chest to rest my forehead on them. The tile floor hurt my butt and made it cold, but I couldn’t rouse myself to move. I was still bone tired.

And my father was still dead.

I waited for grief to strike me but I’d numbed myself so sufficiently the night before, I think I was incapable of feeling much of anything. Dan moved closer and rubbed my back.

“Why don’t you get in the shower? It might make you feel better.”

I lifted my head to look at him. “You stayed with me all night.”

He smiled and stroked a piece of hair off my forehead. I cringed to imagine how I must look, hair glued with sweat, rings under my eyes, skin pale. He didn’t seem to notice.

“Of course I did. I couldn’t leave you alone. I was worried about you.”

The concern in his eyes made my stomach twist a little more, but I didn’t feel like I had to throw up again. He cupped my cheek, then squeezed my shoulder and got to his feet.

“C’mon. I’ll run it for you.”

He made the water just the right temperature, not too hot or too cold. Like an ancient lady, I stood, grabbing the edge of the sink for support. The room spun and I closed my eyes against the sight, gritting my teeth to keep another set of gags from forcing my stomach out through my throat. Shoulders hunched, I shuffled across the tiled inches to the shower. He held my hand and arm to help me in.

Once in the shower, I got down on my knees again to let the water pound against my back. I put my forehead in my hands on the shower floor. This was a favorite position of mine, almost fetal, which allowed water to surround me as I rested. If I wanted, I could lie flat on my back with my legs slightly bent in this shower, which I'd had built oversize during the renovations. I'd slept this way, with hot water blocking out the world and reminding me of what it might have been like cradled in the womb.

I might have slept now, so exhausted was I still, but the rattle of the curtain on its rings announced Dan's presence. He got in beside me. I didn't move over to give him any room.

"Elle, are you all right?"

"I'm fine."

"You're not acting fine."

I turned my face to let water splash on it. "My father just died, Dan, and I went on a bender. How fine do you think I am?"

He rubbed my back. "Okay, I get it. Ask a stupid question—"

"Exactly." I wasn't up to verbal sparring.

He reached for my shower gel and a washcloth, and he started washing my back. It felt too good for me to make him stop. After a few moments he uncapped another bottle and began working shampoo through the thickness of my hair. It couldn't have been easy, especially without me helping him, but he persevered, even rinsing out all the soap using the cup I'd set on the ledge for just that purpose. He added conditioner, working it through the strands and massaging my skull with strong fingers. He massaged my shoulders, too, and my back, the water assisting him like some sort of fancy spa treatment.

By the time the water started to run cold, I was as limp as a rag doll, and he helped me out of the water and dried me with such tender care I wanted to weep again. I didn't. I only wanted to.

He wrapped me in my robe and dried my hair, then took me to my bedroom. He tucked us both into my bed beneath fresh sheets that smelled good. As soon as my head hit the pillow, my eyes closed. I heard the sound of his breathing, but in moments I was asleep.

There was to be a funeral, of course, and a gathering at the house, after. The perfect theater for my drama-queen mother to parade her grief in front of friends and family. I didn't begrudge her, really. She'd never been a perfect mother or wife, and I had my issues with her, but she had been married to the man, after all. She'd chosen to stay with him. She'd earned her martyr's crown.

Considering my father's body had enough alcohol in it to keep him pickled for a year, she nonetheless wasted no time in setting it all up. If she couldn't wait to get him into the ground, I don't suppose I can blame her. I understood that urgency, that sense of having to always get the worst out of the way so as to move on to something else. I'd learned it from her.

"When are you coming home?" Her voice stabbed me through the phone.

"I told you, Mother, tomorrow morning."

"Are you bringing that man?"

I sighed. Light the color of butter streamed through my kitchen window. I traced the line it made on my table with the end of my pencil.

"I don't know yet. Maybe."

She was actually silent for a good thirty seconds. "Don't expect me to let him sleep in your room with you. Just because Daddy's gone doesn't mean I'm going to allow you to slut around in my house."

"I told you, Mother, I'm not staying overnight."

I heard the snap of her lighter and the intake of breath. I imagined her drawing the smoke into her lungs and holding it, letting it stream from her nostrils in twin streams. She slurped, probably coffee, and I closed my eyes against the sudden sorrow that someone I knew so well should be someone who consistently brought me so much grief.

"The funeral's at 10:00 a.m. People will come over right after. It will be late by the time it's over. And you'll be drunk."

"Then it's a good thing I'll have a designated driver, isn't it?" I tried not to let her accusation sting me, but of course it did. She knew just how to stick that needle between my ribs every time.

"Oh, your *friend* doesn't drink?" The emphasis she put on the word *friend* was meant to be insulting, but I refused to take it that way.

"He does. We'll be fine, Mother."

She snorted, and I heard the tap-tap of her long nails on

some hard surface. The side of her coffee mug, the one with the picture of Andrew on it. Her favorite.

"I'm going to need you," she said after a moment, wheedling. "I'll need you to go with me to Mass on Sunday."

"I don't go to Mass. You know that."

"They won't chase you out, Elspeth," she said sharply. "It might do you some good to go to confession, you know. Wash yourself clean."

My fingers tightened on the phone. "I don't have to confess to sins that aren't mine."

She laughed. When I was younger, I had thought my mother's laugh sounded like wind chimes. I thought she was a fairy queen, beautiful and perfect, her love unattainable. Her laugh hadn't changed, but my perception of it had. Now it sounded like a rusted metal gate that refused to open all the way. The kind that would catch your clothes and tear them if you tried to squeeze through it.

"I'll be there tomorrow morning." I told her. "I'll meet you at the church."

"At least I know you'll have a black dress," she retorted. "Put on some makeup, for Christ's sake. Tell me you won't embarrass me."

"No more than you will yourself," I returned and had the guilt and satisfaction of hearing her sniffle.

She hung up on me without saying goodbye. I didn't mind. I had another call to make, one I was dreading only a bit less than the one to my mother. I dialed the familiar number but got Chad's voice mail.

His jovial message made me smile. "Hey, this is Chad. Stop wishing you were me and leave a message, already."

After the beep, I spoke. "Chaddie, it's Elle. Dad died. The funeral is Saturday. Tomorrow, Saturday. There's going to be a wake. I think you should come home, Chad."

I found speaking to his voice mail easier than telling him personally. The news of our father's death slipped off my tongue with no more discomfort than if I'd been telling him about the loss of a pet or a stranger.

"She's going to expect me to go to the cemetery, and I guess I'm going to have to go. I could really use you there, little brother." My throat tightened, and I had to clear it several times before I could find my voice again. "She wants me to come home, and…I'm going to go. I think I should go, I mean, I think I have to, it's the right thing to do. But I could use you there. I know you don't want to come home, Chad, but this is your last chance to say goodbye to him. It might be good for you, too."

I had no idea if his voice mail had a limit to the length of the messages it took, but so far I'd heard no beep to indicate it was cutting me off.

"I'm taking Dan with me," I said into the receiver. "If you come home, I'd like you to meet him. Okay, please call me on my cell, I'll be heading out to Mom's tomorrow. The funeral's going to be at St. Mary's, and everyone's going to Mom's after that. I love you. Call me."

I hung up, and though my phone rang a couple more times, it was never my brother returning my call.

"I'm not Catholic. Does it matter?" Dan eyed the front of the church with apprehension.

"Not to me." I took in a deep breath and adjusted the

lapels of my black suit one more time. I hadn't had to buy something new, my closet was filled with black and white, but I hadn't worn this in a while and it had gotten loose. It was not so much that I cared how it fit for vanity's sake, but because I knew the Dragon Queen would be eagle-eyeing me for loose threads, missing buttons, runs in my hose, worn soles on my shoes. I wouldn't have been surprised if she held a color wheel up to my face and told me my shade of lipstick wasn't in my palette.

"You look fine." Dan rubbed my shoulder. "Are you ready to go in?"

"You should leave." I turned to face him. My hands twisted my handkerchief into a ball and released it, over and over. "Go. You don't need to sit through this. It's going to be long and really boring."

Dan's brow creased. "Elle, I don't mind. I want to be here for you."

Faster my fingers twisted, as I looked from him to the church and the line of people slowly filing in. "Dan, I appreciate it, I really do, but I think maybe I should do this alone. My mother—"

"Your mother needs you to be here," he cut in smoothly. His hand rubbed my shoulder again, then slid down to take mine, hanky and all. "But you need someone to be here for you. You want me to stay."

I couldn't refute that any more than I could any of the other things he'd shown me I wanted. I sagged, shoulders hunching, and he put his arms around me. His embrace was matter-of-fact, nothing sensual about it. An embrace without lust. And he was right. I needed it, and I wanted it.

"Are you ready?" He asked after a few moments, his mouth moving against my hair. "It looks like everyone's gone inside."

I nodded against the front of his suit. Today he wore a somber black tie. I missed the trout and the hula dancers. I ran the soft material between my fingers, up and down, then let go.

"I'm ready."

He put a finger to my chin to lift my gaze to his. "Elle, I'm here for you. Okay? If you feel like you need something, let me know."

I nodded, voice stolen by emotion I wasn't ready to face. Dan smiled. And, as I usually did when confronted with Dan's smile, I smiled, too.

St. Mary's is not a large church, but it is lovely. It had seen my first communion. My confirmation. It had heard my first confession and all the ones that had followed. I'd spent my childhood here under the gaze of the Blessed Virgin and, stepping through the heavy wooden doors to breathe in the scent of incense and holy water, I was transported.

Dan's hand fit neatly under my elbow, guiding me. I dipped my fingers into the holy water font, the odd oily slickness of the water proof to me it was more than just water but something else, something divine. I pressed wet fingers to my forehead, the hollow of my throat, each shoulder, then rubbed them together until they dried.

Father McMahon had already begun, and more than one head turned as Dan and I walked down the aisle toward the first pew where my mother's black-garbed figure awaited. It might have been sacrilege to imagine this was how Hansel and Gretel had felt walking through the forest toward the witch's house, but I figured if the holy water font hadn't started to boil when I dipped my fingers into it, God would surely overlook a little harmless imagination. Besides, I thought as I genuflected and made the sign of the cross, the analogy was faulty. Hansel and Gretel hadn't known they were heading to their doom. I, on the other hand, had a pretty good idea about what awaited me.

Dan hesitated behind me, not making the quick, one-kneed motion that Catholics have perfected before sliding into the pew beside me. I heard Mrs. Cooper, my mother's neighbor, murmur something to her husband Fred in the pew behind us, but I didn't turn around to look at her. Mrs. Cooper used to bake me cookies and had taught me how to crochet. I hadn't seen her in at least ten years.

My mother grabbed my arm the moment I sat down and clung to me as though she were hanging over an abyss and I the only rope that could save her. Considering I'd often imagined my mother as hanging from a rope over an abyss, the irony of her sudden dependence on me wasn't lost, but rather made me smile in an entirely inappropriate way I hid behind my hanky.

She ignored Dan, and Mass was not the time for introductions. Once more I was transported. I'd forgotten how the familiar words used to soothe me, or how the bars of colored light coming in through the stained-glass windows always added up to numbers with perfect square roots. I'd forgotten the ebb and flow of religion and how it could make you mindless, and that wasn't necessarily bad. My head might have forgotten how to pray, but my heart had not. I murmured the words, counting the beads of my rosary. It was learning one could pray using numbers that had first convinced me everyone must have never-ending calculations in their heads. I'd been astounded almost nobody else did.

I was aware of Dan beside me, but he sat quietly without saying much of anything. He didn't hold my hand, nor did he reach for a prayer book. He watched with interest on his face, like he'd never been to a Mass before, his eyes following the priest's back-and-forth meandering around the altar as though he were viewing a particularly interesting tennis match. At the waving of the incense burner, he let out one stifled sneeze.

I looked at him. We both smiled. I gave him my handkerchief. After that, he held my hand even though my mother sniffed and muttered and stepped up her wailing on my other side.

My father was one of seven children and the first to die, so there was much commentary given about him before the Mass had ended and we could "go in peace to love and serve the Lord." I couldn't avoid being part of the line of mourners at the door, shaking hands and accepting the sympathies of those who filed by us. Dan kept to my side, gamely taking hugs and shaking hands and murmuring thanks to those who must have assumed he had a right to be there. I was glad to have him at my side, a buoy helping me keep above the water my mother would have dragged me under. She kept her glare mostly hidden beneath the veil of her hat or her gigantic handkerchief, but every so often in a lull between mourners she'd turn and shoot me with venom, always adding an extra dose for Dan, who either didn't notice or was calmly unconcerned.

By the time the last person had left the church and headed to cars for the procession to the cemetery, my feet and back ached, and my face hurt from trying to smile and look woeful at the same time. My head hurt, too, from tension that radiated from my skull down the back of my neck and knotted between my shoulder blades.

"I've rented us a car," my mother said stiffly. "Since I knew I couldn't expect you to drive."

"I'll be happy to help you to it, Mrs. Kavanagh." They were the first words Dan had spoken to my mother, and I tensed, waiting for her to snap his head off.

Ah, but she was the queen of many things, the art of lulling her prey into a state of false security only one of them. "Thank you, Mr….?"

"Stewart."

"Mr. Stewart," she said with an imperious lift of her chin to indicate the disgrace of having to even ask.

The car she'd hired was big, black and ostentatious, but while I might have rolled my eyes another time, I was glad for her pretensions this time. It meant there was plenty of room for the three of us. There would have been room, even, for two more…but those two weren't here.

"So, Mr. Stewart," said my mother without preamble. "What did you think of the Mass?"

"It was very nice." Dan's answer was diplomatic.

"I noticed you didn't pray along," my mother continued.

I groaned. "Mother, for God's sake—"

"I'll thank *you,*" she said sharply, rapping me on the knee with her knuckles, "to watch your mouth."

Precious advice from a woman who had once stood in

the doorway of my room and told me I was a no-account whore whose lying tongue would rot and sprout maggots on my way to Hell. I glared at her, but Dan seemed unfazed.

"Well, no. I'm not Catholic. I didn't think it would be appropriate. I was there to support Elle."

She sniffed, sitting back against the expensive leather seat. "What are you, Lutheran? Methodist? Don't tell me you're one of those Evangelicals."

"No." Dan smiled with a small shake of his head. "I'm Jewish, actually."

For once my mother seemed to have nothing to say. My own jaw dropped, though I recovered quickly. He looked at us both with a hint of amusement in his shining eyes.

"I see," my mother said, though I was sure she didn't. I was also sure she'd never met a Jew in her entire life. I was surprised she didn't ask him to part his hair and look for the horns.

Dan met my eyes, his mouth quirked in a tiny smile. He gave a small shrug, which I returned. The revelation kept my mother quiet until we got to the cemetery. Not as many people came to the graveside service, which was fine with me. Fewer hands to shake. Fewer hugs to suffer.

We got out of the expensive hired car on a small hill of grass, and my stomach fell away. This time I was the one hanging over the abyss, and Dan was my rope. While my mother marched her completely competent self down the small gravel path toward the pile of dirt and open grave that awaited her approval, I gripped Dan's hand so hard my nails gouged his skin. I had to turn away from the sight.

"Roses," I said through gritted teeth.

He looked down the hill and put himself between me and the sight. “Doesn’t she know you’re allergic?”

I had forgotten I’d told him that lie, because really, what’s one amongst so many?

“She knows.”

He put his hands on my upper arms, rubbing lightly. “Then we won’t go down there.”

“I have to go down there, it’s my father’s service, she’ll be expecting me…”

I was babbling and knew it but couldn’t seem to stop. Dan shushed me, his hands stilling. I looked up at him.

“You don’t have to do anything you don’t want to do, Elle.”

I sucked in a deep, shuddering breath. Sunshine streaked his face, showing his freckles and the lines around his eyes. In bright light like this I saw the gold flecks in the blue-green irises.

“We can listen from up here,” he told me. “You don’t have to go down there if you don’t want to.”

He was right, but what’s more, wouldn’t budge. I babbled some more about duty, respect, honor, and expectations, and he listened to all of it but did not step aside to let me move toward the service that had begun without me.

“You don’t have to go down there,” he insisted. His hand came up to smooth my hair. “It’s all right.”

It was not all right. None of it was. It was wrong, all of it, and I knew I’d pay the price for my cowardice if not then, then later. I always did.

My family is large and boisterous, happy for the most part and, for the most part, drunks. Alcohol is the thread that ties them all together, the jolly Irish aunts and uncles from my father's side and my mother's sentimental Italian relatives. I have all four living grandparents and a slew of cousins, many of whom are now married and starting families of their own. I hadn't seen any of them in years, though a lot of them still lived close to the town in which my mother still lived. They probably saw more of her than I did, spent more time in her house with its never-changing decor and my father in his chair in the corner of the den.

The chair was empty now and looking forlorn, and though there were more asses than seats to put them in, nobody sat in it.

"Like some sort of shrine," I muttered from my spot by the wall. I had indeed been drinking, but only one glass of wine. A drink at which my father's family would scoff and my mother's sing odes. "This whole house is a fucking shrine."

Dan had been welcomed in with open arms by everyone but my mother, who was too distracted in her role as Grieving Widow to make much of a fuss. He'd shaken hands and suffered through good-natured ribbing with an aplomb I envied. He'd fetched and carried drinks and plates of food for the old ladies, flirting with such chivalry he set them all to tittering.

He leaned against the wall next to me. "Your family seems nice."

I didn't answer him right away, sipping wine and letting it fill my mouth before swallowing. "Most families do, don't they?"

He didn't have much to say to that. He looked around.

My mother hadn't changed much since I'd lived there. Her frenzy for having the latest and the best was reflected in her appearance less than the house's. The television, a big screen that dwarfed the room, must have been my father's idea.

My cousin Janet appeared in front of us, her face and form rounder than I'd seen her last but the infant in her arms the clear reason for it. She smiled at Dan and reached to give me a one-armed hug that didn't jostle the baby. I admired her skill and supposed new mothers got used to doing things that didn't wake their babies.

"Ella," she said warmly. "It's so good to see you. How… how have you been?"

"Good. You're looking good. Congratulations." I peeked down at the sleeping baby. "I got your announcement."

"We got your gift," she said. "It was lovely. You made it yourself?"

I glanced at Dan and my cheeks heated at his look of interest. "Yes."

"It's beautiful." She turned to Dan. "She knitted us the most gorgeous baby blanket. Hi. I'm Janet."

I made a quick introduction. "I was glad to do it."

"We'd hoped to see you at the baptism," she said. "Your mother said you were out of town."

"Oh…yeah. I travel a lot." Another lie.

She nodded sympathetically. "Well, don't be a stranger. You know where we live."

She looked across the room at Sean, her husband, who had graduated from high school with me. "We'd love to see you. And you, Dan," she added. "Any friend of Ella's is a friend of ours."

The beauty of Janet's words was that she meant them. She gave me another hug, this time one that woke her sleeping angel, and with a murmured apology about breast-feeding and diapers, she moved off through the crowd.

More family and friends came through, most of them pausing to talk to me and tell me how good it was to see me. I nodded and smiled at all of them, because I did appreciate their sentiments. I did. It wasn't their fault I had run away and didn't want to look back.

"Why," Dan asked after another round of relatives had faded for the moment, "do they call you Ella?"

My third glass of wine had left me with flushed cheeks and a pleasant tipsiness I didn't want to become full-blown intoxication. "It's my name."

Another cousin interrupted us. By the time she was done reminding me I owed her a phone call, my bladder had begun to twinge. The small powder room off the kitchen had seen a steady stream of action, and I'd just seen Uncle Larry heading into it. I couldn't wait for Uncle Larry. That left the bathroom upstairs.

"I'll come with you," Dan said when I told him where I was going. "I need to go, too."

We wove through the throng, most of them well on their way to being soused on my father's gin. I put my foot to the bottom of the stairs, looking up. I hadn't been up there since leaving home, but my hand found the light switch with unerring ease, proving once again the body remembers what the mind tries to refuse.

Sixteen stairs. I'd counted them too many times to forget that. What once had been white shag now was bare, polished wood with a stapled runner of beige and gold flowers running up the center. It's nearly impossible to get blood out of white shag carpet.

"You all right?" Dan said from behind me.

"Fine." I took a step with him close behind.

Faces followed us up the stairs. My mother had hung pictures in matching wooden frames, each in its place the same precise distance from the next. One was askew, possibly knocked by a stray elbow as people passed each other on the narrow stairs, and I reached a finger to straighten it.

"Is that you?"

The gap-toothed smile and ponytails were mine, indeed. "Yes."

"You were a cutie."

I looked at him with a raise of my eyebrow. "Sure. If you like kids who look like monkeys."

Dan laughed. "You didn't look like a monkey, Elle."

I'd have been more than happy to keep moving, but Dan studied all the photos. Elementary school pictures. Photos of my mother and father in bad 1970s haircuts and polyester fashions, grinning with an infant in front of them. Sports teams with the individual photo set off to one side. She had so many pictures hung it seemed impossible that any could be missing, but I knew they were. She'd taken them down, every hint or reminder she'd had two sons, not just the perfect one. It was as though Chad had never existed, and I was an afterthought, my smile captured behind glass as though to prove a point and not because of maternal pride.

Dan was smart. It didn't take him more than a moment or two to scan the wall of photos and see there were few of me and many of another. His brow furrowed in concentration as he looked at frames filled with the same smile. The one that did not belong to me.

At the top of the stairs was the final set of photos. A triptych, a threefold frame. The first held a picture of Andrew, grin broad, skin tanned, eyes twinkling. The second slot was a photo of me, a girl with long dark hair and puffy cheeks, skin flawed with pimples. No smile. The third slot was empty.

"Elle." Dan looked from the frame to one a bit farther down in which I held up a fish for the camera, my head tipped back with laughter. There had been only three years difference in time between the pictures but a lifetime had happened. "Is this you, too?"

"Yes," I answered and kept moving to the hallway above.

He caught up to me, followed me down the hall. His hand caught and turned me gently. "What happened?"

"I stopped smiling" came my answer. "And nobody asked me why."

We stood like that for one of those eternal moments that last seconds but seem like hours. A shadow passed across his gaze. I put my hand on the doorknob directly behind me, pushed open the door, stepped inside.

"Want to see my old room?" The words came out sounding like a challenge rather than an invitation.

"Sure."

He followed me inside. Emotions cascaded over his expression as he looked around the space that had been left untouched for ten years. I saw interest, then awareness and discomfort, but it was the flash of pity that turned my heart hard.

"Roses," Dan said.

"Yes. Roses."

I'd slept in a room full of roses. Roses on the curtains, the wallpaper, the bedspread, the pillows. Big red roses like something from a fairy tale, only not even the thorns had been enough to keep the monsters from this room.

"There used to be a rug, too," I said carelessly, pointing at the bare wood. "But it got stained. I guess she threw it away."

"Elle..."

"You can call me Ella." My voice was like stones tossed against a windowpane. One thrown too hard could break the glass. "They all do. Or Elspeth. It's my real name."

"It's pretty," he said, moving closer as though he meant to hug me, but I stepped away. "I'll call you whatever you want."

He looked around the room at my collection of dolls and model horses, set high on their shelves and yet free of dust. My desk. My closet, where he might find my ballet slippers and cast-off crown if he opened the door.

He didn't open the door. "What happened to him? The boy in the pictures?"

I think he already knew, but wanted to hear my answer. Maybe he hoped it would be different. Maybe he hoped I'd lie. And maybe I should have, except that I was so weary of lying. Tired of hiding behind a wall of thorns.

"I told you what happened to him already," I said, voice flat and sounding very far away. "He slit his wrists and bled to death while I watched from the doorway. He's dead."

Chapter 18

I didn't wait for his reaction. By that time, my bladder threatened to explode and I thought I might also puke, so I pushed past him and locked myself in the bathroom where I peed for what seemed forever and held myself from vomiting by reciting the multiplication tables over and over. Once that bathroom had been white, but apparently blood is also impossible to get out of towels and curtains. My mother had changed her color scheme to dark blue with yellow accents. Wallpaper decorated with sailing ships had replaced the stenciled pansies that had once danced along the white-painted walls. I touched the merry little boats, counting them. If I peeled it away, would I find the blood still beneath? Or had she tried to bleach it first?

"Elle?" The doorknob rattled. "Let me in. Please?"

I took a deep breath. "Dan, please go away."

Silence. I washed my hands, taking time to scrub each individual finger and rinse them, over and over. I went to the door. "Dan?" I knew he was still there, but I asked, anyway. He didn't jiggle the knob. I imagined him standing on the opposite side of the door, and I flattened a palm against the wood like maybe I could touch him through it. I pressed my forehead to it, my eyes closed.

"I'm still here."

I had to swallow, hard, before I could force myself to speak without my voice crumbling. "I need you to go away."

"Oh, Elle." He didn't ask me why.

I didn't want to tell him. What could I say? That shame was easier to bear alone? That seeing his face and knowing he knew what had happened was too much, right now, with my father's death still so raw?

"You don't want me to leave you." The steadiness of his voice was a comfort that could break me, if I took it.

"That won't work this time. I do want you to go. I need you to go, Dan."

A soft shuffle on the other side of the door made me think of him, standing as I did, pressed up against the wood. He sighed so heavily I had no trouble hearing it. I heard the clink of keys.

"I don't want to go, Elle. Won't you just let me in? We don't have to talk about anything you don't want to—"

"No!" My shout echoed in the bathroom, and I winced at the way it bludgeoned my ears. "No, I mean it. I want you to go away! I have to be alone right now!"

"You don't have to be alone," he said quietly.

"But I want to be," I told him.

To that, he seemed to have no answer. I waited, but at last the sound of footsteps led away from the door, the jingle of keys getting fainter and at last, fading away. By the time I came out, most everyone had gone home, leaving behind them the remains of casseroles and cakes I knew I'd be expected to put in containers and freeze.

Mrs. Cooper had stayed behind. I found her in the kitchen, putting the kettle on and tying an apron around her waist. She turned when I came in, and her smile was meant to warm me but missed a big icy section in the middle of my chest.

"I put your mother to bed, poor dear, with one of her headache pills. She's resting. I'll just get these dishes started."

"You don't have to do that, Mrs. Cooper."

"Oh, but, my dear, it's no trouble, really. What are neighbors for if not to help each other out in a time of need?" She smiled and reached for the bottle of dish soap.

I bent to find the neat stacks of butter tubs my mother used as storage containers, but found instead a cupboard full of matching containers and lids. My muffled noise of surprise drew Mrs. Cooper's attention.

"Oh, God love her, your mother," she said with a chuckle. "She had one of those parties, you know? And she went a bit hog wild, I'd say. She'll never use more than a few of those at a time, what with it just being her now, but well, I guess they'll come in handy, won't they?"

She indicated the table groaning with the offerings of potato salad and meat loaf, pierogies in butter sauce and carrot cake. "People were so generous. Look at all that food!"

"You should take some," I told her. "Maybe Mr. Cooper would like some."

"Thanks, honey." Mrs. Cooper started scrubbing while I started packing. I smoothed a spoon over the top of a mound of tuna salad to finish filling the container.

"Where's your young man gone?"

"I think he had to leave." Dan had gone, like I'd asked him to. He gave me what I wanted, the way he always did.

"He seemed nice." She gave me a birdlike glance. "Your mother seemed to like him."

I looked up, startled. "She did?"

"Oh, yes." Mrs. Cooper smiled. "Your mother is so very proud of you, you're all she ever talks about. How well you're doing with your job, how you're always getting promotions. How you fixed up that house of yours all on your own, without her help. Yes, she seemed quite impressed by your young man. He has a good job, she said, and is very polite."

That didn't sound like my mother, but I didn't argue with Mrs. Cooper. I kept my attention focused on filling containers with food and stacking them to be taken to the freezer in the basement.

"It was so good to see you. It's been so long. I'm sorry it had to be such a sad occasion. We miss you around here, Fred and I."

The stack in front of me doubled and tripled, and I blinked away tears. "That's nice to hear, Mrs. Cooper."

"Ella," she said gently, but I didn't turn, "you know we were all sorry about what happened."

"My father dug his own grave," I said. "Not to be rude, but you know it as well as I do."

"Not about your dad," said the woman who'd given me my first copy of *The Little Prince*. "About Andrew."

Sometimes when things break, you can hold them together for a while with string or glue or tape. Sometimes, nothing will hold what's broken, and the pieces fly all over, and though you think you might be able to find them all again, one or two will always be missing.

I flew apart. I broke. I shattered like a crystal vase dropped on a concrete floor, and pieces of me scattered all over. Some of them I was glad to see go. Some I never wanted to see again.

I sobbed, and Mrs. Cooper rubbed my back and let me do it.

It is such a secret place, the land of tears. That is what the narrator of *The Little Prince* says after the little prince argues with him the first time about matters of consequence. And he was right. My land of tears had been a secret for a very long time.

"It wasn't your fault," Mrs. Cooper told me, stroking my hair the way she'd done when I was a little girl and had run into her kitchen for a cookie and tripped and scraped my knee instead. "None of it was your fault. Stop blaming yourself, honey."

"What good is it to stop blaming myself," I sobbed, "when she still does?"

And for that Mrs. Cooper had no answer.

Dan left ten messages before I called him back. I know the number of times I lifted the phone to return his calls, but I'm too embarrassed to say it. I couldn't bring myself to do it. It was fine for Mrs. Cooper to tell me not to blame myself, but I couldn't do that any more than I could face

Dan. I didn't want him to see something different in his eyes when he looked at me.

"I can't see you anymore," I said finally when I'd managed to finish dialing and stay on the line long enough for him to answer. "I'm sorry. I just can't do it. I can't do this. Us. I can't do it, Dan."

I heard the sound of his breathing, this time separated by a far greater distance than a wooden bathroom door.

"I don't know what you want me to say."

"I want you to say okay."

His voice hardened a bit. "I won't say it's okay, because it's not. If you want to break up with me, Elle, then do it. But I'm not going to make it easy for you."

"I'm not asking you to make it easy for me!" I bit out the words, pacing as I talked.

"That's exactly what you're doing."

"So then do it!" I cried.

"No," he said after what seemed like forever. "I can't, Elle. I wish I could. But I can't."

I sat down on the floor because the chair was too far to walk. "I'm sorry, Dan."

"Yeah," he said, like he didn't believe me. "Me, too."

I wanted to hang up, but couldn't make myself do it. "Goodbye, Dan."

"You don't have to be alone" was his answer. "I know you think you do, but you don't. When you change your mind, call me."

"I won't change my mind."

"You want to change your mind, Elle," Dan said.

I couldn't deny the truth of it, so I hung up instead. I let him go. I let him slide away. I convinced myself it was better that way…to say goodbye to something before it had a chance to start. I didn't have time, in my grief, for more.

The days passed, as they do. I went back to work, because I could and because it helped me not to think so much about my father, Dan, my mother, my brothers, both of them. One dead and one so far away. I still hadn't heard from Chad, and I stopped calling.

It didn't seem as if it ought to have been a good time in my life, but the introspection and time alone, undistracted, proved to be the best thing I could have done. I stopped trying to forget what had happened in our house, and instead started trying to let it go. I wasn't very good at it. I'd cloaked myself in my secrets for a long time. They'd become habit, too, one I was at last ready to shed.

Summer ended and fall began. Apples came into season, and I went to hunt some at the Broad Street Market. As I bent over a display of local-grown fruit, a voice once familiar made me turn.

"Elle?"

My smile tried to fade, but I forced it to remain in place. "Matthew."

He was still tall. Still handsome. Gray streaked his hair at the temples now, and when he smiled I clearly saw lines around his eyes and on his forehead.

"Hi," he said, like we'd seen each other only yesterday. Incredibly, he moved forward, like he meant to…what? Hug me?

I drew away. His eyes flashed; his ready smile grew a bit strained. He put his hands in his pockets.

"Hello," I said carefully.

"Elle," he sighed. "It's good to see you."

I lifted my chin a bit. "Thanks."

"You look…fantastic."

I hadn't seen him in more than eight years. "You know what they say. Best revenge is looking good, right?"

He frowned. He'd never really understood my sense of humor. I'd forgotten how he pouted. "Elle."

I shook my head and put the apples back on the stand. I had no appetite for them now. "I'm sorry, Matthew. It's been a long time. You look good yourself."

We stared at each other for a long time while the tide of patrons surged and ebbed around us.

"Have coffee with me," he suggested, and how could I really say no?

So I let him buy me coffee, which warmed my fingers, and I sat across from him at one of the tiny tables at the Green Bean, a small coffee shop just down the street. We chatted about work and mutual friends, all of whom he still saw and none of whom I did. He told me about his wife, their kids, his job, his life, which I couldn't help envying, even if the car-pool and soccer-mom lifestyle seemed more than a bit stifling.

"And you? How are you?" He reached for my hand. I turned it so I could hold his, and I looked into the eyes I'd once loved so much I thought I'd die if they didn't look at me every day. "Are you happy?"

"Are you asking because it will make you feel better to know I am?"

"Yes. But also because I'd like to know you are."

I smiled. He stared. I shrugged, a little.

"You won't even tell me you're happy," he said, resigned, and pulled his hand away. "Listen, I'm sorry, all right? I'm sorry for the things I said and did. I was young. Anyone would have done the same thing. You lied. You weren't honest with me. What was I supposed to think?"

I smiled again.

"Elle, I'm sorry. I'm really, really sorry."

"You don't have to be," I replied. "It was a long time ago, and hardly matters now."

"You're so beautiful," he said in a low voice. "I wish—"

"You wish what?" The words came out harsh, not curious.

"Do you want to go somewhere?"

I gaped but couldn't find the words at first. "Like a motel, somewhere?"

He looked miserable, guilty, but also flushed with the excitement I recognized from old. The thumb of his left hand turned his wedding band at its place on his finger. "Yes."

Not so many months ago, I might have said yes, but now I stood. "No."

He stood, too. "Sorry."

I clenched my fists. "You accused me of cheating on you. You said being unfaithful was the worst—an unfaithful person was worse than anything. What would you tell your wife about this?"

He looked uncomfortable, and I understood it hadn't only been the letters he'd found, but the knowledge of who'd sent them that had made their end. Furious, I left. On the street he caught me by the elbow, turned me, left a mark that would likely bruise.

"I'm trying to tell you I was wrong!"

"You said you loved me, but guess what, Matthew, I've heard better lines from worse men, and if you had loved me you wouldn't have left me like you did."

A grimace twisted the mouth that had once kissed me all over. "You should have told me the truth."

I laughed, low and full of bitterness. "I did tell you the truth, and you turned me away."

I could still recall the look on his face. Disgust. The way he'd backed off, the way he'd never kissed me again.

"It wasn't my fault," I said. "I didn't make it happen. I didn't let him do those things, Matthew, he just did them. I didn't ask him to write those letters to me. He just did."

He said nothing.

I yanked my arm from his grip. "I did not let my brother do what he did," I said, glad to see him wince. "He just did it. And I counted on you to love me anyway. And you didn't. So tell me something, Matthew, who really fucked me, in the end?"

Then I turned and walked away, sick to my stomach, and when he called after me, I didn't turn.

"Great job on the location, Bob." I looked around the mall courtyard, which teemed with families attending the festival.

Bob smiled at me. "Yeah. We'll get a lot of traffic here."

Triple Smith and Brown didn't need to do something like this. The company had enough business without having to actively solicit it. I liked that the senior Smiths allowed us to take part, though. It was good to be part of a company that didn't only care about its employees, but also the community in which we lived and worked.

I haven't been around children much. I don't have nieces or nephews, and while my cousins have all begun having children, my experience with them has been admiration from afar. I'm never quite sure how to speak to kids. I hate the smarmy face adults put on, like children are stupid, and yet the way young humans act usually baffles me.

"Hi," I said to a little girl holding on to her younger brother's hand. "Would you like a treat bag?"

Nothing. Not a smile, not a nod, not word. The little boy grunted, but the girl was silent as a tomb.

"Kara," said the woman with them, I assumed was their mother. "The lady asked you a question."

She nudged her forward. I held out the bag encouragingly. I felt like Dian Fossey, tempting a shy primate to accept her. The little girl still stared. The brother stuck his finger up his nose. I recoiled and handed two treat bags to the mother.

"You can give them to the kids," I told her. "There's a pack of tissues in there."

She didn't get it. Maybe nose-mining was such a commonplace occurrence it no longer shocked. She took the bags, though, and thanked me, and then moved off into the crowd.

"Hi," I said, turning from my box of treat bags to confront the next festival-goer. "Would you like a treat bag?"

The boy who stood in front of our table was a bit too old for minitablets and crayons, though I supposed the tissues might come in handy. Gavin shifted from foot to foot, his hands thrust deep into the pockets of his oversize sweatshirt. His hair had grown longer and obscured his eyes, but I didn't think he was looking at me.

"Hi, Miss Kavanagh."

He'd hit us at a lull in the crowd. I glanced over my shoulder at Bob, who was opening another box of treat bags. Marcy had defected from her post at the popcorn machine to grab us all some snacks. I straightened my spine and kept my voice neutral.

"Hello, Gavin."

"I saw you over here, and I just wanted to say…I wanted to say…"

I didn't help him out. I kept my eyes fixed on a spot just over his shoulder. The accusations from his mother had cut too deep for me to smile at him.

"My mom, she kinda got out of control."

I nodded and fussed with the literature set out on our table. He shifted some more. The front of his sweatshirt featured a grinning skeleton with a dagger through its skull.

"My mom, she…she just got a little upset about me not doing my chores when I was spending so much time with you, and she wanted to know what we were doing over there."

"I see." I looked up and right into his eyes beneath the fringe of his hair. "And you told her, I guess."

He chewed his lip. "Yeah."

I nodded and went back to tidying the piles of notepads and stacks of pencils in front of me. "Interesting, then, that she thinks it's something else."

He didn't say much else, then the defensiveness kicked in. "Hey, you're a pretty lady and I'm a kid—"

I looked up again and my glare must have struck him because he cut himself off. "I don't think you understand, Gavin, exactly how much trouble you could get me into."

I kept my voice pitched low. I handed out another couple treat bags to a set of identical twins wearing matching outfits. Chocolate ice cream stained their matching smiles. Their parents urged them away, and I turned back to him.

"Do you understand?"

He shrugged. "Mom said she knew I was a horny teenage boy and if I had the chance to do something dirty, I would."

Dirty. That word again. The feeling of it was worse. I crossed my arms over my chest as Bob told me he was off to the bathroom. He left us alone, and I was glad.

"I never did anything dirty to you." My words clunked like ice between us.

He stared at his shuffling feet. "It got her off my back. So she didn't ask about the other stuff."

"I thought we were friends," I told him, at last, without sympathy. "Friends don't betray other friends to save their own butts."

He shrugged again. "I'm sorry."

"I'm working," I said. "You need to go away now."

And he did, looking over his shoulder with a mournful glance I refused to acknowledge.

"Pardon me for saying so, honey, but you look like six kinds of shit on a splintered stick."

"Gee, Marcy. Thanks so much." I added sugar and creamer to my mug of coffee and sipped. Awful. I drank it anyway.

"Seriously, punkin." She shook her head. "Tell me what's wrong or I'll force you to listen to stories of my vacation in Aruba."

Marcy had convinced me to go out to lunch with her and take advantage of the last bright days to eat outside. Now I couldn't escape her, and not even the four coats of mascara she wore on each eye could keep her from peering right inside me.

"When did you go to Aruba?"

"I haven't, yet, but I'm going there on my honeymoon."

I drank more coffee, though by this point I was so wide-eyed from caffeine I wouldn't have been surprised had my lashes met my hairline. Then it registered, what she'd said, and I looked to her left hand at the new diamond ring she wore. I put down my cup with a thunk.

"Marcy! You're engaged?"

She beamed. "Yep."

She told me how Wayne had gotten down on one knee and proposed. Our food came and she talked as we ate, her fork waving animatedly and earning her bemused looks from the table next to us. I sat and listened and nodded, her pure, giddy joy infectious.

Finally, with cheesecake clinging to the tines of her fork, she paused for air. "This is my last cheesecake until after the wedding. I want to lose at least ten pounds. But, Elle. How are you doing, honey?"

I studied my own, half-eaten dessert. "I'm all right. Thanks for the card and the plant."

She smiled. "Wayne thought you might like the plant better than flowers."

"I did. You can tell him so." I poked a hole in my cake. "It was very thoughtful of both of you. I really appreciate it."

"Sure." She chewed, swallowed, sipped her coffee.

I felt the weight of her eyes on me but didn't look up. Marcy, however, was not to be deterred by something so simple a social-avoidance technique like avoiding eye contact.

"You know you can talk to me, if you want. About anything."

I nodded. "Thanks, Marcy, but my dad was sick for a while. It wasn't a surprise."

Her concern hadn't made me look up, but the aggravated sigh she gave now did.

"I wasn't talking about your dad."

"You weren't?"

She shook her head and popped the last piece of cheesecake between her lips. "Nope."

I sat for a moment, staring, then forked a bite of cake into my mouth. Sweet sugar, gooey chocolate…my mouth applauded.

"I saw Dan downtown last weekend." Marcy wiped her fingers on her napkin.

I made a noncommittal noise. Marcy pinned me with her bright-blue gaze, her spangled shadow glittering. She wore a new shade of lipstick, today, her mouth pursed. I braced myself for the lecture.

"He said you two broke up. That you wouldn't answer his calls."

I meant to laugh, I really did, but the sound came out somewhat strangled. "Broke up?"

"Did you?"

"We weren't—"

"Elle." Marcy put her hand over mine, and I put down my fork. "What happened?"

"I don't want to talk about it." I looked into her eyes.

She squeezed my fingers. "Okay."

"I mean, even if I had anything to say about it, which I don't, really." It wasn't often that my mouth outraced my mind, but it did that day. The more I said, the more I felt I had to say. To explain. To deny, postulate, consider. To justify.

Marcy sat and listened, silent for once.

"He wasn't my boyfriend. We were just having a good time. It wasn't serious. I don't get serious. I told him right up front, that it wasn't going to be a relationship. I don't do that. I told him that. He said it was all right." Words, like raindrops on a windowpane, sliding down, dividing, branching out, always one more showing up when it seemed they'd all disappeared. "It's not my fault he misunderstood, I was honest with him. I was always honest, right from the start. He knew. I knew. We both knew. And now it's over, but really, can something be over that never started?"

"You tell me," Marcy said gently, sitting back in her chair and looking as calm as though someone verbally drenched her *every* day.

"Yes," I said firmly. "I mean…no."

She smiled. "Elle. Honey. Sweetie-pie. What's so wrong with being happy?"

I didn't have an answer for that at first. The cake sat in

my stomach like a rock. I finished my coffee, even though it was cold.

"I'm afraid," I whispered at last, ashamed.

"We're all afraid, honey."

I looked up at her with a heavy, heavy sigh. "Even you?"

She nodded. "Even me."

That made me feel better, a little, and I smiled. She smiled back. She reached for my hand again, linking her fingers through mine.

"Look at those two old guys over there," she said. "They're anxiously awaiting some girl-on-girl action."

She won a laugh from me. I didn't let go of her hand. "Except in their version, there'll be pudding involved."

"Oooh, pudding," Marcy said. "I could get into that."

We shared another smile, and something in me eased. I reached for my fork again. We signaled for the check.

"Listen, I can't pretend to be the queen of good advice, here. I've had more boyfriends than I can count, and I'm not so sure that's any better than not having any. But I do know this. When you find someone who makes you smile and laugh, when you find someone who makes you feel safe…you shouldn't let that person go just because you're afraid."

"Is Wayne that person for you?"

She nodded, and every line of her expression softened with joy. "Yep."

"And you're not afraid of it ending?"

"Sure I am. But I'd rather have something this good for a little while than have nothing forever."

I finished my dessert and wiped my mouth. "Thanks for the advice, but I think it's over. Dan, I mean."

"He's a good man, Elle. Won't you give him another chance?"

Her assumption that I was the one who had the right to give him anything surprised me. "There's nothing to give. He didn't do anything wrong. He's not the one who…he didn't—"

While only moments before, my mouth had spewed word after word, now my lips moved but nothing came out. I was wordless. I couldn't think of what I meant to say.

Marcy, heaven bless her, didn't need me to say anything.

"You could just call him, you know. Talk to him. Work it out."

For a moment, the thought of doing that lifted my spirits, but it passed as soon as it came. "No. I don't think so."

"Oh, Elle." She seemed disappointed in me, and that stung more than I expected it to. "How come?"

"Because," I said after another long pause. "I don't have enough of myself to give to anyone else. And until I do, Dan deserves better than someone with only half to give him."

She studied me, then nodded slowly. "Did you kill someone?"

"What?" My cheeks bloomed with heat and I coughed. "Jesus, Marcy!"

"Did you?" She asked calmly. "Because I can't really think of anything else that would be so bad you couldn't forgive yourself for it."

I gaped, my mouth working but nothing coming out for a second. "What if I said yes?"

"Did you?"

"Maybe I did!" I cried. "Yes."

"Did you?" She asked again, frighteningly perceptive. "Shot them? Stuck a knife in their guts? Poison?"

My voice sounded flat and faraway. "No. I just didn't pick up the phone and call an ambulance when I knew I should."

"That's not killing someone," she shot back. "That's letting someone die. There's a difference."

I blinked, wishing for a drink to wash away the taste of sugar and coffee and anger. "There was still blood on my hands."

Her steely gaze gave me no release. "Nobody likes a martyr, Elle."

My body reacted faster than my thoughts could catch up. I pushed my chair back and stood so fast my hand knocked my mug to the floor. It broke with a solid "thunk," and a splash of coffee colored the brick.

We stared at each other across the table, me with heaving chest and pounding heart and Marcy looking as cool as spring water. She took a slow, deliberate sip of her coffee. I clenched my sweating hands into fists.

"Why are you taking his side?" I asked her finally, my voice shaking. "You're supposed to be my friend!"

"I wouldn't be much of a friend if I didn't try to help you. Would I?"

"You think this is helping me?"

She nodded. "Yes, Elle. I do."

"You don't know anything about me," I told her. "Not a damn thing."

"Whose fault is that?" she shot back.

My mind couldn't seem to decide between anger and

despair, and both filled me. I backed away from her, my hands up like I was pushing her away. Marcy didn't move.

"Falling in love doesn't make everything else magically disappear, Marcy. Finding your knight in shining armor is a fairy tale. It doesn't change anything, and you're fooling yourself if it does. You go ahead and live in your rainbow-glitter sunshine and marshmallow fantasies. I'm happy for you. I'm happy that you found Wayne and he filled up all those places inside of you that needed filling. Good for you. I hope you live happily ever after. But it's just a dream, it's not real. Love doesn't make everything all better like a fucking fairy wand, Marcy, it doesn't change things just like POOF, there you go, hey, I love you, now let's run hand in hand through a field of fucking flowers!"

The venom in my voice burned my throat. Marcy flinched, her cheeks turning pink in an uncharacteristic show of discomfort. She blinked rapidly, and I should have been ashamed to see that she had tears in her eyes.

"And so what if it does? What if falling in love does make everything else seem better? Is that a crime? Is it a sin to let someone else help you out a little, once in a while? But no, you have to be a damn martyr and carry it all on your own shoulders, all the time! You just keep on hating yourself so everyone else will too, okay? Keep on being miserable because you're too afraid to let go of it! Jesus H. Christ," she cried. "Don't you want to be happy?"

"Yes! I want to be happy! But don't try to hand me Dan on a platter and try to convince me that he's the magic key! Okay? Him or any other man. It doesn't work that way. True love isn't going to transform me, Marcy. Not everyone works the way you do."

"I'm only trying to help you," she said.

"I know you are." I took a deep breath. "And I appreciate it. But this is my thing, okay? It has nothing to do with Dan. It's not something that he did or didn't do. It's not about him. It's something I have to work through on my own."

"You don't have to do it on your own. You've got friends. People who love you. Whatever it is, Elle."

I knew she was right. I knew she would listen, offer advice, hold my hand. I knew she would do what she could; but what it all came down to was that in the end I needed to rid myself of the infection inside me. Cut it out, if I had to. Tear off the scab, open it to the air, get it clean.

"I'll see you back at the office."

She nodded. "Fine."

There were things to say that would make this better, but I couldn't make myself say them. I've never been good at building, only breaking. I left her at the café, and later that day I saw her giggling over her ring with Lisa Lewis in the copy room. They both stopped and looked up when I came in, and Marcy smiled at me as if we barely knew each other.

Chapter 19

Marcy was wrong. I was not a martyr. At least, I didn't think so. I did not want to parade my pain for all to see, to bolster myself with pity, to beat my breast and bemoan my sorry state. That was my mother's agenda, not mine.

It was why I never spoke to anyone about what had happened in our house the years of my life between fifteen and eighteen, when Andrew died. I didn't want anyone, ever, to be able to excuse me because of my past. I did not excuse myself because of it. Bad things happen all the time. Worse than what I endured. Everything in my past was a piece of my self puzzle, the punctuation in the sentence of my being. Without it I would not have become the woman I am today. I'd be someone else. Someone I might not recognize.

She was right, however, about pushing people away. I knew it. I had for a long time. So I pondered getting "someone" the way my brother had, and I decided, instead, to go to church. God didn't reach down his hand and pull me off my knees. I'd abandoned religion for a reason. I didn't believe God could solve my problems any more than therapy could or booze or drugs. Or sex. There was much for me to carry, and I had to let it go.

St. Paul's was larger than St. Mary's and a more modern church, advertising "folk Mass" and "contemporary worship" on the billboard in front. They did offer confession, however, and while I'd never believed it should be up to a man to decide if I'm worthy of forgiveness, the act of confession preyed on my mind so persistently that I at last decided to go.

Father Hennessy had a nice voice. A little rough, but quiet. He sounded kind and interested, at least, not bored, though I'd waited until the church was empty before I entered the confessional, and he was probably tired of listening at that point.

"Bless me, Father, for I have sinned. It's been a long time since my last confession."

I spoke for a long time.

"Are you able to forgive yourself?" he asked at last. "Because you know I can forgive you and the good Lord can, but if you don't forgive yourself it's no use."

I nodded, my fingers aching from being clutched together so tightly. "Yes, Father, I know."

"Have you sought professional services?"

"Not recently, Father."

"But you've had counseling."

I laughed, low. "When it happened, yes."

"And you didn't find it helpful?"

"They could give me medication, Father, but..." My voice trailed off.

"Ah." He seemed to understand. "You know you're not at fault, don't you?"

"I know. I do know."

"And yet you can't let go of the guilt?"

"I can't seem to, no."

We shared silence for a moment before he spoke again. "Like our Lord, you've been pierced with thorns and nails. You can take them out, but each leaves behind a hole. And you, child, have so many holes you're afraid that's all you'll be. Nothing but holes. Am I right?"

I put my forehead on my hands and whispered a reply. "Yes."

"When they pulled our Lord from the cross, he had holes, too. But he rose again with his Father's love, and you can too."

Hot tears leaked over my fingers, but a strangled laugh escaped me. "You're comparing me to the son of God?"

"We're all children of God," the priest said. "Every one of us. Our Lord Christ died for our sins so you don't have to. Do you understand?"

I envied those who could accept that answer, who could let the light shine in and let the blood of their Savior wash it all away. It seemed like another fairy story to me, but I didn't tell the priest that. He believed it, even if I could not.

"I'm tired, Father, of feeling this way."

"Then let our Lord take it away for you."

He sounded so sincere. Genuine. Again, I wished I could

do as he said. Open my heart. Believe in something that would make all the rest seem bearable.

"I'm sorry, Father, I just can't."

He sighed. "It's all right."

He sounded despondent, and I thought maybe the Church business wasn't as satisfying as it had been years ago when Catholics didn't question, they just prayed.

"I'm sorry, Father. I want to believe you."

He laughed. "The fact you're here says that. And if you don't believe, don't worry. God believes in you. He won't let you fall away from him so easily."

I'd never heard a priest laugh in the confessional before. "It's not that I don't know where to place the blame. Or that I think it's my fault. I know it's not."

"But you're full of holes."

"Yes."

"And you're looking for something to fill them."

I wiped my face with my hands, feeling my tears on my fingertips. "Yes. I guess I am."

"It's my job to tell you to find it in the Church," the priest said. "I hope you'll at least consider it."

I liked Father Hennessy, who had a sense of humor. "If anyone could convince me, Father, I think it would be you."

"Ah, that makes me feel better. Are you ready to finish your confession?"

"Yes." I paused. "Go easy on me, Father, I'm out of practice."

He laughed again. "Say one Act of Contrition, my child."

"It's been a long time. I'm not sure I remember the words."

"Then I will say them with you," said Father Hennessy, and he did.

There could be no point in continuing this way. I didn't like it, didn't want it, couldn't stand it. So this is what I did.

I went to visit my mother.

Since my father's death she'd redecorated the den. The big television still squatted in the corner like Shelob waiting for a tasty hobbit to devour, but all other signs of my father's habitation of the space had disappeared. She'd replaced his chair with a love seat and stripped the striped wallpaper for a cheery yellow paint.

She showed me around the room, but didn't actually let me sit in it. She took me to the kitchen, made us both coffee and pulled an apple pie from the freezer. I recognized it as one left from the wake and didn't want any.

"I've got some boxes for you." She lit a cigarette and held it between her French-manicured fingertips. "If you don't take them, I'm giving them to the thrift store."

"What's in them?"

She shrugged. "Bunch of junk."

I stirred sweetener in my coffee in lieu of the sugar she didn't keep. "What makes you think I want a bunch of junk?"

"It's your junk," she said, like that made a difference.

If my visit surprised or pleased her, I saw no sign of either. She drew in the smoke and let it out, squinching her eyes shut in a way that feathered wrinkles around her eyes.

"Fine. I'll take a look through it before I go."

We sipped our coffee in silence. I'd never sat at her table like this, two adults drinking coffee. I waited to feel strange about it, and then I did.

If my mother did, she kept it to herself. "So, Ella. Where's your friend?"

I gave her a look. She tossed up her hands. "What? What? I shouldn't ask?"

"Do you really care?"

She took another drag. "It would be good for you to have a man."

"You didn't seem to think so when he was here."

My mother has always been good at rewriting history to suit herself. "What are you talking about? He seemed very nice for a Jew."

I let my head fall forward with a groan. "Oh, Jesus."

"Not in this house," she warned. "Don't take the name of our Lord in vain."

"I'm sorry." I drank some of her coffee, which was too strong.

"You know I think it's long past time you got married. Had some children. Had a real life."

The rant was an old one, but for the first time I allowed myself to listen not only to her words but to the meaning behind them.

"I have a life. A real life. I don't need to be defined by a husband or children to have a real life."

My mother scoffed. "You need something other than those damned numbers, Ella."

"Yes, because I've had such a good role model," I retorted.

She stubbed out her cigarette and crossed her arms over

her ample chest. Her expertly applied makeup couldn't hide the circles under her eyes. "I wish you weren't so smart with me all the time. I wish you took better care of yourself. I wish you saw I was only trying to look out for you instead of jumping down my throat every time we talk."

I'd been holding both hands around my mug to warm them, but I put it down and spread them flat on the tabletop. I looked at her, trying hard to see myself in the curve of her jaw, the color of her eyes, the style of her hair. I tried to find myself in my mother, some thread of connection to prove I had once swum inside her womb and was not just an afterthought. That once upon a time she had looked at me with something other than disappointment.

"I wish I was fifteen again, and I had told Andrew no when he asked me if I loved him. And I wish he'd listened to me instead of getting into my bed."

The color drained from her face, leaving two bright spots of blush high on her cheeks. For an instant I thought she was going to pass out. Or maybe scream.

Instead, she slapped my face hard enough to rock me back in my chair. I put my hand over the heat the blow left behind on my cheek. Then I looked her in the eyes.

"And I wish you would stop blaming me for it."

I tensed for the next slap, or the coffee in my face, or the shrieks and accusations. I was not prepared for what she did next. She started to cry.

Real, fat tears welled in her eyes and left tracks in her foundation. They dripped off her chin and left dark marks on her navy silk blouse. She drew in a slow, hitching breath as her mouth trembled to let out a sob.

"Who else could I blame?" my mother said, the words striking me harder than her slap. "He's dead."

I wanted to get up but didn't have the strength to do it. "You knew, didn't you?"

"I knew." She reached for a napkin and blew her nose, then took another to pat her eyes. Her mascara left half circles of black on the white paper.

"You called me a liar and a whore." The words stuck in my throat before I forced them out. They felt sharp, like they left scratches.

I had never seen her look so bleak. So unconcerned with how her tears might have smudged her makeup and turned her nose red. My mother wiped her eyes again, removing more of the eyeliner, shadow, mascara. She looked naked without it. Vulnerable.

"Do you think I was a liar and a whore?" I wanted to sound demanding. I only sounded pleading.

"No, Ella. I don't."

"Then why did you say it?" I wept, too, but didn't bother wiping my face. I kept my hands anchored flat on the table. "Why?"

"Because I thought maybe saying it would make it true!" She cried. "Because I didn't want to believe he would do those things to you! I didn't want to believe it, Ella, that my son could work such evil! I wanted to make you a liar because that would mean it wasn't true. Because I would rather have a daughter who's a liar and a whore than a son who raped his sister."

"Like you'd rather have a son who is gay?" I asked, more gently than I had ever thought I'd be able to. "You'd rather have one son dead by his own hand and a daughter who doesn't have a real life than a son who's alive and well but likes men?"

It didn't make me feel good to watch her flinch and crumble, shrivel like the legs of the Wicked Witch of the West when Dorothy took off those shoes. I had always thought confronting her would leave me more triumphant. It only left me sad.

"You don't understand what it's like, to have children. How they disappoint you. You don't understand what it's like to give another person life and watch them throw it all away. You don't understand what it's like, Ella, to be me."

I studied her for another long, long moment in which she wept and my own tears slowed. At last I stood, not filled with triumph but with something else I had longed for. Acceptance.

"No, Mother," I told her kindly. "I don't. And I guess I never will."

She nodded, focusing again on her coffee and her smoke, and I saw for the first time she was not a fairy queen I'd dreamed of as a child, nor the wicked witch I'd made her out to be later, but a woman. Just a woman, after all.

I hugged her, the smoke from her cigarette burning my eyes. At first she didn't hug me back, but after a moment she did, patting my back. Her fingers tugged my hair.

We said nothing else, too fragile for words, and I left her there at the table. I thought maybe I would come back and see her again. I thought maybe we would talk again. But for the moment, what we had done was enough.

I didn't get religion, though I did attend Mass once or twice. The contemporary service was nice, though not quite the comforting, mysterious ritual of my youth. I found it lacking, in the end, though I enjoyed Father Hennessy's sermon about the challenges facing young people today. After, when I shook his hand as I left the church and murmured, "thank you, Father," he pressed my hand with fingers gnarled by arthritis and looked into my eyes when he answered, "You're quite welcome."

I didn't stop "not hating" my mother, either, and when she called I made more of an effort to pick up the phone and talk to her. Our conversations were strained, though. Distant and polite. She stopped asking me about Dan and started telling me more about her life. She'd taken up a membership in the gym and joined a reading group. If I found it odd to speak to her of such inanities, I'm sure she found it equally as strange not to rant and rave at me; but both of us were trying, at least, and I for one had accepted we might never have more than that.

I spent my nights the way I mostly had for years, alone. I read a great deal. I knitted. I repainted my kitchen and steam cleaned my carpets. I had a lot of time that had seemed insufficient before, when faced with all the tasks I wanted to accomplish, but which now, without anyone to share them with, seemed vast and empty and bereft.

I could have called him. I should have. Pride stopped my fingers from dialing, and fear, too. What if I called and he didn't call back? Or worse, hung up on me?

I'd lived a long time without a Dan in my life, and there was no good reason I couldn't get on without one, now. No good reason other than that I missed him. He had made me laugh, if nothing else. He'd made me forget myself.

The night my doorbell rang I went to my door with my heart in my throat, wishing I'd worn makeup instead of leaving my face bare and wearing my hair in a messy tail. The man on the other side of the door couldn't have cared less, though. He swept me into his arms and squeezed the breath out of me, then knuckled my sides until I couldn't breathe.

"Chad!" I wriggled out of his grasp so I could get some air in my lungs, then squeezed him again before holding him at arm's length to look him over. "What are you doing here?"

"Luke convinced me I should see my big sister." Chad grinned.

He looked good. My little brother, who'd been taller than me since hitting puberty. Blond to my brunette, brown eyes to my blue, tan to my fair skin, we didn't look much like siblings except in our smiles. I searched him for the changes time had made and saw a few.

"I can't believe it's been so long," he said.

"I can." I took his hand and drew him inside. "I just can't believe you're here."

Even as he sat at my kitchen table rattling off his latest adventures, I had a hard time convincing myself it was really him. He paused in his narrative to stare at me, his grin softening as he took my hand.

"What's that look for, sweetness?"

"Just glad you're here, Chaddie." I held his hand, tight, and we shared another look.

Survivors.

I wouldn't hear of him staying in a hotel, of course. I wouldn't send my little brother to stay in a hotel when I had two empty bedrooms. It was nice, having him there. Having someone to share coffee with in the morning. To make eggs for. Someone who knew me so well I never had to explain anything. We went out to dinner at night, to the movies, I took him dancing. We spent hours on my couch talking. We watched episodes of *The Dukes of Hazzard* and argued over who was the hotter cousin, Bo or Luke. Chad maintained their hotness would only be magnified if they tongue-kissed, which made me laugh so hard I spilled the popcorn.

"I've missed you so much," I told him over mugs of hot cocoa topped with marshmallow fluff. "I wish you'd think about moving back home."

He rolled his eyes at me. "You know I can't."

I sighed. "I know. Luke."

"It's more than Luke. I have a job. I have a house. I have a whole life."

"I know, I know." I waved my hand. "You're just so far away, that's all. I don't get to see you enough."

"You could visit more often. Luke adores you, doll. We'd take you shopping."

I raised a brow. "He says, as though I need a new wardrobe or something."

Chad laughed. "You said it, not me. We'd put you in something other than black and white."

"My clothes are fine."

"Ella, baby. Honey. The world's not made up only of black and white." My brother looked around my living room. "This place could use some color, too. The dining room is fabulous. Spread some of that around."

He wasn't wrong. "I like black and white, Chad."

"I know you do, muffin." He reached for my hand and kissed it. "I know."

"Are you going to tell Mom I'm here?" He set his mug on my coffee table.

I didn't answer right away. "Do you want me to?"

He shrugged. It was a rare moment when Chad wasn't smiling or cracking a joke. He looked up and our eyes met, and I saw myself reflected in them.

"I don't know."

I nodded, understanding. "If you don't want me to, I won't."

He sighed, rubbing at his face. "Luke says I should. My counselor says I should."

I took his hand. "Chad, I know better than anyone why you don't want to. But maybe it's time."

He squeezed my fingers. "How about you? Have you kicked the ass of the past?"

I laughed a little. "Kicked the ass? No. Stubbed its toe, maybe."

"Elle. What happened to your fella?" My brother stuck his fingers through the holes in my afghan and wiggled them.

"He went home with me when Dad died. He met Mom. She wasn't nice."

"He went home with you? To the house?"

I nodded. Chad sat back, impressed or shocked, I couldn't tell. He rubbed his face again.

"You went back to the house."

"It's just a house, Chaddie. Four walls and a door."

We shared another look, and he didn't hesitate, he leaned over and hugged me. I didn't mean to cry, but I did, wetting the shoulder of his shirt. It was all right. He cried, too.

"I didn't want to leave you, Ella," Chad whispered, holding me tight. "You know that. I didn't want to leave you alone with him. But I had to get out."

"I know. I know."

I handed him a napkin to wipe his face, and I wiped my own. We talked so much our throats got hoarse and so long our stomachs started to rumble because we'd forgotten to eat. We cried. We screamed. We threw things. We cried some more and held each other, and sometimes we even laughed.

"There should be one good thing," Chad said. "One good thing we can find to remember about him, Elle. So we can find a way to let it go."

We'd ended up foot to foot on my couch, under the knitted throw. Tissues littered the floor and my pillows had suffered our wrath. The remains of sandwiches prepared between rants dried on the coffee table.

"He was good at sports," I offered. "All-American Boy."

"He didn't let the bigger kids pick on me."

"That's two, Chad. We found two good things."

He smiled. "My counselor would say that's very good progress."

I smiled, too. "He's right."

"It's easier to remember the bad things he did. The drugs. The stealing. The other stuff."

"You can say it out loud," I told him. "It might be better if you did."

My brother's eyes welled with tears again. "I tried to get him to stop. That's when he started getting mean. That's when he told Mom I was gay."

"I remember." I lined up our feet, our knees bent in an old game. Choo-Choo train. Back and forth beneath the blanket.

"And even when you cut yourself, she didn't listen. She just covered it up." His fists clenched and my heart swelled with love for his love of me.

"I don't blame you, Chad. Please don't blame yourself. You were just a kid. You were only sixteen."

"You were only eighteen, Elle."

"And now we're both older. And he's dead."

"I still feel guilty for being glad when I heard. When Dad called me at Uncle John's place to tell me Andrew had killed himself, I laughed at first."

I hadn't known that. "Oh, Chad."

He shrugged. "I should have come home then."

"You couldn't have changed anything. And she'd only have made your life hell, too." I shook my head. "But listen, we've both made it through, and look at us. We've got great jobs. We've got houses of our own. Lives. You've got Luke. We're making it, Chad. We're doing all right."

"Are we?" He asked softly. "Are you?"

"I'm trying," I answered. "I'm trying hard."

"Me, too."

Being understood by someone who had been there did more for me than any amount of counseling could have. We had both survived that house and what had gone on inside it.

"He made Mom laugh," I said after a moment. "And when she was laughing, she loved all of us as much as she loved him."

"Yeah," Chad said. "I guess that's worth forgiving him for, then, isn't it?"

And for the first time, I thought it might be.

I took flowers to the cemetery. Lilies for my father's grave and sunflowers for my brother's. My mother had buried them side by side, and the grass over both of them was soft and well tended. The carving on the headstones had their names, dates of birth and death. My father's said beloved husband and father. Andrew's said beloved son and brother. I knelt in front of them with my hands on my lap, shivering a little in the sudden fall breeze, and I tried to pray.

It didn't work so well. My mind wandered as my fingers thumbed the rosary beads, and at last I put it away. I sat quietly in the soft, brown-turning grass, and I wept slow, effortless tears.

It seemed wrong, somehow. Incomplete. I had not attended the graveside services for either of them. I hadn't been asked to speak. Now, faced with two slabs of marble and a bouquet of wilting flowers, with fall winds tugging my hair, I needed to find the words I had denied myself for so long. I told my father I loved him and that I forgave him for choosing distance and drinking instead of me, and I didn't merely mouth the words. I meant them.

They didn't come any easier than anything else ever had, and when I'd finished I still wasn't done. I sat in silence for a while, trying to make a list of good things to remember. Something to hold on to in place of the bad.

And then I did it.

"You're the one who taught me how to find the Big Dipper, Andrew," I said aloud. "When I was six. It was the first time I looked up into the night sky and saw something other than numbers, something to count. You're the one who taught me there could be beauty there, too."

The trees lining the cemetery had already begun turning red and gold, and the wind rustled the leaves. I didn't imagine it as something else, an angel's touch or my brother back from the dead to accept my forgiveness. I was too practical for that. I watched the leaves ripple, their colors so vibrant and lovely and yet harbingers of death still to come, but I took solace in the thought they'd return to life in the spring and be renewed.

That's what I wanted. To be renewed. Sitting in front of the graves of my father and brother, the two men who had most shaped my life, I thought maybe I'd be able to do it, too. Come to life again. Make my own spring.

I waited for something to happen. Like for the heavens to open up in beams of rainbow light, or a hand to thrust out of the ground and grab me. All that happened was the breeze blew, and my teeth chattered.

But I felt better. I had faced another demon and come out unscathed. How many more could there be?

I got to my feet, dusting off the crumbles of grass from my long skirt. I bent and arranged the flowers in a prettier fashion. I cleared away some weeds sprouting up at the corners of the headstone. I traced the letters of their names with the tip of my finger and thought how insufficient the inscriptions were to describe the lives of the men whose bodies lay beneath the ground.

"He loved British comedy," I said aloud, my hand on my father's headstone. "He loved Irish music. He used Old Spice cologne and liked to fish, and he always ate what he caught. He was born in New York City but moved away when he was three and never went back."

There was more. Memories of my dad. My tribute to him, the best one I could give. The one for Andrew I thought would be harder, but maybe remembering about the stars had opened the way for me.

"He played games with us even when he was too old for them. He taught me how to ride a bike with no hands. He was the first one to tell a story about Princess Pennywhistle." I spoke on, not caring if I sounded like a loon talking out loud to a grave. I wept again, the tears not so effortless this time. They wet the throat of my sweater and made me cold. "He was my brother, and I loved him. Even when I hated what he did."

The something I'd been waiting for happened, though it wasn't as dramatic as an angel chorus from above or a cheap horror movie thrill. I let go. Not everything, and not all at once, but I took in a breath of crisp fall air that didn't weigh me down. I wiped my face. I took in another breath.

Then I walked away.

When offering an apology, it's always better to bring a peace offering to smooth the way. For me it was a box of chocolate éclairs and a thermos of hazelnut coffee to replace the sludge we usually had in the break room. I knocked on Marcy's door, the bright-pink box announcing the arrival of sugar-filled treats.

She looked up from her desk with a pinched smile. "Elle. Hi. C'mon in."

She'd breezed into my office plenty of times and plopped into my chair. I wasn't quite as relaxed, but I did slide the box toward her. "I brought you something."

She leaned down to sniff the box, then slit the tape with one manicured fingernail. "Oh, God, you bitch. I've been on a freaking diet…"

The moment she called me a bitch, I knew things were all right between us. Coming from Marcy, it was almost a term of affection. I held up the thermos.

"I brought good coffee, too."

"Oh, my God, I love you." She twirled around on her chair and pulled down a mug from her shelf and held it out. "Caffeine's supposed to slow weight loss, but I'll be fucked in fudge if I can understand how."

I'd brought my own mug and filled them both. "Wouldn't that get messy?"

She gave me a blank look at first, then laughed. "It might."

We raised our cups and she pulled out éclairs, one for each. She bit into hers right away and moaned so long and loud I laughed. A moment later, biting into my own pastry, I managed an enthusiastic echo of her exclamation. Together we stuffed ourselves with sugary goodies and strong coffee.

"Marcy," I said when the feeding frenzy had eased. "I'm sorry."

She waved a hand. "No big whoop, hon. I'm a nosy bitch. I admit it."

"No. You were trying to be my friend, and I wasn't being a very good one. I'm sorry."

"Don't fuss yourself!" she cried.

"Marcy, damn it! I'm trying to apologize, would you let me? Please?"

She laughed but nodded. "Yes. All right. I was a nosy bitch and you were an uptight shrew. We're square?"

"Square." I sat back in the chair. "I missed your gossip."

She clapped her hands. "Oooh, and have I got some for you!"

She certainly did. A full half hour's worth of time we both should have spent working, but instead spent giggling over speculation about the new guy who worked in the mail room. Marcy was convinced he was a stripper on the side. I hadn't noticed him.

"What do you mean, you haven't noticed him?" She crowed. "Are you blind? Are you dead? Are your legs glued together?"

"I thought you were getting married!"

"I am getting married, but I'm not dying. It's okay to look, Elle." She paused. "I wouldn't tell Wayne, of course."

"Of course not."

She scraped some chocolate from the side of an éclair and licked it off her finger. "So…how're you doing? Aside from tempting me with disgusting pastry and trying to make me so fat I can't fit into my wedding dress."

"I'm all right." I reached for another éclair and bit into it. Yellow cream oozed out onto my fingers, and I licked them.

"Okay."

I pretended not to notice what a good job she was doing about not being a nosy bitch, but after a moment I had to give in. "I'm good, Marcy, really. And no, I haven't called Dan."

She threw a wadded napkin at me. "Why not? Call him!"

"It's too late," I told her. "Some things aren't meant to work. That's all."

"How do you know if you don't try?"

I licked some chocolate and studied her sincere expression and thought back to when she'd told me she'd seen him downtown. "What, exactly, did Dan say when you saw him?"

"Just that you'd broken up."

"Uh-huh. Was he alone?"

She didn't say anything at first, then gave a too-casual shrug. "No. But that doesn't mean anything."

"Marcy, I'm sad to tell you, it does."

"Elle, it doesn't. He was miserable with that girl, I could tell."

I wiped my fingers with a napkin and warmed my fingers on my coffee mug. "You don't have to save my feelings. Dan and I broke up. He has the right to go out with anyone he wants to."

"But nobody can make him as miserable as you can," Marcy said with a wicked glint in her eyes. "Elle. Call him."

"Marcy," I said. "I can't."

She sighed and tossed up her hands. "Okay, okay, I'll stop bugging. I can't stand not having you to talk to around this place. Nobody else gets me."

"I'm the only lucky one?" I gathered up the trash and tossed it in the pail, then grabbed my mug and the thermos. I left the other éclairs for her.

"I like you," she said without a hint of teasing or mockery. "That's something."

I reached over to squeeze her shoulder. "I like you, too, Marcy. And yeah. It's something very good."

We smiled at each other. I slid the box toward her. "You keep these," I said, and ducked out of the office with Marcy's epithets following me down the hall.

My street had been turned into a scene from a crime television show, with the whirling red and blue lights of a squad car and the harsher red strobe of an ambulance. I hurried closer to my house, my eyes scanning Mrs. Pease's windows, but the light shone in the living room as it always did at this time, though it looked dim compared to the bright lights outside.

I jogged up her stairs and knocked on her door, which she opened immediately to expose her worried face. It smoothed a little when she saw me, and she reached out her arms. I let her hug me, relieved to find her all right.

"Oh, Elle, it's not you."

"No, Mrs. Pease, I thought it must be you." I looked her over. "The ambulance is parked right out front of your house, and I was worried."

"No, they showed up about forty minutes ago and ran up and pounded on your door," she told me.

"My door?" I turned to look onto the street. No police officers or emergency personnel maintained stations at their vehicles. "Are you sure?"

She nodded. "They pounded and pounded, but I guess you didn't answer. They must have gone next door to the Ossleys."

My stomach sunk. "Gavin."

"Oh, I hope not," Mrs. Pease said.

We didn't have to wait long to find out, because the Ossleys' door opened and the paramedics came out wheeling a stretcher. The bulky form beneath the sheet could have been anyone, but the white face belonged to Gavin. Mrs. Pease let out a small, sad noise that hurt my ears. She clutched my hand, and hers felt soft and papery against mine.

"Oh, that poor boy. I hope he's all right."

Mrs. Ossley appeared in the doorway with the ubiquitous Dennis at her side. She clutched a handful of tissues and her face looked tear streaked. He patted her back over and over. A moment later a police officer, the same one who'd brought Gavin home before, came out and watched the medical crew putting Gavin into the ambulance.

They murmured and mumbled, and I couldn't hear what they said but gathered it was something about going with Gavin in the ambulance. She shook her head. Dennis said something to the cop, who shrugged and put away his pad and pen. After another moment Mrs. Ossley got in the ambulance and it drove away.

"I hope he's all right," Mrs. Pease said again from my side.

"Me, too, Mrs. Pease."

Together we watched the ambulance pull away, its lights still flashing but no siren blaring. She invited me in for tea and cookies, and I accepted. I stayed and chatted, but though we spoke of recipes and the upcoming holiday season, my mind stayed filled with the sight of a gurney and a white face.

Several days passed before I steeled myself to knock on the Ossleys' door. Mrs. Ossley answered. If she'd spent the past few days overwrought with grief, she showed no sign of it. Her hair and makeup had been immaculately done, and she seemed still dressed for work in a neat linen suit and fashionable pumps. I remembered I didn't know what she did.

"What do you want?" she asked, and I hoped whatever career she'd chosen wasn't anything to do with customer service.

"I came to see if Gavin's all right."

She lifted her chin and crossed her arms. "My son is fine, thank you."

"You're welcome."

That seemed to take her aback, and she sniffed. "You'd like to know what happened, I guess."

"Mrs. Ossley," I said gently. "I know Gavin's been having some problems. He was cutting himself. I think I can guess what happened."

The color leaked from her face. "Don't you blame me!"

I held up my hands, trying to make peace. "I'm not blaming you—"

"Because if you knew," she continued, agitated, "you

should have done something about it! Said something! You should have…you could have…"

She trailed off, sputtering, and I let her silence fill the space between us on her doorstep. I remembered what my mother had said, about how blaming someone else had made it easier. My shoulders were broad. I could take Mrs. Ossley's blame, if she needed me to.

"He told me," she said after a very long minute, "that you'd never done anything to him."

I nodded, relieved. "Thank you."

She nodded, too, hers stiffer and looking as if it hurt her neck, but an acquiescence I appreciated, anyway. "He's at the Grove. He'll be there for observation and counseling for about two weeks, and then he might be able to come home."

The Grove was a well-established mental health facility in the next town. It had a great reputation and wasn't cheap. Whatever problems Gavin and his mother had, she wasn't skimping on getting him help now.

"I didn't want to know about it," she said stiffly. "It's been hard without Gavin's dad around. I hoped having Dennis here would help."

I didn't want to hug her or reach for her hand. I might have made great strides in my own issues over the past few weeks, but they didn't extend to becoming a casual hugger. I settled for another nod, one I hoped seemed meaningful.

"Blaming yourself can't help him, Mrs. Ossley," I told her. "The most important thing is that he's getting help and that you're willing to listen to him."

"Yes." She rubbed her arms as though chilled. "If you want to visit him…"

"Would that be all right with you?"

She didn't nod right away, and when she did, she didn't soften it with a smile. Yet she did nod. "Yes. I think Gavin would like it."

"Then I will," I told her.

There seemed like there could be more to say, but neither of us said it. We shared an awkward silence for another minute before I excused myself. She'd shut the door before I even got down the first step.

My visit with Gavin took longer than I'd thought it would. I went after work, traffic was horrible, visiting hours hadn't begun when I arrived and he at first wasn't available. It was worth the trip and the wait, though, to see him. We didn't say much. I didn't ask him about the bandages on his wrists or the new haircut. I took him a bag full of books, which he accepted eagerly and with more enthusiasm than I'd seen from him in a while.

"Hey," he said as we cracked open cans of soda from the vending machine. "How's the painting going?"

"I finished the dining room. I painted the kitchen, too. A color called Spring Green."

"Miss Kavanagh," Gavin said with a grin, "you're becoming the Martha Stewart of Green Street."

We both laughed at that, more so when I told him I'd been taking baking lessons from Mrs. Pease. It was good to hear him laugh. Good to laugh myself.

We didn't have long before I needed to go. Bedtime came early for the patients in the program, and they were strict with it. He thanked me again for the books and we hesitated, not sure of how to say goodbye until at last Gavin held out his hand. I offered mine, and he shook it firmly. Still holding it, he turned it to show my wrist, and he looked at the scar there before looking up at my eyes.

"And you're okay now, right?" He did a good job of pretending not to worry. "I mean…it all got better, right? After that?"

I nodded and squeezed his hand, and then I pulled him closer and gave him the hug I really had wanted to give him all along.

"Yes," I said as I let him go. "It all got better after that. And I'm okay now."

I hadn't lied to Gavin, but the visit had left me with a taste for something a bit stronger than soda. I found it at The Slaughtered Lamb, where I had no problem flirting with Jack and even less of a problem turning him down when he asked me right out if I'd like to go home with him.

"You sure?" He flashed me the charming grin.

"I'm sure."

We shared a smile and he gave me a one-armed hug as he moved around me to serve some other customers, but he didn't ask again. I had three drinks while I ate a late dinner and played a video trivia game. I contemplated a fourth and realized I didn't want to get drunk, after all, and I left the Lamb feeling better than I had expected to.

I passed Dan on the way out. He had his arm around a girl who could've been older than twenty-one but didn't look it. She was giggling. He was smiling, but when he saw me, he stopped. In the moment's comedy of errors, Jack pushed through the doors behind me to hand me my sweater, which I'd left on my chair.

The four of us froze for a moment as the men eyed each other and Dan's companion babbled on. Then Jack nodded at Dan, and Dan nodded at Jack, and both of them ignored me, and I wished I'd had the fourth drink.

Instead I took a walk. A long one. I got a blister and I didn't sober up too much, but the pain in my heel was a good distraction. By the time I made it home I thought maybe I wouldn't even have to cry.

Dan was waiting for me when I got home. His shadow loomed on my front steps. He stood aside to let me get to the door. My keys chattered in the lock, but for once it opened like magic.

"I didn't even say 'open sesame,'" I said.

Dan stepped aside while I went in and closed the door after us. I made my way toward the kitchen, intent on getting a couple glasses of water in me to fend off the possibility of a hangover. I shed my bag, my coat, my keys, a trail behind me as though I might lose my way to the door and needed a trail to find my way back. The thought made me laugh a little, under my breath.

"Did you fuck him?"

"What?"

His words stunned the laughter right out of me, and I turned. The room spun a little, and I reached for the door frame to steady myself. "What did you just say?"

"I said, did you fuck Jack. Have you been fucking him?"

I got sober very fast. We stared at each other across a room that had once seemed small and now loomed between us larger than the Grand Canyon. His face was stony, and I hated that he assumed the worst.

"What sort of question is that?" I gave him my back and went to the sink. The first cup I picked up dropped into the metal bowl and shattered. Blood oozed from a cut on the tip of my finger.

"I want to know, Elle. Did you?"

I knew he'd come up behind me, but I didn't turn. I ran water from the tap, scooped it up and drank it down, unheeding of the blood streaming down my hand. Dan moved closer.

I turned, water dripping from my lips. "I don't think that's a question I need to answer, considering you weren't alone tonight, either. It's not my business."

"It is my business!"

He grabbed my upper arms. I thought he meant to kiss me. Or push me. I wasn't sure. I froze, automatic, muscles clenching and going stiff. He shook me, instead, once, twice.

"It's my business, Elle!"

"Let go of me!"

"Answer me!"

"You've already decided I have, haven't you?" I cried. "If you thought I didn't, you wouldn't care! You wouldn't have waited for me, to find out if I did! You've already judged me, Dan, so why should I bother answering you?"

He shook me again, hard enough to rattle my teeth. "Did you, Elle? Tonight? Ever? Is he in love with you? Is that why you broke up with me? Because of him?"

"Why do you care!" I screamed, alcohol and fury making me rage.

"Because I love you." His fingers tightened on my arms, hurting. And then he let me go. Pushed me away from him like touching me had burned him. "Because I love you, Elle."

Then he turned around and stalked away.

I let him go. I watched him go. I stood in stunned silence at the sight of his back his words echoing in my ears.

"You weren't supposed to," I managed to find the breath to say.

He stopped at the front door and turned to look back at me. I have never seen a look so desperate. I have never seen eyes so bleak.

"But I do," he said. "What are you, Elle? Are you a ghost? Are you an angel or a demon? Because you can't be real."

He'd said those words to me the first time his touch had made me shudder with fulfillment. When he said them now, I had to sit. My knees bent, and I went to the floor like a puppet whose strings have been cut. A rag doll. Broken.

"I'm real," I whispered.

"Not for me," he said. "You won't let yourself be real for me."

I looked down at my white shirt. Red flowers had bloomed on it. My blood, from the wound on my finger.

Blood, like crimson roses, blooming on my white shirt.

I began to shake. My hair fell down around my shoulders and over my face. He couldn't see me. I didn't want him to see me, could not bear it, couldn't stand to have him see my tears.

"Did you go to bed with him tonight?"

The words, spoken no more as a challenge but bleakly, made me shake my head.

"No, Dan. I didn't."

He was suddenly beside me. "Look at me."

I did.

"I love you, Elle."

"No," I said. "You don't."

"I do. I love you."

I shook my head. Tears scalded my skin, slipping in hot trails down my chin and down my throat, puddling in the hollow there. He took my hands in his, ignoring the blood.

"Why won't you let me inside?" he asked.

There are always choices in this life. Move forward. Retreat. Leap. Fly. Fall. Succeed…fail.

Trust.

"I want to," I told him. I shook harder, though I wasn't cold.

"Then do it. It will be all right. I promise you." He put my fingertips to his mouth and kissed them. Licked the trace of blood away. Made them clean.

Then I knew the truth I had been denying. He made me clean. Dan made me clean and shining and bright. He made me beautiful, and I did not want to lose him.

"I promise," he told me, and I believed him.

This is what I told him.

Andrew was always my mother's favorite. I think he was meant to be her only, as well, because there were six years between his birth and mine, and she'd never made any secret of calling me her "little surprise." I'd been spared, at least, of being referred to as the "mistake," which was what I'd heard her call Chad once to her gaggle of girlfriends when she'd had them over for cigarettes and cards.

Andrew was her favorite and deserving of it. Smart. Popular. Teachers and priests adored him. Schoolmates admired him. By the time he was in high school, the girls giggled and chased after him.

We loved him too, Chad and I, and he was the perfect older brother. He never minded if we tagged along. He took us everywhere he went. He played games with us long after he'd outgrown them. Clue, Trouble, Uno, Hide and Seek, Ghost in the Graveyard. He made time for us in his life when he didn't have to, and we idolized him. He defused our mother, who swung between suffocating us with love and whirlwind rages. He ignored our father, whose drinking increased steadily, year after year.

I didn't connect my mother's fits of temper with my father's consumption of alcohol until I was older, but by then it didn't matter. We'd all lived so long with the white elephant by then that it was easier to keep pretending we didn't see it.

Something changed when Andrew turned twenty-one. His friends took him out. Got him drunk. Sent him home singing and banging doors at 3:00 a.m. I don't know if he'd ever had alcohol before that, though he'd have had ample opportunity to try it at our house. I think, though, that he hadn't. Drinking was one of those things we never discussed but the results of which we could only pretend to ignore.

He started doing poorly in school, where he'd almost completed a degree in Criminology. In fact, he flunked out of college with only one more semester to go, and he came home to live with us again.

He'd changed. He drank. He did drugs. He stole money to pay for it. He let his hair grow long and he didn't shave. He pierced his ears. He no longer tried to make our mother laugh.

The games he played were different now, too.

He ignored Chad except to call him a sissy and a faggot. Chad, who was having trouble with bullies in school, retreated behind his black clothes and eyeliner, and his Goth punk music. It didn't help anything. He was thirteen.

I was fifteen. Awkward. My body had changed and grown, the braces had come off, I'd sprouted up taller than a number of boys in my class. Andrew told me I was beautiful. That he loved me. And that if I loved him, I would be nice.

I did love my brother. I wanted to please him. I wanted things to go back the way they were, before, when he'd camp out with us in a tent in the backyard and keep us up all night telling us stories about monsters.

Now Andrew had become the monster. Once, he'd vowed to protect me, but he didn't protect me from himself.

I did what he asked for three years. I thought it would make him better. It didn't. He still drank. Still lost job after job. Still got surly and angry at the world for reasons I couldn't understand. He'd leave home for a few months and return, hollow-eyed and sneering, and our mother turned the house upside down to accommodate him.

Chad got bigger, the makeup heavier, the clothes blacker, the music louder. I stopped smiling. Counting helped, and counting food helped more. Bites of cake. Pieces of popcorn. I shielded myself in layers of fat and clothing, hiding the beauty my brother had seen and couldn't seem to forget.

Nobody asked me what was wrong.

Chad knew, the same way I knew the magazines he hid beneath his mattress had pictures of naked boys, not girls, in them. We didn't talk about it. Chad and I barely talked at all. We passed in the hall and sat across the breakfast table with each other, and for three years our eyes shared secrets neither of us dared to speak aloud.

I didn't really want to die, but cutting my wrist seemed like a good idea at the time. It bled a lot, and it hurt worse than I expected. I only did the one because the sight of the blood made me feel faint, and I had to sit down, and because Chad opened the door to my bedroom to tell me it was time for dinner.

I hadn't planned it very well, you see, my suicide attempt. My mother ranted at me the entire time she yanked me down the stairs to the kitchen, where she stanched my wrist with a tea towel. The carpet on the stairs was ruined, and she threw away the rug from my room. She kept me home from school for the rest of the week, but we never told anyone else what had happened.

She didn't tell me not to, I just…didn't.

The only person who asked me why I had done it was Andrew, who let himself into my bedroom and into my bed and kissed the white bandage right over the small red spot that had bloomed on it.

"Why, Ella? Why would you do this? Is it because of me?"

When I answered yes, he started to cry. And I pitied him, my beloved brother, because he sounded so forlorn, and I envied him because I had been unable to weep for years. He buried his face against me and his sobs rocked us, rocked the bed as he'd rocked it before for different reasons, and I stroked his hair over and over with my good hand until he tried to kiss me.

And then I told him no.

"No?" He asked in a voice like broken glass. "You don't love me?"

"No, Andrew. I don't love you."

I thought he might hurt me, then. He'd done it before, even when I didn't resist. He liked to pull my hair or pin my wrists. He liked to pinch.

I didn't flinch. I waited.

He asked me again. "No?"

"No."

Then he got up and out of my bed and left me there, and I thought it was over. I was wrong.

I woke to the sound of my mother's shouting. In the kitchen Chad hunched his shoulders to shield himself from her smacks. Across the table were spread the magazines from his room. *Cowpoke. Beef. Hung.* She'd rolled one of them up and was hitting him with it the way you'd smack a dog for shitting on the floor.

Andrew sat at the table, arms crossed, saying nothing. Doing nothing but watching as my mother called Chad names so horrible I couldn't believe they didn't burn her tongue. Andrew looked at me when I came in, and I saw nothing in his eyes. Not one thing.

Chad ran away that night. He spent a few nights on the street before seeking refuge with my uncle John, my mother's brother. Uncle John lived alone. He'd never married. He took my brother in, gave him food and clothes, registered him in school. Kept him safe. Uncle John also loved my brother and taught him it was all right to be himself. I think he saved Chad's life.

I'd thought my world had fallen apart before, but I was wrong about that, too. Chad was gone. My father didn't bother getting sober any longer. My mother became the Wicked Witch full-time.

I hadn't even taken the bandage off my wrist when I came home to find the house empty and quiet. My father hadn't come home from work. My mother was out, probably picking out new carpet to replace the one I'd ruined. I climbed the stairs past the stains gone brown on the rug, and I'd put my hand to the door of my room when I heard the thunk.

I turned in horror-movie slow motion to face the door to the bathroom at the end of the hall. I wasn't alone, after all. I heard another thump and, ignoring everything that told me not to, I went to the door and I opened it.

He'd sliced deeper, both wrists. Made more of a mess. Blood had arced up in splashes on the walls, the ceiling, the sides of the tub. It dripped off the mirror and the shower curtain. It puddled on the floor. The smell of it, meaty, fresh, made me put a hand to my mouth to quell a gag.

He was in the tub with all his clothes on. Water enough to keep the wounds from clotting and closing covered him. He must have gotten in after the cutting. The razor glittered on the tiles.

He opened his eyes when I opened the door and he said my name. I didn't think, I just went to him. I skidded in the blood, went to my knees, opened the wound I'd given myself a week before and it began to weep again.

I took his hand. His blood covered my fingers, made roses on my skin and on the white fabric of my blouse. He'd gone cold, though the water in the tub was still hot enough to steam.

He was alive when I found him, but I didn't call for help. I looked into my brother's eyes and saw nothing in them, and I sat with him and held his hand while his blood leaked out of him and he died.

That was the story I told Dan, and all of it is true. Much happened after that. I went away to school. I met Matthew. I learned I could love someone and make love with someone, and I learned that fucking and drinking could replace counting, and I learned to be careful about who I trusted with my secrets.

And then I met Dan.

He didn't say much during the tale, just let me talk. His hand moved in soothing circles on my back when I got to the rough parts, and he held my hand tight through others.

When it was over, I took a deep breath, then deeper. I looked at him. I felt as if I'd just vomited up something that had made me sick or cut away a scab that had been festering or dropped a load of stone I'd been carrying on my shoulders.

I felt lighter. Cleaned out. Exhausted and a little numb but…satisfied. Relieved.

"There's not much more to say," I told him. "That's the way it was."

I had never told anyone the entire story. I couldn't do more than that. I couldn't be more than what I was.

But I'd learned I could not be less, either.

He didn't say anything for another moment. Then he asked me simply, "Would it be all right if I hugged you?"

When I nodded, he put his arms around me and held me for a long time in silence. His breath stirred tendrils of my hair, and I timed mine to his. In. Out.

I put my hand to his chest and felt for the beat of his heart. The steady thump-thump, strong, unfaltering, soothed me. His hands on my back soothed me. His lips brushed my hair.

I kissed him first, and he let me do it. Let me lead. I nudged his mouth open with mine and swept my tongue inside to taste him. I took his hands and put them on my breasts. I unbuttoned his shirt and slipped my hand inside to brush the curling sandy hair with my knuckles.

He whispered my name against my mouth. His thumb rubbed my nipple to aching tightness while his other hand slid down to cup my ass and pull me closer. He stroked my tongue. Our teeth clashed, lips slurped and nibbled. Hands groped.

I got to my feet, pulled him by the hand, took him to my bedroom where I pulled down the blankets and let him lay me down on crisp white sheets. My hair fanned out around us; his stood on end when he pulled his shirt off over his head. He bent to kiss me again as my fingers worked his belt, the button and zip, the denim waistband of his jeans and the smoother elastic of his boxers.

He got naked faster than I did with my complication of

buttons, snaps and hooks, and, naked, he bent over me to smooth each button of my blouse apart, revealing my skin inch by inch and following with a kiss.

He spread the cloth open and traced the line of my bra with his fingertip, his eyes following his actions but glancing up to mine every so often. He paid attention to me, to my every detail, but he didn't immerse himself in me. He kept me connected, aware. Kept us together so it wasn't him just doing to me or me to him, but mutual exploration and admiration.

"I love the way your skin changes color here." His fingertip drew a light line along the curve of my breasts. "Just above your bra."

I knew my body well enough to understand how the skin went from pale to paler there. He unhooked the front clasp and parted the wisps of lace and elastic. I drew in a breath when he did, and my breasts rose under his hands.

Dan circled my nipples with his finger. "And pink, here."

They went tight and hard under his touch. He smiled. He bent his head to take one in his mouth, suckling gently, and my clit throbbed in response. He moved to the other, kissing and sucking, and I put my hand on the back of his head.

He kissed between my breasts, then held them close together to kiss the plumped flesh, both at the same time. He helped me sit long enough to push the shirt and bra off and then laid me back down. The sheets were cool on my skin.

He kissed his way down my body, making murmuring sounds of appreciation, his hands as busy as his lips and teeth and tongue. He unbuttoned my skirt and eased it off, but did nothing with my panties for the moment but stare. They were nothing special. No sexy thong or revealing lacey bikinis. I hadn't been expecting anyone to see them. Plain white cotton with high cut legs that revealed enough thigh for him to kiss my bare skin over my hip bones.

He stroked a finger along the small jutting bump of my clitoris through the soft cotton, and I jumped. He kissed my belly just above the waistband of the panties, his finger continuing its motion.

This was all that lay between us now. A thin layer of white cotton. He rubbed me through it again, then fastened his mouth against me and blew hot, damp breath through it. The fabric barrier was enough to keep the sensation dull but delicious, anyway. A tease. Tantalizing.

He did it again, and I felt the wiggle of his tongue against my clit. It was pressure rather than direct stimulation, and I parted my thighs to lift myself harder against him.

He hooked his fingers in the edge of my panties and pulled them down, following their path over my thighs and knees with his hands and mouth. He kissed my ankle and moved up my shin to my knee.

"Fuzzy," he murmured, and I laughed.

"I didn't shave today."

"I like it." He rubbed the stubble of hairs on my kneecap and kissed the part of my body I'd always found the ugliest. "Au naturel."

My thighs were fuzzy, too, the hair there softer. He gave each of them the same attention. His mouth left wet trails on my skin, heat that cooled in the air.

He parted my legs and settled between them. He looked

up at me, but I didn't balk him. He kissed me, soft mouth on soft skin. His tongue slid out to flick my clit, the motion gentle but not tentative. He caressed me, kissed me. I swelled for him. Responded. My body opened and he slid a finger inside, then another, as he licked me.

I gave myself up to it, his lips and tongue. The slickness of his spit mingled with my own fluids, easing the motion of his fingers, and he added a third. I rocked against his mouth, helping him find the rhythm and motion that best suited me.

His moans aroused me. Hearing his pleasure in what he was doing, listening to him murmur my name and words of love as he licked me, sent me higher and higher.

My belly jumped as I rocked my hips, pushing my cunt against his mouth and his fingers. Stars burst behind my closed eyelids, and I remembered to take a breath. With the air came a new level of excitement. Threads of pleasure slid down my legs, into every toe. In my arms and every finger. It suffused me, carried and lifted me. Swept me away.

I came under his tongue and he held me close as my body bucked and jumped. I cried out, his name like candy on my lips. Sweet and fragrant, licorice and whiskey. His name. Dan. Who had listened when I wanted to speak. Who had cared about why I didn't smile.

He nuzzled me for a second before kissing my throbbing clit. He moved up my body to bury his face in my neck, his hand on my heart. I put my hand over his, our fingers laced.

His body radiated heat. His erection pressed my thigh, and I reached between us to stroke him wherever I could reach. His sigh was muffled on my neck, but he didn't otherwise move.

"Dan," I whispered. "You want to make love to me."

He looked up then, his familiar smile speeding up my heart again though it had just started to slow. "You want me to make love to you."

"I do."

He kissed me. I was already so wet he slid inside too fast, stabbing me. We both winced, but I held him tight and didn't let him pull out. I hooked my heels around his calves and put my hands on his rear, cementing him to me.

"Make love to me, Dan."

He did, with slow, leisurely thrusts. In. Out. The shift and lift of our hips matched the way our breaths had joined earlier. Give and take. Advance and retreat.

He bent to kiss my mouth, then covered me with his body to kiss my neck. He anchored me with his mouth, his hands, his cock. Sweat slicked our bodies. I embraced him with my arms and cunt. We were aligned.

His breath became ragged. He added a twist to every thrust that ground his pelvis against my still sensitive clit. The pressure made me gasp aloud, at first in apprehension at imagined discomfort but soon enough with arousal. Thrust. Twist. I arched my back to meet his thrusts and grind myself harder against him.

He moved faster. His teeth found my shoulder. I gripped his ass and pulled him against me harder. Faster, but not rougher. Still smooth. He pumped in and out of me.

I went over the edge again in slow, cascading ripples. I clutched his shoulder blades, as the muscles of his back tensed. He shuddered, and we came together with low gasping cries and wordless murmurs of joy.

Later, in the dark, he held me close and stroked my hair. The scent of sex covered us, and the sheets stayed damp beneath us, but we didn't get up. We lay in the dark and held each other, saying nothing and needing nothing to say.

We didn't run through fields of flowers, hand in hand. No music played when we kissed. No house landed on my mother. I didn't let go of everything all at once and become some bright and shining example to prove all it takes is a knight with a hammer to break the glass tower. Life doesn't work that way. We tried, though, as we still try, every day, to make this work. To be honest and faithful to each other. To listen. To look ahead to things that lie before us instead of always staring behind at what we've left behind. I don't know what the future brings.

All I know with utter certainty is this. Dan tamed me. We need each other.

He has become unique to me in all the world.